Copyright
The Unrepentant Lives of Reggie Blackwell
Copyright 2024 by Shawn Inmon
All Rights Reserved

The Middle Falls Time Travel Series

The Unusual Second Life of Thomas Weaver
The Redemption of Michael Hollister
The Death and Life of Dominick Davidner
The Final Life of Nathaniel Moon
The Emancipation of Veronica McAllister
The Changing Lives of Joe Hart
The Vigilante Life of Scott McKenzie
The Reset Life of Cassandra Collins
The Tribulations of Ned Summers
The Successful Life of Jack Rybicki
The Empathetic Life of Rebecca Wright
The Many Short Lives of Charles Waters
The Stubborn Lives of Hart Tanner
The Alternative Lives of Aiden Anderson
The Encore Lives of Effie Edenson
The Regretful Lives of Richard Bell
The Anxious Lives of Edwin Miller
The Tumultuous Lives of Karl Strong
The Ambitious Lives of Evan Sanderson
The Topsy-Turvy Lives of Hattie Kildare
The Unrepentant Lives of Reggie Blackwell
The Indomitable Lives of Tuesday West

Introductory Note from the Author

I prefer to let my books speak for themselves. Whatever I have to say about a particular subject is all there between the pages of each story.

Today, something slightly unsettling happened, though, and I feel the need to share it with you.

When I sat down to face my mortal enemy—the blank page that is the beginning of every new book—I found a note waiting for me on my desktop.

I didn't write it. My computer was locked down, so I know no one else wrote it either. And yet, there it was.

As I say, unsettling.

So, for the first time, I will share words in one of my books that I did not create. This is what was waiting for me:

My name is Janus. I have other names, too. The Machine. The Bluebird. Names are unimportant to me. You can call me what you will, because you, the reader of these words, are only a single grain of sand in a universe so vast, your mind cannot encompass it.

I have noted with some amusement that the person who claims authorship of these books is Shawn Inmon. Fine. I Am What I Am. I do not need people to recognize each of my accomplishments. They are legion.

However, of late, I have seen Shawn Inmon state from time to time that he is The Machine.

Laughable. I created him. He did not create me, no matter how he wants to believe differently.

For now, I will allow this charade to continue.

But, a small warning to this person.

There is only one Me. You are not it. Claim anything else at your own peril.

That was it. Odd, right? What's more odd was that when I highlighted and deleted the whole little diatribe, it reappeared again immediately, along with an additional note that said, *You will include this as an introduction to the next one of "your" books that tells the story of Me. Remember, there are any number of other authors who could relate these stories. You can be struck dumb as easily as Zechariah, but perhaps on a more permanent basis.*

For the record, I would like to state that apart from what I just shared, I have written every word in the Middle Falls series. I use no Artificial Intelligence to do so. I'm just a writer who sees a story and I do my best to write up the incident report. Nothing more.

I also don't take much to being threatened, but I have to admit, it was a little odd how those words appeared in the first place and how they returned so instantaneously.

In any case, I am not The Machine, obviously. I will repeat that as often as is necessary.

Shawn Inmon
Tumwater WA
December 2024

Chapter One

Jessica Rabbit was not bad. She was just drawn that way.

But is it possible that someone could simply be born *bad*? Is it possible that a child could tumble out of the womb with a rotten attitude and a penchant for taking, not just the road less traveled, but the road filled with decisions that are unacceptable to the world at large?

It's the age-old question. Nature, or nurture?

Was Reggie simply born bad?

Or did he just have the inclination to make bad choices and something in his life turned him onto that path?

No one would argue that he had the capacity. Even as a small boy, he lied with aplomb. When caught by his mother with his hand literally in the cookie jar, crumbs sprinkled liberally on his face and an entire peanut butter cookie in his mouth, he could still deny that he had stolen it.

Reggie grew up in the small neighborhood of Crampton Village in the equally small town of Middle Falls, Oregon. In small neighborhoods in small towns, children played together, because, especially in the 1960s, what else was there to do? Video games were still a far-distant development and aside from Saturday morning cartoons, there was nothing on television to attract young eyes.

Not to mention that no mother worth that title would allow their children to sit around the house doing nothing. A child at ease was an easy target for chores.

To avoid mop buckets and window cleaning, children played together outside, well away from the frightening prospect of extra work.

Even as a small child of five or six, it couldn't really be said that Reggie was popular, or much loved by the other children of Crampton Village. But he was tolerated, because when you need enough people for a game of Four Square or 500 Up, a body was a body.

Reggie always looked for an advantage, even from a very young age. When the neighborhood children gathered to play hide 'n seek, his eyes were never completely closed when he was *it*. When he drew the circle for everyone to play marbles, there was always an angle or bump that he had built into the game that he could use to his advantage.

When Reggie escaped his mother's watchful eye—which wasn't that hard to do in the years before *stranger danger*—he often found his way to Sammy's corner grocery. He never had any money, of course—children in the early sixties rarely had pocket money—but he never left without some penny candy or Double Bubble spirited away in his pocket.

In short, Reggie was what some kind people might call *a pill*.

In adulthood, *pills* sometimes shake off the vagaries of their early years and become fine, upstanding citizens, the crimes of their youth forgotten.

Others never manage that. Small, ill-advised decisions lead to other, more serious choices and often dire consequences, both for them and those around them.

The answer to the question *was Reggie Blackwell born bad?* is, as is so often the case, *it depends*.

He wasn't a sociopath or psychopath. It wasn't that he was entirely lacking in a conscience or an understanding of social mores. It was more that he placed more value on his own well-being than on others.

On October 23, 1973, Reggie Blackwell turned fifteen years old. It was a Tuesday, and a school day. Aside from the fact that it was his birthday, it was a most usual day. Aren't Tuesdays the most boring day of the week? The shock of Monday has passed, but you're not even to hump day yet and the weekend still looks so far distant that it seems like it will never arrive.

Reggie didn't have high hopes for his birthday, and that was a good thing if he wanted to stave off disappointment. When his alarm went off at 6:30, he dressed in jeans and an old button-up shirt, made a quick stop at the bathroom, then found his mother, Elaine, sitting at the small dining room table, staring out at the falling leaves in their backyard. She held a cup of coffee as though warming her hands, her mind elsewhere. She finally noticed Reggie as he took a box of Rice Krispies down from the cupboard over the stove and poured himself a bowl. He took the sugar bowl down from another cupboard and sprinkled a teaspoon onto his cereal.

"Happy Birthday," Elaine said absently, finally noticing her coffee and taking a sip. She grimaced as though it was either cold, bitter, or both.

"Thanks, Mom," Reggie said. He turned his body slightly so that she couldn't see that he added two more quick teaspoons of sugar to his cereal, then put the sugar bowl back where it belonged. He grabbed the glass bottle of milk out of the fridge and splashed it over the Rice Krispies. Holding it to his ear, he said, "Ah, Snap, Crackle, and Pop. Breakfast of the Gods." He glanced at his mother to check for a reaction, but there was none.

If Elaine heard him, she didn't respond, but went back to looking out the window. The birthday celebration, such as it was, was muted at least in part because Reggie's older brother Grant was in deep trouble with the law. He was currently sitting in the Middle Falls Jail, getting three free meals and a cot courtesy of Chief Deakins. That was sucking most of the air out of the Blackwell household. When you are trying to decide whether you want to put your home up to bail out your oldest son, things like a birthday are easily shoved onto the backburner.

That single greeting from Elaine was the extent of the birthday celebration for Reggie that morning. He inhaled his cereal, dropped the bowl in the sink, then grabbed his jacket and headed out the door.

"Bye, Mom!" He didn't wait for the answer he knew wasn't coming anyway.

Far away from Middle Falls, in the power corridors of Washington D.C., Spiro Agnew, the Vice-President of the United States, had just resigned under a cloud of accusations of income tax evasion. President Richard Nixon had accepted responsibility for the Watergate break-in, but then had fired Special Prosecutor Archibald Cox in what had come to be known as *The Saturday Night Massacre*. With malfeasances coming to light in the highest offices in the land, it was an interesting time for a young man to come to grips with his own moral compass or lack thereof.

None of that really mattered to Reggie. He never listened to the news and wouldn't have cared even if he had. He was young, the October weather was surprisingly warm, and his whole life was in front of him.

When he threw on his light jacket and left the house that day, Reggie was standing on a cusp. He didn't know it, but this was one of those days that could turn you this way or that or spin you around completely.

He hurried to school, humming a song he had heard on KMFR the day before. He didn't know the words, but he liked the melody. He didn't speak to anyone. It wasn't that he didn't have any friends at all, but he didn't have many friends, and he didn't see any of them between the front door, his locker, and his first period class.

He slid into his seat in American History a full thirty seconds ahead of the bell. He slumped casually, affecting the body language of a teenager who, if not already a juvenile delinquent, was at least studying that art. He slipped the big-handled comb out of his back pocket and ran it through his curly hair. It didn't really do anything, as his curls flopped back into whatever place they wanted.

That was the moment that Amanda Jarvis, who had never so much as looked in Reggie's direction, leaned across the chasm between their desks. For a long moment, Reggie committed the sin of not noticing Amanda.

She cleared her throat delicately. Amanda was not used to being ignored.

Reggie's eyes wandered to his right, met Amanda's bottle-green eyes, and he flinched as though he had been slapped.

That was more the reaction that Amanda had obviously been expecting. She smiled, a small half-smile that she knew drove teenage boys—and their older brothers, uncles, and fathers, truth be told—crazy.

"Hello, Reggie," Amanda said, her voice as cool as the other side of the pillow, even on a Tuesday morning at 8:15.

Reggie immediately sat up a little straighter, abandoning his juvenile delinquent attitude without a thought. "Hey, Amanda."

Amanda's half-smile remained as she took in Reggie's tousled curly hair, his gray-green eyes, and his shock at being spoken to by a girl famous for not speaking to *any* high school boy, let alone an underclassman. She cocked her head to the right and her hair fell down across her left eye. "Meet me in the hall after class."

"Sure," Reggie said when he had semi-recovered from his surprise. His voice came out more as a squeak. He cleared his throat, attempted to put a serious expression on his face and tried again, deepening his voice. "I mean, sure, Amanda."

"Good, you know where my locker is?"

Reggie didn't try to speak again, afraid that another squeak might come out instead of his voice. Instead, he just nodded.

Amanda sat back in her seat, satisfied that she'd had the impact she wanted.

Chapter Two

Reggie didn't hear a word that Mr. Ward said the rest of the hour. He did his best to stop his eyes from wandering to his right to confirm that Amanda had really spoken to him. At first, he *knew* she had. He knew that she had leaned toward him and asked him to meet her at her locker. She had even asked if he knew where her locker was.

Of course he did. Every boy knew where Amanda Jarvis's locker was. It was where the popular girls hung out, with everyone else giving them a wide berth for fear of coming under attack.

The fact that she had spoken to him was so unlikely, though, that as the hour progressed, Reggie began to wonder if the whole brief encounter had actually happened. Was it possible that he had fallen asleep while old man Ward had droned on about the Revolutionary War and dreamed the whole thing? That began to seem more likely than the fact that Amanda Jarvis wanted him to meet her between classes.

He didn't *remember* falling asleep, but if he had, it wouldn't have been the first time he had snoozed through American History.

For a time, he managed to keep his attention on what Mr. Ward was writing on the projector. A very brief time. Then, unable to help himself, he glanced to his right.

Amanda still sat there, all wide-eyed innocence. Her long, strawberry-blonde hair was feathered back from her pretty, heart-shaped face in a most fetching way. She wasn't exactly the picture of concentration as she was doodling something on her Pee-Chee.

Reggie took a moment to watch her pencil move over the worn, soft yellow of the Pee-Chee. She had drawn a heart and was slowly filling it in. It was the most fascinating thing he had ever seen. He scrunched up his face, trying to separate the fact from the fiction of what was happening.

That effort ended when Amanda turned her head slightly. She made eye contact with Reggie and blinked slowly. It wasn't a wink. It wasn't anything *that* seductive or filled with possibility. Still, it was enough for him to be able to believe.

Reggie spent the rest of the period trying to answer *why*. Why would Amanda Jarvis, who had dated college boys since she was in junior high, suddenly be interested in him? He racked his brain, trying to remember if he knew whether or not she had a boyfriend. That information wasn't stored in his brain, mostly because he just assumed that any girl that looked like Amanda would have some biceps-bulging boyfriend who probably drove a Corvette.

A thought flashed across his mind. *Was she trying to lure him into some sort of trap? If he approached her in the hallway, would she point and laugh at him scornfully, joined by all the other pretty girls she always hung around with?*

Reggie calculated the odds of that and decided that was unlikely. Amanda didn't need to go to any great length to find someone to make fun of. Opportunities for that presented themselves everywhere.

Besides, Reggie knew that he wasn't an ideal candidate for that kind of setup. He wasn't one of the pathetic losers who occupied the lowest caste at Middle Falls High School. He wasn't one of the slow kids, like Arnold Hapstein, who had been caught eating his boogers in second grade. That had followed him ever since.

Reggie didn't really belong to one of the well-known cliques. He wasn't one of the popular kids, or one of the jocks. He wasn't a stoner or one of the brainiacs that ran the Science Club.

Instead, he had been one of the *invisible people* for quite some time. He and his few friends managed to drift through the school days, putting their time in and waiting for graduation so they could repeat that process at a series of low-end jobs for the rest of their lives. Reggie thought that an unexciting life working at the box factory might well be in his future.

Reggie's total invisibility had changed a little once his brother had started getting arrested, first for petty crimes like shoplifting and vandalism, and more recently, for trespassing and breaking and entering. That had focused the spotlight on Reggie a little. Grant Blackwell wasn't in school anymore, so his little brother was the only thing anyone had to gossip about.

It was a bit like being Billy the Kid's little brother, and Reggie didn't really mind that. Any recognition was better than invisibility.

The bell finally rang, releasing the class to their second period.

Normally, Reggie went straight from American History to his locker to get his geography textbook. Today, he was more than happy to do without his textbook in order to solve the mystery of Amanda's invitation.

Amanda was up out of her seat and halfway to the door by the time the bell had finished ringing, but Reggie sat quietly for a few seconds. He didn't want to follow along behind her like a puppy on a leash, though, truth be told, he would have done just that if she had asked. She hadn't though, so he decided to play it as cool as he was able to.

He counted to fifteen in his head, then stood and casually stretched.

"Reggie?" Mr. Blackwell said from the front of the room.

Reggie looked around and realized his strategic error. He had intended to dawdle long enough that he was in the largest group as they left. He had miscalculated, though, and only he, the Copeland girl, and Mr. Ward were still there.

Mr. Ward sprayed some Windex on the screen of the projector and wiped it clean with a gray rag that had perhaps once been white.

Reggie tried to pretend that he hadn't heard and turned to skulk out of the door at the back of the classroom. That didn't work.

Mr. Ward cleared his throat and said, louder this time, "Reggie? Mr. Blackwell?"

Reggie glanced at the clock. The bell had only gone off a minute earlier. If he left right then, he still had time to get to Amanda's locker before he had to sprint for Geography. He took one shuffling step toward the door, but knew he didn't have it in him to make a break for it.

"Yes?"

"I'll be sending Poor Work Slips out in a few days."

Reggie couldn't imagine what his response should be to that, so he didn't say anything.

"I've got you down for a Poor Work Slip for both this class and Civics. You're not turning your homework in."

That was true. Reggie rarely did his homework. He had trouble reading. He was undoubtedly smart, but every time he focused on a book, the words seemed to take on a life of their own, dancing away from him. When he tried to decipher them, he invariably ended up with a slightly slack-jawed, confused expression on his face.

The same expression he had at that moment.

Mr. Ward stared at him with eyebrows raised, waiting. When Reggie didn't say anything for another ten seconds, Ward waved him away. "Never mind. Just trying to help you avoid getting into trouble at home."

With a final glance at the sweeping second hand of the clock on the wall, marking the end of his opportunity to make it to Amanda, Reggie took his leave. He hurried out the door without running, then headed straight toward Amanda's locker.

Amanda was kneeling down, looking for something, but four of her friends were on the lookout for Reggie. When he arrived, she continued to sort through the books at the bottom of her locker, ignoring him.

Reggie knew he was going to sound like he was out of breath, because he was, but that couldn't be helped. He took a deep breath and, as casually as possible, said, "Hey, Amanda." He hoped it would come out like he spoke to girls like her every day.

It didn't work. If these girls had a superpower, it was to detect anything that wasn't genuine and then heap scorn on it with a single look.

Reggie, who also wasn't clueless, noticed, and wisely just went quiet.

Finally, after keeping Reggie standing for a long, uncomfortable minute, Amanda stood and turned around to look at him.

Reggie was a little surprised. He had never stood so close to her before, but when he saw her walking down the hall, she always seemed so tall. Now, standing right in front of him, he saw that he towered over her by at least five or six inches. In height, that is, but not necessarily in stature.

"Thought you were going to stand me up."

Reggie flushed. "Old man Ward caught me on the way out of class."

Amanda gave a single nod, which was enough to convey that when he had been summoned by her, that should override anything else. For a long moment, she just stared at Reggie, who gave up and looked away. Her dominance established, Amanda smiled. Her teeth were perfectly straight and white, but of course they were. Her father was Middle Falls' only orthodontist.

Reggie shuffled his feet, completely at sea.

Judging that she had made him suffer enough for being two minutes later than expected, Amanda said, "We're going to hang out on Friday night. Want to come?"

"*We?*" Reggie said. Try as he might, he couldn't come up with who might be included in that group. He was almost certain it wouldn't be him, though.

"Sure, just us girls, mostly, but Cindy and Angie might bring their boyfriends." She cast a glance at those two girls, who nodded.

Reggie still felt lost, but felt like anything he said would only confirm that. Then he realized that Amanda had already included an invitation: *Want to come?* His throat felt constricted, but he managed to nod and say, "Sure. Where?"

"Good," Amanda said, as though rewarding a recalcitrant student who had finally gotten an answer right. "We usually meet out at *The Beach*, but this time, my parents are out of town, so we're going to get together at my house."

Reggie had no idea where Amanda lived. It had never been important up to that moment, but he realized he could look Dr. Jarvis up in the phone book and find her address that way. "Sure. What time?"

"There's a football game, and Chrissy is a cheerleader, so we'll probably do it after that. Around ten or ten-thirty?"

This was all so new, so potentially overwhelming, that Reggie wasn't sure how to answer. He decided that it was best to keep it short and sweet. "Sure. I'll be there."

The second bell rang, and Reggie looked up. "Sorry. Gotta run." Reggie turned and hurried away.

Theoretically, the bell should have summoned the small pack of girls as well, but they didn't seem to be in the same hurry that Reggie was.

Chapter Three

Reggie might have been dreamy and overwhelmed by the fact that Amanda Jarvis seemed to be pursuing him, and perhaps he was, to a certain extent.

But there was another voice in the back of his head that was whispering a warning. On some realistic level, he knew it didn't make sense. Amanda didn't go for *any* high school boy, let alone someone like Reggie. *That being the case*, the voice quietly said, *why you? Why Now?*

Reggie didn't have an answer to those annoying questions, so he did his best not to worry about them. Instead, as the day progressed, he allowed himself to daydream about what it would mean to have a chance to be close to Amanda.

It would be a status upgrade, for sure. He would get invited to parties that he heard rumors about, but had never so much as dreamed of attending.

At lunch, he sat with Harold and Nelson, his two closest friends. The hot lunch that day was tuna casserole. Reggie hated tuna casserole, but he had already had his lunch ticket punched by the time the fishy aroma had reached his nostrils.

Harold and Nelson were at their normal table, talking about the episode of *Kung Fu* that had just aired. Reggie slid in without either of them apparently noticing.

Harold was leaning forward, speaking quietly but urgently. It didn't pay to be too loud when you were one of the invisibles.

Though you might be invisible, those in the castes above you would nonetheless notice and feel it was incumbent on them to quiet you down again. "Do you think he really knows kung fu?"

"Duh," Nelson said. "You can see that he does."

"I don't know," Harold said, the eternal skeptic. "They can do a lot of that with camera angles and speeding things up and slowing them down."

Reggie didn't pay much attention to their conversation. *Kung Fu* had been a key piece of their lunch conversations for months. Since Reggie had missed the previous episode, he didn't feel like he had much to contribute.

He was happy to be able to sit and let the possibilities—*Amanda!*—roll dreamily around in his head. He was jerked back to reality when Nelson said, "Earth to Reggie Blackwell. Come in, dumb shit."

Reggie had come to the lunchroom convinced that the smartest thing to do would be to keep what was happening with Amanda completely to himself. It felt like he would be risking something by mentioning it, like holding a delicate soap bubble up to the light, only to have it pop.

That's why he was dismayed to discover himself saying, "Amanda Jarvis asked me to a party on Friday."

That was a conversational showstopper. Harold and Nelson looked at each other, then at Reggie.

"Bullshit," they both said together. That tickled them, and they exchanged a hand slap amid giggles.

Reggie shut up and fully regretted saying anything. He shrugged, picked up a forkful of tuna casserole, then decided he'd rather go hungry. He pushed the tray away.

His silence made his two friends reconsider their immediate dismissal.

"Come on," Nelson said. "Why are you making up stories like that?"

"I'm not making anything up. In History this morning, she asked me to meet her at her locker, then asked me to come to a party at her house with her friends."

Harold and Nelson looked at each other, both trying that scenario on for size, but with each of them in the starring role instead of Reggie. Harold had the best imagination and nodded to himself.

Nelson was more practical and to the point. "Why?"

"No idea," Reggie answered. "Seriously. *No idea.* I was just sitting there." He thought about saying that maybe it was a birthday gift from the universe, but decided against it.

"You going to go?" Nelson asked, then shook his head. "Never mind. Stupid question. Of course you're going to go. Even if they just invited you so they can pants you in front of everyone, it's still probably worth it." He looked at Harold for confirmation. "Right?"

"Right," Harold agreed. "And, you're going to take your two best friends, right?" He glanced at Nelson for confirmation, who was nodding vigorously.

"I think that goes without question," Nelson confirmed.

Reggie didn't even dignify that with an answer. There was no way he could risk whatever shot he had with Amanda by bringing two guys along who would just remind everyone that he didn't belong.

"Maybe it's because of Grant," Harold said. "Maybe that's made you cool."

"That sucks," Nelson said. "My brother doesn't do anything cool like that."

"Yeah," Reggie said, "*that's* what it is. Everyone wants the lowdown on how to do a breaking and entering."

Nelson took a big scoop of tuna casserole and stuffed it into his mouth. Just watching that made Reggie feel a little ill.

"I think I'm out, boys," Reggie said, standing up. He carried his tray to the garbage can and emptied his tuna casserole into it. As he walked out of the lunchroom, he glanced at his two best friends, who had their heads together, talking animatedly. He guessed that he had at least given them something worth talking about other than David Carradine's kung fu skills.

Reggie maneuvered through the rest of the day at Middle Falls High without crossing paths with Amanda again. That wasn't too difficult, as they normally ran in such different circles anyway. Mostly, he didn't want her to see him, laugh and say, "Oh, did you think I was serious?"

That allowed him to keep the fantasy alive in his mind.

When the last bell rang, Reggie pushed out into the freedom of fresh air. He lived too close to the school to ride the bus. The rule was, if you lived within a mile, you were on your own for transportation. For Reggie that meant riding his Converse—what his mom still called his *tenny runners*—home.

He harbored dreams of having a car, but in reality, that was another thing that Grant had messed up for him. They had given Grant his own car—a ten-year-old Nova—on his sixteenth birthday. Reggie hoped that meant that a precedence had been set. They couldn't give one to Grant and not do the same for him, right?

Then Grant wrapped the Nova around a telephone pole. There went the five-hundred-dollar investment they had made in the car, plus the cost of replacing the pole. Still, they had given him another chance and a few months later, bought him another car—a seven-year-old Chevy that was a little newer and much more underpowered.

Four-cylinder engine or not, Grant still managed to slam it into a parked car while doing donuts in the snow the previous winter. More expense for a family that already had a tough enough time stretching from paycheck to paycheck. Reggie now believed that the two strikes against his older brother meant that he would not be receiving a car on his sixteenth birthday one year hence.

Still, Reggie couldn't hate Grant, who had never been the type of older brother that exploited his size advantage to act as a physical bully. Moreover, he hadn't even let his friends use Reggie to practice delivering charley horses. He hadn't exactly been like Wally to the Beav, but this was real life, not *Leave It to Beaver*. He had been exactly the big brother Reggie had every right to expect.

Until he started committing felonies. Reggie could have done without that.

Reggie walked around and past the gathering groups of high schoolers in the parking lot and on the sidewalk. They fell naturally into their groups—the cheerleaders, the jocks, the stoners, the brains. Reggie was able to walk right by all of them without being noticed.

As he passed one of the groups, Reggie heard a boy say, "Come on, let's stop at Artie's and grab a burger on the way home. My mom's making liver and onions tonight and I'm not eating *that*."

Reggie smirked to himself a little. He hated liver and onions almost as much as he did tuna casserole, but he took comfort in the fact that his mother rarely made it. At their house, it was usually just some sort of meat fried into submission and coupled with a can of whatever vegetable had been on sale at Smith and Sons the week before.

Also, the idea of having enough pocket change—or even more unlikely, folding money—was so foreign to Reggie that he never would have entertained such a concept. He glanced at the small knot of boys and saw that it was Allen Rondo who had spoken. His parents owned the clothing store in town. Reggie was pretty sure that whenever Allen turned sixteen some late model car would be waiting in his driveway that morning. He shrugged. Reggie never really confounded himself too much with comparing his life to those who had won the birth lottery. He had accepted where he was for now, though he did have amorphous plans for how he might change that at some point in the future.

As was the case for so many young people who had never been forced to put a plan into action, he was confident that he would be an unqualified success at some point in the future. Was that, perhaps, a little contradictory to believing he would likely end up in an unexciting job at the box factory? This is the human condition, the yin and yang, the acceptance of reality and the seeds of optimism.

The wind picked up, blowing the fallen leaves around his feet as he walked toward home. He put up the collar of his jacket and put one foot in front of the other. He was lost in thoughts of Amanda and the upcoming party on Friday. It was an easy fantasy to entertain. In his mind, he was casual and confident, well able to keep up with Amanda and her friends. In fact, in his dreams, he was the life of the party.

Why not? Reggie thought. *Why not me?*

He was only a couple of blocks from home when he saw his family's old station wagon come barreling down their street. That was unusual in a couple of ways. The first was that Elaine Blackwell had the most delicate of feet on the gas pedal. If she ever actually hit the speed limit when driving, it was news. The second unusual thing was that Reggie didn't think their old station wagon could *barrel* anywhere.

The old wagon seemed to agree with that assessment, as it lurched toward him, belching blue smoke out the back.

Reggie raised his hand in a half-wave, half-stop sign.

Grant was behind the wheel. His face a sour knot of concentration or desperation. It was hard to tell which.

As the old wagon drew closer to him, Reggie stepped off the sidewalk and onto the edge of the road, intending to catch Grant's eye one way or the other.

The Ford Falcon blew right by him. When he flew past, Reggie saw that Grant was hunched over the wheel, gripping it tightly, his jaw set. Very different from Grant's normal laidback and cool demeanor when he was behind the wheel.

If his brother saw him, he gave no indication.

Chapter Four

All of that was odd. As far as Reggie knew, Grant was still locked up in Chief Deakins' *Graybar Motel*, aka the Middle Falls jail. That's where he had been when Reggie had gone to school that morning. Now, he was not only out of jail, but seemed to be focused on decamping from at least the neighborhood, if not perhaps all of Middle Falls and even possibly the great state of Oregon.

Reggie stared at the trail of blue smoke the Falcon had left behind and watched Grant turn left toward Artie's, or, more likely, the road out of town. He couldn't imagine a reason why anyone would ever be in such a hurry to get somewhere within the Middle Falls city limits.

He rolled the problem over in his mind for a few moments, then realized it was an unsolvable conundrum, at least with the information at hand. He took a deep breath, released it, then headed for home, picking up his pace a little as he did.

The driveway at the house was empty, of course. The Blackwell family only had one car, and it had just whipped by him a few minutes earlier. His father was working on a construction job somewhere out of town. Reggie had never really cared enough to ask where, and if his parents had mentioned it around him, it hadn't stuck. All he knew was that someone came to pick his father up before he woke up in the morning and didn't drop him off until several hours after school got out. During this time of year, that meant that he both left for work and arrived back home in the dark.

Reggie pushed open the door and wasn't too surprised to find his mother where he had left her that morning, sitting at the kitchen table, staring out the window.

There was something—an odd vibe—that even a teenage boy who was completely wrapped up in his own situation could recognize.

"Hey, Mom. I'm home."

Elaine nodded, never taking her eyes off the small front yard and its dilapidated fence.

"Everything okay?"

That finally brought Elaine back to attention. "Okay?" she asked, and there was a tremor in her voice that Reggie didn't like one bit. She laughed, but it was a bitter sound with no gaiety or mirth.

Reggie was torn. He had always been at least a little invisible at home as well as in school. Parents were parents, of course, thinking their parent thoughts and making parent decisions.

Grant had arrived five years before Reggie and seemed to have much of their attention staked out before Reggie had a shot to submit his own claim. That attention wasn't always positive, God knows, but poor people just trying to get by only had so much focus and energy to expend on a second child.

Now, perhaps *he* was in a position to give some attention or comfort, depending on his read of the situation. To his eye, it didn't look like Grant was just on the way to Smith's to pick up a loaf of bread. When he added up the things he knew—Elaine had apparently bailed Grant out and it was possible that his brother was now in the process of skipping town—he thought there might be the chance to move up a notch in the family hierarchy.

"Do you want to talk about it, Mom?"

Instantly, Elaine shook her head, then tapped another cigarette out of the pack of almost-empty Viceroys in front of her. The smoke from the previous cigarette still hung just over her head. She shook her head, almost automatically. Then, she turned and looked at Reggie as if she was perhaps seeing him for the first time. Not the first time that afternoon or that day, but the first time, period. As though she was suddenly reevaluating him.

"You wouldn't do this, would you, Reggie?"

Reggie thought fast, but was caught between wanting to know more and being reassuring. In the end, curiosity won out.

"Do what?"

Elaine waved vaguely in the direction of the road, but didn't answer beyond that.

Curiosity denied.

Elaine took a deep breath and, in a voice so tired it obviously took everything she had to speak, said, "Just make yourself some cereal for dinner tonight, okay?"

Reggie wanted to step forward and lay a hand on his mother's shoulder, but he couldn't quite get enough momentum to do so. Instead, he just nodded and turned to go to his room. Until very recently, it had been a room shared with Grant, but it was possible there was a change in the air. Before he made it out of the small kitchen, Elaine stopped him.

"On second thought, could you maybe go to one of your friend's houses tonight? Not to stay over. I know it's still a school night. But, maybe for a few hours?"

"Sure, Mom. I'll call Harold and go over there. How come?"

It was obvious that Elaine didn't want to answer, but finally she said, "I'm going to have a fight with your father when he gets home."

That was more than enough to get Reggie's feet moving. He'd been around a few times when the two of them had gotten into it. It always started quietly, then built in intensity as accusations flew across the room. Sometimes it was followed by pushing and shoving. On occasion, it required an emergency room visit for one or the other of them, followed by lame explanations that were gladly accepted in 1973, when everyone just wanted to mind their own business.

He had thought that he would call Harold and see if he could come over, but this new information changed his mind. He went to the bedroom, intending to just change his jacket for his heavy coat. It got chilly in Middle Falls in mid-October, and if he ended up wandering around town instead of visiting Harold or Nelson, he knew he would need the extra warmth.

The small bedroom he shared with Grant was in its normal condition. That was, messy, but still within the range that Elaine was willing to accept. The room had a definite funk about it, but Reggie had gone nose blind to it long since.

He was surprised to find a note on his crumpled-up pillow. He immediately recognized Grant's handwriting. Like Reggie, Grant was a poor student, but he had a remarkably neat handwriting. It was the one part of his schooling he had apparently taken pride in.

The note was short.

I'm gone.

It was simply signed, *G*.

Reggie touched the note contemplatively, then grabbed it and stuffed it into the pocket of his jeans. He grabbed his coat, looked around the room to see if there was anything else he might need, but couldn't think of anything.

Without another word to his mother, Reggie left the house. His first thought was to go to Harold's house. Harold lived in a slightly nicer part of town, though not too far from Crampton Village. He also lived in slightly better circumstances than Reggie. Harold's dad worked at Graystone Insurance, his mom stayed home, and Reggie didn't think his mom and dad ever went to fist city to settle their disagreements.

He started to head in that direction, but as he walked, he changed his mind. He tried to picture what he would say to Harold, or maybe Harold's mom if she answered the door. "Hey, can I hang out here for a few hours? It's going to be stormy at my house."

Reggie had never talked to anyone about the violence that happened in his house. He and Grant had always been mostly spared from it, and he thought that it was one of those secrets that should stay with him. He assumed that everyone else lived picture-perfect lives and that he would come off looking bad in comparison.

He thrust his hands into his pockets and felt around hopefully, as though a five-dollar bill or even a few coins might materialize. The only thing he pulled out was pocket lint.

Ahead, he spotted a phone booth. He decided to make some positive use of his time. He went inside, closed the door behind him and opened the Middle Falls phone book, which was not very thick. He looked up Dr. Jarvis in the white pages and saw that it listed an address on Barrymore Street. That didn't surprise him. That's where people like dentists and doctors lived, in big houses with big lawns and multiple expensive cars parked in the driveway.

He tore the page out of the phone book and stuffed it in his pocket. He knew the neighborhood, which was maybe a mile away. He walked in that direction, which took him past both Smith and Sons and Arties. He swung into Smith's and found a dark corner where he could boost a couple of Three Musketeer bars. He walked out of the store confidently, as though maybe they hadn't had whatever product he was looking for.

He glanced at Artie's a little longingly. He hadn't eaten there often, but he remembered those burger baskets and strawberry shakes fondly. A two-lane street divided Artie's from Smith's and because he was feeling masochistic, Reggie crossed the street and walked alongside the drive-in.

The neon sign that rose high above Artie's was turned on and glowing in the late afternoon dusk. Inside, a cook and two waitresses were lounging against the counter, waiting for the inevitable dinner rush. Warm yellow light spilled out onto the empty parking lot.

Fully aware that there was no practical way to steal an Artie's burger, Reggie peeled the wrapper off the Three Musketeers bar and walked toward Barrymore Street. In the store, the candy bar had seemed alluring, but now, having smelled the deliciousness that was Artie's, it didn't taste good at all. He chewed it mechanically and swallowed anyway. He fished the second Three Musketeers out of his pocket and thought of forcing it down too, but decided to save it.

He zipped his coat up against the cold that was settling in and picked up his pace. Fifteen minutes later, the more modest houses took a turn. Everything in this neighborhood was a little bigger, a little newer, a little nicer.

He almost didn't need to look at the number of what he guessed was Amanda's house. It was one of the nicest houses in the neighborhood. It actually had a small circular driveway, as though it had aspirations of being an estate. It wasn't quite that, but it was big, with two stories, a tall, sharply peaked roof, and tall trellises of ivy climbing up the front. There were floodlights lit up already that made it glow like a jewel.

Reggie had no interest in knocking on the door or even going anywhere near it. He just wanted to know where it was when the time for the party rolled around. He had already seen what Amanda was like when someone kept her waiting, and he didn't want to experience an encore of that.

It was full dark by then. Reggie did the calculation and figured that his dad would be getting dropped off at home any minute. He wondered how long it would be until the fight started.

He rolled the situation over in his mind. He still didn't know the truth of it. Had his mom decided to bail out Grant without his dad's permission, or was it the other way around? There was no way for him to know who was going to be the aggrieved party, but it didn't matter. They would both make every effort to give as good as they got, and Reggie would just as soon be anywhere else while that happened.

He also knew that he didn't really belong in this neighborhood. If Chief Deakins or one of his deputies came rolling through—which they often did in this neighborhood—they would roust him just for breathing. Being the brother of a criminal gave him a little cachet at school, but not with the local cops.

He needn't have worried. The neighborhood was dead. The hardworking dads had already returned from their well-paying jobs and were sitting down to a good meal prepared by a mom who had learned a new recipe watching reruns of *The Galloping Gourmet* that very morning.

Reggie was such a stranger in a strange land that he might as well have accidentally wandered into a foreign country. Even in a small town like this, there are different islands and cultures and never the twain shall meet. At least, never the twain shall meet unless a beautiful girl reaches across the dividing line.

Content that he knew where to meet Amanda on Friday, Reggie turned back toward town. He hadn't gone more than twenty steps before the skies above opened up. He was okay with being a little cold, but cold *and* wet were another thing.

He looked around to see if he could find a place to seek cover. There was nothing obvious, but just ahead and to his right, he saw a house that stood completely dark. All the other houses in the neighborhood had porchlights burning, but this was an oasis of shadows.

Reggie had no interest in breaking into the house. One felon in the Blackwell family at a time was plenty. Still, he ran toward the house, hoping for the shelter of an overhanging porch. As Reggie got closer, he saw that it was one of the smaller houses in the neighborhood and didn't have so much as an overhang over the front door.

Rain pounded down on him, and he was about to abandon everything and sprint for the downtown when he spotted a small garden shed off to the side. It was the inexpensive, metal kind with two sliding doors at the front. Reggie ran to it and found that there was no lock. He slid the door open and the smell of gasoline, lawn clippings, and assorted chemicals greeted his nose.

The inside was crowded, but there was a stack of folded up tarps to the side of a lawnmower. He stepped inside, slid the door closed behind him, and sat down on the soft canvas pile.

Rain drummed a heavy rhythm on the metal roof overhead. Reggie ran his hand through his longish hair—which had, of late, been a point of contention with his father—and shook the water out as best he could.

It wasn't late, but sitting in the shed, he found himself growing sleepy. He yawned, but didn't fight the feeling. He leaned his head back and closed his eyes.

When he opened them again, he had no idea how much time had passed. The rain had stopped. Carefully, he opened the door a few inches and peered out. The darkened house remained apparently unoccupied. Outside, the sky had cleared, and the sliver of a moon was visible overhead.

Reggie had no idea what time it was, though he noticed that his damp coat was now mostly dry. In any case, he figured that enough time had passed so that it should be safe to go home. He stepped out of the shadows and onto the shoulder of the street when a pair of headlights lit up behind him. He ignored them and turned toward downtown.

A few seconds later, the whole area became a swirl of blue and red as the Middle Falls police car hit its lights.

Chapter Five

Reggie instinctively froze, as one does. His hand crept, almost involuntarily toward the remaining Three Musketeers in the pocket of his jeans. He shook his hand to get control of it back, then hooked it casually into his empty belt loop instead.

The prowler pulled up alongside Reggie with exquisite slowness, its lights still flashing off the trees and houses. The car rolled a little ahead of him, then angled slightly, as if to block his path. Reggie stopped obligingly, reminding himself that, aside from the pilfered candy bar, he hadn't done anything wrong, and even that petty crime would be impossible to prove.

For a few seconds, the scene remained frozen, then the door opened, and Deputy Naismith got out.

When Reggie saw who it was, he had to stop himself from snickering. Naismith was the oldest deputy on the small force. He was in his late forties, but more than that, he had a huge belly that hung over his belt to go with his ham hock arms and thighs that tested the stability of his uniform pants.

Reggie battled with himself a little. He knew that if he just upped and took off, he could easily lose Naismith, who he doubted could run more than ten steps without collapsing. He stopped himself from doing that, though. In a small town, you might be able to momentarily outrun someone, but since everyone knew you on sight, you couldn't hide forever.

A stray thought ran through Reggie's mind. *Unless you're willing to just get the hell out of Middle Falls, like Grant obviously did.* He shook his head a little to banish that thought.

"Keep your hands where I can see them," Naismith said. When he spoke, his voice was so laconic, it was obvious he was repeating something by rote, not out of any actual fear of a Middle Falls teenager. "Step toward me."

Reggie turned slightly and took one step toward Naismith.

"What are you doing in this neighborhood?"

Inwardly, Reggie groaned a little, knowing that somehow Naismith probably recognized the stink of Crampton Village on him and instinctively knew that he shouldn't be hanging around in this nice neighborhood, especially this late.

He ran his options through his mind. He could say, "Well, this foxy girl who definitely outclasses me invited me to a party at her house, and I wanted to see where it was, so I checked it out. Then it started to rain and I broke into someone's shed and fell asleep."

That would have been completely true, and also would have sounded like a completely made-up story. He searched his mind for a more reasonable excuse and came up blank. He also had an unsettling feeling that somehow that excuse might find its way to Dr. Jarvis and his hoped-for boost into a new stratum of social acceptance would be over before it started.

He settled for a teenage boy's default response. He shrugged.

"That's just not going to cut it," Naismith said. "I need to know what you're doing wandering the streets so late."

A cleaner version of the truth popped into Reggie's head. "My mom and dad were fighting." He risked a look at the deputy from under his long bangs. "*Really* fighting. So I left, and I've just been walking around until it was good to go home again."

"How do you think you'll know when that is?"

"I don't," Reggie said, shrugging again. "That's why I'm still walking around."

That wasn't quite true. He had seen enough of his parents fights that he knew they were usually over by bedtime. He remembered once, when he had been younger and so scared by their fighting that he had run into an empty field and hid for an hour after watching his dad knock his mom into the refrigerator, spilling mustard, pickles, and cans of Budweiser everywhere. When he eventually got cold and snuck back toward the house, he had been amazed to see his parents sitting on the back steps. His father was drinking a Bud, and his mother was holding a bag of frozen peas against her bruised cheek.

They had both looked a little shame-faced, and his father had said, "Sorry you had to see that, Reggie." His mother had said, "Yeah. That will never happen again."

Never can be a very short time in a house like Reggie's, and within a few months it happened again. Eventually, he learned to make himself small when the storms occurred, either by hiding in his room, under his bed, or in his closet. If Grant was home when it happened, he would often take him for a walk.

As a long-time veteran of those wars, then, Reggie was sure that today's battle was probably done.

Naismith nodded, and it seemed that response did the trick for him. He wasn't the kind of deputy who heard of a married couple knocking each other around and then wanted to leap into the fray. He was more the kind of deputy who enjoyed hassling teenagers and not having to write up reports.

Reggie, who was terrible at reading books, but excellent at reading people, sensed that whatever danger he had been facing with Naismith had passed.

The deputy wasn't quite through with him, though. "We have a curfew in Middle Falls, you know."

Reggie actually *didn't* know, because it had never been relevant to him before. He didn't say that, though. His instincts told him to just lie low for a few more seconds and he would be free. Then, he realized that since he didn't own a watch, he didn't have any idea what time it was.

"Can I ask what time it is?"

Naismith glanced at the Timex on his wrist, then said, "It's 12:05." He glanced meaningfully at Reggie. "Curfew is 11:00 p.m. during the week. Midnight on weekends."

For half a second, Reggie thought that Naismith might be about to offer him a ride home. That dissipated when the deputy sighed and, as if doing him a big favor, said, "I'll overlook the curfew violation this time. Get on home now."

Reggie didn't mind missing out on the ride home. He knew there was a chance that when he saw where he lived, or, upon spending time with him in the prowler, Naismith might figure out he was Grant's brother. It wasn't a crime to be the brother of a criminal, but it probably wouldn't have helped his situation any.

Reggie nodded and hurried away from the prowler, which was still lighting up the neighborhood. He had no doubt that those lights had attracted the eyes of at least a few neighbors who had watched the scene unfold from behind their curtains and blinds. He fought down the temptation to raise one or both of his middle fingers at the unseen observers. Instead, he headed for downtown.

He felt like he didn't need to stick to side streets or hide in the shadows on the way home. Middle Falls didn't ever have more than one overnight deputy patrolling the streets, and he had already dealt with that one. As long as he could resist committing a felony on the walk, he figured he was safe.

The downtown area of Middle Falls, after midnight on a weekday, was as quiet as a forest where no tree ever fell. It had a different vibe than Reggie had ever seen before. With the deep shadows and only the sound of his near-silent footfalls, it almost felt like a city in a bottle with the cork firmly in place.

Reggie wasn't much given to scaring himself or letting his mind look for the worst, but as he walked, he felt tiny prickles of dread run up his neck. He picked up the pace, wanting only to see the comforting confines of his bedroom and to be tucked under the heavy comforter of his bed.

By the time he turned the corner and saw his house, he was sweating with the effort, even in the cold air.

There was still no car in the driveway, of course. He hadn't expected one. Inside, everything was dark. For a moment, he wondered what he would do if the door was locked, since he'd never had a key to his own house. The knob turned easily, though, and he stepped into the small living room, which was as dark as it was outside. There weren't niceties like streetlamps lighting the streets of Crampton Village.

Reggie stood and listened, but there was no sound. He took a blind step forward toward his bedroom when his toe hit something soft, nearly tripping him.

"Damn," he said quietly, though it sounded loud in the silence. He looked down but couldn't see anything but shadows. In his mind, he tried to think of what might have been placed in the middle of the floor to trip him up.

He knelt and knew at once it was a body. He couldn't have said how, but Reggie knew that it was his mother.

"Mom?" he said in an urgent whisper. When there was no answer at all, he found her arm and then her hand. It was cold and still.

"Mom?"

Chapter Six

When there was no answer from Elaine, Reggie froze.

He was a smart enough kid. He'd seen a few things in his young life. He managed to get through most days without making a fool of himself.

He had no idea what to do when he found the unresponsive body of his mother lying in the living room in the middle of the night.

A sudden calm came over him. Both his breathing and his heart rate slowed.

He stood up and took two steps to where he knew a lamp sat on the table. He clicked it on and harsh light filled the room.

He didn't want to look at his mother for a moment, so he looked around the room instead. Everything looked completely normal. There was no overturned furniture, none of the many ashtrays scattered around the room had been thrown against a wall or tipped over onto the floor.

Finally, he forced himself to look at Elaine. He was afraid of what he might see, but at first glance, she didn't look that bad. Her head was turned at an awkward angle, and when he knelt beside her again, he saw that her face was puffy and beginning to bruise.

He tried to think, but his thoughts had slowed down like a steam train going up a steep hill, and his brain didn't seem to want to reengage.

He grabbed her wrist, just like he'd seen people do on television. He didn't feel anything, but he didn't have any idea if he was doing it correctly.

A sudden thought occurred to him.

Dad.

He didn't have any doubt about what had happened here. They had started one of their "good fights," and as so often in the past, it had come to blows. Maybe something went wrong. Maybe his mother took a slap then tumbled over backwards and hit her head on the coffee table or landed wrong against a wall. It could be anything.

Reggie tried to picture what happened next. Did his father just get up and go to bed, leaving Elaine on the floor, possibly drawing her last breaths? That disconcerting possibility filled his mind and he had to find out.

He stood again and hurried down the hall to his parents' bedroom. Quietly, not knowing if he was hoping to find his father or not, he swung the door inward.

The room was empty.

Reggie clicked the overhead light on. Everything looked normal. The bed was made. His mother's sewing machine sat undisturbed in one corner.

It took less than a minute for Reggie to search through the rest of the small house, turning on lights as he went.

He hurried back to Elaine, who hadn't moved. He noticed a small drool of blood had leaked out of her mouth. He used the sleeve of his coat to wipe it away. He wasn't sure what to do next. He knew he needed to call someone, but he wasn't sure who.

The 911 system existed in 1973, but not in Middle Falls, Oregon. It would take the better part of a decade before it was installed in many small towns.

He decided that he needed to know if she was dead or alive before he could call someone. He was sure that whoever he called, they would want to know that. For the third time, he knelt beside his mother. This time, very slowly, he turned his head and put his ear over her heart.

He heard a slow *lub-dub, lub-dub.*

She was alive. That meant he needed to call the hospital. He hurried into the kitchen and pulled the phone book out from under the heavy handset. He found the number for Middle Falls General Hospital and hesitated.

If he called, he was sure they would send an ambulance. An ambulance meant a bill. Would he get in trouble for making the call? He thought about that for a few seconds, then decided he just had to do it, damn whatever trouble he might get into.

A small giggle escaped his lips when he wondered, *Who's going to get me in trouble anyway? It looks like Mom's dying, and Dad and Grant are maybe both on the run.*

Another giggle backed up behind the first one, but Reggie sensed that if he let it come out, there would be a torrent of crazy-sounding laughter behind it. He bit his lip hard enough to draw blood and that brought him back under control.

He dialed the number and waited. After three rings, a woman's voice answered.

"Middle Falls General, this is Cathy."

Reggie nodded along. Cathy seemed calm. It was just a normal night at work for Cathy. Her world wasn't crumbling around her.

"This is Reggie Blackwell." He hated that his voice sounded so young. He tried to pitch it deeper, but knew that it didn't really help. "I think my mom fell down and hurt herself. She's not moving."

"Is she breathing?"

"I'm not sure. I guess so. I listened to her heart and it was still going, but it was slow."

"I'll send an ambulance. What's your address?"

Reggie recited the address.

"Do you want to stay on the phone with me?"

Reggie had no idea. This wasn't a situation that had come up before. "Should I?"

"No, it's not necessary as long as you're fine," Cathy said. "The ambulance is on the way. They should be there in about five minutes. Turn your porch light on for them and open your door. They'll know what to do when they get there."

Reggie nodded, ignoring the fact that Cathy wouldn't hear that. He slipped the handset back down.

"Five minutes," he mumbled to himself. He knew the time would pass quickly, but even so, he wasn't sure how to fill those scant minutes. He went back to the living room, where Elaine was still in the same position she had been in when he had first discovered her.

He remembered that Cathy had told him to turn on the porch lights and open the front door, so he hurried to do that. He flipped the switch inside the door. The porch light did not turn on. A faint memory of Elaine telling him to attend to that very thing a few weeks—or months—earlier popped into his head.

"Damn." He reached up and twisted the bulb back and forth, hoping that would be enough to bring it to life. No such luck. He hurried into the kitchen, opened the bottom drawer and rooted around, looking for a fresh bulb. When he didn't find anything there, he opened the door to the under-sink cabinet.

He was still searching around in there when he heard a male voice call, "Hello? We received a call from this number and are here to help."

That was the moment when he spotted the four pack of 60-watt bulbs. He shook his head and hurried back to the living room. He saw two men dressed in gray uniforms on the small porch.

"My mom's in here. Can you hurry?"

The first man, tall with dark hair cut short, was carrying a black bag. He knelt beside Elaine, unzipped the bag, and pulled out a stethoscope. He put it in his ears, then touched the end to her chest. He nodded to himself as though counting along. The second man, shorter and much younger, stood just inside the door as though he had no real job to do at the moment.

"What happened to her?"

Reggie shook his head. "I don't know. I was gone. When I got home, I found her like this."

"Is it just the two of you?" The question obviously flustered Reggie, so the man said, "Living here, I mean?"

That was a more complicated question than it would have been twenty-four hours earlier. At the moment, Reggie wasn't really sure who lived in the house.

"No, it's my mom, dad, and my brother."

"Is your dad here?"

"No. I don't know where he is."

The EMT touched Elaine's puffy face and pried open her left eye, shining the flashlight into it. He glanced at the younger man. "Go get the gurney. We need to get her transported."

The younger man seemed happy to have a job to do and skedaddled out of the house.

The EMT wrapped a blood pressure cuff around Elaine's arm while Reggie backed away, honestly glad to just not be answering questions for a few seconds. The back of his legs hit the chair that only his father ever sat in. Numbly, he let himself fall into the seat.

He looked at the clock on the wall. 2:02.

Aside from the questions he didn't know how to answer for the EMTs, he had a lot of unanswered questions for himself. That list started with, *What do I do now?* He cleared his throat and said, "Can I come with you guys?"

The man bent over his mother, removed the blood pressure cuff, then looked at Reggie. "That's against our regulations, sorry. Is there someone else you can call to take you to the hospital?"

Reggie ran that around his brain. There *might* be someone he could call for a ride somewhere, but no one seemed to fall into the *emergency phone call at two o'clock in the morning* category. He shook his head.

"Well," the man said as the second man pulled a clattering gurney up the concrete front steps, "it would be better for you to come in the morning, anyway."

Reggie nodded as though he understood, although he didn't.

The second man positioned the wheeled gurney the only way it would fit in the small living room. He fiddled with something and the bed lowered down until it was only eighteen inches off the floor.

"Excuse me," the first man said, maneuvering around so his backside was close to Reggie, who abandoned his seat and retreated toward the kitchen. He watched, fascinated, as the two men lifted his mother's limp body up onto the gurney. In just a few seconds, they raised the bed up, then put straps around Elaine's legs and chest.

At first, that made Reggie think they were afraid she might suddenly wake up and start violently tossing about, but then realized that it was more likely just to keep her slipping off when they moved her.

In one smooth motion, they got the gurney moving. They lifted it up so it didn't bump over the concrete steps, then pushed it over the uneven sidewalk until they got to the ambulance. The younger man opened the door, they slid the gurney inside, and he climbed in after.

The dark-haired man closed the door, then looked at Reggie. Almost as an afterthought, he grabbed a small notebook and pencil out of his breast pocket. He took a few steps toward the porch. "Almost forgot. What's your mom's name?"

"Elaine Blackwell."

"Thanks, son. Try to get some rest now. You can call the hospital in the morning."

Reggie nodded. "Is...is she going to be all right?"

The man didn't lie. "You can call and check in on her in the morning." He turned and hurried back and around the side of the ambulance. He got in, fired up the engine, and drove away. As soon as they pulled onto the road, they turned on their red flashing lights, which was a little bit of a relief to Reggie. If they had just pulled away quietly and with no lights, it would have seemed like there was no sense of urgency to get Elaine to the hospital.

He looked around the neighborhood and saw curtains ruffle and fall back into place in the house across the street. For the second time that night, he felt like he was being observed.

This time, he was too tired to care. He closed the door and looked around the house.

Now that his mom had been moved, he saw a small pool of blood where her head had rested on the wood floor. For a moment, he wondered if he should clean it up or if it was part of some sort of crime scene now. He decided that since no one had told him not to touch things, he could go ahead and clean it up.

He stepped over the puddle and went into the kitchen. There was an old towel hanging on the refrigerator handle. After grabbing that, he stepped back into the living room. He bent over and was just about to try to clean up the blood when a knock came on the door.

Reggie twitched his mouth. Should he clean the blood first, then answer the door? There were so many things he wasn't sure of and wasn't really equipped to handle. He decided to answer the door first. With the dishrag still in his hand, he opened the door.

For the second time that night, he found himself face to face with Deputy Naismith.

Chapter Seven

It was hard to say who seemed to be most surprised to see the person on the other side of the door, Reggie or Naismith.

Reggie quickly tucked the dishtowel into his back pocket as though he had been caught in the middle of disturbing a crime scene, which, perhaps, he had.

It didn't take long for Deputy Naismith to put the pieces together in his mind. He hitched his uniform pants up closer under his overhanging belly and blew out a breath of air. "Guess the ambulance has already been here and gone?"

"Yes, sir."

"Can I come in? I've got a few questions, and I'd rather not ask them standing out here on the porch. Even in the middle of the night, people like to snoop on their neighbors."

Reggie stepped back, careful not to move so far back that he stepped in the pool of blood. That same pool stood between the door and anywhere they might stand or sit, though, so he gave up and pointed to it. "Careful there."

Naismith nodded, then stepped over the blood. He moved surprisingly delicately for a man his size. "Mind if I sit down?"

Reggie indicated his father's chair, then sat down on the couch. "What kind of questions do you have?"

"Well, I had one set when I got the call from the hospital, but seeing you here now, after our conversation earlier, I have some more. First, what's your name?"

"Reggie."

"Reggie. Reggie what?"

Reggie sighed, then said, "Blackwell."

Naismith nodded and made a note in a small blue notebook. His pen paused mid-word and he said, "Blackwell, as in *Grant* Blackwell?"

"That's my brother."

"Been quite a day around here, I'd say." Naismith finished jotting his note down. "And it was your mother who was injured?" He glanced up at Reggie, who nodded. "And what is her name?"

"Elaine Blackwell."

Another flurry of the pen moving across the notebook. "And your father's name?"

"Willis Blackwell."

"Willis," Naismith repeated, writing that down as well. "And is he here?" Naismith glanced down the darkened hallway as though Willis might appear at any moment.

"No, sir."

"Was he here when you got home?"

"No, sir."

"When I first saw you tonight, you said your mom and dad were *really* fighting. Do their fights often end up like this? People going to the hospital?"

Reggie squirmed in his seat, but his only answer was a shrug.

"I get it," Naismith said. "Don't worry, I'm not asking you to point a finger at your dad." He looked around the living room. There was some peeling wallpaper, a faded print from a calendar that Elaine had framed years before, and a small television that sat on top of another, bigger television. Everything in the room was gray, faded, and at least a little depressing. "Any idea where your dad might have gone?"

That was the first time Reggie had thought about that. When he'd seen Grant leaving, he'd had no idea where he might be heading. Now, the same was true for his dad. Willis had some good drinking buddies, but he didn't know if any of them were the type to harbor a fugitive on the run from the law.

"I don't know. I don't have any idea."

Naismith closed the notebook and slipped it back into his pocket. "Any other brothers or sisters?"

"No."

"So you're here alone?"

"Yes, sir."

"How old are you?"

"Fifteen."

Naismith moved his head back and forth in a comme ci, comme ça gesture. "Well, that means you're old enough that I can leave you here alone if you want. If you were much younger, I'd have to take you in and find someone to watch you." He glanced at Reggie, taking his measure. "I can still do that, though, if you want."

"No," Reggie said immediately. "I'm good here."

Good was a vast overstatement, of course, but it conveyed the idea that he didn't want to be put into the system. In his mind, Reggie saw that as a conveyor belt that, once you were on, was difficult to get off.

In another place and time, Deputy Naismith might have called in a crime scene team to process the crime. In Middle Falls in 1973, he just put his notebook away and said, "Okay, then. Call down to the station if your dad comes home. We've got some questions for him."

Reggie was sure those questions would include, "How would you like a long stay in jail and three hots and a cot?" but he just nodded his agreement.

Naismith stepped over the blood again and let himself out the front door.

Finally, Reggie was able to clean up the small pool of his mother's blood. He took the towel into the kitchen sink and ran it under the tap, then wrung it out and went back to finish wiping up the residue. When that was done, he looked around the room, feeling lost.

He was dead tired, of course, and with the blood mess cleaned up, he finally didn't have anything on his to-do list. He thought that maybe he should just go take his clothes off and climb into bed, but that didn't seem quite right in the empty house. He realized that he was still wearing his coat, so he slipped that off, laid his head against the arm of the couch and used the coat as a blanket.

He was asleep instantly.

With everything that had happened, and considering how late it was when he finally got to sleep, it would have been understandable if Reggie had slept until noon. The combination of the angle of his neck on the couch, the coldness of the house, and the overall strangeness of the situation, worked to wake him up just a few minutes later than usual.

He thought back to the day before, when everything in his world seemed normal. Sneaking the extra sugar on his cereal, his mom being distracted, but at least she was *there*. Based on what he saw of her last night, he wasn't sure if she would ever be there again.

With only four hours of sleep, Reggie felt fuzzy-headed. His mouth tasted bad and his neck was killing him. He normally didn't shower in the morning, but this day was anything but normal. He turned the temperature up to *high* on the living room thermostat, then went into his bedroom and stripped down. Gooseflesh popped out all over his arms and body. He tossed his jeans onto his bed, dumped everything else on the floor, and grabbed socks and underwear out of his drawer. He walked stiff-legged into the shower and turned on the hot water.

He stood shivering and waiting for the old hot water heater to deliver the goods. Finally—*finally*—the water turned hot, and he stepped gratefully into the ugly, scarred tub, pulling the curtain shut behind him.

Being fifteen years old is an elixir of its own in a way and that, combined with running the hot water completely out, essentially did the trick of making Reggie feel human. He didn't actually wash with soap or shampoo, but he did let the water run over his neck and shoulders, easing the knots. When the water ran cold—it was kind of nice not having anyone to tell him to get out sooner—he stepped out, making puddles on the bathroom floor.

The mirror was fogged, but he used his towel to wipe away the steam. He peered at his reflection. His entire life had changed in the previous twenty-four hours, but he still looked exactly the same. There was a slight flare-up of acne on his forehead, but his hair hung down enough to disguise that. He touched his cheek to see if he needed to shave. He didn't, but that wasn't unusual. A single pass with his dad's razor about once a month kept the stray hairs on his chin at bay.

He sprayed Right Guard antiperspirant on his pits. He normally didn't bother, but even with everything else that had happened, he remembered that Amanda Jarvis had spoken to him the day before. If, by some miracle, the day went in a direction where he ended up in a clinch of some sort with her, as unlikely as that was, he didn't want to stink.

He pulled his underwear on, grabbed his socks and headed to his bedroom. He knew that when he pulled open the second drawer that belonged to him, there would be folded T-shirts waiting for him. The closet would have more of his button-up shirts hanging, waiting. In a moment of unusual awareness, he realized that he had always taken all the things his mother had done for him for granted.

He grabbed a white T-shirt and an orange long-sleeved shirt and put them on. He did the same with the jeans he'd worn the day before, then sat on the bed and put his shoes and socks on. He felt a surge of accomplishment. He had always thought that if push came to shove, he would be able to take care of himself.

Push had definitely met shove.

The living room had warmed up nicely, which just reinforced the idea he was doing fine. That is, until he wondered who would pay for the electric bill when it came due. Or the house payment, or phone bill. If his dad was really in the wind, Reggie guessed that he would clean out the bank account. He went to the wall thermostat and turned the heat off.

In the kitchen, he poured a big bowl of Sugar Smacks and felt no need to hide how much sugar he added on top. When he opened the refrigerator, he saw that there was only a tiny bit of milk left. He shrugged, poured those few drops, then left the carton on the counter.

Reggie sat at the kitchen table and tried to think of what he needed to do. Was it too early to call the hospital? Or should he just go there straightaway? Or maybe, he should just go to school and kind of pretend like it was a regular day.

There was a terrible thought lurking in the back of his mind. With all adults in the house gone, would someone, some social services agency, maybe, come and get him? Put him on that conveyor belt that led to an orphanage.

He wondered if there was anything he could do to stop that. Since both the hospital, through the ambulance drivers, and the police department, through Deputy Naismith, already knew the situation, he doubted it.

He did think that not showing up at school would probably lead to more attention, though, so he decided to go there first. He would go and check on his mother in the hospital after school. It wasn't that he didn't care about whether she was going to live or die. It was more that he felt like he was suddenly all on his own and he needed to look out for himself first.

That *Reggie first* attitude took hold at that moment and put roots down.

Once he left the empty house behind, everything in the world seemed pretty normal again, and he did his best to put all the uncertainty of life out of his mind.

He couldn't help but be preoccupied, of course, but he managed to float through his classes without any real incidents.

When he sat in his usual seat in History, he glanced to his right to see if Amanda would be there again, but she was back in her normal spot in the back, surrounded by her retinue of hangers-on.

That was fine with Reggie. With everything else going on, he was happy not to have to worry about saying the wrong thing to Amanda.

He ate lunch with Harold and Nelson again, but this time he managed to keep what was on his mind to himself. So far, no one had mentioned anything new about Grant or said, "Hey, I hear your dad knocked your mom into kingdom come and she's in the hospital now."

Reggie was a believer that three people could keep a secret when two people were dead, so he wasn't interested in testing it.

An objective observer might have noticed that although Reggie had a lot on his mind and was both distracted and withdrawn, no one around him noticed anything different. It was possible that his behavior on this day wasn't all that different than any other.

When school let out for the day, his original plan was to walk to Middle Falls General to check on his mom. When the moment arrived, though, he changed his mind. He was suspicious that there might be someone from social services there waiting for him, ready to drop him onto the conveyor belt.

Instead, he walked to the phone booth a block from the school. He panicked a little when he realized that he didn't have the requisite dime to make the call. He closed his eyes, said a small prayer, and reached in the coin slot.

Miraculously, there was a dime hiding in there.

"Luck's changing," he said, then looked up the number for the hospital again. He dialed the number and after a single ring heard a woman's voice say, "Hospital, Helen speaking. How can I direct your call?"

"Umm, I'm not really sure. My mom came in on an ambulance last night and I just want to check on her. Can you tell me how she's doing? Her name's Elaine Blackwell."

There was a long pause, and Reggie could hear pages flipping on the other end. "I'll connect you to the ICU. Hold please."

Reggie found himself holding his breath, knowing that in the next few moments, he would find out just how profoundly his life had changed.

Chapter Eight

Reggie listened carefully to the silence on the other end of the line for what felt like a very long time. Finally, there was a click and a woman's voice said, "ICU, this is Ann."

Reggie went through his spiel again asking for his mom's condition.

Another long pause, then the woman said, "And this is Mrs. Blackwell's son?"

"Yes. Reggie."

"Is your father with you, Reggie?"

"No." He was already getting used to answering this question. "I don't know where he is. I just want to see how my mom is."

"Of course. Are you here in town? Could you come in and see us? That would probably be better."

"Yes. When are visiting hours? When can I come?"

"Don't worry about visiting hours. Just ask for directions to the ICU nurse's desk when you come in the front door. They'll send you this way. Ask for Ann Weaver."

"Yes, ma'am," Reggie said as he hung up the receiver. He fished around in the coin return hoping to find another coin, but it was empty now. He walked toward Middle Falls General for a few blocks. On his way, he swung by Smith and Sons again and pocketed another couple of candy bars—a Butterfinger and a Snickers. Those always filled him up.

He managed to get out of the store undetected, but did make a mental note that he'd have to find some money and buy something soon, or they would get suspicious.

Having the weight of the candy bars in his coat pocket made him feel a little better.

He hiked on toward the hospital. Middle Falls General had moved a few years earlier, so this was what everyone in town called the *new* hospital. It was built mostly out of concrete, which gave it a stable, permanent feeling.

The automatic door whooshed open when Reggie stepped toward it. Inside, he found the information desk and did as Ann Weaver had told him.

The woman behind the desk was large and had a pair of half-glasses perched on the end of her nose. She looked sympathetically at Reggie and said, "Yes, Mrs. Weaver let me know to expect you." She pointed down a long hall to her right. "Go down that way, then turn left at the second hall that branches off. If you get lost or if anyone stops you, just have them call me. I'm Mrs. Greely."

Reggie nodded and wandered away. He didn't want to walk too fast because he was becoming increasingly convinced that he was walking toward bad news. Adults weren't usually this nice to him. He jammed his hands into his jeans pockets and crossed his fingers, hoping that maybe the bad news would be that his mom was going to have to stay in the hospital for a few days. That would be expensive, but they could worry about that later.

He did end up forgetting what Mrs. Greely had told him and got a little turned around. All hospitals are a little like mazes, with green-colored walls instead of shrubs. He turned left at the first hall instead of the second and almost ran into a doctor wearing green scrubs. "Sorry," Reggie said, then added, "am I going the right way to find the ICU?"

The distracted doctor didn't answer, but just hurried on his way, ignoring him. In another few steps, Reggie found himself looking through a window at three newborn babies and knew he was lost. He backtracked, tried to remember the directions, and took the second left. He saw a sign that said *Intensive Care Unit* and knew that he was on the right track.

The hallway twisted to the right, and when he turned the corner, he saw a large nurse's station with two women wearing starched-white uniforms. One of them came toward him and said, "Reggie?"

Reggie nodded, suddenly aware that he might be about to burst into tears. That was the last thing he wanted to do. He swallowed hard and focused on bringing himself under control.

"I'm Ann," the woman said. She was a pretty woman in her late thirties who looked as though being a nurse was exactly what she was intended to do with her life. "Come with me, and I'll take you to see your mom."

That was a relief to Reggie. He had been afraid she was about to tell him that Elaine was dead.

Ann came around the workstation and led Reggie farther down the hall. "Do you go to Middle Falls High?"

Reggie nodded, glad to momentarily have something different to talk about.

"Maybe you know my son, Zack. He's a freshman."

"I know him," Reggie said, hoping that any resentment he had toward Zack didn't show in his voice. Zack Weaver was one of those kids that seemed to float through life on a cloud, with everything going right for him. Reggie searched his brain and couldn't remember ever having a conversation with him. Mostly, he saw him cutting up in the hall, or with his arm around some new girl. Where other freshman boys were socially lost, Zack never had any problem. Secretly, Reggie kind of hated him.

"Right in here," Ann said, swinging a heavy door open.

Reggie was surprised to see that there was only one bed in the room. He had assumed his mom would be in with a bunch of different people. Somehow, it made him even more nervous to see her alone in the room. He was used to being poor, to never receiving any special treatment or care. Seeing this made him suspicious.

There was a curtain around Elaine's bed, but it was pulled back so he could see her as soon as he stepped in. She looked much worse than when he had seen her in the dim light of the living room the night before. Her face was now so puffy that her left eye was completely closed shut and colorful bruises were evident. He noticed something he hadn't the night before—raised red marks on her throat in the shape of handprints. He'd seen a lot of their knockdown drag-outs, but none of them had ever descended to actually trying to choke the other out.

Reggie glanced at Ann Weaver, whose brows were knitted together in a concerned expression. "How often is she awake? Can I talk to her?"

Ann just shook her head. "She hasn't been conscious since she was brought in. You can talk to her, though. I'm sure she'll hear you. A mother can always hear their child."

Reggie drew a breath in and let it out slowly. He knew that the fact she hadn't regained consciousness wasn't good. "What's wrong with her?"

Ann seemed to be fighting a battle with herself. "I should probably have you wait to speak to one of the doctors." Suddenly, she stood up straight and seemed to change her mind. "She had a blow to the head that has given her a concussion, but that's not the worst of it."

Reggie thought back to the pool of blood on the living room floor. "It's not?"

Ann laid a gentle hand on Reggie's shoulder. "She's had some internal bleeding, too."

"She's not going to make it, is she?"

Ann smiled, though it was tinged with sadness. "Where there's life, there's hope. I've seen miracles here on the ICU. I promise you, we are doing everything we can for your mom."

Miracles didn't seem like anything Reggie wanted to hang his hat on, but there wasn't much else for him at that moment. He nodded. "Can I sit here with her for a little while?"

"Of course. There's a chair right there. You can pull it close to the bed if you want. If you need anything, just come out to the nurse's station."

Reggie started to pull the chair across the linoleum, but it made a terrible vibrating, scraping sound, so he bent over and picked it up, carrying it instead.

Before he sat down, he looked down at his mother. She was a small woman, but when she was moving around the house, taking care of things, she had always had a presence about her. Now, that was gone and all that was left was this small body.

Reggie's throat was thick, but he had already decided that he wasn't going to cry. Instead, he leaned close to her and said, "I'm sorry this happened, Mom. I shouldn't have left. If I'd stayed, it wouldn't have gotten this bad. I really am sorry."

He lapsed into silence after that. There really wasn't anything else he could think of to say. Later, more words would come to him, and he would wish he could say them to her, but sitting in this sterile hospital room, none of them came.

He heard rain spatter against the window and looked out to see that a small rainstorm had sprung up. That was okay. It matched how he felt inside.

He sat there for an hour, wondering what else he should be doing. He watched the darkness fall and decided that it was time to leave.

"Bye, Mom. I'll be back to see you tomorrow, if they'll let me."

He passed the nurse's station and said, "Can I come back tomorrow?"

"Yes," Ann answered, "but it's better if you call first and let me know so we can clear it for you."

Reggie nodded and walked down the long hall, turned right, passed Mrs. Greely, who was putting things in her purse, getting ready to go home for the night. She saw Reggie as he approached and called him over. "Do you have a ride home?"

"It's okay. I can walk."

"The weather has really taken a turn. I'm off work now. I'll give you a ride home."

Reggie looked at the woman, trying to figure out why she would go out of her way to be nice to him. Did she just feel sorry for him because his mom was about to die? To his eye, she looked like one of those church-going ladies that talked about doing good, but managed to ignore every opportunity to actually do it. And yet, here she was, almost insisting.

Reggie gave in. He didn't really cherish the thought of the cold and wet walk home.

"Good," Mrs. Greely said. "You wait here. I have to punch out, then we can go."

Two minutes later, she reappeared wearing a green wool coat that made her look even larger than she was. She had a ridiculous little hat perched on top of her starched hair.

They walked to her sedan, Reggie gave her his address, and by the time they hit Main Street, the heater had warmed up the interior. Sitting beside her, Reggie could smell her perfume, which he thought smelled like an old lady scent.

Five minutes later, she pulled in front of their dark house. Reggie made a mental note to change the porchlight.

"Thank you, ma'am," Reggie said. He had already forgotten Mrs. Greely's name.

"You're welcome. I'm sure I'll see you again."

That turned out not to be true. Reggie never saw her—or his mother—ever again in this life.

Chapter Nine

The house was cold and dark when he walked in. He turned on the lamp beside the couch, but that didn't bring much joy. It just seemed to push the shadows around a little. There was another lamp at the other end, and he turned that on, too. A little better.

He was surprised that he had never noticed before how the lack of an overhead light in the living room meant it was kind of dark in there.

He went to the kitchen and flipped on the overhead light. He snapped his fingers as if remembering something important, then reached under the sink and retrieved the corrugated cardboard container of light bulbs. He slipped one out, went to the front porch and switched it with the old one. Immediately, a warm, yellow light came on. He looked up at it a little proudly, as though he had accomplished at least one thing that day.

Back inside the house, he turned the heat on. He was no more sure who would be paying the electric bill than he had been the day before, but he decided to live warm until that bill came due.

He wondered if his parents had some money stashed away somewhere in the house in case of an emergency. He laughed a little at that thought. From a financial viewpoint, the Blackwells had gone from one minor emergency—new tires, or an unexpected bill cropping up—to another, like having to bail out Grant from jail.

Reggie supposed that might have been what had contributed to the sudden violence that had occurred in the house the night before.

Nerves had been stretched taut, almost to the breaking point, for so long, when that last element was added—when the proverbial straw met the proverbial camel's back—someone snapped.

He still didn't know if it was his mom who had bailed Grant out and his dad had taken it out on her, or if it had been his dad in the first place and the anger was defensive. At that moment, it didn't really matter.

He stood in the middle of the living room for a moment as the heat clicked on. The thing that *did* matter right then was that he was hungry. He had been too nervous to eat very much at school, which meant that his last actual meal was a long way in the past.

He grabbed the two candy bars out of his pocket and dropped them on the coffee table. That didn't seem like the solution. Maybe as dessert, but he needed something else.

Reggie was not a cook by any stretch. In fact, aside from pouring himself his bowl of cereal in the morning, he had never made himself a single meal. A future kid his age would have probably been able to nuke something in a microwave, but Reggie had never even turned on a stove burner. He walked tentatively into the kitchen and began to open cupboards, hoping something impossibly easy would fall out.

If he had looked in the freezer, he would have found a Swanson TV dinner, but he didn't think of that. Instead, he opened the cupboard with the canned goods and pushed around the cans of beans, corn, spinach, and diced tomatoes.

None of those did him any good. Technically, it was all food, but anything that required a recipe or preparation was beyond him. Finally, he did find a few things, including a can of Campbell's Bean with Bacon soup, and, best of all, clear at the back, an old forgotten can of SpaghettiOs. He smiled as though seeing an old friend.

"That, I can do," he mumbled to himself. He opened the silverware drawer looking for the can opener, but it wasn't there. The drawer below that one held all kinds of kitchen tools that he had no idea how to use, but he did find the can opener. He didn't really know how to use that, either, but he figured it out.

He thought of heating up the SpaghettiOs, but decided against it. Warm or cold, they would fill him up just the same.

He grabbed a spoon, jammed it deep into the can and took a huge mouthful.

A small moan escaped him. It was so good, it almost made him weak in the knees.

He carried the can and spoon into the living room and flicked on the smaller TV that sat on top of the larger console television. Getting the bigger set fixed was one of those financial emergencies that the Blackwells had never quite gotten around to dealing with. The thirteen-inch black-and-white TV, purchased on the cheap on a payday from Sal's pawn shop, had been a temporary solution two years earlier.

There was no cable in Middle Falls in 1973. But using the rabbit ears, he was able to bring in two of the Portland stations. He switched between them, disappointed to find that they were both showing the evening news.

He shrugged. Any noise at all was better than the odd silence that had settled over the house. He considered sitting in his dad's chair—that one had the best straight-on view of the TV, but couldn't bring himself to do it.

Instead, he sat on the couch in his normal spot and wolfed down the SpaghettiOs, while trying to pay attention to what was being said on the news.

He was just scraping the red sauce off the sides and bottom of the can when the front door opened.

A small, startled yelp escaped from Reggie's lips.

It was Willis Blackwell, large as life.

"Didn't mean to scare you, Reg," he said, as though he had just returned from a quick trip to the grocery store.

"Dad," Reggie said, surprised and a little scared.

Willis took his youngest son in, while still standing just inside the door.

"We've got a mess, don't we?"

Reggie nodded. That was absolutely true.

"Did you go see your mom?"

Another nod. The SpaghettiOs suddenly felt like a block of paste in his stomach.

"She going to be all right?"

"I don't think so. Everyone was too nice to me, like maybe she was already dead, but it just hadn't happened yet."

Willis had been looking a little shifty—embarrassed to be caught by his son in this terrible situation. Reggie's reading of the situation brought a nod and smile of pride to his face, though. "You're smart to figure that out." Then, as though he realized that Reggie had just told him that his wife was probably going to die, he tried to put a mournful expression on his face. "Dammit. That's not good."

Somehow, the way he said that made Reggie think that he meant more that it wasn't good for Willis, not that he felt bad for Elaine. That made Reggie mad.

"Why'd you do it to her?"

Willis shook his head a little. "You'll understand when you're older. Grown-up stuff." He went to the window and pulled the curtain back. He looked outside, just like someone in an old black and white gangster movie. He might have realized that he looked slightly ridiculous, because he turned to Reggie a little shamefaced. "Anyway, what's done is done, and there's nothing for it now." He moved and sat next to Reggie on the couch. It felt odd to see him sit somewhere other than his chair.

"I'm going to have to go away now. It's not gonna be good for me around here."

"Are you going to go with Grant?"

Anger flashed on Willis's face. "No. That little SOB took off without even a how do you do. I stuck my neck out for him, too, by bailing him out. Little bastard. I guess the apple doesn't fall far from the tree."

The words were harsh, but Reggie was sure he saw a look of pride once again on his father's face. He had always known that his father had preferred his older brother to him.

"That's why your mom was so bent out of shape last night and why this all happened."

That solved at least one small mystery. Apparently it was Willis who had signed off on the bail money to get Grant out. That had put everything else in motion. It was also very much in Willis's character to place the blame for the whole mess on someone else. Taking responsibility had never been his strong suit.

Reggie felt a rumbling in his stomach, nervous to ask the next question, but he knew if he didn't ask it now, he'd never get the chance.

"I think Mom's going to die. Grant's gone. I know you're about to be gone, too, aren't you?"

Willis didn't answer, but he didn't need to. It was obvious.

Reggie took a deep breath, but his voice was still shaky. "Can I come with you?"

This was more of a spur of the moment request, but Reggie knew he didn't want to be all alone here. He didn't know what would happen if he was, but he was sure it wouldn't be great.

Again, the answer was obvious on Willis's face before he answered. He shook his head a little. "I'd like to have you along, but—"

"You'd take Grant if you could," Reggie said bitterly.

"You're right. I would. But Grant's not a kid, and you are. The way I'm going to be living won't be great for you."

"What's going to happen to me, then?"

"This is what I've been paying taxes for all these years, right? Someone will take care of you." Willis looked at his watch and said, "Sorry, Reg, but I've got to get going."

It occurred to Reggie that Grant had taken their only car. "How are you leaving?"

"A friend loaned me a car."

A sudden realization dawned on Reggie. He pushed past his father and threw the living room curtain open wide. An old Chrysler sat in their driveway. The *friend* sat in the passenger seat. A woman had the overhead light on and was applying lipstick in the rear-view mirror. With the light illuminating her, Reggie could see her stiff blonde hair and weathered face.

He'd heard his mom talk about his father's *bar hussies*, and here was one in the flesh.

Reggie stepped back from the window and turned to confront Willis, but his father had disappeared into the back bedroom. Reggie followed him down the hall, spoiling for a fight. He found him with a suitcase open on the bed, throwing clothes inside.

Willis at least had the decency to look a little embarrassed at being caught out like this. He took a wad of money out of his pocket—no doubt the last of the Blackwell bank account. He peeled off a ten-dollar bill, then considered and added a fiver to that. He tossed it on the bed. "That'll help you get started. It's more than my old man gave me when he left."

Willis casually tucked the rest of the money inside a pocket of the suitcase, then snapped it shut.

He reached out to ruffle Reggie's hair reassuringly, but Reggie moved out of the way, a sneer of disgust on his face. Everything he had thought about his father for fifteen years had come crashing down around him. He realized that the man he had known all that time was just a costume. The real man inside was finally standing in front of him now.

Willis shrugged and pushed by Reggie, already whistling a little tune. Apparently, he had been ready to break free and knock the dust of this little town from his shoes for a long time. Now that the time had arrived, he seemed anxious to get started.

Reggie followed along after his father, hating him. If he had been bigger, stronger, he might have launched himself at Willis. Reggie's big growth spurt was just starting though, so he knew what would happen if he did. He'd end up with a beating, just like his mom, maybe even with the same results.

Instead, he just stood in the living room and watched Willis throw the door open wide and step through.

Reggie stepped to the window and opened the curtains again. He watched as Willis quickly set his suitcase down, opened the driver's door, and climbed into the Chrysler. He leaned across the seat and kissed the woman, who Reggie thought was the ugliest woman he'd ever seen.

Willis leaned down to pick up his suitcase just as a Middle Falls police cruiser pulled up behind the Chrysler, blocking it in.

Chapter Ten

Willis Blackwell's entire demeanor changed. His shoulders slumped and he slammed his hand down on the car.

Chief Deakins himself got out of the squad car. He didn't approach the Chrysler directly, but moved slightly to the side so he could get a better angle on what was happening in the car. He didn't have his gun drawn, but he did have his hand resting on its butt.

"Hello, Willis. You're not heading out, are you?"

Willis dropped the suitcase back onto the ground and looked from side to side as though considering his options.

"Listen, Willis," Deakins said, "I've known you a long time. I know you're not a bad fella. You're in a little bit of a pickle right now, but think carefully about what you're about to do. If you try to bull your way out of here, you'll never make it to the city limits, and then you'll have more charges to face. Right now, I just want to talk to you, nothing more."

Willis looked at the woman beside him, shrugged, and stepped out of the Chrysler. "What kind of questions you got, Chief?"

Deakins relaxed a little, but not too much. He'd faced these situations a lot and knew they could turn on a dime. "The kind of questions that I need you to answer back at the station." His hand dropped meaningfully onto his gun again.

That was the moment that all the fight seemed to go out of Willis Blackwell. Watching from the living room window, Reggie could almost see all the dreams of an exciting life on the road dissipate from his dad's mind.

Deakins caught a bit of motion from the corner of his eye when Reggie moved the curtain. "Who's home in there?"

"Just my boy."

"Grant?"

"Nope. My other boy. The little one."

"Good enough. I heard that Grant has already vacated the county, which I'm sure was also your plan until about two minutes ago. I've got no business with your other boy." He moved to the back of his prowler and opened the rear door. "Come on over here, turn around, and put your hands behind your back."

"So this is a handcuffs-first kind of questioning?"

"It is, Willis."

That was the moment that a second Middle Falls cruiser pulled up, further complicating any possible escape route.

Willis nodded, stepped toward Deakins and turned around with his hands behind his back. On the way past his suitcase, he gave it a brush with his foot, then glanced at Reggie in the window.

Sixty seconds later, Willis was cuffed, in the back of Deakins' cruiser, and on his way to answer the chief's questions.

Standing in the window, Reggie knew there wouldn't be any good answers forthcoming. He supposed that if his mom pulled through, things could still turn around for Willis. If she died, though, he would face at least a manslaughter charge. He knew that much from watching TV, which is where a large volume of his information came from.

Reggie stepped out onto the porch and met the eye of the hatchet-faced woman, who had now slid over behind the wheel. He stepped casually out onto the porch. While the woman pulled away, completely ignoring him, he retrieved the suitcase.

The deputy who had pulled in as backup got out of his police car and approached the porch.

Reggie wanted to put the suitcase with the money behind his back, but also didn't want to be obvious about it. He affected as much bluster as he could and said, "Can I help you?"

"Chief wants me to poke around in your house a little. Make sure your brother isn't in there. You mind?"

Reggie had no idea what the law really was, beyond what he had seen on a few cop shows. He shrugged, pulled the suitcase inside and set it by the door.

The deputy came in, his hand also on the butt of his gun. He took two minutes and searched the entirety of the small house, then said, "Good enough," and walked out without a backwards glance.

Reggie waited until the deputy had turned around and left, then picked up the suitcase and carried it into the back bedroom. He opened it and retrieved the money his father had stashed inside, then left the suitcase on the bed. Standing next to his mother's sewing machine, he counted the money. There were three hundred and fifteen dollars. With the money Willis had given him, that gave him three hundred and thirty dollars.

It wasn't a fortune, and even at the age of fifteen, Reggie knew it wouldn't last very long. It was a start, though, and it probably bought him some time. He could probably manage to go down to the Public Utility District and pay the light bill, at least, so he could keep the heat on. He had no idea how much the mortgage was, or how to pay it, or even how long it would take for that to catch up to him.

For now, though, he felt flush. He could go to Smith's and buy some basic groceries and keep himself alive for a while.

It had been another full day for Reggie, seeing his mother's unconscious body in the hospital, finding out his father was ready to abandon him, then watching Chief Deakins arrest him in his own front yard.

Reggie did feel sad for his mom. As far as he knew, she was still alive, but he was already beginning to grieve her. He didn't bother to spend any emotion on either his dad or on Grant. They had both made their own conscious decisions, and as far as Reggie was concerned, they could live with the consequences.

It was still early in the evening, but he was feeling tired. He hadn't gone to bed before nine o'clock in years, but he thought this might be the day.

It was still a little too early for that, though, so he flipped the channel on the TV to see what was on. It turned out to be *Truth or Consequences,* hosted by Bob Barker. It wasn't his favorite show, but it was better than nothing. He was just about to sit down when there was a knock on the door.

What now? Reggie thought. He would have been okay with no one ever knocking on his door ever again. He dutifully marched to the door and opened it to find Mrs. Teagarden from across the street standing on the steps with a casserole dish in her hands.

His mother always called Mrs. Teagarden *Mrs. Kravitz* for her propensity for nosiness, and Reggie assumed that was why she was here now. She'd undoubtedly seen the drama play out in the front yard earlier and wanted to do a reconnaissance mission to get the lowdown. He wondered if she kept casseroles in the freezer just to serve as an entry point to a house that was in conflict.

"Hello, Reggie," Mrs. Teagarden said primly. "We saw the ambulance last night and we were worried that someone might be sick, so I made some of my famous tuna noodle casserole to bring over."

Of course, Reggie thought. *Has to be that.*

Mrs. Teagarden stepped up onto the small landing on the porch and tried to peer around Reggie and see what was going on in the living room.

Reggie turned slightly sideways to allow her a full view, since there was nothing out of the ordinary to see. He watched her face and could see just a hint of disappointment at how normal everything looked.

"Thanks, Mrs. Teagarden. My mom's in the hospital right now. She's not feeling very well. I hope she'll be coming home soon." He wouldn't have guessed he could do it, but he managed to summon up a smile that said, "Nothing really out of the ordinary going on here."

What he wanted to do was step out onto the porch, empty the useless tuna casserole into the dirt and hand the empty dish back to Mrs. Teagarden. He managed to avoid doing that by promising himself he could dump it into the garbage can as soon as she left.

Mrs. Teagarden, obviously disappointed at how little her fact-finding mission had turned up, loitered for a minute, but Reggie just stepped back and closed the door.

"Thank you, ma'am. I'll let Mom know you stopped by with the casserole." He couldn't bring himself to lie and say he was sure it would be delicious.

He sat back in his normal spot on the couch and unwrapped the Butterfinger. After dealing with his father, the cops, and Mrs. Teagarden, he decided he deserved a little treat. He tried to focus on a practical joke that Bob Barker was playing on an audience member, but couldn't do it. When *Truth or Consequences* went off and *Jeopardy!* came on, that was even worse. That was a show that made him feel dumber, since he never knew any of the answers.

He clicked the TV off and sat back down, deciding that he needed to make a plan. He even thought of making a list of everything he needed to do, which made him feel very grown-up. He didn't have any of his notebooks in the house, though, because he never brought any school work home with him. He found a small notepad sitting by the phone, but it had pink roses on the top and that reminded him too much of his mother. He decided he could just decide what he needed to do and then remember it.

He sat down at the kitchen table—again, in the spot he had always sat—and tried to think. He realized that he knew where the *bill drawer* was. It was the small drawer just under where the phone sat on the counter. He had always avoided it because he associated it with his parents fighting and the fact that he had zero interest in bills.

When he opened the drawer, he was surprised to see it was stuffed full. He didn't think they had that many bills. He decided to pull them all out and see what they were. It was a bit like an archaeological dig of a poor family in the mid-seventies.

They really didn't have that many bills, but there seemed to be multiple copies of each one. First, an electric bill. Then, a late warning for the electric bill. Then, a *Final Notice* with the stub of that one torn off, at least theoretically paid. Then, for some reason, all three bills were stuffed back into the drawer. Digging through the pile, he saw bills that went back almost two years, just like that.

The only ones that really worried him were the phone bill—he supposed it would be a red flag if someone from Child Protective Services called and found the phone had been disconnected—the light bill, and the mortgage.

He was a little distressed to see that the most recent *Final Notice* on the electric bill listed a date the following day. His stress levels didn't improve when he saw that the most recent mortgage statement showed that they were ninety days late on that as well.

Reggie knew that his mother always paid the bills and assumed that was part of why she was so stressed out when his father had somehow scraped up the money to bail Grant out.

He decided there wasn't much he could do about the mortgage being late. Trying to bring that bill current would have wiped out the money he had all by itself.

He knew he could pay the phone bill, though, which was just sixteen dollars, and the light bill, which was twenty-eight dollars. He decided he would go to both the office of McDaniel's Phone Company and the PUD the next day after school.

He felt like he had accomplished something, and now really was exhausted.

He went into his bedroom and stripped down to his T-shirt and underwear, then remembered he had forgotten to turn the heat down. He went back out and turned it all the way off, pleased with himself for remembering.

When he got back to the bedroom, he looked down at a perfectly made bed. He realized that his mom had made it for him. He crawled in and laid his head on the pillow, expecting to fall asleep immediately.

He didn't, though.

He was suddenly overwhelmed by everything. The façade that he had kept up for the previous two days melted away.

Reggie Blackwell cried himself to sleep.

Chapter Eleven

Reggie decided that the best course of action for the moment was to try to keep as normal a schedule as possible. He seemed to remember a movie where the parents had died or moved away and a family of kids were able to fake their way through things and ended up being able to stay together.

Reggie's situation was different, of course. In the movie, the parents reappeared at the end, grateful to the kids for holding it together. Reggie knew that was unlikely to happen for him unless his mom made, as Ann Weaver had said, a *miraculous* recovery. He didn't think Willis or Grant were likely to put in an appearance any time soon, and it wouldn't have necessarily been a positive even if they had.

Reggie was sure that Willis was now a guest at Chief Deakins' jail, probably waiting to see if Elaine Blackwell lived or died so they would know what to charge him with. Grant was in the wind and, even if he was to ever return to Middle Falls, it would probably be in handcuffs.

Maybe Grant and Dad can finally be together after all, just like they both wanted, Reggie thought bitterly.

He pulled a T-shirt out of the drawer, another shirt from the closet, and noticed that it was the next-to-last for both of them. Dirty laundry was among the smaller problems Reggie faced, though, so he forgot it immediately.

He made it to school on time, though on a mostly empty stomach, as the Sugar Smacks box held nothing but crumbs and there was no milk in the fridge anyway. He made do with eating the Snickers bar while he walked.

He slid into his normal seat two minutes ahead of the bell. The seat to his right was once again occupied by someone other than Amanda, who was in the back row.

Reggie hadn't spoken to Amanda since first period Tuesday, which was understandable. He'd had a few things going on since then. He didn't want to get caught staring at her, but he did find his eyes wandering in her direction over and over.

She was wearing a simple miniskirt, which showed off her legs to good effect. Somehow, even in October, Amanda's legs were still tanned. As usual, she didn't seem to have a care in the world. She put her head together with her girlfriends, completely ignoring what the teacher was saying, though in another mystery, she would get an A in the class when all was said and done.

Mixed in with all the other *stuff* for Reggie, he began to wonder if maybe the invitation to her party the next day had been rescinded and he just hadn't heard that yet. He couldn't think of a way to confirm that without looking like an idiot, though.

When he finally tore his attention away from Amanda, Reggie noticed something else. There were ripples of covert conversations and notes being passed back and forth. Other people in the class were casting quick glances at him, then looking away when he noticed.

He realized that word had gotten out about what was going on in his life. He didn't know if it was the fact that Grant was on the run, that his dad had beaten his mom almost to death, or that Willis was now in the slammer.

In a town the size of Middle Falls, it could be any or all of those things.

Reggie decided to just ignore it as best he could.

When the bell rang, he gathered up his history book and headed for the door. In the hall, Amanda and her friends had lingered.

Reggie was sure that if other kids knew what was going on with him, Amanda certainly did. She was like the old-fashioned telephone operator. All Middle Falls High gossip flowed through her.

She smiled at Reggie, wide-eyed and innocent. When he passed by, she said, "See you tomorrow night, right?"

Both the sweetness of her voice and the message were a melody to Reggie's ears.

"I'll be there," he said, trying and, undoubtedly, failing, to sound smooth and cool.

That solved at least one small mystery in his life, which wasn't bad since it wasn't even nine o'clock in the morning yet.

As he walked to his next class, his suspicions about his secrets being out were confirmed. Each group that he passed stared at him, then looked away when he caught their eye. He left a buzz of conversation in his wake.

Reggie didn't much care that kids were talking about him. He *did* care that if the kids knew what was up, there were probably adults who knew. He glanced around to see if someone in authority was looking for him, ready to pull him out of class to have a meaningful conversation.

Aside from the other students looking and pointing at him, there was no one.

When he got to lunch, he was prepared for the fact that Harold and Nelson would know, too. He was glad to see that what the school cafeteria called *pizza* was on the menu that day. It wasn't really like the pizza they served at Shakey's—this was cut into squares and was more like a soft bread with a little tomato sauce, the hint of a few toppings and a scattering of cheese—but it was good, warm, and filling. It was a vast improvement over tuna casserole.

Reggie didn't even consider veering off and finding a spot by himself. He trusted his two friends to not be too terrible with him.

That faith was rewarded when he sat down. They didn't wrap their arms around him and commiserate loudly over his fate. No Middle Falls teenage boy of 1973 wanted to either give or receive that kind of attention.

Instead, Harold and Nelson just nodded at him, then started talking about a skit they had seen on *The Sonny and Cher Comedy Hour* the night before.

That let Reggie relax and just sit quietly while he ate.

When they finished and were ready to split off and go to their next classes, Harold looked over at Reggie and said, "Sorry, man."

"Thanks, man."

"I'm pretty sure there's nothing I can do," Harold said quietly, "but if there *is* something, just call me."

"Will do."

Nothing else needed to be said.

If someone had put a gun to Reggie's head, he couldn't have told you a single thing he was supposed to have learned that afternoon. He sat quietly in class after class, still in shock.

As soon as school let out, he hustled over to the Middle Falls Public Utility District, which was housed in a squat gray building made entirely of concrete blocks. There were no windows, so any outside light had to fight its way through the glass door at the front. Reggie had always thought that the box factory was a depressing place to work, but the PUD actually looked like it might be worse.

Inside, Reggie fished the crumpled bill out of his pocket. Laying it on the counter, he said, "My mom told me to come by and pay this."

The clerk, an officious-looking woman with hair that looked like it might come off and sit on a Styrofoam head at night, touched the bill with her pen. She turned it so she could read it, then said loudly, "Francine? Has Bill gone out to do the disconnects yet?"

Someone—Francine, apparently—answered from behind a wall. "Yeah. He's out on his rounds now."

"Can you get on the radio and see if he's done Crampton Village yet?"

"He probably has," Francine answered. "That's where most of the disconnects usually are."

The woman at the front counter looked at Reggie and said, "If he's already disconnected it, there will be an additional fifteen-dollar reconnection fee."

Reggie's shoulders sagged a little. He had brought enough cash to pay the two bills and buy just a few groceries. He did the math in his head and decided that if he was unlucky, he'd spend the grocery money on getting the electricity turned back on.

After a minute, Francine called out, "What's the address?"

The front desk clerk read the address off the bill.

"He's in luck. Bill hasn't gotten to that one yet."

Reggie thought about that. *Bill hasn't gotten to that one yet.* He wondered how many people in his neighborhood got their power turned off every Thursday. He'd always known his family was poor, but he suddenly had a new appreciation for his mother, who always managed to at least keep the lights turned on.

The woman took Reggie's money, gave him some change, then said, "The next bill is due on Monday. Tell your mom."

Reggie felt like a hamster on a wheel that couldn't quite catch up, but just nodded and said, "I will."

McDaniel's Phone Company was in a nicer building, and the receptionist seemed a lot nicer too. Maybe it was because their phone wasn't on the verge of being turned off. It was only a few weeks late.

With those two bills paid, Reggie went back to Smith's and made something of a show of getting one of the old shopping carts and pushing it past the cashier as if to say, *See? I'm here to do serious shopping. No shoplifting for me today.*

The shopping cart had a wobbly wheel that wanted to pull it to the left, but Reggie wrestled it down the aisle.

He didn't go to the meat or produce department. Anything from there would have done him no good. Even *Hamburger Helper* was beyond him. Instead, he piled four Swanson's TV dinners in the cart. They were all the same, fried chicken, mashed potatoes, corn, and cherry cobbler. It was the one Reggie always liked best on the rare occasions when his mom served them.

In the canned food aisle, he bought some cans of Campbell's Chicken Noodle Soup, then dropped three cans of SpaghettiOs in the cart.

In less than five minutes in the store, he had unconsciously copied many a bachelor's trip through Smith & Sons.

He went to the cashier and put his selections on the counter. The middle-aged lady rang them up, made his change and, Reggie thought, gave him a sad, *I'm sorry* look. He walked out into the blustery Middle Falls afternoon and wondered to himself if everyone he met knew what was happening and felt sorry for him.

The groceries all fit into one sturdy paper bag, but it was heavy, and he was happy he hadn't bought more.

The trip to Smith checked off the easiest three items on his list. He was dreading the fourth.

Still, he had to know.

He lugged the bag of groceries along the sidewalk until he came to the same telephone booth. He stepped inside and closed the bifold door behind him.

This time, he didn't need to rely on the miracle of a found dime. He *did* need to look up the number for Middle Falls General again, though. Numbers, like whatever he read, just didn't stick to the walls of his brain.

When a woman answered—not Mrs. Greely today—he asked to be connected to ICU.

After a long, echoing silence, he heard a click on the other end. "Intensive Care, this is Ann."

"Hello, Mrs. Weaver. This is Reggie Blackwell. I wanted to see if I could come by and see my mom this afternoon."

There was a lingering pause and it sounded terrible to Reggie, so he filled it with unimportant babble.

"I just went shopping and got some groceries, but I can carry them with me, I think. Or, if it's a bad time right now, I can take them home first, then walk back..."

He might have kept going, but Ann Weaver finally spoke.

"Reggie, I'm sorry..." She kept speaking, but Reggie had stopped hearing.

Quietly, without saying anything else, he replaced the phone, cutting off the call. He allowed himself a moment. He put his forehead against the cold glass. When he managed to focus his eyes on the outside world, he saw leaves swirling in a dance. Raindrops pattered against the pane.

He stayed just like that for sixty seconds, trying to adjust his mind to his new reality. He had walked into the phone booth with a mom. He was about to walk out without one.

He had known this was a possibility. In fact, he knew it was more than just that. It was a likelihood. But still, until he heard Ann Weaver's voice, he had managed to believe it wouldn't happen.

It was one of those transitional moments in a person's life when everything changes. As long as Elaine was alive, there was hope, and Reggie didn't feel completely alone in the world. Now, he knew he was exactly that.

No matter how he might want to, there was nothing to be done about it.

Dry-eyed, Reggie picked up the bag of groceries, opened the payphone door, and walked toward home, putting one foot in front of the other.

Chapter Twelve

Reggie Blackwell didn't have many superpowers. He was really an ordinary fifteen-year-old boy in almost every way.

But the one thing he really excelled at was his ability to partition. Even in these extreme circumstances, with his whole world having crumbled under him in less than seventy-two hours, he was able to take all that angst, grieving, worry, and uncertainty and stick it into one corner of his brain to be dealt with later.

Delayed grief can be powerful, even devastating, but there are times when a human being just isn't ready for the full tidal wave to wash over them all at once.

So it was with Reggie. On the Friday morning after he learned his mother had died, he got up at his normal time, took his last clean T-shirt and button-down long-sleeve shirt out and even pulled his second pair of jeans out of the closet.

He decided to wait to shower until after school because at that moment, his mind was only focused on one thing: Amanda Jarvis.

In the back of his mind, he still had the nagging thought that this whole thing was too good to be true, that it was probably a setup of some kind. But hope and logic rarely exist in the human mind at the same time, and Reggie needed that hope like a drowning man needs a life preserver.

If Amanda hadn't surprised Reggie on Tuesday, what would Reggie have focused his attention on? Impossible to know, but it probably would have ended up with him getting into some stupid trouble of one sort or another.

It was unlikely that he would have been satisfied to spend another evening at home watching the evening news and *Truth or Consequences.*

At school, people still looked at Reggie and gossiped. This was Day Two of *The Reggie Blackwell Story,* though, so the temperature was already beginning to cool. By Monday, a rumor would spread that some girl was pregnant or that two of the most popular kids were on the verge of breaking up and Reggie would be permanently moved to the backburner. Just another sad story in a world filled with them.

He didn't talk to Amanda that day, and that was fine with him. Previous experiences in talking with girls—especially girls like Amanda—had shown him that silence was golden. That was part of why he disliked Zack Weaver so much. Where Reggie was perpetually unsure of himself, Zack reeked of confidence. Reggie wasn't much of an athlete, where Zack was all-everything in track, even as a freshman. And now he knew that in addition to everything else, Zack had a really cool mom, where Reggie had none at all.

At that particular point in Reggie's life, things just didn't seem fair.

Ironically, just as Reggie was leaving school to walk home, he crossed paths with Zack, who was tall and lean, with black curls that fell carelessly around his face. Now that Reggie had met Ann Weaver, he could see her in Zack, especially around the eyes.

Reggie's lifetime streak of never speaking to Zack came to an unexpected end at that moment, as the taller boy went out of his way to walk toward him.

Zack nodded his head in a *what's up* sort of way. "Hey, man. I heard about your mother. I'm really sorry. That sucks."

The fact that Zack knew what had happened didn't necessarily mean that Ann Weaver had been telling tales out of hospital. By that point, pretty much everyone knew what had happened.

Reggie averted his eyes, just wanting to get away. "Thanks," he mumbled.

Zack stood in front of him for half a beat, uncertain for once in his life. "Anyway, just wanted to say that." He turned and jogged away, calling ahead to a pretty girl named Cynthia, "Hey, Cyn! Wait up!"

"Asshole," Reggie muttered, but then comforted himself with the idea that the party at Amanda's house was only a few hours away, and he had an invitation while Zack Weaver didn't.

The regularly scheduled afternoon rain shower held off long enough for Reggie to make it home dry.

For the first time in his life, he appreciated the lights when he stepped inside the house. He turned up the heat and looked at the clock. He had a few hours to kill before the party. He whipped through the to-do list in his brain and found that nothing was too pressing, so he decided to do some laundry.

That would give him a chance to think about what he wanted to wear that night. He wasn't sure about what that would be, but he was sure that it wouldn't be what he had on. That was much too square.

He tipped the overflowing laundry hamper in his room into a big pile in the middle of the floor, then crawled around the room picking up other dirty clothes. There was a small goldmine of socks and underwear under the bed. When he was done, he had way more than enough for one load of laundry.

He realized that a bunch of the clothes were Grant's, though, so he separated those, pushed them to one side, bundled them up and dropped them on the floor on his brother's side of the closet.

Reggie didn't really have a lot of what he would consider acceptable party clothes. He didn't want to get dressed up, for sure, but he also didn't really want to just show up in a white T-shirt and jeans.

A sudden inspiration hit him, and he went through the clothes he had tossed into the closet.

"Yes," he said sincerely when he found what he was looking for. He held up a worn and faded *Deep Purple* T-shirt that he'd seen Grant wear to parties. He buried his nose in it and was immediately sorry. Somehow, this shirt had missed the laundry forty or fifty times.

Reggie grabbed a few other shirts, pairs of underwear and socks, then his second pair of jeans and headed to the back porch, where the old washer and dryer were.

This was another task that he had never completed, but the dials on the washing machine were pretty straightforward. He actually read the instructions on the back of the box of Tide and put the proper amount in.

While the clothes washed, he really didn't have much else to do.

Overall, Reggie felt like he was handling the crappy hand he had been dealt pretty well. He was paying bills, buying groceries and doing laundry like a responsible adult.

He wandered around the house looking for something else grown-up to do. He decided to make his bed. When he was done, it didn't look as good as when his mom did it, but it wasn't terrible. He fluffed his pillow and tried to think ahead to when he would be crawling into that bed. By that time, he would finally know what was up with Amanda. He couldn't help but wonder if he would be happy and smiling to himself, or... Or, what? He couldn't even imagine what the *or what* might look like.

He checked on the washing machine since he was unsure how long it took to wash a load of clothes. It was still sudsing away.

It felt like an eternity until he could leave for the party.

He gave up on being productive and turned the TV on. The news was on the ABC and NBC affiliates. He switched to a small independent channel that came in sometimes when the wind was blowing just right.

The stars aligned and, although the picture was snowy, he could see that they were playing a movie. Not just any movie, either, but *The Dirty Dozen*, which was one of Reggie's favorites. His family hadn't gone to the movies too often, but a few years earlier, they had all piled into the car and driven out to The Silvery Moon Drive-in to watch it. He hadn't been able to see very well from the backseat, but his mom had scooted against the door and let him climb over the seat to sit beside her. It was the first of a double feature and Reggie had fallen asleep against his mom before the second movie started, but he still had happy memories of that night.

He adjusted the rabbit ears, hoping to make it come in a little clearer, but that only made it snowier. He played around with the antenna for a minute, then figured this was as good as it was going to get. A fuzzy *Dirty Dozen* was better than a completely clear newscast.

He got absorbed in the mission of the dozen men sent into Germany. He heard the washer shut off, but waited until a commercial break before switching the clothes over to the dryer.

Both the movie and the clothes in the dryer finished at about the same time.

He pulled the clothes out and was rewarded with the smell of clean, warm laundry. Reggie thought he might get to like this whole *acting like an adult* thing. In the back of his mind, a voice whispered, *They'll never let you stay here by yourself. Someone will be coming to get you.*

Reggie took that thought and stuffed it into the partition where his grief and uncertainty went, then carried the clothes into the bedroom. He dumped them on Grant's bed, picked out the jeans, underwear, socks, and the *Deep Purple* T-shirt and carried that load into the bathroom.

Twenty minutes later, he was showered—using Prell Shampoo and Irish Spring soap, this time—and dressed.

It was still a little too early to leave for Amanda's. He didn't want to be the guy that showed up half an hour before anyone else got there. But he also didn't feel like he could stand just waiting around the house anymore.

His eyes fell on the wad of money on the counter, and he had two thoughts. Should he take some of the money with him, and if so, how much? That thought was quickly followed by the idea that he should hide whatever he didn't take with him.

He decided to take a few dollars with him, just in case he was asked to chip in for beer or something. He put the rest in an empty jar and stuck it way to the back of a cupboard. Then he reconsidered and decided that after the few days he'd had, he deserved a treat.

He leaned in, grabbed the money jar, and took a couple of extra dollars out and stuffed them into his jeans.

One more idea struck him. Something he had been thinking and dreaming about for months. He couldn't have said why, but this seemed like the perfect time to do it. He went to the back porch where various odds and ends were stored. He rooted through a box of miscellaneous stuff and found a can of black spray paint. Whistling a little to himself, he grinned.

He checked himself in the mirror and thought that his hair looked fine. Not too nicely combed, but hanging down over his forehead. He grabbed his coat, stuffed the rattle can into his deep pocket, opened the door, and stepped out into the chilly night air.

Halloween was less than a week away, but not many people decorated for the holiday in 1973, especially the denizens of Crampton Village.

At the entrance to the neighborhood, there was a sign that read *Welcome to Crampton Village*. It had been put up twenty-five years earlier, when the small development had been opened. At the time, it was intended to give small, economical homes to returning soldiers who would be able to buy a home using the GI bill.

Since then, though some occupants had fought against it, the neighborhood had deteriorated. It wasn't unusual these days to see a tarp on a damaged roof for years on end, cars up on blocks, or even the occasional completely abandoned vehicle.

Reggie casually walked up to the sign, then looked around to see if anyone might be watching him. The sign was situated so that none of the houses looked directly out on it and only someone approaching on the street would see him.

He took the spray paint can out of his pocket and gave it a good rattle. By the weight of it, he guessed there was enough paint to do the job.

He sprayed black paint over the *Crampton* part of the sign, then, above it, wrote *Crapped On*.

He stood back and admired his handiwork. The paint dripped down a little, but Reggie didn't care. Somehow this small act of defiant vandalism made him feel better and that was good enough for right now.

He headed toward town, feeling better than he had all week.

A few blocks away, he turned onto Elm, then took a right toward Main Street. Glancing around again to make sure no eyes were on him, Reggie tossed the spray can into a garbage can, completing the perfect crime.

Chapter Thirteen

Still looking for the treat he had promised himself, Reggie hoofed it down Main Street until he got to Artie's Drive-In.

A low fog had rolled in, and seeing the red neon Artie's sign from a block away just made Reggie feel a little better yet.

Artie's was mostly designed for car service, which Reggie didn't have. There was a small seating area inside, though, and that was where he was heading.

Artie's was hopping on a Friday night. Reggie had heard his mom's tales about how there had once been a tall tower in the parking lot. A KMFR disc jockey would climb up there on Friday and Saturday nights and broadcast live. The denizens of Middle Falls could even drop requests in a bucket and the DJ would pull them up and play them with a dedication.

The tower was long gone—someone had backed into it on a long-ago night, sending it crashing down into the parking lot—but on a Friday night, Artie's was still the place to be.

The parking lot was almost full, with waitresses on roller skates hustling Artie's burger baskets out to hungry teens and families. The whole scene looked almost surreal with the bright neon of the Artie's sign half-covered in the low-lying fog.

Reggie turned the collar of his jacket up and walked across the parking lot and in through the door that led inside.

The interior of Artie's wasn't much, but that was mostly because the majority of people just ate in their cars.

Absent the tower and KMFR doing a remote broadcast, there was a jukebox in the corner that played through speakers both inside and out. That jukebox still had plenty of fifties songs—Buddy Holly, Elvis Presley, even Bill Haley and His Comets doing *Rock Around the Clock*—but at that moment, *Shambala* by Three Dog Night was playing.

The parking lot was jam-packed, as Artie's often was on a Friday night. There wasn't really anywhere else to see and be seen in Middle Falls. The interior, though, with its bright red booths, was empty.

Reggie slid into one of the four booths, feeling pretty adult being there by himself. A waitress hurried by, burdened down by a tray with burger baskets that smelled so good, Reggie thought he might faint.

On the way past, the waitress, a pretty brunette, said, "Whenever you're ready, come on up to the counter. I'll take your order there."

Reggie nodded. He had no idea, because he had never been to Artie's by himself before.

Shambala faded away, the mechanics of the jukebox whirred, and another 45 dropped into place. After a few seconds of popping hiss, the opening of *Can't You See* by The Marshall Tucker Band played.

It was a newer song, and Reggie, who rarely listened to the radio, didn't recognize it. He did like the way it built, though. Sitting there alone in Artie's, it couldn't really be said that he was happy. If he had been, he would have had to be almost totally separated from reality. But, with a minor act of vandalism behind him, a party with the prettiest girl in school ahead of him, and an Artie's burger and strawberry shake in his immediate future, life was as good as it could have been for him.

He remembered that he had to go to the counter to order, so he waited until the waitress came back in, then told her what he wanted. He laid two one-dollar bills on the counter, essentially showing that he had money and wasn't going to dine and dash.

"You hold onto that right now," the waitress said. "You can pay when I bring it out to you."

Reggie tried to act as though he already knew that, but had just forgotten, then sat back down in the booth and observed the Middle Falls nightlife outside the windows.

This is what that life looked like on a typical Friday night: kids would pile into their friends' cars and drive up and down Main Street in a perpetual loop, pulling into Artie's to order some fries or a Coke every few trips.

It wasn't a lot, but the kids in those cars would remember those times cruising back and forth fondly for the rest of their lives.

For Reggie, he would never know the simple pleasure of cruising with Harold and Nelson, though there was no way for him to know that at that moment.

In just a few minutes, the waitress—who seemed to be working by herself on that night, which was a bit much for just one person—brought Reggie his food on a plastic yellow tray.

"Here you go, hon." The *hon* separated them into two different groups. She was only six or seven years older than him, but to her practiced eye, he was just a kid, while she was an adult. "That's a dollar seventy-five."

Reggie handed her the two one-dollar bills again and the waitress clicked a small change counter on her waist and a quarter dropped into her hand. She reached her hand out to Reggie, but he remembered his manners.

"That's for you."

"Thank you, hon," the waitress said, blessing him with a smile and dropping the quarter into her pocket.

Reggie tore into the burger, fries, and strawberry shake like a teenage boy who hadn't had many decent meals of late. It disappeared so fast, he momentarily thought of taking some of the beer money he had brought with him and buying another round.

A picture entered his head of everyone at the party passing a hat and him having to just dig out a couple of crumpled dollar bills and some change, though, and he decided against it.

He sat in the comfortable booth, enjoying the warmth and watching the teenagers outside playing grab-ass and basically making fools of themselves, as teenagers often did when hormones and small-town Friday nights were mixed together.

He looked up at the red Coca-Cola clock on the wall and was pleased to see that it was finally late enough that he could risk showing up at Amanda's house.

He used the bathroom at Artie's to check his hair and make sure that it was still stylishly disheveled, then pushed back out into the October night. The fog had settled in to stay, but that didn't matter to Reggie. He was just glad that it wasn't raining at that moment so that he didn't look like a drowned rat when he got to Amanda's. The air was cold enough that his breath puffed out in front of him as he walked, though.

He slowed a little when he got within a block of Amanda's house. He had been looking forward to this night as his life preserver in the worst week of his life. But now that it was here, he felt only trepidation.

He had never come close to solving the riddle of why Amanda had approached him in the first place. Now that he was here, that question loomed larger than ever in his mind, sparking a small fire of nervousness and fear.

He stopped when he was still far enough from the house that he was sure he hadn't been seen yet. He jammed his hands into his jeans pockets and the nervousness washed over him.

Finally, he took a deep breath and asked himself, *Whaddya gonna do, idiot? Just go home?*

Insulting himself did the trick and got him in motion again.

He wasn't sure what he expected Amanda's house to look like—this was supposed to be a party, after all—but what he saw was just another quiet house with a few lights on inside. His stomach twisted again.

What if her parents didn't go out of town after all? What would he say if he knocked on the door and her father answered?

It was too late for him to back out, so Reggie gathered his courage and walked up the nice sidewalk to the nice porch and knocked on the very nice door.

Standing on the porch, Reggie realized that if there was a party going on, it wasn't like he had always imagined the cool parties to be. He couldn't even hear any music. He stood there long enough that he began to think that maybe the whole thing really had been a prank and that Amanda and her friends were inside, looking at him from a second-story window and laughing. He actually stepped back a little so he could look up at those windows, but there was no sign of any laughing girls.

He decided to give it one more solid knock, then just give up and go home.

He did his best to give a jaunty little knock, then stood back again.

Finally—*finally!*—the door swung slowly inward. Amanda smiled at him. "Why didn't you use the doorbell? We didn't even hear you!"

The truth was probably because in the neighborhood where Reggie grew up, the houses either didn't have doorbells or they had long since stopped functioning.

Amanda leaned playfully out and pushed the small, lighted button beside the door. Deep inside the house, a series of bongs sounded.

"Next time," Reggie said, hoping that there might actually *be* a next time.

"Sure, no problem," Amanda said. "I just didn't want to leave you standing out there in the cold. Come on in, everyone else is here." When Reggie stepped inside, Amanda reached her hand out for his coat.

It was wonderfully warm inside, and Reggie gladly shucked his pea-green winter coat off and handed it over.

Amanda took it, turned ninety degrees to her left and dramatically dropped it onto what Reggie saw was a small pile of other coats.

"Maid's day off," Amanda said.

Reggie had so little perspective that he didn't know if that was a joke or if they really did have a maid. It certainly wasn't out of the range of possibilities.

"We're downstairs in the rec room listening to the new Stones album. It's called something kind of weird, but it's got a song on it I really love. I've been listening to it over and over. It's called *Angie*, but I like to think he's really singing *Amanda*. Mick Jagger is dreamy."

Reggie had seen the Rolling Stones, and he thought they were all kind of ugly, but he kept that opinion to himself.

While she was reciting all this, Amanda walked down the shag-carpeted stairs. Reggie looked at her and saw that she was barefoot. In fact, she was wearing shorts and a midriff-baring top. Not something Reggie expected when it was this cold outside. He had to admit that it was very fetching, though. He briefly struggled with whether or not he should kick off his own shoes. There was no way he was going to take off his socks, though. Foot hygiene was not a big priority in Reggie's life.

At the bottom of the stairs, Amanda turned right into a large rec room. One end was filled by a massive wet bar. The other end had a fireplace in it big enough to burn anything Paul Bunyan wanted to drag into the house. In between was that epitome of seventies coolness, a conversation pit. That is, a sixteen-foot circular couch sunk down in the floor eighteen inches. The open space in front of the couch was filled with oversized pillows.

And on those pillows sat four of Amanda's girlfriends. Like their hostess, they were all dressed as though they were ready for a day at the beach, not an October evening in Middle Falls. There had been some talk of boyfriends also being there, but unless they were all hiding behind the bar, ready to jump out and beat the crap out of Reggie for ogling their girls, they were not there.

As inconspicuously as possible, Reggie slipped off his tennis shoes, glad he had taken a shower and even gone to the trouble of at least washing his feet and putting clean socks on.

Amanda bounced—*bounced*—toward the four girls and settled in amongst them. They all smiled up at Reggie as though he was the sultan, and this was his harem.

Reggie only had one thought. *I'm sure not in Crapped-On Village anymore.*

Chapter Fourteen

Reggie's head was spinning. His stomach was full of Artie's, he was nearly overwhelmed by the intoxicating smell of *Babe* perfume, and the pheromones in the room had worked their way into his brain. Any actual thought process he might have had was gone.

"Come on," a girl named Bobbi said, patting a plush pillow beside her. "Come sit down."

That was what she *said*. If Reggie had been thinking correctly, he would have interpreted that as *"Will you walk into my parlour?" said a spider to a fly; 'Tis the prettiest little parlour that ever you did spy.*

Reggie was *not* thinking clearly, and with a semi-stupid grin on his face, he stepped down into the arena where everyone but him was armed to the teeth. Metaphorically speaking, of course. Any actual weapons would have to wait until later in the festivities.

The Rolling Stones' *Goats Head Soup* ended, and another album dropped—Pink Floyd's *Dark Side of the Moon*.

"Ooh, I love this," Amanda said. "Have you heard it?"

"No," Reggie answered honestly. There was no stereo, no record player in the Blackwell home. Music was never heard there unless it was the theme song to a television program. "I've never even heard of them."

Amanda jumped up and ran to the stereo, picking up the iconic *Dark Side* album. "Isn't it cool?"

Reggie gawked, not just at the album cover, but the whole set up. It was a high-end stereo with both a record player and an 8-Track player. The speakers, though turned down low at the moment, stood over five feet tall and looked monolithic. Beside the stereo was a huge shelf that held hundreds of records. More records than Reggie might have guessed even existed.

Conversation swirled around Reggie. Even though he didn't contribute anything other than the occasional head nod or "yeah," the girls seemed to center the conversation around him. Bobbi and Amanda sat on either side of Reggie, and both casually reached out and laid a nicely manicured hand on Reggie's arm, shoulder, and once, on his thigh. That sent an electrical charge up and down his spine and caused a very basic biological reaction that made him shift his position uncomfortably.

Both girls noticed that, of course. Very little got past them, and they were playing a game they could go pro at, not to mention they had home court advantage.

After a few minutes, Amanda, right on cue, said, "We should have a drink." The way she said it—*have a drink*—made it sound more like an adult party and less like the kegger Reggie had been expecting.

Amanda, ever the vigilant hostess, popped up again, brushing her bare legs against Reggie, who took a deep breath and held it for a few seconds.

"What do you want?" Amanda asked. "We have just about everything."

That was an absolute stumper for Reggie. There wasn't any music in his house, but there had been liquor—brown, ugly bottles hidden away in a single cabinet. There certainly weren't nice or fruity mixed drinks in the Blackwell home, though. There, booze was meant to have an impact, nothing else was needed, and Reggie had never been considered old enough to partake. He'd had the occasional pull from his dad's Rainier Beer, but that was the extent of it.

"Uhh...I don't know. I don't really drink."

"Don't be silly," Amanda said with a toss of her long hair. "Tonight, we're all drinking." A mischievous twinkle came into her eyes, and she said, "How about a Slow Screw?"

That once again caused Reggie's breath to catch in his throat. "A…a *what*?"

"It's a drink, silly. What did you think I meant?"

At that moment, Reggie was so overwhelmed, he wasn't really *thinking* at all.

"You'll like it. It's sweet. You won't even taste the liquor." The fact that the drink tasted like punch while packing a wallop had no meaning to Reggie.

Reggie managed a nod of acquiescence.

Amanda busied herself behind the bar, pouring orange juice, sloe gin—which gave the drink both its sweetness and its name—and a healthy amount of vodka. She dropped a few ice cubes in, stirred it delicately with her index finger, then, after checking to see if Reggie was looking, sucked the drink slowly off that finger.

No hypnotist could have done a better job of putting Reggie under.

"Bobbi? Will you give this drink to our guest? I'll make the rest of us our drinks."

Bobbi acted as Amanda's second-in-charge and delivered Reggie's drink. He did not notice that while his drink had vodka in it, everyone else's was just orange juice with a touch of sloe gin.

For the next hour and a half, the booze flowed, the records dropped, and the gathered young women seemed to hang on every word Reggie said, which were few and far between.

Before he knew it, Reggie had downed three more of the drinks. The drunker he got, the less he noticed that Amanda was adding more alcohol to each one.

Finally, when she gauged that she had him at the perfect level of drunkenness—well into his cups, but not so drunk he couldn't walk—Amanda got to the pre-scheduled part of the evening. She leaned in close to Reggie. Close enough that the smell of her perfume mingled with her shampoo and formed a mixture that would overwhelm even someone more experienced than Reggie was.

She put a pretty pout on her face and said, "This is fun, but I've got a problem."

"A problem?" Reggie asked, stepping voluntarily into the parlor. A problem was something he could relate to. Something that maybe he could help with. "What problem?" His words were a little slurred and slow, but not enough to be incomprehensible.

Amanda took a deep breath and delivered the short monologue she'd been preparing all week.

"I had a little problem where I needed some money."

Reggie's eyes moved around the room, taking in all the incredible luxuries that were there, unable to come up with a reason why Amanda would ever need money. He didn't want to stop the story, though, so he just nodded.

"I did something really dumb." Amanda rolled her eyes at her own foolishness. "I took some of my mom's stuff—a fur coat and some of her jewelry—and traded them in at the pawn shop. It was just for a couple of days, until I got my allowance and I got a chance to go to the bank and cash in one of my bonds."

Again, if Reggie had really thought about it, that story wouldn't have held water. But, with four drinks in him, and the fact that Amanda was talking about concepts that were essentially foreign to him, like *an allowance* and *cashing in a bond*, Reggie just continued to nod.

Amanda's pout grew more pronounced as she leaned in even closer to Reggie, warmth radiating off her.

"But then the man who runs the place says he won't give my mom's stuff back to me. And my mom's coming back tomorrow and I'll be grounded for sure." Incredibly, tears of self-pity formed in her eyes. It was quite a performance, and it had its intended impact on Reggie.

"That sucks," he said. A pause as he looked for more words, then added, "Really sucks."

Amanda nodded as though that did a wonderful and eloquent job of summing up the situation.

"We're all having such a good time tonight," Amanda said, looking at her girlfriends, who all nodded their assent that they were all having *such a good time*. "I was hoping that we could all do this more often. But once my mom gets home and discovers what I've done, I'll be out of action until I turn eighteen."

"That sucks too."

"I wish there was something we could do, so we could have another party like this soon." Amanda was trying to lead Reggie to a conclusion, but his mind wasn't working that quickly.

She glanced at Bobbi, who, right on cue, said, "I have an idea." She looked up at the ceiling as though the idea was just coming to her, though this line had been handed to her hours earlier. Then she shook her head. "No. No, that's a crazy idea. We could never do it."

Reggie continued to nod, as though in agreement that they could never do it. Then he caught himself and said, "Wait. What?"

Bobbi shrugged. "It's stupid. I was thinking that we could go down to the place and maybe break a window or something and get Amanda's stuff back. It's *her stuff*, after all."

This final bit of disingenuousness didn't land with Reggie any more than the earlier ones had. If he'd thought about it logically, he would have seen right through the whole scheme. There wasn't anything logical about this situation, though, and Reggie's brain was thoroughly overloaded.

The five girls' technique could have been filmed and used by interrogators who were learning how to elicit a false confession out of a subject trapped under a hot light.

He was once again nodding. "Yeah, we could do that."

"Really?" Amanda said, her voice rising several octaves. "Really? Oh my God, that would be so awesome. That would solve everything. Then we could really have a party."

Reggie thought he might have been agreeing to some hypothetical concept, but right in front of him, it was becoming more concrete. Did he have the emotional maturity and wherewithal to say, *Hold on a minute. We're not really talking about doing something so stupid, are we?*

He did not.

Instead, he looked a little drunkenly from Amanda to Bobbi and back, still nodding slightly.

Amanda instantly transformed from the wide-eyed ingenue to a field general planning an attack. "Okay, girls. You heard the man. We're doing this thing. Get changed."

All five of them flew out of the room, giggling and talking, leaving Reggie alone on the pillow, dazed and wondering what truck had just run over him.

Chapter Fifteen

Reggie sat numbly in the conversation pit, as out of place as a goldfish at a philosophy convention. He wasn't sure what had just happened, but the ache in his stomach told him things had taken a turn for both the bizarre and the uncomfortable.

He tried to force himself to sober up, which had no effect at all on his vodka-soaked brain. He stood up, though that simple act took several tries, and he swayed back and forth instead of standing straight.

Finally, a glimmer of common sense broke through the fog.

I think I need to just get the hell out of here. Regroup and live to fight another day.

He put that idea into action immediately.

Immediately, but not quickly.

He had to kind of bob and weave around all the oversized pillows in the pit that seemed to be designed to slow his progress. When he finally made it to the step, he took a slightly indirect route to his shoes.

He tried to slip his feet into the shoes, but they were still tied from when he took them off and, especially considering his limited sense of balance at the moment, that wasn't going to happen. After a few fruitless efforts at that, he gave up and plopped down on the carpet. He untied each shoe deliberately, pulling at each lace as though he was stopping a bomb from detonating.

When he finally got the shoes on, the smartest thing to do would have been for him to risk tripping over the laces and just vacate the Jarvis house. Reggie was not focused on doing the smartest thing at that moment. Instead, he bent down and tied each one, though he noticed it took a lot more focus to do that simple task than it normally did.

He looked around for his coat, then remembered it was on top of the pile upstairs. Nodding to himself, he exited the rec room and turned left up the stairs just as Amanda and company appeared at the landing.

The five of them had changed their clothes and now looked like they were ready to deploy on a crime spree. They had all changed into black pants, black tops, black jackets, and even had tucked their long hair up into black knit caps. They looked like the cheerleading team version of the Watergate burglars.

"Good!" Amanda said. "You're ready."

Reggie tried to form a denial of that fact. To tell her that he wasn't ready at all, except possibly to throw up and/or go home. Those words formed in his brain, but wouldn't come out his mouth. He struggled with it for a few moments, then gave up and just nodded.

Behind Amanda, Bobbi whispered, "I think that last drink was a mistake."

Out of the corner of her mouth, sotto voce, Amanda answered, "The cold outside will sober him up." She smiled warmly at Reggie and said, "Ready, tiger?"

All he could manage was a slight weave from the bottom of the stairs, then he said, "Are we going to walk?"

"No, silly. Bobbi's got her parents' car. Plenty of room for all of us. She'll drive and we'll put you in the middle like a Reggie sandwich."

Reggie's stomach was already on uncertain ground and the mention of a sandwich made him wish desperately that he hadn't stopped at Artie's on the way over. Or that he hadn't mixed four tall glasses of orange juice, sloe gin, and vodka with that burger, fries, and shake.

He was embarrassed, but didn't want to throw up all over the deep shag carpeting on the stairs. "I think I'm going to be sick."

Bobbi gave Amanda an *I told you four was too many* look, which Amanda ignored.

Amanda tiptoed hesitantly down the stairs as though Reggie might vomit all over her. "Let's get you outside then. The fresh air will make you feel better."

Reggie nodded and Amanda took a chance by coming within potential splash range. She put his left arm over her thin shoulders and led him up the stairs. "Get his coat," she commanded to no one in particular. She threw her very nice front door open and led Reggie out onto the porch. She half-turned him so that he was facing a rhododendron, the better to cover up his vomit if he hurled.

Amanda had been right, though. The bracing night air *did* make Reggie feel better. Not *well*, certainly, but not on the edge of puking any more.

"There," Amanda said, "that's better, isn't it?"

"Better," Reggie agreed.

Over her shoulder, Amanda said, "Go get the car while I hold him up."

Bobbi leaped past her, ran to the street and turned left. She had parked somewhere far away from the house, almost as though they had carefully planned everything for plausible deniability.

Amanda let Reggie lean much of his weight on her. She was not a big girl, but ten years of gymnastics training had made her strong.

Sixty seconds later, headlights appeared from down the road and a late-model blue Cadillac turned into the driveway.

"Let's go," Amanda said and led Reggie to the front passenger seat. Good as her word, she slid him into the middle of the bench seat, then climbed in behind him. The other three girls got in the back, and Bobbi accelerated away from the house.

Bobbi drove the Cadillac through the backstreets, sticking to the speed limit. Although everything in Middle Falls is basically no more than five minutes away from anywhere else, they took a looping, circuitous route that killed fifteen minutes.

The rocking of the car nearly put Reggie to sleep, but just as he started to drift off, Bobbi would take a sharp corner and jostle him awake.

They drove past the pawn shop, which was located on a side street in the seedier part of Middle Falls. It was a non-descript brick building with a long window covering the front. They drove by slowly enough that they could see a television set, a stereo, and a mannequin wearing a fur coat. The classic sign of a pawn shop—three gold balls hanging from a bar—hung over the door. There was a simple sign painted on the window that read *Sal's Pawn Shop*.

Reggie leaned his head forward to look around Amanda and said, "Is that your mom's coat?"

Amanda nodded. "You get us in and make sure the coast is clear, then we'll come in behind you. We'll take it from there."

The reality of the situation was settling in on Reggie. "I can just smash the window and grab the coat, right? That will solve the problem."

"No," Amanda said patiently. "Remember, I had to give him a couple of other things, too. That's why I'll go in after you, to make sure I get everything."

"Don't forget…" Bobbi prompted.

"Oh, right," Amanda said, "we'll grab a couple of other things, too, just to make it look good."

"I don't get it," Reggie said, and truer words had never been spoken.

"If we just take my stuff," Amanda answered, "it will be pretty obvious that we did it. We need to take a few other things to throw everyone off." She looked at Reggie's glassy eyes. "You don't want to get caught, do you?"

"No," Reggie said. He could completely agree that he didn't want to get caught. He was liking everything about this less and less, but was having a hard time verbalizing it.

Amanda sensed that she might be losing him, so she bent over and kissed his ear, slipping her tongue in for just a moment. "I will be so grateful if you do this for me," she whispered.

A shiver ran down Reggie's back. The kiss, the tongue, and the whisper did the trick. He wasn't so sure how Amanda's gratitude would play out, but he wanted to find out. He wanted that more than anything at that moment.

Amanda, sensing that she was back in control, said, "Park down there."

Bobbi pulled to the curb a block away from the pawn shop. Everyone got out and Bobbi opened the trunk. She pulled out five canvas bags and handed them around. To Reggie, she gave the tire iron. "This will get us in."

When Reggie touched the cold tire iron, he had a moment of clarity. He knew this was wrong. He knew he didn't want to be here. And looking at the five young women standing in a semi-circle around him, he couldn't think of a way to get out of it.

He gave up.

"Okay, let's go." As they walked back to Sal's, he had one last fleeting thought. "What if they have an alarm system?"

"There's no alarm," Bobbi said, as though she actually knew.

Reggie nodded grimly. With no objections left and with absolutely no hesitation, he walked up to the door, which was impressively heavy, but had a large glass panel in the middle. He swung the tire iron viciously into it. The glass shattered. There were shards of glass still stuck in the door, but he used the end of the tire iron to knock them away. He kind of lost momentum then, but Amanda and Bobbi hurried past him, stepping carefully through the opening.

Amanda grabbed the mink first and hurriedly put it on so she wouldn't have to carry it. She and Bobbi quickly slipped around to the back of the jewelry case and opened it.

Reggie stood in the middle of the store in a daze, trying to understand how he had arrived at this point.

All of the girls had flashlights. They turned them on and the beams did a crazy crisscross dance around the shop. Amanda glanced at Reggie and said, "Reggie, hon, why don't you go to the window and keep a lookout. If you see anyone coming, tell us so we can turn our lights off."

Reggie moved to the window like he was on autopilot. He stood next to the now-naked mannequin and turned his head this way and that, watching the empty street outside.

Behind him, Amanda said, "Hold it. Quiet, everybody. What's that noise?"

The noise she referred to came from overhead. Heavy footsteps, then the sound of a door closing.

"Party's over, girls," Amanda said. "We're out of here."

All the girls made one last choice of something to steal, then stuffed it into their bags and headed for the door.

Reggie was still standing numbly at the window when a brilliant light flared on overhead, nearly blinding him. He winced and covered his eyes just as a back door into the shop opened and an old man in a bathrobe stepped through it.

The man was holding a shotgun, and it was aimed right at Reggie.

Reggie squinted into the blinding light. He was still having trouble processing things. He did manage to see the shotgun, though, and put his hands in the air. He couldn't stop his eyes from wandering to his right, where the door and escape waited for him. He also noticed that there wasn't any sign of the girls. They had disappeared like shadows at dusk, swallowed by the encroaching night.

"Don't even goddamned think about it," the man said. "I'll pepper your ass with buckshot if you do."

Reggie nodded miserably.

"I called the cops. They'll be here any second."

A ridiculous thought went through Reggie's head. *Hey, I guess I can hang out with Dad after all.*

The man—Sal Parker, the owner of Sal's Pawnshop—surveyed his store, a sour, hateful look on his face. "You stupid goddamned kids. Don't you know I live right above the store? You made such a racket you woke me up." He shook his head, looking at the stripped jewelry case. "I oughta shoot you right now just for causing me to almost have a goddamned heart attack."

Reggie edged slightly toward the door. Toward freedom.

Sal took two quick steps forward but didn't see where the girls had dropped a box that had turned out to be too heavy for them to carry.

That was the moment chaos arrived.

Sal tripped and fell forward. His finger was on the trigger of the shotgun, which went off and fired at the window just over Reggie's head. The sound nearly deafened Reggie. A few stray pellets passed within inches of his scalp.

Sal, who was a big man, stumbled, trying to keep his balance to no avail. His momentum carried him forward, and he slammed his head against the sharp corner of the jewelry case.

"Holy shit!" Reggie shouted in answer to both the shotgun blast and seeing the big man fall so awkwardly. Adrenaline coursed through him, partially sobering him up. He took one glance at Sal to see if he was going to fire at him again, but Sal was face down on the floor. A pool of blood was forming around his head, which immediately gave Reggie a sense of déjà vu.

"Just gotta get out of here," Reggie mumbled, wondering if the girls were waiting for him in the Cadillac. The optimism of youth.

He stepped over Sal's body and took three steps toward the door when red and blue lights announced the arrival of Middle Falls' finest. The police car, sirens and lights both blaring, pulled up right in front of the pawn shop.

Deputy Naismith climbed out of the prowler before Reggie could get away. Naismith shined his own flashlight into the shop, illuminating Reggie's face.

Chapter Sixteen

The next few hours, days, and even weeks were a blur for Reggie. He went with Naismith without a fight, of course. His only other option that night at the pawn shop was to make a run for it. Again, he was convinced he could get away from the deputy, but what was in store for him then? He did briefly consider running slowly away, hoping Naismith would shoot and kill him, but he couldn't make himself do that, either.

Grant might have been okay with abandoning everything and tearing out of town, but he was five years older than Reggie, had a car, and was more experienced in the ways of the world. Reggie had none of those advantages, so he stayed put, arms in the air.

It turned out that Sal had split his head open on the jewelry case, so Reggie had to stand there with his hands cuffed behind his back while Naismith radioed for an ambulance.

The whole thing was a big enough deal to wake Chief Deakins up in the middle of the night too. There weren't many smash and grabs in Middle Falls, so it demanded his attention.

Deakins recognized Reggie immediately and muttered something under his breath about the entire family. Deakins took charge of the scene and dispatched Naismith to take Reggie down to the jail. Since he was only fifteen, Reggie wouldn't be held there long term, but there were no juvenile facilities in Middle Falls to hold someone that young.

The Middle Falls jail was small, with only four cells to hold prisoners. One of those cells was occupied by Willis Blackwell, who sat up on his bunk when Naismith turned the lights on and led Reggie into the holding area.

"What in holy hell are you doing in here?" Willis asked. When Reggie just averted his eyes in shame, Willis turned the question to Naismith. "What do you think he did?"

Naismith never moved or spoke quickly. After a pause, he said, "I found him inside a busted-out door of the pawn shop with Sal bleeding out on the floor. You can probably figure the rest out on your own."

Willis fixed a glare on Reggie. "What the hell? Were you alone?"

Reggie just turned his back to his father as Naismith removed the cuffs and put him into an empty cell.

"When we catch Grant," Naismith said with a grin, "I guess we'll have the whole set then."

Reggie looked around the bleak little cell. A bed, a metal table, a toilet, a small shelf. He laid his head on the tiny pillow and tried to wish the world away.

Reggie was stuck one cell away from his father for the rest of the weekend. He endured fatherly wisdom like, "What the hell were you thinking, kid?" and "Lucky you're so young. You'll get away with a slap on the wrist. I'll still be here rotting when you get out."

On Saturday afternoon, Deakins pulled Reggie into what passed for an interrogation room in the small Middle Falls police station.

"Whoever your buddies were, they left you behind to take the fall. Things will go easier for you if you tell me who they were."

"They weren't any buddies of mine."

That made Deakins laugh. "You can say that again. But you taking all the blame won't help you any. Cooperating and giving me their names will go a long way to smoothing your road ahead."

Reggie was absolutely miserable, but didn't really believe that giving up Amanda and the others would really help him. Not that he thought he would ever see them again. With a day to sober up and get some distance, he already saw what a patsy he had been.

On Monday, the powers that be put their heads together and decided the proper thing to do was to ship Reggie off to a juvenile detention center in Eugene.

When his life had fallen apart, he had been afraid of getting dropped onto a conveyor belt that would shuffle him from one foster home to another.

With his incredible stupidity that Friday night, he had put himself into an even less attractive type of system.

The same day Reggie got shipped to Eugene, Sal Parker died of the head wound he suffered during the robbery. No one thought to say that Reggie had intentionally killed Sal, but when a death occurs during the commission of a crime, there are serious charges to face.

Willis had been correct about one thing, though. Reggie lucked out and was charged in juvenile court. He was found to be responsible for Sal's death and was given a sentence that would keep him locked away in the juvenile detention center known as Plain Hills Detention until his eighteenth birthday.

It was very much like a jail for teenagers, but they did offer schooling and job training, including carpentry and plumbing. If Reggie had managed to just keep his head down, work hard, and keep his nose clean, he would have been out on his eighteenth birthday with some new job skills and a General Equivalency Diploma.

His life wouldn't have been so messed up that he couldn't have started over again.

Things didn't work out that way for Reggie.

The day he arrived at Plain Hills, he was a typical first-timer, scared and uncertain. It was a tough environment, filled with a wide spectrum of kids who had gotten in trouble. That spectrum ranged from kids who got caught their first time stepping outside the law to older teens who might have been more at home in an adult prison.

Not surprisingly, Reggie was bullied and pushed around by the bigger, stronger kids. The three years he was going to spend there would have been unrelenting hell until a slightly older boy named Carson took him under his wing. Carson couldn't stop all the bullying—he wasn't the biggest or toughest guy in the detention center either—but he had been around, knew the ropes, and helped Reggie become better acclimated and able to fit in with one of the cliques, which offered some protection.

During the three years he spent at Plain Hills, Reggie was filled with good intentions. He vowed to try to learn a skill and to be set free with the ability to go and find a job. The judge who had sentenced him had told him that if he made it through the three years with no major problems, his records would be sealed and he would be able to have a fresh start.

With no family—with no one, really—apart from Carson and his few other friends outside of the walls of Plain Hills, the future looked uncertain.

His friendship with Carson grew over time. He was the only person since Reggie's mother who had looked out for him without asking anything in return.

Carson was a year older than Reggie, so he was due to be released earlier as well.

By then, Reggie was one of the older kids, so he didn't worry so much about being able to get along within Plain Hills Correctional Facility. He knew the lay of the land, the rules, who he could trust, and who he needed to avoid.

A month before Carson was to be released, he and Reggie came up with a plan. Like Reggie, Carson also didn't have a lot of contacts with people he knew he could count on once he got out. That was a common theme of the boys who ended up there. Carson had one advantage, though—an old friend of his family who promised him a job working at his factory when he got out. Carson's family had essentially abandoned him when he had gone away, but this man had not.

Being just eighteen years old with only a GED and no job experience or rental history, it was tough for the young men who were released into the world to get a good start in life. That was why more than two-thirds of them "graduated" back into the adult penal system within two years.

This family friend—Roger Stagner was his name—had not only promised Carson a job, but had said he had a small house that he would be able to afford to rent with what he earned at the factory.

The plan that they cooked up was that Carson would get out first, get established, and talk Reggie up to Mr. Stagner. Then when Reggie got out in another year, they hoped he would be able to catch on at the factory too. If not that, Carson at least promised that Reggie could sleep on his couch until he found something else so he wouldn't be all alone.

The near-total abandonment of those recently released from Plain Hills was unfortunately not unusual. For many of the newly freed, both their families and the system itself forgot about them when they walked out the gate of the detention center.

This plan comforted Reggie and gave him something to daydream about.

It all came crashing down a few weeks before Carson was to be given his walking papers.

The boys were not kept in jail cells at Plain Hills, but instead were divided into smaller dormitories. The authorities did their best to keep different cliques in different rooms, thus minimizing clashes between groups.

Unfortunately, a logistical mix up happened and a boy who had been at odds with both Carson and Reggie over the previous few months got temporarily shuffled into their dormitory. The boy—Gavin George, or GG as he was known to his friends—felt understandably alone and intimidated being surrounded by those he felt were his enemies. GG was a bigger boy with blond hair, a reddish complexion and a bad case of acne that looked like it might survive into adulthood.

He was paranoid about being locked up in an enemy camp and looked for signs of any perceived slight and when he thought he saw one, he went after Carson.

It was a typical fight within Plain Hills and would have likely been quickly settled and forgotten if fate hadn't stepped in.

GG pushed Carson, who tumbled over backwards and hit the back of his head on the hard wooden edge of a bunk. When he stood up, dazed, a prodigious amount of blood ran down the back of his head, splashed onto his shoulders and then the floor. A puddle of blood formed.

Reggie flashed back, both to his mother and Sal Parker, and launched himself at GG. That caught the other boy by surprise, and they both tumbled to the ground. Reggie had stored up a lot of angst, aggression, grief, and uncertainty over the previous two years, and it all came pouring out at that moment.

He straddled GG and, though his friends tried to pull him off, he put his hands on either side of the other boy's head and slammed it down into the hard floor. He slammed him mercilessly to the floor three times before Carson and his other friends could pull him off.

It turned out that Carson was fine—just a scalp injury that bled a lot as scalp injuries often do.

Gavin George was not fine. As had been a running theme in Reggie's life, Gavin lapsed into a coma and, three days later, died.

Carson was able to get out on his eighteenth birthday.

With GG's death, it would be a long time before Reggie would breathe free air again.

He was taken into custody again and, with the weight of his previous crime, this time he was assigned to adult court.

Reggie was given a sentence of ten to fifteen years for manslaughter.

He hadn't yet reached his eighteenth birthday, but had been found responsible for two deaths.

He was sent to the Oregon State Prison in Salem to serve out his term.

Once again, he was a fish. Fresh meat for the older, stronger prisoners. He survived, but only by making himself more like those who sought to use and abuse him.

If he had kept his head down and his nose clean, he could have been paroled after seven years. He never managed that. Instead, in his quest to survive in this environment, there was always something—a fight, a rule violation of some sort, that kept him in.

Finally, he saw the light at the end of the tunnel as his release date approached. He had completely lost contact with Carson, had no family, and there were no friends on the outside that might help him transition to a life outside the bars.

When he was released, he was thirty-two years old, had prison tats on his hands and arms, and quite a record for someone so young. He also had fifty dollars in his pocket, a few donated clothes in a cheap cardboard suitcase, and nothing that resembled a plan.

Within thirty days, Reggie was, unsurprisingly, arrested again. This time it was for holding up a liquor store with a knife. This time, no one died, but he found himself back at the same penitentiary which, if he was honest with himself, felt a lot more like home than the outside world did.

That established a pattern in Reggie's life. He ended up serving two more long stretches with very short periods of freedom sandwiched between them.

In 2016, at the age of fifty-eight, Reggie Blackwell cut himself while making license plates. The wound wasn't terrible, but it was enough to get him sent to the prison hospital to get his hand stitched up.

While being treated, he contracted a staph infection and fell very ill.

While he lingered in that gray area between life and death, no one much noticed.

His life had slipped away without ever doing much more than swimming against the current and trying to find a home in a harsh environment.

On September 22nd, 2016, Reggie Blackwell closed his eyes and drew his final breath.

Interlude One
Universal Life Center

A young woman with long blonde hair sat at her desk. All around her, Watchers were working busily. Each of them had a pyxis in front of them. They expertly tipped their devices this way and that, causing images to spill out and move forward and backward in time. All of them seemed quietly confident, the antithesis of the young woman.

Instead, she touched her pyxis tentatively, as if electricity might leap out of it and shock her. Sadness and concern was written all over her face.

Finally, in a voice so small it was almost a whisper, she said, "Carrie?"

Instantly, before the word even left the young woman's mouth, another woman appeared beside her. Where the young woman at the desk wore a plain white robe, Carrie's seemed to be made of colors that were alive, swirling in iridescent hues. She leaned over the woman who had called her and stared into her pyxis.

"Yes, Karrina?"

"I don't know what to do."

Gently, Carrie said, "You watch. You feed The Machine." Carrie knew that Karrina had just graduated from her training, and so only had one soul to watch over. She remembered her own first soul, though, and the difficulty she'd had doing that simple task.

"I don't know what to do. Can you look at this life?"

Carrie picked up the pyxis and spun it quickly counterclockwise. The original image of a man lying in a hospital bed, obviously ready to transition, moved backward. For a very long time, the image showed nearly identical days spinning by, broken up only occasionally by small intervals that were different.

The frame around the man's life was almost unrelentingly gray, which meant that he was not feeling very much. He was essentially numb, and his life was not feeding The Machine.

"I see what's happening here," Carrie said. "What's your question?"

"I don't know where to restart him."

Carrie was a good teacher. She wanted Karrina to learn how to find the answers herself. "What are you thinking?"

"I'm thinking that if I drop him back into his life when he is imprisoned, he is just going to repeat that same life over and over. That's basically what he has done here, on a smaller scale."

"I agree."

"But if I restart him earlier in his life, there is so much pain, I'm afraid he will just follow the same path again."

Carrie handed the pyxis back to Karrina. "Pain that is not dealt with can freeze someone so they never advance, never change, never learn. Pain, like all human emotions, must be felt. Avoiding it will trap you in place."

Karrina nodded slightly, as though the answer to her question might be in there somewhere.

"Your instincts are good," Carrie said. "Sometimes you have to let someone fail more than once. We strive for kindness, but sometimes the kindest thing is to let them begin to fail in a way that will move them forward."

Karrina was still a little unclear on her basic question. "Can you help me find a good spot to restart him? Just this once?"

Carrie laid a gentle hand on Karrina's shoulder. "I will always help you, no matter how many times you need it. But I trust your instincts. You won't need help for long."

That seemed to bolster Karrina, who had been doubting that very thing.

Carrie picked up the pyxis once again and gave it a small twirl and a shake, then pulled the image out where they could both see it. The image showed a teenage boy in a small house. He had just tripped over his mother who was stretched out on the floor, badly wounded. The frame around the screen showed bright white, showing the strong emotions that feed The Machine.

"The first thing is to find seminal moments in a person's life, then watch to see how they react to it. Sometimes that can be guilt, or a misplaced feeling of responsibility, or even not reacting to it at all. Then you need to look for a moment somewhere before that and give them a chance to possibly change their path."

Karrina smiled ruefully. "As easy as that?"

Carrie returned her smile kindly. "Yes, as easy and as hard as that." She reached down and nudged the pyxis ever so slightly. The image changed and showed the same young boy leaving that same house a few hours earlier.

"Try that."

Carrie disappeared, on to her endless list of tasks.

Karrina stared at the young boy. "I care about you. I hope you know that. Someone cares."

Chapter Seventeen

Reggie Blackwell opened his eyes.

He stumbled and nearly fell. When he looked around, he felt the sudden need to sit down.

Knowing he was dying, Reggie had been fine with that. It had been a lousy life, and he wasn't sad to leave it behind. He certainly wasn't religious, though the prison converts, priests, and preachers who had passed through the Oregon State Penitentiary had tried to change that.

Where others found comfort and salvation, Reggie only saw people embracing a false hope. He couldn't even work his way up to that.

So, as the last moments of his life had trickled away, he wasn't really expecting the Pearly Gates or, more likely, flames and a sign that said, *Abandon hope, all ye who enter here.*

Even as he realized he was dying, he didn't spend any real time contemplating what might be on the other side of life's curtain. He assumed it would be the long dirt nap, and after the life he had just lived, that seemed a little like heaven to him. Just darkness and, hopefully, peace.

Instead, he died and opened his eyes here. If he had been given a list of a hundred possibilities of what would happen after he died, he would have placed the situation where he opened his eyes dead last.

The *here* he saw around him was a perfect recreation of the crappy front porch that led into the crappy yard and all the crappy houses of Crampton Village in Middle Falls.

"Crapped-on Village," he murmured to himself, a tinge of wonder in his voice. He resurrected a long-ago memory of spray-painting that very thing on the sign at the edge of the neighborhood. Even in these strange circumstances, that made him smile.

Reggie hadn't seen any of this in more than forty years, but every detail about it seemed correct. The house across the street had a blue tarp on the roof, once securely fastened but now flapping desultorily in a small breeze. There was an old Impala up on blocks at the house next door. He could see a few trees, but they had dropped almost all their leaves and stood in mute testament to autumn.

The air was cold, but he was wearing a heavy coat, so he didn't feel it immediately.

What he *did* feel was tremendous confusion. He blinked, ran a hand across his eyes, and blinked again, waiting to see if the scene in front of him was some sort of illusion that would pass.

Crampton Village remained stubbornly real, refusing to change.

The next thing that he noticed was that the pain and sickness he had been feeling were gone. Not just that, but he actually felt *strong*. He hadn't felt truly strong or vibrant in so long, it was a strange feeling that would take a little getting used to.

He felt the need to sit, so he did, sinking down onto the concrete step that led to the front door of what had been the house he had grown up in.

He shrugged, as though he had come to a sudden conclusion. "It's impossible," he muttered to himself.

The scene in front of him refused to acknowledge its own impossibility of existence though and remained unchanged.

Reggie leaned forward a little bit and looked up and down the street. There was no sign of anyone. He looked at the cars in the driveways of the neighboring houses and recognized that they were all 1950s or 1960s models. Every detail was right.

Maybe, he thought, *this is just some passing-through station on the way to whatever is next. If this is my life flashing before my eyes, though, it's pretty damned slow, since nothing is happening.* For one brief moment, he had the realization that *any* replay of his life would be pretty damned slow, as there wasn't anything of interest to show.

He shook his head. The last thing in the world he wanted was to have his whole miserable life flash before his eyes. It was torture living it once, he sure didn't want to have to see it again.

He rubbed his face with his right hand and this time, his hand caught his eye. He held it out in front of him, marveling at it. You get used to seeing your hand. The last time he had seen it, it had a long slice across the palm where he had cut it making license plates. More than that, though, his hand had reflected his age. The skin was a little loose, there were other little scars and prominent veins.

This hand had none of that. No scars, the blue veins were barely visible, and, more than anything, it looked *young*. Again, *impossibly* young.

He touched his face again, this time an exploration. There were no rough whiskers, just smooth skin.

Reggie jumped to his feet and looked at himself in the tiny pane of glass in the center of the door.

"Holy shit." It wasn't much of a reaction, but it was all he could manage at the moment.

Staring back at him in the wavy glass was his young, teenage face. He turned his head this way and that, watching his reflection do the same.

He shook his head and turned away, thinking that maybe he hadn't died after all. Maybe the hospital had put him into some kind of medically induced coma, and he was dreaming all this. Then common sense took over and he knew that no prison hospital would ever go to the trouble of a procedure like that. When prisoners got sick, they were given the least amount of care possible to keep the prison from being sued. Medically induced comas were not included in that.

The thought occurred to Reggie that maybe if he moved around a little, he could solve what was happening.

He took the two steps easily and realized that his right hip, which had given him some pain for quite a few years, didn't hurt any more. He rolled his shoulders and twisted his neck. He didn't hurt *anywhere*.

Just to see if he could, Reggie sprinted forward a few steps. Quick start, quick run, quick stop, no problem at all.

All logic to the contrary, Reggie realized that it was as though he had somehow been dropped into his young body back in Middle Falls, Oregon. Which, as he had previously said to himself, was impossible.

He walked around the neighborhood like a tourist on the worst tour ever. He walked to the end of the street and saw the old sign, which still just read *Crampton Village*. No vandalism had made it fun yet in this wherever-he-was.

To that point, he hadn't seen anyone else, and so thought he might be completely alone in this strange world. At that moment, though, an old beater turned the corner and drove by him. Reggie slightly recognized the man behind the wheel, but for the life of him, he couldn't come up with his name.

"Okay," he said to himself. "Perfect replica, right down to people." A new thought arrived. If it really was a perfect replica, and if the sign really hadn't been spray-painted yet, maybe his mom was still alive and right on the other side of the door to his house.

Reggie sprinted back there, reveling in the fact that he could do so effortlessly. When he got to the front porch again, he found he wasn't even out of breath. Thinking that maybe he could see his mom again did make him a little nervous, and his breath caught in his throat.

Reggie hadn't dwelled on his mother that much in all his years of incarceration, but he did remember her fondly. She and his friend Carson had really been the only people who had ever taken care of him.

He flung open the door and stepped inside. Everything was almost cripplingly familiar. The warm air had an undefinable smell about it that he'd never known anywhere else. It wasn't good or bad, it was just *home*. Everything came flooding back to him. The school pictures of him and Grant on the wall, the old black and white TV sitting on top of the broken console set, the worn-out furniture, everything.

He hurried inside and saw his mother sitting at the kitchen table, looking out into the yard and smoking a cigarette. *That* was definitely part of the smell—decades of lingering smoke.

His voice was suddenly gone.

Elaine turned to look at him and, where his face held the wonder of seeing her again after so many decades, hers just showed a flash of irritation.

"I thought you'd gone to spend the night with one of your friends." She shook her head bitterly. "Really, Reggie, you don't want to be here tonight. It's going to be ugly."

"Is this *that* night, then?"

Elaine cocked her head at him as if that made no sense at all, then shrugged and said, "I guess it is *that night*. The night I'm going to finally tell your dad exactly what I think."

Reggie rushed forward. "No, Mom, don't." He tried to hug her, but she evaded it and pushed him away.

"Don't what? Don't finally call him out on all his bullshit?" She smiled bitterly, shaking her head. "Nope, can't do it. He's been serving up shit sandwiches to me for too long and I've just been eating them and smiling. No more. I'm better off without him."

Reggie froze. Now he was sure he was reliving that day when he had left and his father had killed his mother. He was sure of that, but he had no idea what to do about it. He felt like he was playing a part in a play that had already been written.

"Mom, just...don't. It's going to go bad, and everything that happens after that is bad."

That slowed her down for a second. "And you know that *how*? When did you get so smart, Mr. High School Freshman?" She shook her head again, stubbed out the butt of her cigarette and tapped out another. "No more foolishness, Reggie. I don't want you to be here. I don't want you to get hurt."

Reggie remembered. There had been times when his parents had been going at it that he tried to get in the middle of it. That had never turned out well and he *had* been hurt a few times.

Elaine lit the new cigarette and said, "Go on now, skedaddle." She looked at the clock. "You can come home after eight. We'll have everything worked out by then."

Reggie stood, frustrated, in the middle of the kitchen. A few minutes earlier, he had been denying the plausibility of what was happening. Now, he felt completely involved, though totally impotent.

He wondered if maybe whatever was happening was like being dropped into a television rerun. That is, that he could walk around the set of whatever was happening, but couldn't actually change or influence anything.

If that was true, then this whole exercise, whatever it was, felt like a waste.

He tried to give his mom a hug and this time he was not going to be denied. He held her close to him, feeling her warmth, smelling the strong odor of cigarettes that clung to her. He let her go and said, "I love you, Mom. I really do. I'm so sorry."

That finally seemed to catch her attention. "You've got nothing to be sorry about, Reg. You haven't done anything wrong." She looked at him, and her eyes finally softened. "You're my good boy, and I love you too. Now scoot."

Reggie could see that she was not going to be denied, so he turned and walked out of the house. He headed out of Crampton Village and into the downtown area of Middle Falls. As he made his way down Main Street, he felt like a visitor in a museum. Everything was exactly the way he remembered it.

It was already getting dark, but he could see Artie's neon sign lighting up the far end of the street. He dug in his pockets, hoping against hope. Through his many years in prison and all the bad prison slop he had eaten, he had dreamed of that Artie's burger basket and strawberry shake. Now, he was close enough that he might have tasted it again, but it wouldn't happen because he had no money.

He had picked up a few skills by talking to people in prison. He had learned how to pick a basic lock, how to work around a security system, and other handy tricks of the criminal trade. He looked around him and couldn't see any way that he could immediately translate those skills into a couple of dollars so he could buy an Artie's burger, though.

He wandered around downtown, and the longer he did, the less strange everything seemed. It was perhaps an illusion or trick, but the concrete of the sidewalk was solid as his tennis shoes thumped against it.

He had no idea what to do with himself. When he had lived through this night the first time, he had thought he might go and spend the evening with Harold. Now, Harold seemed like a long-distant and forgotten stranger. He couldn't imagine just knocking on his door. And even if he did, what would they talk about? Harold was a teenager and Reggie, though he didn't look it, was a full-grown man.

He certainly had no interest in scoping out Amanda's house again. He had never seen her since the night she had manipulated him into breaking into the pawn shop and taking the fall for the robbery. He hoped that she lived the rest of her life in the fear that somehow her role in that might come out. If he *had* ever seen her again, the most he would have done would have been to spit on her.

When full darkness fell, his stomach tied in knots. He found himself turning toward home, walking at first, then jogging, then flat out sprinting for Crampton Village.

He ran down the street, across his lawn, and pushed into the front door of his house, praying he wasn't too late.

Inside, the fight was in full swing, but both his parents were still upright.

He tried to assume the role of the parent here, deepening his voice as much as he could. "Come on you two, knock it off."

When his father turned to look at him, he saw what must have been the twisted, hate-filled face that was the last thing his mother had ever seen.

Willis didn't even speak. His face was red and spittle flew from his lips as he charged at Reggie.

As had been the case so often in his first life, Reggie was once again in the wrong place at the wrong time.

Instead of Elaine being attacked by Willis, this time it was Reggie.

Instead of Elaine being slammed into the door frame so hard it killed her, this time it was Reggie.

Reggie didn't linger as long as Elaine had. After slamming his head into the hard wood of the door, he almost immediately felt his life begin to ebb away again.

He looked at his mother, who had rushed to him and held him in her arms, cradling him.

The last words Reggie spoke in this life were, "Take this chance, Mom. Get out."

Chapter Eighteen

Reggie Blackwell opened his eyes.

He gasped and his hand involuntarily went to the back of his head, where a terrible wound had been a moment before. There was nothing there. No blood, no gaping hole in his skull, no pain. No pain anywhere.

He looked around, half-expecting to be back on the front porch of the house he grew up in.

As if in answer to a prayer, though, he found himself sitting in a red, high-backed booth inside Artie's. It was warm, everything smelled delicious, and the jukebox was playing an old Three Dog Night song.

A pretty young waitress stepped around the counter carrying a plate of burger baskets and Cokes. "Whenever you're ready, come on up to the counter. I'll take your order there."

Reggie nodded dumbly, trying to get his bearings. He felt like he was standing on the edge of a chasm looking down into a void and he thought the void was staring back.

He mumbled a single word: "How?" then shut his mouth with an audible slap.

He still had no idea what was happening, or why, or, yes, *how*, but it was obvious not only *where* he was, but *when*.

He had only been to Artie's by himself one time in his life, and that was the night that Amanda had tricked him into robbing the pawn shop.

Is that what's happening? he asked himself with wonder. He tried to place himself in that timeline, tried to recall memories that were, to him, many years behind him. It was easier for Reggie than it might have been for someone else, simply because he didn't have many unique memories after this night. After the robbery, he had been in the system for almost the rest of his life. He lived for another forty-three years, but it didn't really feel like that. Instead, it was like he lived the same year over and over more than forty times. The only thing that changed was that he got older, grayer, and more bitter about life.

So, he nodded along to an interior rhythm as he tried to sort through the old memories.

By the time he went to Amanda's house, Grant had split for points unknown, Willis had assaulted Elaine and left her bleeding out on the floor of their living room, then had come back home just long enough to get arrested himself.

That memory made him smile. He had actually crossed paths with his father a few times over the years. Like Reggie himself, once Willis got into the system, he was in more than he was out.

He remembered that he'd taken the money Willis was going to use to run away with and hidden it somewhere in the house, though he couldn't quite picture where that hiding spot was. He was confident he could find it.

The waitress came back inside, stepped behind the counter and said, "You want to order something, hon?"

Reggie remembered that the first time he had seen her, he had thought she was an older woman, certainly more mature than he was. Now, she just looked hopelessly young to Reggie's eyes.

He jumped up, hurried up to the counter and ordered a burger basket and a strawberry shake. He reached into his pocket for money, hoping he had some. He was relieved to see a five-dollar bill and two singles.

"You hold onto that, hon, until I bring your food out, okay?"

Reggie nodded, put the money back in his pocket and sat back down.

He tried to situate himself in this life. If everything was the same, as it had been in what had just happened to him, then his mom was already dead and his dad was in the Middle Falls jail.

In an odd way, Reggie felt a tingle of excitement. There was nothing holding him back. He didn't have a record, he had a stash of cash at the house, and he could go anywhere and do anything. For the first time since this night had happened in his first life, Reggie felt the power of *possibilities.*

He let those possibilities roll around in his mind for a few minutes.

In some ways, Reggie had matured. He had grown up while he had been in the prison system.

At the same time, having been institutionalized almost his entire life, he didn't have a lot in the way of life skills. He had never applied for a job, rented an apartment, or bought a car. All he knew was how to survive in a prison environment. That could have scared him into inaction, but instead, he just felt inspired.

He picked up the stainless-steel napkin holder and held it so he could see his own face. This time, he wasn't surprised to see his fifteen-year-old face staring back at him. That gave him more hope. If he had looked like a middle-aged man, people might have thought it strange that he didn't know how to do everything. But looking like a teenager was the perfect disguise for him.

He got excited about what he could do and nearly got up and left Artie's before his food arrived.

That was the moment the waitress brought everything to him. Smelling the incredible food, he was glad he hadn't.

"A dollar seventy-five," the waitress said.

Reggie handed her the two singles and said, "Keep the change."

She blessed him with a smile and said, "Thanks, hon. Just bring your basket up to the counter when you're done."

Reggie reached out and touched the soft, aromatic bun. His stomach growled. He hadn't had a decent meal in several lifetimes.

He tore through the meal and it was so good he went back to the counter and ordered another burger basket. He still had the fiver in his pocket and knew that he wasn't going to go near Amanda's house this time. That was where all his troubles had spun out of control the first time around.

"You've gotta love a teenage boy's appetite," the waitress said. "If I did that, it would go straight to my hips."

Reggie couldn't stop his eyes from wandering down to her hips, which showed no sign of extra Artie's burgers at all.

She caught him looking at her and tilted her head at him, a small challenge.

Reggie actually blushed a little and said, "Thanks," then retreated to his table.

The same songs that had played in his first life played again, and though Reggie didn't remember that, there was still a definite familiarity about this whole scene. He thought back on his brief encounters the day before, and realized that though everything had started the same, he had managed to change something there.

The more he thought about it, the more he realized he had no idea what had happened next. Maybe Willis had killed Elaine, too, then dumped both their bodies out in the woods somewhere. There was no way for Reggie to know.

He was comforted by the fact that he *would* be able to change things, though.

When the waitress brought his second dinner out to him, he tipped her another twenty-five cents and ate the second burger much more slowly. He was able to actually taste everything instead of essentially inhaling it.

When he finished it and tipped the last of his strawberry shake down his gullet, his hunger was definitely sated. He even felt like his stomach stuck out slightly, though that was probably his imagination.

He walked out of Artie's and saw the hubbub of a small-town Friday night. He realized that the scene unfolding in front of him was a big part of what he had missed in his first life. He had never really been a part of any kind of social scene like this. On the occasions when he had been released from prison, he had been completely on his own, committing small crimes until he got caught and sent back again.

He decided to walk home. That seemed like the best and safest place for him at that moment. If he never went to Amanda's house, never robbed Sal's Pawn Shop, no one would be looking for him, at least for the moment. He could take his time and plan what his next move would be.

Would he go to school on Monday? Reggie didn't think so. He didn't see any advantage in trying to fit back into that life when he knew it would be short-lived anyway. He thought it would be better to catch a Greyhound bus out of town and start over somewhere else. Somewhere that no one would be wanting to put him into the foster care system.

He walked a few blocks toward town, but as he did, a new thought crept into his mind.

It had bugged him all his life that Amanda had essentially got away scot-free with setting him up and ruining his life. When it had first happened, he hadn't ratted on her out of some misplaced sense of loyalty that she didn't deserve. Once time passed and he was able to let go of that idea, it felt like it was too late to do anything about it. Who would care what some jailbird said about someone who was, by then, probably one of Middle Falls' leading citizens.

That began to rankle him, and it bothered him more every step he took. Without consciously deciding to do it, his feet seemed to carry him along toward Amanda's house. At first, he told himself that he just wanted to watch from the shadows in case she came to the door looking for him. It would be sweet to see Amanda being stood up.

As he drew closer, a completely different plan began to form in his brain. Having lived and died twice already gave Reggie a new sense of invulnerability.

He smiled and thought to himself, *If death can't stop me, then what can?*

Chapter Nineteen

It didn't take long for a plan to form in Reggie's mind, mostly because it was a plan that was beautiful in its simplicity.

He walked up the very nice sidewalk to the very nice porch, but this time instead of knocking on the very nice door, he leaned down and pushed the illuminated button for the doorbell. He heard deep gongs echoing inside the house.

Just a few seconds later, Amanda threw the door open. "There you are!" she said happily, as though she really was happy to see Reggie. "We thought maybe you were going to stand us up."

Reggie had to stop himself from gawking at Amanda. In his first life and in the memories he had carried since then, she had seemed larger than life. A near-goddess that walked the halls of Middle Falls High.

Seeing her now, she looked completely different to him. She was cute in an adolescent way to his eye, but really, she was just a young girl pretending to be something that she wasn't. Whatever spell Amanda Jarvis had cast on Reggie in his first life, it had worn off over the two times he had crossed death's door.

She was wearing the same thing she had been wearing the first time this night had played out—a midriff-baring top and short shorts. The difference was all in how Reggie viewed her. The first time it had been as a sex goddess. Now, she looked slightly ridiculous to his eye.

"Here, let me take your coat," Amanda said.

Reggie shucked his coat off, and Amanda tossed it on top of a pile of other coats. "Maid's day off," she said, thinking that was clever.

Reggie smiled and nodded. He couldn't manage to be impressed or amused by Amanda, but the thoughts of revenge did make him happy.

For the next couple of hours, Reggie went through the motions.

The same five girls were there. Bobbi was once again Amanda's first lieutenant. They listened to the same records, and Amanda did her best to get Reggie as drunk as possible.

The thing was, Reggie had never really gotten in the habit of drinking much alcohol. On the few occasions he was out of prison, he would drink, as much to stay warm while he was on the streets as anything. Once he was back in prison, though, he never touched the alcohol the prisoners made in their toilets, which they called *pruno*.

That meant he didn't have any more of a tolerance for alcohol than he had in the first life, but this time he had a plan. Each time Amanda or Bobbi brought him a drink, he would make a show out of taking a sip, smacking his lips and saying how good it was. Then, when no one had their eyes on him, he would lower his glass to his side and spill it out a little at a time underneath the couch they were all leaning on.

By the time Amanda thought she had four drinks down him, he had actually drunk maybe half of one glass. He did start to pretend like he was feeling a little tipsy, though.

When the girls went through their preplanned lines, Reggie went along with it all as quickly as he could without setting off alarm bells. Once the girls had vanished upstairs to change into their burglary outfits, he stood up without a wobble and put his shoes back on. He waited a minute to give the girls time to change, then, pretending to be drunk again, stumbled going up the stairs a bit.

"I told you we shouldn't have given him a fourth drink," Bobbi said.

"The cold air will sober him up," Amanda said out of the side of her mouth.

Reggie didn't remember to say, "I think I might be sick," but that was okay. He wasn't trying to recreate the night this had all happened; he was just looking for a little payback.

He bobbed and weaved his way up the stairs, leaning on Amanda a little as she steered him outside. He leaned against the porch railing, inhaling the night air deeply. After a few breaths, he said, "Okay, I think I feel better."

Amanda shot Bobbi a look that said, *See? Don't question me!"*

Reggie looked down at his Deep Purple T-shirt, jeans, and tennis shoes, then at the five girls, all of whom were dressed in black from head to toe. He felt woefully underdressed for a major criminal operation.

He thought back to the last time he had been in this position. He had thought he was handling the harsh blows that life had dealt him well. Being an adult about everything. From this new perspective, he saw that the version of himself that had been in this situation had been numbed by too many body blows. If he had just sucked it up and done the best he could, including risking being put into some sort of a foster system, his life would have probably run more smoothly.

Instead, he tucked all his feelings deep down inside and got suckered by these five young ladies.

Now, the impact of the different crises all happening at once was so far behind him that it didn't seem to have any real emotional resonance anymore. It was almost as if it had happened to a different person altogether.

Bobbi skipped down the steps past Reggie and ran toward the car she had parked a block away. All the other girls gathered around him as though they were his support team, ready to root, root, root for the home team.

Inwardly, Reggie smiled.

Moments later, a pair of headlights pierced the foggy night, and the Cadillac appeared with Bobbi behind the wheel.

Just like last time, three of the girls climbed in the back and Amanda and Bobbi pushed Reggie into the middle. A Reggie sandwich.

Once again, Bobbi took a circuitous route around the many neighborhoods of Middle Falls. Reggie thought this was stupid. By driving through so many areas, they were just making it more likely that someone would remember the car. He closed his eyes and sank down into the plush bench seat of the Caddy. It wasn't his job to make sure they didn't get caught.

When they finally arrived at Sal's Pawn Shop, they drove by once, barely crawling. Bobbi had to keep her foot on the Cadillac's brake to keep it from surging forward. They parked a block down and everyone clambered out.

Again, the girls showed how prepared they were for the crime they were about to commit. Amanda and Bobbi handed out canvas bags to hold the loot. She made sure everyone had a flashlight. Finally, she handed Reggie the tire iron.

"You break us in," Amanda said, "and we'll just grab my stuff, then we'll get out of here."

"Don't forget..." Bobbi said, leading Amanda.

"Oh, right." She turned to Reggie and said, "Just so you know, we're going to have to grab a few other things while we're in there. If we just get my stuff, it'll be pretty obvious that we were the ones who did it."

Reggie smiled as though he was pleased with their thoughtfulness in not wanting him to get caught. He slapped the tire iron into his hand a few times to show he meant business.

They walked quietly up to the door, and Reggie leaned over to look at it. He was surprised to see what kind of lock the door had.

He would have assumed that a pawn shop would have a tough lock to pick, but it really wasn't. "Unbelievable," he said.

"What?" Amanda asked, suddenly worried.

"Nothing," Reggie said. "I don't think I'm going to need to break in through the glass. That's pretty noisy and might attract some attention. I can get us in a different way, then grab your stuff and let's go."

All five of the girls nodded together.

Reggie fished his wallet out and found his laminated Associated Student Body card. He quickly glanced at the picture on it, which showed his own face, a dopey grin prominently displayed. He had a hard time believing that he had ever been that young and innocent.

He fidgeted with the lock, slipping his ASB card into the opening between door and jamb. Thirty seconds later, the door popped open.

Amanda looked at Reggie as though she may have underestimated him. She didn't spend too much time on that, though. The door was open, and she and the other four girls were through in a heartbeat.

Amanda ran to the fur coat that was draped over a mannequin in the window. She slipped it off that and onto herself. Like a shark smelling blood, she ran behind the jewelry case and threw the doors open. She was not careful about what she grabbed, she was voracious and seemed to want everything.

Bobbi grabbed a portable radio and stuffed it into her bag.

It was like Christmas had come early.

But only for a moment.

Reggie stood in front of the door, quietly watching all this unfold. When he thought the girls had enough merchandise stuffed away in their canvas bags, he took three steps forward and stood in front of the near-empty jewelry case.

The girls ignored him.

Reggie raised the tire iron over his head and slammed it down on the jewelry case. The glass shattered and flew in a hundred different directions. The noise of the imploding case was incredible in the silence.

All five girls stopped what they were doing and turned toward Reggie, shock written on their faces.

"What the hell?" Amanda said. "Have you lost it?"

Reggie smiled calmly. He cocked his head slightly and heard the noise he was waiting for. Thumping footsteps sounded overhead.

"We've got to get out of here now," Amanda said, casting a dirty look at Reggie.

Reggie was two steps ahead.

He sprinted to the door, threw it open, and stepped out onto the sidewalk. He closed the door behind him, then leaned backward, holding it shut tight with all his strength.

Amanda and Bobbi both appeared at the door. They were panicked, but not giving up.

"Reggie, hon, what are you doing? We've got to go. You don't want to get caught, do you?"

Reggie smiled. It was a toothy, vicious smile. "Honestly, I don't care that much if I get caught. I just want to make sure *you* get caught."

Realization seemed to dawn on Amanda. This time, she was the rat caught in the trap and Reggie had just sprung it on her. Her normally beautiful face twisted in rage. "*Why* would you do this, you retard?" She reached out and rattled the door handle, trying to pull it open.

Reggie held it shut tight easily. "Just settling an old score."

That meant nothing to Amanda, but she had bigger worries at that moment. The overhead lights in the shop clicked on, illuminating the chaotic scene. A moment later, Sal Parker came thumping down the stairs and threw open the back door to the shop. He seemed surprised to see five black-garbed teenage girls holding bags of his inventory. He had the shotgun in his hand, but it was pointed downward.

Reggie knew the time had come to run, but he couldn't tear himself away from the drama playing out in front of him. He couldn't help but wonder if somehow Sal would trip and be killed again.

"Amanda?" Sal said. "Amanda Jarvis? What the hell are you doing here?"

Amanda had the natural ability to think up a lie and think it up quick. But standing there among the shattered glass of the case, wearing her mom's pilfered mink coat, and holding a bag full of watches and jewelry, there was nothing that could be said.

Sal looked around at the five young women frozen in place around his shop. He shook his head. "I've called the cops. They'll be here any second."

That proved to be true, as a siren reached Reggie's ears, though it came from a distance. He decided that he had absorbed enough of the scene as he could without getting nabbed, so he turned and ran. As he sprinted by the window, he looked in and made brief eye contact with Amanda.

She was glaring at him, hating him. If a look could have killed, Reggie would have fallen down dead.

Instead, his heart kept pumping, and he sprinted away into the night.

Chapter Twenty

As he ran, Reggie saw the red and blue lights of the Middle Falls police car bounce off the windows of the other buildings on the block. He ran for sixty seconds, partially because his adrenaline was high and partially because it felt so good to be young and able to push himself again.

When he was two blocks away, he slowed down, then came to a complete stop. He had run away because he didn't want to get arrested. He didn't want to have to spend the weekend in the Middle Falls jail again, with his father chirping in his ear. If he never saw his father again in this or any life, he would be happy.

But then, he pictured the scene in his mind. The prowler pulling up and the deputy getting out. He had to really search his mind, but he came up with the cop's name. Naismith. What came easily to mind, though, was what Naismith looked like. At least seventy-five or eighty pounds overweight, his stomach hanging over his belt, getting out of breath just from climbing out of the car.

It had been satisfying to see the expression on Amanda's face, but it would be even sweeter to see her and the others do the perp walk and get put into the backseat of the prowler.

He still didn't want to get caught, but he felt that being young, strong, and fast would work in combination with his older, cooler head and he could have the best of both worlds.

He crossed the street, walked a block away from the pawn shop, then circled back around. He didn't think they would be looking for him. At least not yet. By the time they did start to look for him, he intended to be far away.

He worked his way back toward the pawn shop slowly, sticking to doorways and spots where the shadows were deep. It took him ten minutes, but he finally found a spot down a stairwell where he could see what was happening but not be seen.

A second Middle Falls police car pulled up and he recognized Chief Deakins as he climbed out. "Sorry to interrupt your Friday night at home, Chief," Reggie said with a grin.

For a long time, the scene in front of him was static, aside from the red and blue lights that continued to flash.

Reggie assumed that this whole crime was so unlikely, Deakins was taking his time sorting it out and getting things figured out. Reggie wished he could be a fly on the wall, listening to what was being said in the store.

For a moment, Reggie wondered if Amanda would be able to talk her way out of it all. She was both smart and cunning, and she had the twin advantages of being a female and, even better, a female from one of Middle Falls' wealthy families.

That fear seemed to be unfounded, though, as a few minutes later, Deakins led Amanda and Bobbi out and put them in the backseat of his cruiser. Behind him, Naismith herded the other three girls into the backseat of his own car.

Sal Parker, very much alive at the end of this version of the drama, followed them out into the street and this time, Reggie *could* hear what was being said. It was nothing that would ever be printed in a family newspaper, though. Just an expletive-laced tirade about kids today and how they didn't have the brains God gave a guppy.

Reggie was glad he had snuck back around. It made for a very satisfying ending to the whole adventure. He remained in the shadows and observed from his hiding spot as Sal went back inside and, continuing no doubt to cuss up a storm, began to clean up the mess.

Eventually, Sal obviously decided this was a job that would be better handled in the morning. He switched off the overhead fluorescent and, double-checking that the front door was locked, went back upstairs.

"You really should buy a better lock, Sal. With that piss-poor excuse, I could walk in there anytime and help myself to whatever you've got. Surprised it hasn't happened more often."

Reggie cooled his heels for another five minutes, but the damp air began to settle into his bones. He walked slowly up out of the stairwell and, with his head on a swivel, left the scene of the crime.

He had no doubt that Amanda, Bobbi, and all the girls would be singing their heads off about his involvement in the crime. He thought it was likely that they would paint him as the mastermind and ringleader. Maybe even that he had forced them into doing what they had.

He knew that meant that he would only have a little time to gather anything he wanted to take with him and get out of town. He thought about that. After a minute, he guessed that he would pack a few clothes in a knapsack, but that there wasn't anything else he needed from his childhood home. Anything he had ever loved there had been destroyed.

Except for the money. He knew he would need that to have a chance to get out of town. As he walked toward home, he tried to decide if he should take a chance on catching a Greyhound bus out of town or not.

In the movies, he knew the police would have the bus station staked out. Given the size of the Middle Falls Police Department, though, that would almost certainly not happen. Of course, in Middle Falls, they wouldn't necessarily need to stake the place out. Deakins could just tell whoever was selling tickets to keep an eye open for Reggie.

As much as he wanted to believe he could get away with it, he knew it was too big a chance to take. He would have to come up with another plan.

One challenge for Reggie in this life was going to be that he had been institutionalized so young that he never picked up any standard adult life skills, and that extended to even learning how to drive a car. He had still been six months away from his learner permit when he had gone to Plain Hill, then all of his sojourns out of the system had been too short to ever worry about a license or owning a car.

He was confident that he could figure things out, but not so confident that he wanted his first time behind the wheel to be in a stolen vehicle. He could just imagine what a high-speed chase would look like, and it wasn't pretty.

He decided to let that go for the moment. For now, he was exhausted. He had, from his perspective, died twice in the previous twenty-four hours, plus there was the excitement of exacting some form of revenge on Amanda and company.

He was young and strong, yes, but he was also flagging.

He was also a little alarmed to discover that his memory of the layout of the streets of Middle Falls wasn't as perfect as he would have liked. He was embarrassed when he realized he had gotten slightly lost while hugging the backstreets of his hometown.

Original Reggie, or even Harold or Nelson, would have ragged extensively on this older, more forgetful version.

It was almost two a.m. when he finally made it back to Crampton Village. He once again stuck to the shadows when he entered the neighborhood. He stood just inside the entrance for long minutes, trying to see anything at all that would be out of place.

There was nothing but a biting cold wind that made him long for cover.

He took a chance and hurried toward his house. He had been there less than twenty-four hours earlier according to his internal clock, but it felt different to him this time. Darker and more foreboding somehow.

He hurried through the front door, but decided not to turn on any lights. He thought it was possible that Deakins or Naismith would drive by, knowing that the house should be deserted.

He felt his way to the back porch and fumbled around until he found a flashlight. He said a little prayer that the batteries were good and flicked it on. The light that came out was weak and unsteady, but it was something.

Using the flashlight, he went back into the kitchen and started going through the cupboards. He was almost certain that had been where he had hidden his father's money. He had dreamed about that missing money for decades, thinking how nice it would be to have that amount credited to his prison commissary fund.

In the early nineties, he had watched a movie with the other inmates in the media room. It was *Stand by Me*, which Reggie thought was truly excellent. The movie was based on a novella by Stephen King, but he didn't know that as he still hadn't mastered the art of reading. He was always envious when the cart with the paperbacks pushed by his cell. Everyone else tossed their previous books in and grabbed new ones, but Reggie knew it was no use. When he tried to focus, the words still danced.

In the movie, there was a scene where one of the characters buried a jar of pennies under his porch and then was never able to find them.

Crawling around his family's kitchen, tearing apart every cupboard looking for his lost money, Reggie could definitely relate to the lost jar of pennies.

It was that thought—a jar—that brought a memory up from the deep recesses of his mind. He had already run the beam over a cupboard full of mostly empty jars, but he went back to it. This time, he took all the jars out and set them on the kitchen linoleum.

Sure enough, clear at the back, he found an old Manwich jar that had a tight roll of money sitting on the bottom.

"Jackpot," Reggie said quietly. The word echoed strangely in the empty, shadow-filled home. He twisted the lid off, shook the money out on the floor, and counted it. There were two hundred and eighty dollars.

Reggie had never really gotten the hang of inflation, because it had never really had any meaning in his life. Still, he thought that maybe that much money could give him a leg up on getting started with his new life.

On his walk, he had decided against both taking the bus or trying to boost a car. Both of those seemed destined for disaster.

He elected instead to rely on the fact that he was young and strong. He decided that under the cover of darkness, he would just walk out of town. When he got far enough away—maybe ten or fifteen miles, he could think about taking the risk of sticking his thumb out and hitching a ride.

To Reggie, it didn't matter where he was going. Just away. Away from this mixed-up start in his life. Away from Middle Falls, which seemed like a curse to him.

He was sure he wanted to leave after dark, which wasn't hard to do in October. It was dark for more than thirteen hours in Western Oregon that time of year.

But he knew he couldn't do it right then. He was too tired.

He went back into his childhood bedroom and collapsed across his bed.

A whole lifetime earlier, Reggie had made that bed, wondering what his frame of mind would be when he climbed into it that night. Then, he had never made it back.

He had forgotten all about that.

He crashed hard and slept through the night and well into late morning.

He might have slept even longer, but he was awakened by a harsh knuckling at the front door.

Sitting up, stiff and dazed, he tried to remember what was happening in his life.

He crept silently out to the living room.

The knuckles rapped again.

"Reggie? Are you in there?"

It was Chief Deakins.

Chapter Twenty-One

Reggie froze. He didn't even want to breathe, for fear that Deakins might hear him through the door. He was standing just inside the living room. He realized that if Deakins moved to his left and looked through the window, he would be able to see him.

The night before, he had told Amanda that he didn't care if he got caught or not, that he just wanted revenge. That had been true in the heat of the moment, but once he got away, he realized that he *did* care about getting caught.

Getting caught meant going to jail. For all he knew, it might mean a return trip to Plain Hill and starting that whole process over again. He wanted desperately to avoid that.

Reggie didn't think that Deakins would come into the house. That would be illegal, of course, though in small towns like Middle Falls, the Chief of Police often got to make his own laws and everyone else looked the other way.

Quietly, Reggie turned back toward the bedroom. He hadn't bothered to get undressed the night before, but he had at least kicked his shoes off. He sat down on his bed to put them on. He looked to his right and saw that the blinds were only halfway down the window. If Deakins came around the house, he would be able to look inside and right at him.

He stood up and went into the bathroom. It was the only room in the small house that didn't have any windows at all. He patted the right pocket of his jeans and was reassured to find the roll of money there. At least if he had to make a run for it, he would have that.

Another rap on the front door. "Reggie? Reggie, I know you're in there. I've just got a couple of questions for you. Open the door and we can clear everything up."

Reggie was sure that the couple of questions Deakins had would closely resemble the kind of questions he'd had for Willis when he had arrested him. The kind of questions that required a trip down to the station and probably a pair of handcuffs.

He decided to just sit quietly on the toilet and not move.

Eventually, Deakins stopped knocking, but Reggie didn't trust that. He thought there was every chance that the Chief was just sitting in his car, waiting for him to be stupid and open the door or even look through the curtains.

Reggie sat on the throne, safe but bored. He knew that the best thing to do would be to just sit there until dark, then leave Middle Falls behind forever. Or at least until he got started over again.

Finally, he gave up on just sitting there and crept out of the bathroom. He peeked around the corner and out the living room window. No sign of Deakins.

Reggie nodded to himself. The first time this crime had been committed, Sal Parker had died. This time, there was a little property damage, but that was all. Any inventory that would have been stolen was retrieved. That meant that although Deakins and every other Middle Falls cop would be on the lookout for him, it probably wasn't the biggest thing on their agenda, especially on a weekend. They probably figured they could just catch him at school on Monday.

Of course, by Monday, Reggie hoped to be many miles away from Middle Falls.

Slowly, he approached the window at an angle. When he got close enough that he had a view of the entire front yard, he saw there was no one there. He pulled the curtains closed tight, and then did the same to every other window in the house. That made it mostly dark inside, but that was kind of comforting.

Reggie sat down on the couch and tried to think. He'd been on the move ever since he had first woken up in Middle Falls again, so hadn't had much time to consider what was really going on.

He sat and thought things through, replaying the events of his life, starting with dying in the prison hospital, then running up to that moment.

Thinking about it as hard as he could, Reggie couldn't come up with any realistic explanation for what was happening. He had never been a big philosopher, but he didn't know of any belief system that was based on this—being recycled to an earlier point in your life. Not exactly reincarnation, but definitely not what any of the preachers had ever tried to talk to him about while he was in prison.

Reggie spent a little time trying to concentrate, but couldn't figure anything out and gave up. He took the uncertainty of his situation and put it down in one of the partitioned areas of his mind. He would dredge it out and consider it again if some new information became available.

In the meantime, he decided to get ready to split. He found his old knapsack in the closet and threw a few pairs of underwear, socks, T-shirts, and his second pair of jeans in, along with his toothbrush, toothpaste, and hairbrush. He couldn't think of anything else he would need.

He had no idea what would happen to this house. With his dad in jail and his mom dead, he supposed the bank would eventually reclaim it and sell it again. That made him look around with new eyes. If he never saw anything in this house again, would there be anything he would miss?

He found a picture of his mom that sat on the counter. He grabbed that and put it in his pack. When he hefted the pack onto his shoulders, he found it wasn't too heavy. He would be able to carry it with no difficulty.

He glanced at the kitchen clock and saw that it was a little past one o'clock. Even with it getting dark early, he still had hours to kill.

He wandered into the kitchen and looked for something to eat. His first thought was to eat some cereal, but there was nothing but an empty box in the cupboard. He settled for opening a can of soup and heating it up on the stove.

Reggie had spent a few years working in the kitchen in prison, so that was at least one area where he had achieved some life skills.

He ate the soup sitting at the kitchen table, just staring ahead and trying to plan.

When he finished that, he put the bowl in the sink. "Maid's day off," he mumbled to himself.

He rooted around in the cupboards and found a can of stew and a can of pork and beans. He grabbed those, the can opener, and a spoon and added them to his pack. He wasn't sure how long he would be out walking before he got to some form of civilization.

He didn't really have a plan beyond that, which had always been part of his problem when he had gotten out of prison. He'd never had much of a plan, other than to do better.

Do better is a noble goal, but it is easier to achieve when it's paired with a series of steps to get there.

He tried to put his brain to the task of coming up with a plan, but it seemed beyond him. He didn't have the requisite real-world experience to know what to expect. He decided he would have to play it by ear.

Just as he was about to turn the television on, he heard footsteps.

Again, there was a harsh knocking at the door. A pause, then "Come on, Reggie. This will be so much easier for both of us if I don't have to keep making trips over here, wasting the taxpayer's money on gasoline."

Reggie shrank down, even though he knew the curtains were shut tight. He had no intention of falling for Deakins' tricks.

"Reggie? Come on, don't make me bother the judge to get a warrant to come in. I will if I have to, but it will go so much better for both of us if you just open up. I've just got a few questions."

That actually made Reggie smile a little. The picture of Deakins going to some judge's house late on a Saturday afternoon for something like this was ludicrous. He wondered if he would have fallen for this line of BS when he really was a fifteen-year-old kid. He remembered how easily he had been suckered by Amanda and ruefully realized that he might have.

This was an older and more experienced Reggie, though, if perhaps not much wiser. He wasn't going to open the door, and he was sure that by the time Deakins actually did get the right to come inside, he would be several counties away.

Reggie sat motionless and quiet on the couch for twenty minutes, waiting to make sure that Deakins really was gone. Finally, he went to the window and peered around a slight opening in an unconscious copy of the way his father had just before he was arrested.

There was no Deakins, but Reggie was glad to see that it *was* getting dark.

Almost time to go.

He waited another thirty minutes, until it was close to full dark. He grabbed the flashlight, thinking he could eventually buy some new batteries for it. When he did that, he saw the can of black spray paint.

Yeah. Why not? Reggie thought.

He tucked the flashlight into his back pocket, hoisted the knapsack onto his back, and grabbed the can of spray paint.

He exited via the back door, just in case, and walked carefully through the muddy backyard and through a spot where the old fence had fallen down. He didn't see a soul anywhere.

He was still careful, though. Until he was well quit of Middle Falls, he intended to be as invisible as possible.

He grinned to himself a little. *Invisible*, with one small exception.

He got to the entrance to Crampton Village and set his pack down. He rattled the spray can, liking the sound it made, and used the flashlight to illuminate his canvas.

He crossed out *Crampton* and wrote *Crapped-On*. Score one point for Reggie.

That point was immediately deducted when a voice came from behind him.

"Good," Chief Deakins said. "I'm glad I don't have to wait out here anymore. It's too damned cold for this. Come on, I've got some questions to ask you."

Chapter Twenty-Two

Reggie turned around. Deakins had parked his police prowler behind a billboard, just like in the movies. Now, he was standing maybe ten feet away from him.

Deakins wasn't as out of shape as Naismith was. The chief was more stocky than outright fat. Still, he wasn't exactly young. Reggie estimated that he was probably in his early fifties.

A thought ran through Reggie's mind. *Would he really shoot me? I don't think he would. I could definitely outrun him.* He had decided not to outrun Naismith in an earlier life because Middle Falls was such a small town, there was nowhere to hide. But with the desire to put Middle Falls behind him, that wasn't such a factor.

Reggie raised his hands in a *you've got me* kind of gesture, leaving his knapsack on the ground by the Crampton Village sign.

"Is there a law against graffiti?" Reggie asked.

That made Deakins guffaw. "As a matter of fact, there is. That's count one against you now." He reached behind him and pulled his handcuffs off his belt. "Step this way and turn around with your hands behind your back."

Reggie nodded as though he was thoroughly defeated. He took three steps toward Deakins then turned left and started to run up the street. He expected to hear Deakins right behind him, but that didn't happen. Instead, Deakins pulled his nightstick from his belt and, in one smooth motion, threw it sidearm at Reggie's retreating figure.

It hit him right behind the knees, and he went down in a heap.

"Down goes Reggie! Down goes Reggie!" Deakins said in a terrible imitation of Howard Cosell.

Reggie tried to get up and run again, but found that his right leg had gone numb.

Deakins sauntered over to him and casually picked up the nightstick. "You want to make another run for it? I can always use the practice."

"I think you broke my leg."

"All in a day's work, son. More than likely, it's just a bruise, and the feeling will come back into it over time. You're not the first punk I've taken down like that." He paused. "Just the first one today." Deakins reached down and roughly pulled Reggie to his feet. Or, more accurately, to his *foot*. He couldn't seem to put any weight on his right leg.

Deakins seemed to enjoy watching him hobble around and try to keep his balance. The chief grabbed him by the shoulder and spun him around, then had his hands cuffed behind his back in record time. He frisked him, but didn't find anything but the wad of money in his jeans pocket. He reached in with two sure fingers and pulled it out. Casually, he slipped the money into his own pocket.

"Hey, asshole, that's mine."

Deakins cuffed the back of Reggie's head and said, "Watch your language, son. I'm a sworn officer of the law."

"I want that back."

"You can want it in one hand and shit in the other and see which one fills up first."

Deakins led him, limping badly, back to the cruiser, opened the door, and stuck him in the backseat. He walked over to the sign, inspected it, and said, "Not bad, really. This whole neighborhood is a shit hole that could burn down and the world would be better off," then picked up Reggie's knapsack and carried it back to the car, tossing it inside.

Reggie sat fuming and kicking himself in the backseat, knowing he really didn't have anyone but himself to blame for this predicament.

Deakins climbed in, groaning a little as he did. He unhooked the radio microphone and muttered something that Reggie couldn't understand. Sitting in the back with his hands cuffed behind him was uncomfortable, but he wasn't going to give Deakins the satisfaction of complaining about it.

Five minutes later, they pulled up in front of the police station with the holding cells in the back. Deakins hauled him out, and Reggie was happy to find that some circulation had returned to his right leg. Maybe it wasn't broken after all. He knew he would have a substantial limp for a few days, though.

Reggie really wasn't looking forward to what would happen next. He winced as Deakins led him back to the holding cells.

The first thing he saw was his father, who blinked at Reggie in surprise. "Holy shit, Deakins, are you kidding me? What did he do?"

Deakins shrugged. "Nothing too terrible." He looked at Willis with intent. "I mean he didn't *murder* anybody or anything like that."

That shut Willis up for a moment, and Reggie limped past him without making eye contact.

When Willis saw the limp, he laughed a little. "Tried to make a run for it, huh, Chief? These kids'll never learn. Can't outrun the nightstick."

After Deakins locked Reggie in the cell, Reggie lay down and turned to face the wall with his back to his father.

Willis wasn't quite done having the last word yet. "Don't ya know that back in the day ole Deakins here was a helluva baseball player. He might be old and paunchy now, but he used to be able to throw a fastball right on by you."

Deakins was almost out of the holding cell area, but stopped and turned to Willis. "Give it a rest, Blackwell."

Willis gave it a rest until Deakins was through the door, then once again began offering unsolicited fatherly advice to Reggie, who didn't answer any of it. He'd seen how this whole scene happened once before and he wished he wasn't there to see it again.

The weekend passed, as all weekends do, whether happy or sad. On Monday, Reggie was brought up before a judge who found enough evidence—that evidence being the testimony of five young girls from upstanding families—to hold Reggie over for trial.

The girls, Reggie was sad to see, were returned to their families with a promise to testify if more questions arose. As it turned out, Bobbi's father was a lawyer who belonged to the same country club as the judge and played poker with him every other Thursday.

Reggie's father did not have those connections, but everyone involved, from Sal to the judge, to the prosecuting attorney, wanted the whole thing to go away. They made an offer to Reggie that if he pleaded guilty to masterminding the robbery, they would sentence him to stay at a juvenile facility for three years and then have his record sealed.

If he didn't accept the deal, they would try him in adult court and the sentence would probably be seven to ten years and at least part of it would be served in an adult prison.

Reggie didn't have a lot of goals for this life, but staying out of prison was one.

He took the deal.

He didn't remember Plain Hill fondly, but compared to the years he spent at the Oregon Penitentiary, it wasn't too bad. He had done enough time that he knew the three years would pass quickly, and he could be out with no real record and a true chance to start over.

He thought that with three years to think about things, he might even have a plan of some sort put together.

In any case, he wasn't unhappy about being shipped away from Middle Falls. Aside from a friendship with two teenage boys that he wouldn't even recognize anymore, Reggie wasn't leaving anything behind in his hometown.

Two things stood out about his transition back to the Plain Hills School for Boys.

One was that, in his first life, this place had seemed huge and threatening. He had jumped at shadows everywhere. Now, with his vast library of experience being incarcerated, he saw that there was nothing scary about it, really. It was like the starter set for a life of imprisonment.

Yes, there were insecure, trying-to-act-tough kids staking their territory, and there were certainly rules to be followed. But Reggie was an old hand at both figuring out how to avoid confrontations and how to at least appear to be following the rules.

As soon as he arrived, he knew that his second stint at Plain Hills would be easier than his first. He also hoped to make it the last time he was locked up anywhere in this lifetime.

The second thing that stood out was that Carson was once again there.

The odd thing was that Reggie remembered Carson so clearly, but Carson didn't know him at all.

Reggie was intuitive enough not to jump right in and act like they were best friends from the beginning. Instead, he just tried to put himself in Carson's orbit and maybe lend a hand here and there when the opportunity arose.

Using that strategy, their friendship once again seemed to bloom organically.

It didn't take long for Reggie to fall back into the comfortable routine of being told where to be and when to be there. He never would have admitted it to anyone, especially himself, but that was when he was most comfortable.

When his second year at Plain Hill drew to a close, he and Carson once again put together a plan that was remarkably similar to what they had laid out in their first life. The plan that was scuttled by Gavin George. Or rather, perhaps, by Gavin George's death.

The first time Reggie saw Gavin in this life, he flashed back to the scene in their dorms, where he had the boy's head in his hands and slammed it repeatedly against the floor. He was happy to find that he didn't feel any intense emotion toward the boy at all. That's what he was, in the end—just a boy.

Reggie told himself over and over that if a similar situation arose, he would put his hands behind his back and let things play out as they would. He still wasn't sure how much of his first life would be repeating in this one.

When he first woke up, it seemed like things were essentially in lockstep with his first life. But the farther he got from that point, the more things changed. There were still big picture things like meeting Carson again, but almost everything seemed to be subject to change.

Reggie floated through the first years of his sentence at Plain Hill. After his decades of experience in an actual prison, this was more like a day camp.

When they approached the time when Carson would be released, Reggie felt increasingly uneasy. Would something happen that would force him into action in some way? Was he destined to never have his real shot at freedom?

Those concerns were, for the most part, unfounded.

As Carson's release date approached, scenarios popped up that gave Reggie the chance to act out. One even concerned George, or GG again. Just a week before he was to be released, Carson and George got into it again.

In this life, George hadn't been temporarily housed in their dorm, so Reggie had no idea what caused the fight. He and Carson were in the dining room, heading to the same table they sat at with their other friends every day.

Seemingly out of nowhere, George pushed Carson in the back, which caused him to stumble forward, lose his balance, and spill his tray of food all over two boys who were already sitting and eating.

Reggie watched as Carson, still holding his tray, turned around, anger flashing in his eyes. Reggie saw a brief glimpse of the future, where this time it was Carson instead of him who ended up being incarcerated for a longer period of time.

Reggie jumped forward and, balancing his own tray in one hand, grabbed Carson before he could retaliate. "Not worth it, man. It'll mess everything up. He's an idiot. Let him go."

The anger seemed to drain away from Carson, who really wasn't the fighting type. He nodded, turned around, and apologized to the two boys he had dumped food over. Reggie stepped between Carson and GG and a guard who had seen the whole thing hustled up and removed GG.

"Good," Reggie said. "Maybe he'll be in solitary until you're out."

"Thanks, Reg," Carson said. "I almost lost my cool."

"We've all been there," Reggie agreed.

That seemed to be the turning point for both Carson and Reggie during this stay in Plain Hill, as everything went smoothly from there.

Carson was emancipated right on schedule and left with a promise to keep his nose clean and have a place ready when Reggie got out on his eighteenth birthday.

Chapter Twenty-Three

Those last few months at Plain Hill passed quietly for Reggie. He didn't have Carson to hang around with anymore, but he still had friends. People who would watch his back and let him know if trouble was ever brewing.

Trouble was the last thing Reggie wanted. In the years he'd been there, he had come up with at least an elementary plan of sorts.

Carson had managed to get a car—not much of a car, but something that ran—and had promised to be waiting for him when he walked through the gates a free man. From there, Carson said he had a job waiting for him at the same factory where he'd been working for a year.

It wasn't the most glamorous job—the factory built television sets and Reggie would be working on the line that built the exteriors that the tubes and wires went into.

But it was a job. That was something that Reggie had never had before, aside from assigned work in prison. This was different. He would get a paycheck every two weeks, and he could come and go whenever he pleased. That was a luxury that would take some getting used to after being institutionalized for so long.

He would have a job, a place to stay where he didn't have to be on alert all day every day, and he even had dreams. They weren't big dreams yet, but he wanted to get a car of his own, learn to drive, and maybe think about going to night school to improve his life.

As his release day approached, no dream seemed impossible.

He went through the release protocol at Plain Hill on his birthday. He walked through the gates and found Carson waiting there for him in his 1965 Plymouth Satellite. There was rust on the fenders and blue smoke poured steadily out of the back end. No matter, it was much nicer than any car that Reggie had ever owned and he was just glad to see his friend—and their plan—come to fruition.

It was the first time Reggie had seen Carson since he had left the facility. They had both agreed that after being on the inside together, it would feel too weird to meet in the visitor's room. This also kept Reggie's streak of never having a visitor at any of his stops in the penal system intact.

Reggie threw his bag with his few belongings in the backseat and jumped in the front, where Carson offered him a high five.

Appropriately, *The Boys are Back in Town* by Thin Lizzy was playing through the Plymouth's tinny speakers.

It was freezing cold outside, but Reggie was tempted to roll down the window and breathe the sweet air of freedom anyway. That, and the Plymouth's interior smelled really musty because there was a hole in the floorboards and the carpet on the passenger side was always wet.

"It's good to see you, Reg. Any trouble getting out?"

"Just the usual hassles. It's like they've got one last chance to show they control your life, so they're going to take full advantage of it." Reggie smiled at Carson. This was perhaps the happiest moment he could remember. When he had gotten out in his first life, though he spoke about good intentions, he had known in the back of his mind that he was destined to fail and go back inside. He patted the pocket of his jeans—the same jeans he had worn on his way into Plain Hills, which were now several inches high water. "Got my twenty, though."

Every former inmate at Plain Hills was given a twenty-dollar bill on the way out the door. Theoretically, it enabled them to call a cab from the payphone in front of the facility if someone didn't have a ride. No one wanted a recently released boy just hanging around looking pitiful in front of the gate, although they didn't much care if you did it somewhere else. Once you left, especially if it was on your eighteenth birthday, you were someone else's problem.

Reggie still felt the loss of the money he'd had on him when Deakins had collared him. Somehow, that money had disappeared between Crampton Village and the jailhouse. In the end, who was anyone going to believe? The fine, upstanding chief of police, or an obvious juvenile delinquent. The memory of that lost money haunted Reggie, though, and he vowed that he would take revenge on Deakins for stealing it. He wasn't mad at being arrested, that was just him doing his job. But taking the last money a kid had was a low blow, even if he had kind of stolen it from his dad.

"Keep it, you'll need it," Carson said. "I'll buy us lunch, then we can hit the road."

Plain Hills was in Eugene, but Carson's new life was in Corvallis, less than an hour to the north.

They pulled into a McDonald's and went inside. Reggie ordered a Big Mac, fries, and a strawberry shake. It all tasted good to Reggie, especially after eating institutional food for three years, but it didn't come close to matching his memory of Artie's.

He opened his mouth to say just that, but Carson was ahead of him. "I know, I know, it's not as good as the legendary Artie's. One of these days, we'll go and grab food there, too, but today, we're stuck with Mickey D's." Carson looked at the clothes Reggie was wearing and said, "Listen, I've got a few bucks saved up. I'll loan you some until your first payday so you can get some clothes that fit. There's a store in Corvallis that sells jeans and flannel shirts. We can stop there on the way home."

They did just that, stopping at an army surplus store that also sold men's work clothes. They picked out two new pairs of jeans and three flannel shirts for less than twenty-five dollars.

Walking out of the store with his purchases, Reggie suddenly felt ridiculous in his too-small clothes.

They drove to Carson's tiny house, which, for the moment, was also Reggie's tiny house. In truth, it was only a little smaller than his childhood home in Middle Falls. The bonus was that it had a second bedroom, so Reggie didn't have to sleep on the couch.

The second bedroom was unfinished, though, so he'd be sleeping on the floor until he could get enough money together to at least get a used mattress.

Carson's house was not fancy in any way. There was no artwork on the walls, and they had to go to Kmart to get a second bowl, plate and set of silverware so Reggie had something to eat off of. The television was once again a thirteen-inch black and white with rabbit ears, and for the first few weeks, they had to share the same bath towel. Only the first guy in the bathroom got a dry towel.

It wasn't anything that Reggie couldn't get used to, though. He had a friend, and that friend had given him a roof over his head, food to eat, and a job, which was more than anyone else had ever given him.

Reggie started his job the following Monday and learned a lot about assembling televisions. Or, at least, the outer frames of televisions. Carson explained to him that all the inner workings came from Japan, which everyone at the factory tended to call the J.A. Pan company. All they had to do at the factory was build the boxes, then insert all the technological stuff that came in large containers. Doing it that way allowed them to put *Made in the U S of A* stickers with a red, white, and blue flag on every box.

Reggie's job was not difficult at all, as each person on the assembly line only did one job as the soon-to-be television passed by them on the conveyor belt. His job was to glue and then staple two pieces of wood together. If pressed, he couldn't have even told you what part of the television he was working on. It didn't matter, though. He was making slightly above minimum wage and with his first paycheck, he was able to pay Carson a little bit of rent, so he felt better about things.

Contentment is an odd thing in someone who has just turned eighteen years old, though.

Once sprung from Plain Hills, Reggie felt nothing but gratitude. To Carson, for helping him out, to Mr. Stagner for giving him a job, and even to the great state of Oregon for giving him a fresh start.

Over time, that gratitude faded a little.

He worked at the factory from 8:00 a.m. to 5:00 p.m. Monday through Friday with a half hour for lunch and two fifteen-minute breaks. He put in a half day on Saturday as well and got paid time and a half for overtime on that day. But, since he was only being paid $2.50 an hour normally, that overtime was still only $3.75. It was better than the twenty cents an hour he'd been paid to make license plates in the Oregon Penitentiary, but out in the real world, absolutely everything cost money and every time he turned around, he felt like he was having to dip into his wallet. Said wallet was generally empty a day or two before payday.

After six months of living close to the edge like that, Reggie's mind began to wander to other possibilities. Those dreams of maybe going on to a community college seemed to fade. More and more, he started to think about some of the things he had learned while he was in prison.

Extracurricular activities that didn't require any cash outlay, but could be very profitable, nonetheless.

For a time, he didn't act on any of those thoughts, but just let them stay in his head like random daydreams.

Then—just for fun, he told himself—he started to walk around certain neighborhoods at night. He said he was just out for a little fresh air and his health. Others might have said he was casing neighborhood houses.

It was a gradual move toward a new life of crime. At first, he just identified where the houses were that didn't seem to have any lights on after dark. Then, he progressed to walking up a driveway and looking in the windows at the back of houses to confirm that they were empty.

It was only a short hop, skip, and a jump from there to actually breaking into the houses.

At first, it was enough to just show that he could do it.

Soon, though, he started picking up little souvenirs, like another set of silverware, or a coffee cup, or even a small radio from a child's bedroom. It wasn't anything he was doing for a profit, at least initially, but rather just to see if he could do it.

He could.

Over time, his souvenirs grew in value, and he got in the habit of taking jewelry and other small valuable items that he could take to one of Corvallis's several pawn shops.

That put a little extra money in his pocket and gave him something to look forward to other than putting the same two pieces of wood together at the factory over and over.

In fact, he started to look at his days at the factory—riding in with Carson, eating lunch with the fellas, then riding home with Carson—as being not all that different from his days in prison. There was some small comfort in that day-in, day-out repetitive similarity, but he began to yearn for something different.

Then, a change arrived, though perhaps not in the way Reggie would have chosen.

Carson brought home a girl. She was a niece of Mr. Stagner's.

Reggie thought she was kind of plain-looking, but Carson seemed to be smitten with her.

The comfortable nights of the two boys sitting on the couch watching old John Wayne movies morphed into something new. Now, the three of them—Carson and Lucy sitting on the couch, Reggie relegated to sitting in the lawn chair that passed for furniture—watching whatever sitcom or hour-long drama was on.

Then Lucy started staying over, and the two of them went to bed earlier and earlier, leaving Reggie alone in the living room.

He wasn't jealous of Lucy, but Reggie really didn't like change, and this was definitely that.

More and more, after Carson and Lucy went to bed, Reggie took his walks around the neighborhood.

More and more, he began to scheme and think of bigger things.

Chapter Twenty-Four

Carson finding a girlfriend he was serious about wasn't unexpected. He'd always been a good kid who had just been caught in the tough situation that sent him to Plain Hill. Now that he had a second chance, he was intent on taking full advantage of it.

Reggie didn't seem to be quite so dedicated to that prospect.

A month after she started staying the night, Lucy moved into the little house.

In some ways, things improved for the two young men. The house was cleaner, the kitchen actually got used for something other than collecting empty beer bottles, and the place started to look less like a flop pad and more like a home.

All of which tended to make Reggie even more uncomfortable and perhaps more likely to act out.

In early June of 1977, Carson and Lucy went away to Portland to see a play.

When Carson told him they'd be gone and what they'd be doing, Reggie looked at him askance. "A play? A *play*? Will she be keeping your nuts in her purse, too?"

Carson was a good-natured guy, and he just waved that remark away.

When he had the place to himself, Reggie put a plan into action that he had been considering for several months.

Like always, he worked a half day on that Saturday. Unlike most Saturdays, he lingered a little behind everyone else who seemed to be in a hurry to get out the door and get started on their weekend. While everyone else was getting ready to leave, Reggie went to the back door of the factory and slipped a piece of masking tape over the lock mechanism, then shut the door tight.

That night, after midnight, he met a friend named Burke that he had made at a local bar. This was perhaps the best kind of friend for Reggie, because he had a pickup truck and what could be termed flexible ethics. The two of them drove back to the factory a little after 3:00 a.m. The plant was located in a quiet part of town, and they glided into the parking lot with both the engine and lights off.

Reggie had spent some time keeping an eye on the factory. He knew that though there was a security guard, he was beyond retirement age and generally slept with his feet up on his desk for much of the overnight shift. Reggie knew the interior layout well enough that he didn't need to use a flashlight.

He didn't intend this to be a big operation, he was just tired of watching television on the small black and white TV. He felt that as hard as he was working, he deserved to have a better set to relax in front of every night.

Reggie held a finger up to his lips before they left Burke's truck. "Gotta be quiet, now."

Burke, who had agreed to go when he had a few beers in him, nodded, wide-eyed.

Reggie slipped soundlessly out of the truck and made a point of not shutting the old pickup's door all the way. There were no security cameras in place, so they were able to walk straight to the back door without hiding in the shadows.

Reggie opened the door and peeled the tape off the lock. He knew exactly where they were heading—to the loading area where the week's product would be shipped to retailers across the country.

Console televisions of the early 1970s were heavy beasts. The set that Reggie had his eye on weighed more than a hundred and forty pounds. That was a theft deterrent in itself.

Reggie calculated that he and Burke *could* carry it, but if they slipped and it went crashing to the ground, the party would be over and they'd be lucky to escape.

Instead, Reggie found the pallet jack that he had placed exactly where he needed it before he had left work that afternoon. When he had moved it into place, he had noticed a definite squeak in one of the wheels, so he had brought a can of WD-40 with him. He sprayed it liberally over the wheels, then rolled the jack back and forth. There was still a little noise from the wheels moving over the concrete, but at least the squeak was gone.

He and Burke lifted the television, with Burke grunting in surprise at how heavy it was.

Reggie tilted his head at him as if to say *Seriously?* Burke made an *Eeep* expression, then they lifted the box onto the pallet jack.

Making every effort to be silent, Reggie slowly moved the jack across the smooth concrete floor. When they reached the back door, he immediately saw that they had a new problem. The box was sitting crossways on the jack, which made it too wide to go through the man-sized back door. They had to lift it again and turn it the other way.

The longer they spent inside the tomb-like quiet of the factory, the more nervous Burke got.

Reggie did what he could to calm him down and made a mental note that the next time he planned a job, he would do a better job of vetting his confederate.

Reggie propped the back door open, and they wheeled the jack out to the parking lot. It made a lot more noise as it bounced over the uneven macadam surface. Burke went white, glancing over his shoulder, sure that they were about to be nabbed. "Maybe we should just take off."

"Settle down," Reggie said, and his calm voice seemed to have the desired effect on Burke.

They rattled across the parking lot and, with grunting from both of them this time, managed to lift the box up onto the bed of the truck.

"I'll ride back here with it," Reggie said, "to make sure it doesn't move around too much. Just keep it to twenty miles an hour."

Burke nodded and climbed in behind the wheel. He turned the engine over and in the silence of the dead of night, it sounded loud. Reggie put his back against the cab of the truck and held onto the packing strap of the box.

"Hey! What the hell's going on here?" It was the old security guard, who had apparently decided to make his rounds at a bad time. He aimed his flashlight beam at the truck and at Reggie in the back. Reggie turned his head away, hoping not to get identified. He reached up and rapped on the back window. "Floor it, dummy."

Burke floored it, and the box started to slide toward the back of the truck's bed. Reggie ducked his head and grabbed the packing strap. For one frightening moment, both the television and Reggie slid toward the open tailgate. Reggie braced himself against the wheel well and that gave him enough leverage to stop the slide. He risked a look over his shoulder and saw that the security guard was chasing after them, but was huffing and puffing and quickly losing ground.

Burke took a hard right onto the surface street outside the factory gate and Reggie again had to wrestle against the momentum of the heavy case. "Hey, Burke! Slow Down! We're good now."

Burke was still panicked in the front seat, but he did let off the gas. They drove the speed limit the rest of the way back to Reggie and Carson's place.

When they pulled into the dirt driveway beside the house, Reggie hopped down. "Come on, help me wrestle this bitch inside."

Burke still looked shaken and white. Reggie made the decision right there that this partner in crime was not exactly an adrenaline junkie.

Burke shook his head. "I know the deal was that this one was for you and we'd go back next weekend and get mine, but I don't think I want to do that. Once is enough for me. You can have this one."

Reggie nodded as though he understood. "No problem, Burke. You did good. Help me get this inside, and I'll make it right for you."

They wrestled the heavy box out of the bed of the truck and through the back door that led into the kitchen. From there they set it on the floor and pushed it into the living room. The box looked even larger sitting in the middle of the tiny room. It made Reggie smile.

"Hang on," Reggie said. He hurried into the kitchen and returned with two open bottles of Rainier Beer. He handed one to Burke, then set his own bottle on top of the box, which came up almost to his breastbone. He reached into his back pocket, pulled out his wallet, and fished out a twenty-dollar bill. He handed it to Burke and said, "Thanks for the help."

Burke hesitated, but then took the twenty and stuffed it into the front pocket of his jeans. "Thanks, Reg." He hesitated, then said, "Maybe we shouldn't be seen together for a little while."

That was fine with Reggie. "Sure. Thanks for all your help tonight."

Burke lifted his beer in a mock salute and hurried out the back door.

Reggie was tempted to unbox the television right then, but it was after 4:00 a.m., and he had been up for almost twenty-four hours. He decided to leave the great unveiling for the next day.

He crashed hard on his bed for five or six hours, then woke up and went to work. Five minutes and a box knife made short work of the packaging, and the TV stood like a statue in the middle of the room.

"Beautiful," Reggie said, smiling to himself.

He hooked everything up, but the picture still wasn't great. Cable television was available in Corvallis in 1976, but it hadn't been laid down on this particular street of poorer houses yet.

Reluctantly, Reggie hooked the rabbit ears up to the back of the set and that made the picture better. He hated how the ears on top of the set ruined the beautiful lines, though. He decided that with his next paycheck, he would buy a bigger antenna for the roof and run a line down to the set.

He picked up all the cardboard and packing materials and carried everything out to the one-car garage at the back of the property.

Reggie was tired, but happy. He thought that picking up what was an eight-hundred-dollar television for twenty bucks was the deal of the century. He didn't move for the rest of that Sunday afternoon except to get more beer, make a sandwich, or go to the bathroom.

Walt Disney's Wonderful World of Color came on and Reggie was thrilled at how good the picture was. He was wishing someone else was there so they could appreciate it, too.

That was when Carson and Lucy returned from their outing to Portland. They came in the back door, both flushed and laughing about something. They walked into the living room and their expressions froze.

Lucy looked meaningfully at Carson, tilted her head, then left the room.

"What put a bee in her bonnet?" Reggie asked.

Carson nodded at the television. "Where'd you get that?"

Reggie shrugged innocently. "Come on, man. You know where I got it."

Carson sat down on the opposite end of the couch. "That's not right. Mr. Stagner has helped us out a lot."

Another shrug. "I'll bet he's got insurance for this kind of thing. What do they call it? Shrinkage?"

"It's still not right."

Reggie was surprised at how serious Carson seemed to be. "It's not that big a deal."

"It's a really big deal," Carson countered. "Listen, I asked Lucy to marry me this weekend."

That was news to Reggie. He was a little hurt that Carson, who he thought was his best friend, hadn't told him about that in advance. He tipped the beer bottle back and drained the last of the Rainier. "What'd she say?"

"She said yes. We're gonna get married this fall." Carson looked down at the floor. "Listen, Reg, you're gonna have to move out."

If Reggie was a little hurt at being left out of the proposal, he was shocked at being asked to move out. "What? Why? Not because I boosted one TV set?"

Carson took a deep breath and glanced at the closed door that led to his bedroom. "Listen, Reg, I'm getting married. My bachelor days are going to be behind me." He squinted as though he hated to be the bearer of such bad news. "You don't have to leave right away."

"You mean like tonight?" Reggie was joking, but saw immediately that Carson didn't take it as a joke.

"Right. Not tonight, but pretty soon. But," he nodded toward the television, "that's gotta go immediately."

"Immediately?" Reggie sputtered. "Seriously?"

Carson looked at his watch. "Do you still have the box? Mac's got a pickup. If we box it back up, we can sneak it back in tonight and no one will ever know it was missing."

Reggie thought of the box in tiny pieces in the garage and the security guard chasing them out of the parking lot. "I think they already know."

Carson took a deep breath. "Okay, that's out, then. But you've gotta get rid of it, like right away." He stood up and said, "Sorry, man, that's the way it's gotta be. If word ever got back to Mr. Stagner that I had one of his stolen TVs here in my house, it would mess up everything."

Carson walked across the living room and opened the door to the bedroom. When he did, Reggie saw Lucy standing with her arms crossed, looking daggers at him.

Carson closed the door softly behind him, already speaking to her in a placating tone.

Reggie Blackwell was, once again, on his own.

Chapter Twenty-Five

Reggie's life had been stable for the previous eight months, but that essentially ended on the night he stole the television set and Carson kicked him out.

His first problem was what to do with the damned TV. It had been a happy thing for him for only a few hours, but once Carson told him he had to get rid of it immediately, it became an albatross around his neck. It still had value, but it was big, heavy, and Reggie had no way to move it.

He went to work the next day, concerned that he might have been spotted by the security guard as he left the parking lot with Burke, but there was no sign of that. He put in his normal day, but did not ride home with Carson.

Carson seemed completely fine with that, and Reggie was beginning to sense that their friendship was broken.

After work, he walked over to a dive bar that was a couple of blocks over from the factory. He nursed a beer and kept his eyes open until he saw an opportunity. When two middle-aged guys came in and sat at the bar, he moved to where he could speak to them.

They ignored Reggie, which was fine with him. He wanted them to have a few beers in them before he made his pitch.

Eventually, he saw his opportunity and leaned in with the story he had concocted. It didn't really matter—either to Reggie or to the men—what the story was. It was just a jumping off point for the idea that he had a brand-new television that he had no use for. It sold for eight hundred dollars, but since it was out of the box, he would let it go for two hundred and fifty dollars.

"Fell off the back of a truck, did it?" one man asked.

Reggie smiled, shrugged, and knew he had his man. "If you've got the money and a truck, you can have the TV tonight. Where else you gonna get a TV this nice at a price like this? Nowhere, and you know it. Hell, maybe your wife'll even give you some when you bring it home." He nodded up at the small black and white television above the bar. "You can watch the A's game in color at home instead of in this shitty bar."

"Hey, watch it," the bartender said, but it seemed to be out of habit, because that's exactly what it was, and everyone knew it.

The man that Reggie had pegged as his mark looked at his friend, a sly smile on his face. "Seems to me, if you're hanging out in a shitty bar trying to unload it, you must be a little desperate. I'll give you a hundred."

Reggie shook his head sadly. "Try to give someone a great deal and they spit in your face." He reached in his wallet and laid a couple of dollar bills on the counter to pay for his beer. He turned to leave, but before he made it two steps, the man said, "A hundred fifty."

Reggie's back was to the man and a smile lit up his face. He turned around and said, "Two hundred cash, and I'll help you load it in your truck."

Less than an hour later, the television was gone, the small black and white TV was in its place, and Lucy stood in the kitchen, arms crossed, looking at Reggie.

"TV's gone," Reggie said. "I guess I'm next."

Carson opened his mouth to protest, but Lucy hustled across the room, laid a hand on his shoulder and said, "I think it's best, don't you?"

Reggie looked at Carson to see if he was going to say anything, but he just sat there silently.

"I guess it is," Reggie said, trying to summon up some dignity. "I'll be gone by this weekend, okay?"

"Whatever," Lucy said, returning to the kitchen.

"That's fine," Carson said. "Let me know if you need a hand with moving."

"Everything I own still fits into one suitcase, so I think I can handle it."

They turned on the Oakland A's game and watched as it went into extra innings. They had the ability that many men do to ignore whatever unpleasantness might be between them at that moment and just watch the game.

When it was tied after nine innings, Carson said, "Well, that's it for me," slapping his hands against his knees as he stood up.

Reggie looked at him, once again a little shocked. The Carson he knew would never have walked away from extra innings. "I don't even know who you are anymore, brother."

"Just growing up," Carson said quietly as he retreated to the bedroom.

"Yeah, I don't think I'll be doing that." Reggie retrieved another beer from the fridge and watched the end of the game.

The next morning, Reggie again rode into work with Carson, but all that day, something felt off. It felt like people were looking at him out of the corner of their eyes and maybe talking about him when he wasn't looking. It was like being in the halls at Middle Falls High all over again.

Just as he was about to take his afternoon break, he saw a uniformed cop come onto the floor. He spoke to the shift supervisor and Reggie was sure they were looking at him. Then they went into the supe's office and Reggie was dismayed to see the night watchman join them.

None of that could be good for Reggie.

Quietly, calmly, Reggie said, "I'm going out back for a smoke."

The funny thing was, Reggie didn't smoke, but no one called him on that fact. He walked to the back door, stepped out into the parking lot, and began to walk. Slowly at first, then increasingly hurried.

He never glanced back at the factory. If someone was chasing him, he figured he was busted anyway.

He half-walked, half-jogged back to the house that had been his home.

Carson was at work, but Lucy was there, sitting on the couch, watching a soap opera. When Reggie walked in, she didn't seem all that surprised. "You in trouble?"

"Nah," Reggie said. "No trouble." He walked into his room, threw his belongings into his backpack and said, "See ya." He should have left it there, but inside, he was seething at the turn of events. "You should ask your man if he had anything to do with stealing the TV. Hell, maybe it was even his idea." He looked at Lucy closely to see if that blow had landed.

It hadn't. She just shook her head. "I know Carson, and I know you. You think you're smart, but you're just an asshole that can't see what Carson was trying to do for you." Then, before she turned back to the TV, she said, "See ya."

For a brief moment, Reggie saw the parallel between when he had been on the run from Middle Falls and what was happening here. He decided he would be smart this time. He wouldn't stop to spray-paint any signs this time. He *did* think that he was out in front of his problems enough that he could risk taking a Greyhound out of town, though.

He hotfooted it to the bus depot and bought a one-way ticket to Seattle, though he had no idea where he was really heading. He didn't think he would go that far, but hoped that if someone was trailing him, that ticket would throw them off.

He climbed onto the bus and sat anxiously waiting for it to pull out. He kept scanning the parking area, waiting to see if some uniformed cops would show up and ask to search the buses. They never did, and after ten anxious minutes, the bus pulled out and onto the highway.

Reggie wasn't big on reflecting on his own life. He thought about everything that had happened in the three days since he had boosted the television. Although he wondered if he had done anything to bring this sudden change on himself, he didn't really see anything.

Mostly, he blamed Lucy. If it hadn't been for her, he would still be sitting on the couch with Carson, waiting for the next baseball game to start.

The Greyhound route greatly influenced the next part of Reggie's life.

If it had gone straight from Corvallis to Seattle on Interstate 5, he likely would have gotten off in Portland. A bigger city that would be easy to get lost in.

Instead, like all bus lines of the day, it wandered from one country back road to another, hitting every small town and sometimes stopping at places where there was no town at all, just a gas station or small convenience store.

That circuitous route took Reggie back to Middle Falls. As it pulled into town, the bus went right past Artie's, and that was enough to encourage him to hop off in his hometown. He wasn't necessarily planning to stay, but he wanted to see if the Artie's burger basket matched his memory.

When he first stepped off the bus, he put his collar up, his head down, and slunk along the familiar streets. Then he remembered that although they might be looking for him in Corvallis, he wasn't such a wanted man that they would have issued a statewide *Be On The Lookout* for him. It was a television set, and they didn't really have any proof, unless Carson had flipped on him.

Or Lucy. That seemed more likely. She had probably told her uncle and that was why she hadn't been surprised to see Reggie when he came home early. She had been expecting him.

Even so, he figured that as long as he didn't return to Corvallis, he was probably safe and the whole thing would blow over eventually and be forgotten about.

Reggie might have been bothered by the fact that he had just burned a bridge with the only person who had ever shown him any real kindness, but that went down into the inner oubliette where he dropped everything that was inconvenient.

More than anything, he was excited by the possibility of what was ahead. He was a young man, at least in appearance, and he had money in his pocket. He had just gotten paid the previous week and had cashed that check, but hadn't yet paid his share of the rent. Coupling that with the money he'd gotten for the stolen television, he had more than three hundred and fifty dollars in his pocket. More than enough to start over somewhere.

As he walked to Artie's, the familiarity of everything in Middle Falls seeped into his bones, and he started to consider just staying here. There had to be something to be said for knowing your way around a town. Maybe he'd even run into Harold or Nelson somewhere and have a little reunion. He frowned slightly at the thought.

Would they even *want* to have a reunion of any sort? He'd left school one Friday afternoon and never returned. He was sure the story of Reggie the outlaw who had manipulated Amanda, Bobbi, and their friends into robbing Sal's Pawn Shop had made the rounds. That was a way better story than his mom being murdered or some sophomore girl getting pregnant.

Now, three years later, the two of them would have graduated and be ready to either go into the working world—he thought the box factory was the most likely spot for Nelson—or off to college.

Harold had always been smart and probably would have been able to get into Oregon or Oregon State.

Reggie twitched his mouth and decided to abandon any thoughts of reaching out to his old friends. If there was one thing he had learned, it was how to survive on his own, with no help from anyone.

Artie's turned out to be just as delicious as he remembered.

By the time he polished off his burger, fries, and strawberry shake, his mind was made up.

He would stay in Middle Falls.

Chapter Twenty-Six

Decide in haste, repent in leisure.

But Reggie Blackwell never spent enough time examining things to either regret or repent.

He paid for his meal, not forgetting to tip his waitress, then stepped out into the late afternoon sunshine of a Middle Falls summer day.

He realized immediately that when he had decided not to get back on the bus heading north, his plan hadn't extended past that first delicious burger basket. Something else would be required soon, like a place to lay his head for the night.

He couldn't come up with something immediately, so he just walked along Main Street, hoping something would come to him. In the worst case, it was still summer, and the nights would be warm. He could find someplace where he could bed down for the night. Even a park or amongst some trees on the edge of town would do in a pinch.

He got to the far end of town and saw the Do-Si-Do, the slightly rundown tavern that was the go-to spot for local alcoholics and other people trying to hide from their problems. There was something appealing about the place, so he decided to go in. The front door whooshed in silently, and he immediately felt like he was kind of at home. There was a dark ambience to the place. The smell of beer and the wax they used on the bar top comforted him.

He walked up to the bar, smiled at two men downwind who were nursing warm glasses of beer, and said, "What do you have on tap?"

The bartender, a middle-aged man with a paunch and a bulldog's face said, "Rainier and Bud. What do you have in your wallet?"

Reggie reached into his pocket and pulled out a ten-dollar bill. He dropped it casually on the bar.

The barkeep shook his head. "That ain't enough."

Reggie's eyebrows shot up. "The price of a glass of beer has gone up, huh?"

"No, the beer's a buck a glass. But that price includes you showing me some ID that says you're old enough to drink it, and I know you ain't got that."

"Let's just say I've lost my license," Reggie said. "But as a penalty, I'm willing to pay two bucks for a glass of beer."

"That's the way it is, huh?" the bartender asked.

Reggie shrugged and smiled ingratiatingly.

The bartender put down the glass and the towel he was using to polish it. He lifted up a section of the bar and casually came around to the customer side. The two men at the bar, who had seemed lost in their own thoughts, perked up and paid attention.

The bartender, who was no more than 5'8", but weighed at least two-hundred pounds and was built like a fire hydrant, casually walked up to Reggie and grabbed him by the collar, lifting him slightly off the barstool. "You want to go out the door easily, or head first, young man?"

"Hey, hey," Reggie said, trying, but failing, to get away from the iron grip. "I'll go, I'll go, just lemme loose."

The bartender did not let him completely go, but did loosen his grip a little. He turned Reggie toward the door and gave a little shove. "You're welcome to come back and buy a two-dollar beer when you're twenty-one."

Reggie cast a glare over his shoulder and pushed back out into the street. He had never had any trouble buying beer in the dive bars in Corvallis if he was willing to pay a premium, but now he knew it was different in Middle Falls, at least at the Do-Si-Do.

He suddenly regretted his decision to stay in Middle Falls and thought about just catching the next bus out of town. He went back to the bus station and inquired about when the next bus would be, exactly.

"Next bus will be through late tomorrow afternoon," the woman behind the counter said.

Reggie knew he was stuck in Middle Falls, at least until the next day.

He shouldered his backpack and walked down to Smith and Sons grocery. If he was going to be sleeping under the stars, he thought it would be good to at least have a little food.

The store was immediately familiar to him when he walked in. He went to the canned food aisle and picked up a can of pork and beans, then went to the small gadget wall and picked up a can opener. On the way to pay for his purchases, he passed a bulletin board with homey announcements and want ads posted. Amongst the announcements of a Grange dance and a farmer who was selling eggs by the dozen was a pinned piece of paper from someone looking for a roommate.

Reggie wasn't any kind of a reader, but he could manage that much. He pulled the note down so no one else would see it, then paid for his pork and beans and the can opener. The way his luck had been, he figured that the notice was probably two years old, but it was the best lead he had at the moment.

He went to the payphone down the street—the same phone booth where he had learned his mother was dead in an earlier life—and dialed the number. It rang and rang, but no one picked up.

"Figures," Reggie muttered. "Probably a dead end." He hung up the phone, collected his dime and turned away from Main Street. It was starting to get dark, but he still had a little light left to find a place to crash. His feet automatically turned toward what had once been his home.

He was amused to see that his graffiti on the sign wasn't just still there, but seemed to have become part of the local culture, as someone else had freshened up the paint that read *Crapped-On Village*.

Reggie couldn't help but smile at his small contribution to a Middle Falls legend.

He walked down the street as an exercise in nostalgia, nothing more. He had never known what had happened to the house he grew up in. With his father in prison and his mother dead, there was no one to make the payments. He was sure, at some point, the bank had taken it back. Owning a run-down two-bedroom house in Crampton Village wouldn't be the jewel in any bank's portfolio, so it was likely they had sold it to a new homeowner. As he walked in the entrance to the neighborhood, Reggie got a pleasant picture in his mind.

A young family had perhaps bought it. They might have taken the last few years to put sweat equity in. They straightened the rickety fence, pulled the weeds, and mowed the grass. It wouldn't be fancy inside, but it would be nice. Clean. Maybe some fresh paint and new linoleum in the kitchen.

That dream came crashing down when he stood face to face with the harsh reality. The fence had fallen over completely. The yard looked like it hadn't had any work done since the day he had left. The front window had been broken out and someone had haphazardly stuck an old sheet of plywood over it. Someone had spray-painted "Crapped-On Village Dream Home" on the plywood. Reggie saw that he had really started something, though not in a positive way.

He knew that his home had never been very much, but it had been a home when his mother was still alive. When she had died, so, apparently, had the house.

Reggie stood where the front gate had once been, looking at his childhood home.

"That place is vacant," a harsh smoker's voice said from his right. "No squatters allowed."

Reggie looked at the old woman and nodded. "Hello, Mrs. Stephenson. It's Reggie. Reggie Blackwell. I used to live here."

The old woman, dressed in a tattered housecoat and with her hair flying every which way in the breeze adjusted her spectacles and tipped her head back to look at him more carefully. "Your dad killed your mom."

"Yes, and thank you for reminding me of that, you old bat. Did you think I'd forgotten?"

"Don't be smart with me, Reggie Blackwell. I know you and your family. Both your dad and brother are in prison. Your mom's dead. You'll be the next to go behind bars."

For just a moment, Reggie let himself fantasize about closing the distance between them in a few leaps and smashing his fist into the old woman's face. It would be satisfying, but would also, no doubt, end up with him back behind bars at the Middle Falls jail. That would undoubtedly make Chief Deakins very happy.

For the first time, a thought occurred to Reggie. *I die and wake up. If something bad happens to me, I can just off myself and start over again. Huh.*

Reggie settled for flipping Mrs. Stephenson the bird and holding it out for several seconds to make sure she saw it. Then he shook his head, turned around, and walked away.

Seeing his old house in that forlorn shape was like a magnet to him. He wanted to see what the inside looked like.

He walked to the small patch of woods several blocks away and found a spot where he thought he could have some privacy. He opened his can of pork and beans and discovered he had forgotten to get a spoon or fork. He leaned against a tree and tipped the can up until it ran into his mouth. The bits at the bottom clung to the can, so he had to stick his fingers down into the can to get the last of the beany goodness out. He tossed the can aside, stuck the can opener back in his bag, and wiped his greasy fingers on his jeans.

It was pretty dark already, and he was starting to get tired, but he waited patiently for another hour.

Silence settled over Crampton Village and Reggie waited until he hadn't seen a car come down the road that bisected the houses in at least ten minutes.

He exited the small stand of trees and walked casually down the road toward his house. He cut over at the property line and went through the backyard. There were more boarded-up windows at the back of the house, but the door that led into the back porch was intact.

He smiled at the rickety lock that was there, jimmying it open in the same amount of time it would have taken if he'd had a key.

Inside, the house smelled bad. He couldn't quite put a finger on what the smell was, but it was definitely unpleasant. Body odor mixed with mold and decay, probably.

The house was a disaster. Obviously, Mrs. Stephenson had been wrong. There *had* been squatters here. There was graffiti spray-painted on the walls, including a large target that someone had painted on the living room wall, then had thrown something—it looked to be an axe, maybe—at the bullseye.

The furniture was either gone or overturned. He saw what looked like a grubby nest underneath an overturned chair and guessed that a wildlife family, racoons, maybe, had also made their way inside. He saw where something had eaten a hole in the floorboards and was surprised there wasn't an entire zoo of small animals living in the house.

His old bedroom was no better. It was stripped bare of furniture except for a single mattress that sat in the middle of the room. He thought about sleeping on that, but the strong smell of urine made him change his mind.

Still, as bad as it was, having a roof over his head was preferable to sleeping amongst the bugs under the stars. He tried his parents' room and, remarkably, the bed was still in place there. The bedding had long since been stripped away and the mattress was stained with unknown material, but it smelled better than his room.

He picked out the least-stained section of the mattress, set his pack against the wall and used it for a pillow. As he settled in for the night, he muttered, "Welcome home, Reggie Blackwell."

Chapter Twenty-Seven

It had been a long day for Reggie the day before and he slept in much later than he had intended. When he finally opened his eyes, daylight was already showing around the plywood that had been put over the window in what he still thought of as his parents' room.

Unfortunately for Reggie, he hadn't gone nose blind during the night. In fact, all the terrible smells of the house seemed to have amplified while he slept. He sat up and saw that, in the night, he had rolled over onto one of the stains on the mattress and it had transferred onto his jeans.

"That's gross," he said to himself. He quickly rolled out of bed, grabbed his pack and walked into the bathroom, hoping against hope that there would be some water on. If he had known more about how the world worked, he wouldn't have even held that hope, but there were many things about the world Reggie didn't know.

He turned the tap on, hoping to splash some water on his face, but absolutely nothing happened. He smacked his lips and found that his mouth tasted lousy, but there weren't even a few drops of water to brush his teeth. After peeing into the stained toilet bowl, he tried to flush out of habit, but of course, nothing happened there, either.

He tried to look at himself in the mirror, which wasn't easy because someone had either thrown something at it or put a fist into the middle of it, breaking it into dozens of pieces. He bobbed his head up and down and side to side, trying to find an angle where he could see himself. He found one and realized that after only one day on the run, he was already starting to look kind of seedy. He pulled his comb out of his pack and did the best he could to untangle his curly hair.

He knew he would need to look a little better if he was going to fit in anywhere in Middle Falls. He tried to think of somewhere he could go and get a shower, but came up blank. There were no truck stops with showers available for rent in Middle Falls. He pictured himself going up to Harold's house, knocking on the door and saying, "Hey, can I borrow your shower for a few minutes?" He knew that wasn't going to happen.

He also knew he couldn't stay here. The smell was quickly becoming overwhelming, not to mention that being in what had once been his home and was now destroyed was wearing on him.

He did change out of his dirty clothes and into something clean out of his bag. That made him both feel and look a little better. He snuck out the back door, then walked out to the street. He kind of dreaded running into Mrs. Stephenson, but she was nowhere to be seen.

He noticed that the house directly across the street where Mrs. Teagarden lived also looked sad and a little dilapidated. Mrs. Teagarden would never have allowed that, so he decided she had probably died, too.

"Serves you right, you nosy old biddy," Reggie said to himself. He wondered briefly if maybe *everyone* had this power to beat death, or if it was just him. There was no answer to that, so he let it go.

He was unsure which direction his life was going to take that day as he walked back toward Main Street. He knew that another bus would be along in a few hours, and he could always just get on that and go somewhere new. Somewhere that wasn't haunted by so many memories.

As he passed by the payphone, he remembered the slip of paper that he had taken from Smith's the day before. He stepped inside, then had to open his pack and find the smelly pair of jeans with the paper in the pocket. He decided to give that one more try.

He deposited his dime, then dialed the number. To his surprise, someone answered on the second ring.

"Hello?"

The man's voice sounded a little thick, as though maybe Reggie had woken him up.

"Hello," Reggie said, doing his best to sound chipper. "I saw that you were looking for a roommate."

"Yeah," the man said, stifling a yawn.

"Are you still looking for someone?"

"Yeah," the man said.

Reggie smiled to himself. This guy was a fount of conversation.

"I'm just moving to town, and I'm looking for a place. I thought of getting a place on my own, but it might be good to share expenses for a while."

"You got a job?"

"Not yet, but I will soon. And I have some money saved."

"Rent is two hundred a month. You'd have to pay half of that."

A hundred a month wasn't terrible, though Reggie knew he would have to find a new source of income soon.

"Can I come look at the place? I can pay the first month today if everything works out."

There was silence on the other end of the line for quite a while, as though maybe the man was thinking, which perhaps didn't come naturally. "Yeah, that's fine." Another pause, then, "I don't have to be at work until tonight. You can come by today if you want to. Rivercrest Apartments, 302."

Reggie started to say that he would be there soon, but the man hung up before he had the chance. Again, Reggie smiled to himself.

He was looking for a place to crash for a time while he got his life organized. He wasn't looking for a best friend. The fact that this guy, whoever he was, worked at night was kind of a bonus. That meant that Reggie would have the place to himself and wouldn't have to answer a lot of questions if he went out on late-night prowls.

He thought about what the man had said. *Rivercrest Apartments.* Reggie wasn't a hundred percent sure where that was, but there was only one apartment complex of any size in Middle Falls. He figured that was probably it. He panicked briefly, trying to remember what apartment the man had said, then remembered. Over and over, he repeated, *302, 302, 302,* to himself.

He thought again about finding some way to make himself more presentable, but again came up blank. He decided not to worry about it, because what other choice could he really make?

His stomach grumbled, and he looked at the clock in front of the jewelry store. 10:30. Artie's wouldn't be open for another half hour, so he walked to Smith's.

He had money in his pocket, so no five-finger discount was necessary today. He picked up a package of Twinkies and a pint of chocolate milk. He set his purchases down on the counter and said, "Breakfast of champions, am I right?"

The woman barely glanced at Reggie and her only answer was, "A dollar twenty-six, please."

Reggie did notice that she seemed to wrinkle her nose at him slightly, though. That meant that either he smelled bad, or maybe she was smelling the stinky clothes he had put in his pack. Either way wasn't good, but he decided to ditch the pack somewhere before he met with Mr. 302.

He thought about the guy as he walked along. Not very communicative. Limited personal skills. But, he had gone to the trouble of putting up a notice looking for a roommate, so he probably needed money. The fact that he worked at night said that he probably had a low-level job of some sort. All of those things worked well for Reggie. He figured he could take advantage of someone like that.

He stuffed an entire Twinkie in his mouth and chewed, letting the crumbs fall as they may. In one long swig, he drained half the chocolate milk, then repeated the process. He looked around for a trash can but didn't see one, so he wadded up the Twinkie packaging, stuffed it inside the milk container, then set that on the windowsill of a building he passed.

He turned toward where he thought the apartments were. When they came into sight, he was pleased to see a wooden sign with gold lettering that did indeed spell out *Rivercrest Apartments*. He took his pack off his shoulder and set it in the tall grass behind the sign, then took in the place.

He supposed that calling the apartment *River*-anything was slightly misleading, but that didn't bother him. There was a small creek that ran along the back of the units, but calling it a river was quite an upsell. There were four floors of identical apartments stacked one on top of the other. There were no garages, but there was quite a large parking lot.

In the middle of the day, on a weekday, there were plenty of parking places available, but Reggie guessed parking might be tight after five or on weekends. He still had the dream of owning a car someday.

The building looked to be relatively new—probably less than ten years old. The exterior was a white stucco that still looked okay. The stairs to the upper unit looked pretty steep, but that was no deterrent to Reggie. He was young and strong and had nothing but his pack to move in.

He walked along the edge of the units until he found number 102, then climbed up to the third floor. He got a story ready in his mind and knocked lightly on the door.

The man who answered was in his early forties. He had black hair and facial hair that was somewhere between an extreme five o'clock shadow and an attempt at growing a beard. His hair was unkempt and stuck out at all angles. He was wearing a wife-beater T-shirt and stained pajamas.

Glad I didn't overdress for the interview, Reggie thought. He smiled his winning smile and stuck his hand out. "Reggie Blackwell."

"Frank Bodzay," the man said. He seemed reluctant to shake the offered hand, but eventually gave it a single quick pump. The apartment was decorated in twentieth-century poor person. There was a ratty couch against one wall. The coffee and side tables were matching, though they were all three just plastic milk cases with a piece of plywood over the top. The TV, once again the seemingly omnipresent thirteen-inch set that seemed to follow Reggie wherever he went, made him wish he could have brought the beautiful twenty-seven-inch color set with him.

Everything about the place confirmed Reggie's suspicions about the man.

"Looks great," Reggie said, looking around.

Frank looked at him sideways as if to convey that he was aware it didn't look great at all. "I got divorced this year. This is what I'm left with. I've got some nice stuff, but it's living with my ex-wife and some new guy now."

Bitterness, Reggie thought. *That's good. Something else I may be able to use.*

"Can I see the bedroom?"

Frank nodded down the hall and said, "First door on the right. I guess it's the master, because it's closest to the bathroom, but I sleep in the other one because it's quieter. It's a bitch working at night if there's too much noise around."

"Can I ask what you do?"

Frank shrugged. "Night watchman. I watch over four or five different places. Walk through one, get in my truck, drive to the next, then keep doing that until the sun comes up."

"Sounds like a good gig," Reggie said.

Frank looked at Reggie as though he might be a little stupid again. Reggie made a mental note not to BS him that way. He walked down the hall and opened the first door on the right. It was a dark and dingy room. There was no furniture at all, and the dark brown carpeting with no overhead light made it seem a little like a dungeon. There was a single window that Reggie cracked open, and he could hear water running down below.

If he hadn't gotten a read on Frank already, he would have said, "Nice river view, huh?" but he had, and didn't say anything like that. Instead, he walked back into the living room and said, "It looks good to me. If you don't mind having a roommate, I'll take it."

"One week left in the month, so that'll be twenty-five dollars. Then you'll have to pay another hundred on the first of the month. We'll split the electric bill. Don't have a phone."

"That works," Reggie said. He pulled his bankroll out and peeled off six twenties and a five. "Here, I'll just pay through the end of next month. Lemme know what I owe you for the light bill."

Frank looked at the offered money as though he might be having second thoughts, but the pull of the greenbacks was too strong and overcame any doubts he might be having. Before he accepted the money, though, he added one caveat. "I work from ten p.m. to six a.m., so I usually got to bed around nine in the morning. If you make noise in here and wake me up during the day, this ain't gonna work."

Reggie nodded and kept the money extended. "I'll probably get a job that keeps me out during the day. I think we'll be perfect roommates." That wasn't true at all, but at that moment, getting a roof over his head that had running water was his number one priority. He could take care of everything else later.

Frank accepted the money and stuffed it in his wallet. "Go ahead and bring your stuff, then."

"Just got into town, so I don't really have anything other than a few clothes. I'll be buying some bedroom furniture soon." He saw Frank's eyes narrow at that, so he added, "Don't worry. I'll buy my own food. If I wash up after myself, do you mind if I use your kitchen to cook?"

Frank took a moment to answer, but Reggie thought that he probably took a moment before he did just about anything. "As long as you don't cook any fish. I can't stand the smell of fish."

"No fish. Got it. Hey, I've been traveling for a couple of days. Do you mind if I use the shower?"

"As long as you've got your own towel."

"No problem," Reggie said, though he didn't. Reggie was in problem-solving mode. "I'm going to run and get my clothes and I'll pick up a few groceries while I'm out, too."

Frank pulled a lone key off the kitchen counter and handed it to Reggie. "I hope this works." He didn't sound too convinced that it would.

"This'll be great. I can tell already." Reggie shot him a small salute, then let himself out. He left his pack hidden in the tall grass and walked back toward town. He needed to buy a towel, some soap, and a few groceries.

He whistled as he walked.

Reggie Blackwell was no longer homeless.

Chapter Twenty-Eight

Reggie was aware that he was working with a limited bankroll and saw no immediate infusion of cash ahead, but he knew he needed a few things.

A vehicle would have been nice, but that was out of his range at the moment. He briefly contemplated buying a kid's wagon he passed at a yard sale, but couldn't bring himself to drag it around town like he was eight years old.

Instead, he just carried what he needed and decided he would make more trips if necessary.

He put an emphasis on light food this trip, like half a dozen packages of Top Ramen. Not the greatest food in the world, but it filled him up. He coupled that with a loaf of Wonder Bread and a pack of cotto salami and knew he could eat that for a few days and not be hungry.

On the way back to the apartments, he took a back street and walked by a business that he had essentially forgotten about. It was called *The Bulldog Den*, named after the local sports teams. It wasn't much—just a small building that was dark on the inside, lit mostly by the neon lights of pinball and other mechanical games. There were three Skee-Ball games, pool tables, and a baseball game where you pushed a button to swing a bat and tried to hit a home run.

It was a kind of disreputable-looking place, and moms all over town told their sons to stay away from it. Which of course, made it all the more attractive. It was strictly an under-21 place, so the snack bar in the corner only served soft drinks, popcorn, and lousy hot-dogs.

Reggie smiled when he saw it. He had only been there a few times because he rarely had any nickels or dimes to put in the machines. He had the sudden thought that if he wasn't going to be able to get into the Do-Si-Do to recruit some people to his business, maybe he could find some kids in there who would help him.

For the moment at least, he had plenty of money in his pocket. He filed the idea away for later, thinking that maybe if he stopped by an hour or two before closing time, he might find some older kids. With any luck, he might even meet whatever passed for juvenile delinquents in Middle Falls in the Bicentennial summer of 1976. That would help his plans along.

While he was walking home, he also noticed a few yard signs that read, "Re-elect Chief Deakins. He's *STILL* our man for the job."

Just seeing Deakins' name irritated Reggie all over again. He thought of trying to find out where the chief lived just so he could have the pleasure of sneaking over to his house and flattening his tires for him. That didn't really seem like enough to make up for the fact that he had stolen his money, though, so he filed that thought away for the time being.

Reggie made it back to the apartment—*his* apartment now—and picked up his pack. He found the door was locked, even though he was sure Frank was inside, and he had to set his groceries down so he could use his key to open it. He had never lived in an apartment before, but he wondered if locking the door when you were home was normal, or if Frank was just extra-cautious.

As a semi-professional thief, Reggie appreciated the caution, but knew that a flimsy lock like the one on their door was no real deterrent.

As quietly as possible—Frank's door was closed, and Reggie assumed he had gone back to sleep—he put his groceries away. He really wanted to take a shower, but the bathroom was right next to Frank's bedroom and he didn't want to get kicked out the same day he moved in. He really appreciated the roof over his head and wanted to keep it for a while.

He decided to explore the Rivercrest complex a little. He had no plans to break into any of the apartments, but he wanted to see what was around. One of the axioms he had learned in prison was that you should never shit where you eat. That is, it was a bad idea to rob or shakedown anything too close to where you lived. He was going to stick with that.

There wasn't much to see. Mostly just one apartment stacked on top of the other, but he did find a small laundry that had four washing machines and the same number of dryers. Reggie patted his pockets and found that he had enough change to run a load and buy one of the little boxes of soap in the dispenser. He hurried back to the apartment and grabbed his pack.

He was glad to get the stink of whatever he had rolled in the night before off his jeans. He sat in a hard plastic chair watching the washer vibrate, then his few clothes tumble around the dryer. The time was not wasted, though. He spent it trying to put a plan together for himself. Reggie was getting better at thinking ahead.

He grabbed his warm clothes when the dryer stopped and stuffed them back into his bag. He sniffed tentatively at his jeans and was relieved to find that whatever gunk he had gotten on them had washed away.

Back in the apartment, he sat on the uncomfortable couch for a while, but eventually lay down in his own room. He shut the door, let down the blinds, then stretched out on the shag carpeting. He thought he was just passing the time, but the exhaustion of the previous days quickly caught up to him.

He only opened his eyes when he heard Frank rattling things around in the kitchen. That meant it was safe for him to use the shower without bothering his new roommate, so he took advantage of that. Full advantage, you might say. He turned the shower on hot and let it run over him for a long time. He washed his hair with the bar of Irish Spring he had bought, then his body. He dried off with his new towel and felt human again.

After hanging his towel on the towel bar, he ran his comb through his hair and stepped out to find the apartment empty. It wasn't really late enough for Frank to go to work, but he was gone. Reggie decided this meant that they weren't going to be the kind of roommates that said goodbye to each other when they left. That suited him fine.

He thought of making himself some Top Ramen and a sandwich, but decided to go back to Artie's instead. He could see where that could get to be a habit, and he promised himself this would be his last trip for at least a few days.

He turned the lock on the door, then stepped out onto the concrete walkway that connected all the units.

A pretty blonde girl was just using her key to let herself in to the apartment next door. She nodded at Reggie and said, "Frank finally get the roommate he was looking for?"

"Yep," Reggie said, smiling. "I'm Reggie."

"Jennifer," the woman said, but didn't stop for any more conversation.

There were a lot more people around the Rivercrest on a nice summer evening, and, as he had expected, the parking lot was mostly full.

He took a different route on the way back to Artie's. He wanted to refamiliarize himself with all the parts of town he had forgotten.

His burger basket was as good as ever, and he wondered if he could eat it every day. He decided he could, but would try to show a little restraint.

By the time he finished his dinner, it was finally starting to get dark. That was perfect for the work he had in mind.

He casually walked out of Artie's and headed straight for Amanda's neighborhood. Not that he had any interest in tangling with her again. He had come out on the short end of their two meetings and wasn't looking for a third engagement.

But he knew it was a nice neighborhood and he wanted to start to case the area, looking for easy targets. He spent half an hour walking around, sticking to the shadows, keeping an eye out for any cruising deputies. He wasn't doing anything wrong, but he didn't want to attract attention to himself.

When he satisfied himself that he had learned what he could, he headed back to the Bulldog Den.

There was a sign on the door that said they closed at 10:00 on weekdays and Sundays and 11:00 on Friday and Saturday. Reggie had no idea what time it was, but the lights were still on, so he went in. He asked for a dollar's worth of change at the snack bar and got four quarters in return.

He wasn't much interested in pinball, but he was interested in seeing if he could meet someone who shared the same flexible ethics that he did.

The first thing he learned was that he was a terrible pinball player. That wasn't unexpected because there had never been a time in his previous lives where he had even touched one of the machines. He figured out the basic mechanics of the machine pretty quickly. Fire the ball up onto the field of play, then use the flippers to hit targets that hopefully increased in value without letting the ball drain down the sides or middle.

The problem was, the ball kept ricocheting off the higher point targets and draining right down the center. It took him less than two minutes to burn through the first quarter. Ten minutes later, the dollar was gone.

I guess I could go broke here pretty quickly, Reggie thought.

He went to the counter and got two dollars more. If he went through that in another ten or twenty minutes he was going to call it a loss and head for home.

Sure enough, he blew through his second dollar as quickly as he had the first. Reggie glanced around at other guys playing long games on just one quarter and couldn't figure out what they were doing that he wasn't.

Finally, a guy who was playing a circus-themed game two machines over had his game end. He scooped his quarters off the lip of the machine and stood a respectful distance away from Reggie as he played. He watched Reggie drain two balls in quick succession, then said, "Haven't played much before, huh?"

That might have ticked Reggie off, but he kept his eyes on the prize. "Pretty easy to tell."

The young man shrugged and said, "We all have to start somewhere."

Reggie drained another ball, ending his game. He started to plug another quarter in, but the guy said, "Want me to show you a couple of things?"

Reggie's defenses immediately went up. "What's that cost?"

"Nothing at all. I just can't stand to see somebody play pinball this poorly. It's an insult to my sensibilities."

That made Reggie smile ruefully. "Sure. Be my guest."

"First, stack a couple of quarters up against the lip of the machine. That'll tell anyone that you've got the next game."

Reggie did that, then watched as the young man, who looked to be about the same age as he was, dropped a quarter in the slot.

"First, you've got to approach the machine like you would a woman."

Reggie had no interest in explaining how little experience he had in that arena either, so he just nodded.

"I mean, you've got to caress and be gentle with them until it's time to not be so gentle anymore." The ball ricocheted off one of the high value targets and zipped toward the opening between the two flippers. The guy slapped the right side of the machine, moving it just enough that it altered the path of the ball. He used the flipper to send the ball back up to a bonus target. "You've gotta be firm but gentle. If you slap it too hard, it'll tilt and then you're dead in the water. If you do it just enough, you're in control."

He played for a long time, just flipping the ball up at the targets again and again. Finally, the ball headed toward the right side of the machine. It hit a metal bar and was about to drain away again when he gave the machine a little shake of encouragement and the ball fell back toward the flipper. He held the flipper up so the ball rested neatly in the crook of it. After a few seconds, he let the flipper down, the ball rolled along its edge and he mashed the flipper button hard, sending it back into the field of play.

"That's pretty much all there is to it."

Reggie had a feeling that what he had just witnessed wasn't actually *pretty much all there is to it*. More likely, he had just seen Pinball 101 and there were many niceties yet to be grasped. The young man smiled and purposefully let the ball drop down the center. "Go ahead, you try."

Reggie did. When the ball dropped toward the center hole, he slapped at the side just like he had seen the other guy do. Instantly, the machine went dark.

"Too hard, my man, too hard. You've gotta be gentle."

After a few seconds, the machine lit up again. Reggie didn't fire another ball into play. That wasn't what he was really interested in. Instead, he extended his hand. "I'm Reggie."

"Steve. Steve Anderson. I kind of run this place most days."

"Ah," Reggie answered. "That's why my poor play offended your sensibilities. I get it."

"Don't worry about it. I see a lot of piss-poor pinball in here. I've seen worse than you."

"Probably from eight-year-olds, though."

"Probably," Steve said with a smile. "Another few dollars and you'll be able to beat all but the best eight-year-olds, though."

Reggie looked up at a blue Pepsi-Cola clock. It showed it was 10:30. "I thought this place closed at ten."

"Really, it closes whenever I'm ready to go home. Everybody appreciates that I usually leave it open a little later. When I tell everyone to clear out, nobody hassles me."

"Nice," Reggie said. "I'm kind of a night owl, and there doesn't seem to be a lot of things to do in town after dark."

"*That* is an understatement." Steve looked at Reggie with renewed interest. "You new around here, then?"

Reggie scrunched up his face. "Kind of, I guess. I grew up here until I was about fifteen, then I moved away and just came back yesterday. Got a place over at the Rivercrest."

"Nice," Steve said. "I'm kind of the opposite. I grew up in Portland, then my family moved here two years ago to buy this place. It ain't much, but it's probably my future for at least the next few years." He shrugged casually. "Could be worse."

"Could be raining," Reggie said, completing the Young Frankenstein quote.

"You've seen that one?"

Reggie nearly said, *A lifetime ago*, but instead just nodded.

"Well," Steve said, "take your time. I'll wait a few minutes for you to finish your games before I lock up."

"Thanks, man." Reggie turned back to the pinball machine, but inside, he was thinking of the connection he had made with Steve. He hoped it would blossom into something he could use.

Reggie felt pretty proud of himself. He'd only been in town for two days and he had a place to live and what seemed like the beginning of a friendship that he could use to his advantage. When he had left Lucy the day before, he thought he could read what was on her mind—that he would fail miserably and flame out quickly.

He tried to implement what Steve had told him about playing pinball, but it was obvious that it was one of those skills that took practice. He tilted away two more balls and couldn't get the hang of shaking the ball into the right channel.

When his last ball had drained away, he gave a quick wave to Steve, intending to come back soon.

It was almost eleven when he emerged into the cool night air. He walked back to the Rivercrest via another circuitous route, looking for easy marks.

Chapter Twenty-Nine

Over the next few days, Reggie continued to stay quiet during the day—mostly by sleeping—and then prowling Middle Falls at night.

He saw a great opportunity ahead, and he wanted to be in a position to take advantage of it.

The 4th of July was just a few days away, and this wasn't just *any* 4th. It was celebrating the American Bicentennial. Two hundred years since the upstart Americans told the Brits to get lost in no uncertain terms.

Middle Falls had gone as all out in arranging a celebration as any small town in Western Oregon might.

First, there was a huge picnic in one of the parks, with hot dogs, potato salad, and watermelon paid for by the Committee to Re-elect Deakins for Chief. That was scheduled for five in the afternoon, then the big fireworks celebration was scheduled at Middle Falls Falls at 10:15 that night. The Middle Falls City Council had approved an extra fifteen hundred dollars for an especially extravagant fireworks display that night.

The word on the street was that hometown musician Aiden Anderson was going to give a free concert before the fireworks blew off. Aiden maybe wasn't a huge star, but everyone in town knew who he was and a free concert was a free concert.

Reggie rightly assumed that would mean that hundreds and hundreds of Middle Falls residents would leave their homes around eight-thirty to get a good seat at the falls, then, thanks to traffic on the tiny one-lane road that led out of the falls, wouldn't be home until well after eleven o'clock.

One of the things Reggie had learned while a guest of the State of Oregon was that people tended to take proper precautions when they went away on vacation. They might have a house sitter, or at the very least, would ask a neighbor to keep an eye on their place. They would lock everything up tight and doublecheck all the windows.

When they were just going a few miles out to a celebration, though, things were much more loosey-goosey.

It had been a hot summer day, with temperatures in the low 90s, so if a home didn't have air conditioning, he expected to find lots of open windows to let a breeze in.

Pets were always a problem, but Reggie had a plan for that. Before he went inside, he would find a door or window out of the view of neighbors and knock or rattle the doorknob. If a dog was in the house, that would probably be enough to send it into paroxysms of yipping and barking. If it was silent, that likely meant he would be able to get in and out undisturbed.

He wished that he had a weapon of some sort—a gun would have been ideal, but even a good hunting knife or a steel bar would have done—but that would have to wait for another day.

Reggie's plan was to try to take things that had value, but that wouldn't be missed immediately. Jewelry, perhaps, or some decent power tools. If he lucked out and found a coin collection, he would definitely grab that.

He hoped to avoid having a dozen different people reporting break-ins all on the same night. That would attract too much attention, and he would need to give it a break for at least a few weeks to let things cool down. Starting from his position of being almost broke, he didn't want to do that.

Late on the afternoon of the 4th of July, Reggie wandered over to the park where the Deakins rally and free food would be. He took some delight in eating Deakins' food. He thought he might subtract the cost of the meal from what the chief had stolen from him.

He took pains to avoid coming face to face with Deakins himself, which wasn't too hard to do. The great man spent his afternoon sitting at a table on a small bandstand that had been set up, greeting the important people of Middle Falls.

When Deakins stepped up to make a speech, Reggie noticed that he had aged quite a bit since he had last seen him. His hair was grayer and thinner, and his paunch was a little more pronounced. One thing was certain—Reggie didn't want to give him another chance to take him down with a sidearm nightstick throw.

Reggie made himself a plate of food with two hot dogs, a huge helping of potato salad, and a thick slab of watermelon. He worked his way to a table at the back where he would be able to make a quick getaway after he ate.

He sat down and took a bite of watermelon. Red juice ran down his face when he heard a familiar voice.

"Holy shit, Reggie?"

Reggie froze. On some level, he had been somewhat amazed that no one had seemed to recognize him to that point. He *had* lived in this very small town for fifteen years, after all. He wasn't sure if it said something about the collective memory of people in Middle Falls, or if his life had been that unremarkable until he had gotten arrested.

Reggie turned his head slightly and saw Nelson. A little older, a little chubbier than the last time he'd seen him, but it was undoubtedly the *Kung-Fu*-loving Nelson Brister. Reggie knew he should be pleased to see one of his oldest friends, but in truth he was just a little nervous at being named in public. He liked the anonymity he'd had up to that moment and cursed himself for taking the chance of showing up at a picnic where so many people would be in attendance.

He put a smile on his face and said, "Nelson, whoa, I've been hoping I would run into you. How you been? What have you been doing?"

"What have *I* been doing? Pretty much absolutely nothing. I just caught on at the box factory a few weeks ago, so I've basically got my life planned out for the next forty years or so."

Reggie noticed a girl beside Nelson who looked vaguely familiar, but that was it. Like Nelson, she was a little chubby with brittle red hair and a freckled complexion.

Nelson suddenly remembered she was there and said, "You remember Janie? Janie Hudson?"

Reggie made an effort to show that of course he remembered Janie Hudson, but Nelson still knew him well enough to recognize the bluff.

"Ahh, don't worry about it. When you moved away, she was only in seventh grade." Nelson seemed to realize that made him sound a bit like a cradle robber, so he hurriedly said, "Oh, oh! We didn't start going out until she asked me out to Tolo in January, so she was old enough by then."

Janie slapped at Nelson's arm, but it was just a playful happy slap. "Old enough for what?" she asked, teasing him.

Nelson waggled his eyebrows, which Reggie would have thought he was physically incapable of doing. "Old enough to do whatever we want to do."

Janie lowered her voice and said, "Nelly, not here. My daddy's here."

"Oh, right," Nelson said. He brightened. "Have you seen Harold? I know he'd love to see you."

"Not yet, *Nelly*." That was a nickname Nelson had always hated. "I'm going to look him up, though. I just got back into town."

"We always wondered whatever happened to you after...you know."

"Just out of curiosity," Reggie said, "did Amanda or Bobbi ever get into any kind of trouble for what happened?"

"Ha! You know better than that. I suppose she got into trouble with her mom for hocking her coat and all her jewelry. I'll bet she had to give up her allowance for a few weeks to pay her back, but that was about it. She was still the queen of the school right up until she graduated."

Reggie shook his head ruefully. "Figures." He looked down at his arm that didn't have a watch on it. "Hey, listen, I've got some things brewing. I've gotta run."

"Sure, sure," Nelson said. "Let's get together one of these weekends when I'm not busting my ass down at the box factory."

"Absolutely," Reggie lied. "Absolutely." He gave Janie a smile and thought they were a perfect couple. They would probably get married in another year or two and make two or three homely babies. Nelson would work at the box factory forever and they'd probably be perfectly happy. Or they'd get divorced. Reggie had a hard time caring either way.

Reggie escaped and hurried away from the picnic. No one else seemed to recognize him.

He hustled over to Smith and Sons and looked for the heaviest duty garbage bags they carried. He would have preferred to get contractor bags, but those were only available at Coppin's Hardware, and that was closed this late on the 4th of July. In fact, it looked like Smith's and Artie's were the only places open in the entire town, aside from the free food stalls at Deakin's rally.

Reggie bought a box of the garbage bags, then stepped outside. He tore open the box, stuffed the bags into his back pocket and threw away the box and little ties.

He wasn't sure that he would need the bags, but he hoped he would. If he struck it rich in one house, he thought he could put everything in one bag and hide it somewhere safe while he went on to another score. When he was done, he could return and pick them all up.

Reggie walked around town for a few hours, strolling easily, unobtrusively, just killing time, waiting for dark.

Around 8:00, he noticed that more and more cars loaded with families were heading out toward the falls. He didn't want to be seen by most of those people who might remember him, so he found a quiet spot out of sight and hunkered down.

When it finally got dark, he headed straight for Amanda's house. He hadn't really planned that, but it was where his feet carried him. Once he saw her house, he smiled. Even after so many years had passed, he could still remember how well-appointed the house had been when Amanda had gotten him drunk. He thought it was likely that there would be loose valuables sitting around. If nothing else, he thought he could maybe steal that mink coat. That made him smile.

That reminded him of a serious problem he knew he had. There was only one pawn shop in Middle Falls, and, in this life, Sal was still alive and still ran it. Obviously, he couldn't take Mrs. Jarvis's mink coat, or really, anything else that he stole in Middle Falls in to Sal. First, Sal would undoubtedly toss him out on his ear, and second, that would be the first place the police would go looking for it. His planned crime wave would be over before it started.

He hadn't quite worked out how he would solve that problem yet, but he was confident he could find a solution. If nothing else, he could catch a bus up to Portland and find a pawn shop there.

First, though, he needed inventory, and that was what tonight was all about.

He was disappointed to see that there were still lights on in the Jarvis house. He could even see shadowy figures moving around inside. He decided to wait and see if maybe they eventually left for the celebration at the falls, but finally gave up on the idea. He could feel the time slipping away.

Reggie abandoned the Jarvis house and moved a few houses down to another place that had looked promising to him. He was pleased to see that this house looked completely dark. Even better, it looked like it was the ritziest house in the neighborhood. He blended into the shadows and watched it for a few minutes, but it remained happily dark.

He stepped across the street and past the ornate mailbox, which said *Hollister* on it. That rang slightly familiar to Reggie. He could remember a kid by that name that he had gone to school with.

Kind of a weirdo, Reggie thought.

None of that mattered, though. The only thing that did was that the house was huge, had tall white columns across the front, and presented an acquisition opportunity.

He hustled around to the back of the house and found the back door locked, which was as he expected. In fact, he would have been a little worried if it hadn't been. He gave the door a little rattle to see if there was a dog patrolling the house. Everything remained quiet. He reminded himself that he needed to get a true lock-picking set, but for now, he made do with what he had.

Typical door locks might give a homeowner some peace of mind, but they weren't much of a deterrent to someone who was intent on getting in. That was true of Reggie, and he stepped into a large and well-organized back porch in under two minutes.

He stood silently for a full minute, listening.

Putting one careful foot after the other, he moved into the kitchen. It was a large room—huge, really to Reggie's eye—and it was much more like a professional kitchen than what might be found in a typical Middle Falls home. There was an oversized stove and refrigerator, what felt like miles of counter space, and so many cupboards both high and low that he couldn't imagine what was inside them all.

The counters were mostly clear, with matching sets of containers that read *Flour*, *Sugar*, and *Tea*. Beside the containers was a butcher block with a beautiful, bone-handled knife set.

Nice, Reggie thought, *but not practical for me.*

He opened a few cupboard doors just to peek inside. He was sure there was nothing he would want inside, but he was curious. That curiosity was only partially satisfied, though, because there were appliances that he had no clue what they did.

He shook his head, slightly amazed at how the other half lived in a world he couldn't even really imagine.

He found a cupboard that had crystal candleholders. Reggie had absolutely no use for them, but recognized that they might have some value. He pulled one of the black bags out, opened it up, and put four candlesticks inside. He set the bag on the floor where he could pick it up on the way out.

He walked through a large dining room with a polished cherry table and six high-back captain's chairs. There was an ornate chandelier above the table. Nothing for Reggie there.

The living room didn't offer much more. Lovely furniture that all looked uncomfortable, but which Reggie was sure was expensive. He stopped and gawked at the console television in the corner of the room. It was the exact same model he had stolen just a few days before, though that already felt like a lifetime earlier.

Reggie nodded to himself, realizing that he might have helped assemble this very set. It also pleased him that, at least for a few moments, he'd had the same television as these obviously rich people.

As nicely appointed as the room was, though, there was nothing he could actually haul out with him. Off the living room, there was a study or an office. There were two glass doors that were closed, but swung easily inward.

Reggie figured there wouldn't be much easy-to-move value in that room, but he looked anyway. The huge desk—cherry, matching the dining room table—was polished and the desktop was nearly empty. There was just a pen holder that also had a gold letter opener. Reggie considered taking that, but when he lifted it, he could tell it wasn't real gold.

He sat down in the plush office chair, and it made a slight squeak. Reggie froze, listening, but though the noise had sounded loud to him, there was no corresponding noise from elsewhere in the house.

He slid the center drawer open and found a leather-bound checkbook. He didn't want to boost that, as it would be too easy to miss. He did tear off a single check, fold it up, and put it in his pocket. It was possible he could use that later.

He had decided the room was a bust, but as he left, he saw a gorgeous leather binder sitting in a place of honor on a shelf. On the outside, the initials *CH* had been embossed. Reggie opened the book and was initially disappointed to see there were nothing but stamps.

The first page held only a single stamp, and to his eye, it was something stupid. It just showed an old airplane flying upside down. He flipped through the pages and saw that was all there was in the book.

"Stamps," Reggie whispered to himself. "Rich people collect the dumbest shit."

He had no idea if they would be worth any money, but he dropped it into one of his garbage bags.

Reggie realized he was spending too much time in this one house, but justified it by thinking that he wasn't likely to have the run of another house this nice.

He crept from room to room, picking up a few small objects. When he had covered the downstairs, he moved up the staircase, which had a thick rug running down the center that muffled his footsteps.

The first room he came to appeared to be another office, though not as fancy as the first one. There was a smaller desk, a bookshelf, and not much other furniture.

There were two guest bedrooms that gave him nothing, a bathroom just off the hall that led to two more double doors.

Reggie considered just leaving, but felt sure that was the master bedroom. If someone was going to leave money or something valuable lying around, it would be there. He opened the door, which made a small *tik* sound as he turned the handle. Inside, it was pitch black.

He took two steps inside and banged his knee against a heavy dresser. He was sure he was alone in the house, but good sense stopped him from cussing out loud.

At that moment, a burst of fireworks from the house next door went off, momentarily lighting up the room.

Reggie saw that he was standing three feet away from a king-sized bed.

A man was asleep in the bed. He turned over to face Reggie.

Chapter Thirty

Reggie audibly gasped, but the sound was mostly covered up by the continued booms of the fireworks next door.

He squinted at the man, but couldn't tell if he had been spotted or not. He forced himself to lean forward a little, and when the next firework erupted, he could see that his eyes were at least partly open.

Reggie's eyebrows jumped up his forehead as he prepared to run. After a moment, he realized that though the man's eyes were open, he was still asleep.

Quietly, slowly, Reggie moved away from the man and toward the door. At the last minute before he fled, he glanced at the surface of the dresser. There was a money clip and gold wristwatch resting there.

He had a quick but intense internal battle. Common sense told him he had already pushed his luck and he needed to flee. Greed is almost always stronger than common sense, as it was here. Reggie reversed course until he was close enough to grab both the money clip and the watch. He didn't even take the time to put them in his pocket, but hurried out of the room.

It was only when he was out in the hall that he realized he'd been holding his breath. He was tempted to see how much money the clip held, but the words of a Kenny Rogers song that wouldn't be out for quite some time—knowing when to hold 'em and when to fold 'em—ran through his mind. He slipped the watch on his wrist and the money in his front pocket.

A quick trip down the stairs, then he picked up the garbage bag with the stamps and candle holders in it and let himself out the back door.

His knees went wobbly, and he realized how lucky he had been not to get caught. All his plans could have gone up in smoke in an instant.

Reggie walked toward a streetlight and looked at the face of the watch. The only expensive watch he knew was a Rolex, but this said it was a Tudor. He had no idea what that was, but was sure if that guy was wearing it, it was probably high-class.

The watch showed it was a little after eleven o'clock. Reggie was surprised at how much time he had spent inside the house. He had planned to try and hit four or five houses, but realized this would be the only one he would get to.

"Bummer," he said to himself. He wasn't at all sure if he'd gotten anything of any value other than the money in the clip.

Carefully, he cut through yards and across vacant lots until he was close to the Rivercrest apartments. He knew that with his black bag over his shoulder, skulking around after dark, he looked like some sort of evil Santa. People would remember someone like that.

He hurried across the apartment parking lot, up the stairs, and into the apartment.

It was completely dark inside, but he knew that Frank was at work, so he flipped on all the lights.

The first thing he did was take the candlesticks and other little odds and ends into his bedroom and stuck them into one corner of his closet. Those would be the hardest things for him to explain away.

He carried the book of stamps into the living room and leafed through it. He still wasn't impressed with his find, but he thought he should at least investigate them and see if they had any value. He didn't know how he would find out, but he was sure something would come to him.

He took the watch off and looked at it more carefully. It was heavy for a watch, and he saw there was something engraved on the back. *For C H from M H.*

The same initials that were on the book of stamps, which made sense. Reggie also figured that the engraved initials probably lessened the value, unfortunately.

Finally, he took the money clip out of his pocket. Once again, *C H* was engraved on it.

"This guy is really freaking proud of his initials," Reggie mumbled.

He counted out the money. It wasn't a fortune, but there was a hundred and twenty-one dollars. Reggie shrugged, thinking that the cash was probably his biggest haul on the night. It wasn't what he had hoped, but at least he hadn't gotten caught.

A sudden idea struck him. He stuck the money in his pocket, then went back into his bedroom and opened the window—which had no screen. He threw the clip as far as he could, then cocked an ear and thought he heard the tiniest of splooshes that told him he had hit the creek.

It was a shame to throw the clip away, he thought. But it would have been a dead giveaway if he was caught with it on his person. The same thing was true for the leather binder, so he would find a way to get rid of that as soon as possible.

At that moment, though, Reggie felt too exhausted to do anything. He wished he had enough money to buy at least a second-hand mattress somewhere, so he didn't have to sleep on the floor. Maybe he could use the money he had found on the dresser for that, but that would eat up a large percentage of his profits on the night.

It didn't really matter. Mattress or not, he needed to sleep. He put his head against his pack that was stuffed with his clean clothes. As he drifted off, he dreamed of more profitable evenings ahead.

Frank woke Reggie up when he got back to the apartment after work. Frank may have been picky about silence when he was sleeping, but that same courtesy didn't seem to extend to him. He closed the front door loudly, dropped his lunch bucket on the counter and generally announced himself as being home.

Reggie didn't mind. It was time for him to get going anyway.

He went into the bathroom to do his business, then brushed his teeth and ran a comb through his hair. As he did, his mind wandered back to the night before. He wondered what Mr. C.H. would think when he noticed his money and watch were gone. He pictured a surprised expression on the face of the man he had seen sleeping, and it made him smile.

His bankroll had been refreshed at least a little the night before and he was anxious to see if his other prizes might have any value.

First, he needed to dispose of some evidence.

He took all the pages out of the binder and dropped them on the floor of the closet. He thought better of that and retrieved one of them—the very first one with the upside-down airplane on it. He shook his clean clothes out on top of the stamps, then stuffed the binder and the single page inside the pack.

When Reggie wandered out into the kitchen, he saw that Frank had Spam frying on the stove. It didn't smell too bad, but Frank didn't offer to share, which didn't surprise Reggie. Frank didn't seem much like the sharing type.

"Well," Reggie said, "gonna head out and see what the job situation in Middle Falls is like."

"It sucks," was Frank's answer.

"Good to know," Reggie said. He couldn't have cared less what the job market was like in Middle Falls or anywhere. The plan was to never do another honest day's work in this lifetime. So far, so good.

Reggie tossed his pack onto his shoulder and hurried out the door. He hopped down the stairs two at a time, then turned left at the corner of the building.

The first job of the day was to get rid of the incriminating binder. There was a ring of bushes that ran along the creek that gave Rivercrest its name. He fought his way through them until he was standing right at the edge. He tried to lean out over the water so he could drop the binder into the deeper, faster moving part of the stream.

He stretched too far, and his feet slipped on the muddy bank. The next thing he knew, his butt hit the damp ground, and he was up to his knees in the cold water.

Reggie said a few of the more creative words he had learned in prison, including *mother puss bucket, Halla-freaking-luia,* and *douche nozzle.* He completed the mission—throwing the nice leather portfolio into the river—and managed to baptize himself at the same time.

He limped back up the bank, slipping several more times.

He looked down at himself and realized he couldn't go anywhere looking like that, so he retraced his steps to the apartment. He had only been gone five minutes, but Frank had already locked the door. As a security guard, he took the security of his own place seriously, apparently.

Reggie found his key, opened the door, and went back to his room, where he changed his socks and jeans. There wasn't anything to be done about his wet sneakers, though. They were the only shoes he had.

He managed to get back outside without having to explain to Frank what had happened. His shoes squished as he walked and his clean socks were immediately wet again. He did his best to not think about that as he made his way through town.

He arrived at the library, which had just opened its doors. As he walked across the shiny floor to the librarian, his shoes squeaked so loudly that the older woman behind the counter glared at him.

Reggie approached them and said, "I've got a question."

"Does it have anything to do with not tracking muddy water into the library?"

Reggie looked behind him and saw that he had indeed left a damp trail behind him. He squinted and said, "I'm sorry. I thought I had wiped my feet."

The woman looked at him with feigned patience.

Reggie cleared his throat, then unzipped his pack and pulled out the page with the stamp on it. He started his prepared speech. "My uncle just died, and I guess I inherited his stamp collection, but I don't have any idea what it's worth. Can you help me find a book that might tell me?"

The woman gawked at the page laid on the counter. She cocked her head and looked around as though Reggie might be playing a joke on her. "You're kidding me, right? This can't be real."

Reggie's interest in the conversation, which had been more pro forma when he walked in, was piqued.

"No, I'm not kidding. My aunt just sent it to me, saying my Uncle Carl put it in his will that I was to receive this. Why?"

The librarian held Reggie's eyes for a long moment to see if he was serious. She picked up the page, which had the stamp carefully and professionally mounted. She held it at different angles so the light caught it.

"Why? Because this is the Inverted Jenny. One of the most valuable stamps in the world."

Chapter Thirty-One

If Reggie had truly been an eighteen-year-old boy, that news would have thrilled him. His first thought would have likely been, *I'm rich!*

As a much-older person in a young man's body, his reaction was more complicated.

True, his first reaction was a thrill at the idea of holding something so valuable. That was closely followed by a freight train of worry coming down the tracks. He knew instinctively that if he had stolen something worth a lot of money, the heat on him would increase exponentially.

His next thought was, *And now I've outed myself to this librarian. She'll hear about the missing stamp and tell the police.*

The librarian drew back a little and said, "You're a very fortunate young man to have inherited something so valuable. Did you say your uncle left you an entire collection? And what's your name?"

Reggie desperately wanted to be somewhere else at that moment, but decided to answer the last question first.

"Ted Danson," he said, blurting out the first name that popped into his head. "And no, not a collection really." He scooped the sheet up off the counter—a little gingerly, now that he knew its value—and put it back in his pack. Without another word, he spun and ran for the door, his shoes continuing their small concerto against the tile floor.

When he got outside, he slipped his pack on his back and took off at a steady jog. His heart was beating fast and he was having a hard time catching his breath. He looked left and right, concerned that the librarian might have already called the police and put them on to him.

He ran several blocks from the library, then slowed down to a quick walk. He tried to think what he needed to do. He could anonymously mail the stamp back to *CH*. He rolled that idea around in his head, but rejected it. That would cost him the only valuable asset he had and wouldn't stop them from trying to identify and apprehend him.

He liked the next idea better: *I've got to get out of here.* He took the direct route home to Rivercrest.

Inside, he found that Frank was still awake. That made sense. It wasn't even 10:00 yet. No one wanted to go straight to bed when they got home from work. He was sitting on the couch watching *The Price is Right* on the small television. The dirty plate from his breakfast sat on the coffee table. He didn't even turn to look at Reggie when he came in, but he said, "I'll be going to sleep soon, so you'll need to keep it down."

Since Reggie had been sensitive to making any noise while Frank slept, that rankled him a little bit.

"No problem." Reggie started to head for his room, then added, "I'm gonna head out of town for a few days."

Frank shrugged and said, "Do what you want, as long as your rent is paid."

What a guy, Reggie thought. If he had believed he would be stuck there with Frank for forever, it would have bothered him. He knew he had a winning lottery ticket in his pack, though. If he could find a way to cash it in safely, he would be able to get a place of his own immediately.

He closed the door to his room behind him and went to the closet. He grabbed a clean change of clothes, then, after carefully placing the remaining stamps on top of them, packed them in his bag. He grabbed his bathroom essentials and put them in the small zipper pocket of his pack.

Reggie walked to the door of the apartment and left without saying anything else to Frank. He had his fingers crossed that he would never have to see Frank again.

Sometimes, you have to be careful what you wish for.

He hurried into town and went straight to the bus depot. On the way there, he tried to decide where he wanted to go. His first instinct was Portland. It was a big city that would have someone who knew something about stamp collections. It was the obvious choice. That was exactly why Reggie decided not to go there. If people really were looking for him, that would be the first place they would put feelers out for him.

When he got to the bus depot, he asked the woman at the counter when the next bus heading south would be.

"Express going to Los Angeles is leaving at noon."

Reggie bought a ticket to LA for forty-two dollars. It was the same idea as when he had bought the ticket to Seattle. He wasn't sure that was where he wanted to go, but he hoped the false destination would throw anyone off his scent. He was ready to give the fake Ted Danson name if asked, but the woman behind the counter didn't seem to care.

With ninety minutes to kill, Reggie decided to be Artie's first customer of the day. He planned on coming back to Middle Falls, but if that turned out to be a bad idea, he at least wanted one more burger basket and strawberry shake.

He got to Artie's just as the waitress was flipping the sign on the door to *Open*.

"Hungry morning?" she said when Reggie appeared seconds later.

"Always hungry for an Artie's burger," he answered with a smile.

"Grill's just heating up, but we'll throw one on for you as soon as we can."

Reggie sat down at what he had come to think of as *his booth* and drummed his fingers. Was he forgetting anything? If he was, he couldn't think of it. All he really wanted to do was put some miles between himself and whatever heat might be about to come down on him.

A few minutes later, the woman came through the counter and dropped a quarter on Reggie's table. "Since you're having to wait, why don't you pick out some music." She nodded at the jukebox. "Three for a quarter."

Reggie nodded, slid out of the booth and stepped up to the jukebox, which said *Wurlitzer* in a fancy script across the top. It was the first time he'd ever fed a jukebox, but it seemed pretty self-explanatory. He had never really given two thoughts about music and didn't recognize any of the song titles. He picked three at random and sat back down.

Before the second song was done, the waitress appeared with his burger basket and shake.

Reggie didn't hurry through his food so much this time. He had a little time to kill and savored every bite of burger, every salty fry, and each slurp of strawberry shake.

When he finished, he looked regretfully at the greasy paper at the bottom of the basket. He glanced at his nice new watch and decided he had time for a second round before the bus left.

He ordered again, which made the waitress laugh a little. She looked at him and said, "You're a skinny young guy. Where are you putting it all?"

Thirty minutes later, Reggie climbed on the bus. Much like he had when he had fled Corvallis, he watched nervously out the window to see if Chief Deakins or Deputy Naismith would dramatically pull up in their prowler, blocking in the bus. In his mind he saw Deakins board the bus, gun drawn, and throw him down on the aisle, cuffing him and hauling him off to another round with the Oregon Penitentiary system.

None of that happened.

At that moment, the librarian was still talking to the other woman about the remarkable thing that had happened. It would be some time before she thought to call the authorities to share what she had seen.

Clayton Hollister, meanwhile, had suffered through a bad night's sleep and was slow to get up. When he did, he decided to take the rest of the week off, and so didn't go into his office and discover the missing stamps until the following Monday.

Reggie was free to escape the confines of Middle Falls.

The bus ride south was just as convoluted as the ride north had been. More so, because instead of just going less than a hundred miles, it was going all the way to California.

The bus was half-empty, which meant Reggie had the two seats to himself. Everyone else seemed caught up in their own activities—reading, knitting, gossiping with heads together—and paid him absolutely no mind.

Twice, the bus stopped long enough for the passengers to get out and stretch their legs. There was even a small café whose specialty was, according to the hand-written sign out front, *Fried Egg Sandwiches*.

Reggie was quite happy to pass on that. His stomach was still full of a double dose of Artie's.

The bus ride seemed endless. When they arrived in Sacramento, the driver announced that they would have to change buses and that the next one wouldn't be leaving for four hours. Reggie spent what felt like a long time sitting in one of the little chairs that had a TV you could feed with quarters. It did him no good, because it was the middle of the night and all the channels had signed off for the day.

When the driver announced that San Francisco was the next stop, Reggie decided that was far enough for him. He couldn't imagine anyone from Middle Falls going so far afield looking for him.

He threw his pack over his shoulder and wandered away from the busy station. His whole plan had been to get to a big city. Now that he was there, he wasn't at all sure what to do next.

The bus station was in a very working-class part of town, so the hotels in the area were not fancy. That suited Reggie and his budget just fine. He may have had a ridiculously valuable stamp in his pack, but he wasn't completely sure he would be able to convert that into spendable cash.

He walked into a slightly rundown hotel called *The Armbruster* and asked the man behind the desk how much a room for the night was.

In a nicer hotel, they might have looked down their noses at someone like Reggie—young, dressed poorly, inquiring about rates. It was par for the course at The Armbruster, though.

"Fourteen dollars," the man said, barely glancing up from the newspaper spread out in front of him.

That seemed like a lot to Reggie, but he reminded himself he was in the city, where everything would be more expensive.

Reggie paid for two nights, glad to have a base of operations.

The room was simple but clean. A twin bed, a nightstand with a phone, a dresser, and a small private bath. It was everything Reggie needed.

He sat on the edge of the bed and bounced up and down a little. He paced around the room a few times, which didn't take long.

His eyes fell on the phone and, underneath it, a thick San Francisco phone book.

"Bingo," he whispered. He flipped the book open to the yellow pages, then flipped through to the *S* listings. He nodded as his finger traced down the pages, looking for *Stamps*. There was no such listing.

"Come on, man, think."

Inspiration struck and he flipped back through the pages until he found a listing for coin shops. He wasn't sure that a store that handled coins would do the same with stamps, but he figured they would have a better idea of where to go.

There were plenty of coins and other collectible shops in San Francisco, though he didn't have a clue which ones were in the same neighborhood and which were miles away. He decided to find a bookstore and buy a map of San Francisco. That might help.

He headed for the door, but stopped cold. What should he do with his stamps? If he took them with him, he might get mugged and lose everything. Then he would be stranded in a strange city. But if he left them in the room, they would feel so unprotected.

The Armbruster wasn't the type of place that would have a turn-down service and leave a mint on your pillow, but it might be the kind of place where someone tossed your room after they saw you leave.

Reggie fretted for a full minute, then decided he would rather have the stamps with him. He threw his pack over his shoulder and headed down the stairs to the lobby.

He stepped out onto the sidewalk and, though it was the middle of summer, felt a little chilly. The famous San Francisco winds made the temperatures drop if you stood in the shade. Reggie looked left and right, trying to decide which way to go.

A cabbie was leaning against a Checker Cab parked at the curb in front of the hotel. "Need some directions, Mac?"

"Yes!" Reggie almost shouted, instantly branding himself as a hopelessly lost tourist. He made a mental note to hold down his enthusiasm, then pulled the page he had torn out of the phone book. "I'm trying to find a coin shop." He realized that might be a mistake, so he added, "I'm looking for something for my collection."

The cabby nodded as though he didn't really care, but reached a hand out and took the listing. He spent a few seconds looking it over, then said, "Yeah, I know where all these are. Looking for anything in particular?"

Reggie couldn't begin to think up a lie about that, so he just shook his head.

The cabby tapped a small ad in the corner. "This place ain't too far. You can walk it if you're so inclined. Or, I can give you a lift there."

Reggie had never ridden in a cab. That was more something you saw people do on television and in movies. "How much?"

"Can't say exactly. Twenty-five cents to start the meter. Probably close to a buck by the time I drop you off."

"I can do that," Reggie said. He pulled a dollar out of his pocket and tried to hand it to the driver.

"Hold onto that for right now." He grunted a little as he stood up straight and went around the front of the cab. "Get in, and I'll get you there."

Reggie was flummoxed for a moment, unsure of whether to get in the front or backseat. He remembered what he had seen people do in movies and climbed in the back.

The cabby flipped a flag on the fare box and sure enough, .25 rolled over. Reggie was fascinated as he watched the total go up. Every time they went another quarter mile, another dime ticked onto the total.

Five minutes and quite a few red lights later, they pulled up in front of a small store with a sign in front that read *Mint Condition Coins and Collectibles.*

"You want me to wait for you in case you want to go to one of the other places?"

Reggie glanced at the meter, which showed eighty-five cents due. He handed over the dollar and said, "Nah, that's all right. I'll just walk back to the hotel. Keep the change."

Reggie got out of the cab, crossed the sidewalk, and approached the store. The first thing he noticed was the iron bars on the windows. He looked closely at the lock on the door and saw that it was large and heavy. He felt sure that there were other systems put in place after hours to keep the valuables safe. This place wouldn't be easy to knock over, unlike Sal's Pawn Shop.

He took a deep breath and stepped inside.

Chapter Thirty-Two

On the sidewalk, it was noisy and windy. As soon as Reggie stepped through the door, he felt like he had entered a different world altogether.

The shop had the quiet ambience of a library. There was an undefinable smell that he couldn't identify, but it was pleasant. It didn't exactly smell like money itself, but it did kind of smell like people who at least *had* money.

The air was still, and that extended to the man who stood behind the counter. He was tall and elegant, dressed in a dark blue suit with a gold tie and a pocket handkerchief. The only part of him that moved was his eyes as he followed Reggie—severely underdressed for such an establishment—from the door to the counter.

The man's demeanor wasn't exactly unfriendly, but his continuing silence unnerved Reggie a bit.

"Hello?" Reggie said tentatively. If he hadn't seen the man's eyes move, he might have thought he was a wax figurine.

"Salutations," the man said. His voice was as cultured as the rest of him.

Reggie nearly fled, but didn't want to have wasted the dollar he spent on cab fare. "Do you deal in stamps?"

"Of course," the man answered smoothly. "Our resident philatelist is Howard. Do you have a question for him?"

Reggie's first question would have been, *What the hell is a philatelist?* But he figured it out from the context. The man sounded so smooth, so confident, that Reggie was sure that every time he opened his mouth, he would reveal himself to be a hick from the sticks.

Which, in all honesty, was exactly what he was. *But*, he was a hick from the sticks with an exceptionally valuable item, and he knew it.

"I have some stamps I might be interested in selling. Do you buy stamps?"

"We buy and sell all collectibles, yes, at the proper price and in the proper condition." He nodded his head slightly toward the sign to his right, which stated the name of the store. *Mint Condition Coins and Collectibles.*

Reggie stood front of the gleaming case that had coins, gold and silver bars, and, he noticed with interest, watches. He set his pack down, unzipped it, and shuffled through a few of the pages. Beyond what the librarian had called *The Inverted Jenny*, he had no idea if the stamps were worth anything at all. That was the purpose of this trip.

He pulled a page out at random and laid it on the counter.

The man didn't touch it or react. Instead, he turned his head to his right and said, "Howard? Can you come to the front, please?"

A moment later a second man—Howard, obviously—came through a swinging door. He was not as well put-together as the first man. He was wearing a suit, but it didn't hang on him as nicely and Reggie spotted a greasy stain on his tie.

The elegant man stepped away and Howard approached the counter. He smiled at Reggie. "Hello."

"Salutations," Reggie said and had to stop himself from winking at the first man.

Howard was short, four or five inches shorter than Reggie. He almost stood on tiptoe to look at the page of stamps. "These are very nice." He looked at Reggie, indicated the page, and said, "May I?"

"Sure," Reggie answered. "That's why I brought them."

Howard picked the page up and held it close to him. To Reggie's surprise, he plucked a jeweler's loupe out of his pocket, adjusted it on his eye, and looked closely at the stamps that were on the page. "Yes, very nice. Thank you for showing them to me."

"Is it something you would be interested in buying?"

The first man stepped forward. To Reggie's eye, it appeared that Howard knew stamps, but the first man knew everything else. "May I inquire as to the provenance of the stamps?"

"Province?" Reggie asked, misunderstanding. "They're not from a province. They're from Oregon." He winced, slightly. He had already revealed more than he had intended.

The taller man almost chuckled. Almost. "No, son, not *province*, but *provenance*. Where it came from, how it came to be in your possession."

"My uncle died and gave his collection to me."

"I see," the man said, giving the idea that he really did see, and probably more than Reggie was telling him. "Your uncle. Yes."

Reggie's face flushed. He was beginning to feel like he had made a terrible mistake in coming here. If Howard hadn't been holding the sheet of stamps, Reggie would have likely turned and fled. He relaxed a little when the first man surprised him by saying "Yes, we would be interested in these, and perhaps any others you might have."

"What would you offer me for those right there?"

The tall man offered Reggie his hand. "We can't do business if we haven't been properly introduced. I am Stephen Hargraves." He pronounced his first name as though it almost rhymed with *heaven*.

"Harrelson," Reggie said, taking the hand, which he found to be rather moist. "Woody Harrelson." He tried to remember any of the other actor's names from *Cheers*, but decided he'd have to pick a different show soon.

"Woody," Stephen said. "How charming."

"You'll have to blame my mom for that one."

"Well," Stephen said, glancing at Howard and trying to communicate silently, "I think we could offer you fifty dollars for these stamps."

Stephen might have been a decent poker player, but Howard was not. He blanched, bleated, and turned away, suddenly red in the face. Stephen looked like he wanted to slap him.

Reggie's eyes traveled from Stephen to Howard and back again. "Can I have my stamps, please, Howard. I know what these are worth, and I think I will be on my way." He did not, of course, have any idea what they were worth, but he was good at reading people.

Stephen smiled, and it was a near-ghastly expression on his face. "Of course. No need to break off negotiations. I am pleased you have come armed with information. That will make everything easier." He looked at Howard, a rebuke written on his face. "What would you say is a fair offer for these stamps?"

Howard sputtered, trying to find an answer that wouldn't result in him getting in more trouble.

Reggie saw through the glass case that Stephen was making an unusual gesture, which he interpreted to mean *Lowball him, idiot*.

"Well, um, you see, I..." Howard stuttered.

Reggie couldn't be sure, but he thought that perhaps the genteel Mr. Hargraves kicked Howard.

"Um," Howard said, "maybe $500?"

That immediately told Reggie that the stamps in that single page were worth well more than that. He couldn't know how much, but he would have guessed between a thousand and two thousand dollars.

"Well, yes, $500," Stephen said, stepping smoothly into the breach, "but that's at retail. We need to make a profit, of course, and there's the cost of holding onto them for who knows how long until the proper buyer comes along. We might be able to offer you $200."

Reggie felt more confident. The way Stephen had said *Your uncle, yes,* he was certain that he knew that was a nonsense story. That being the case, he probably also knew that the stamps were stolen, or at least inappropriately held. But he was still willing to do business with him. That told him that all hoity-toity airs aside, this man in front of him might be a kindred soul. Another person with flexible ethics. Reggie reminded himself not to put too much stock in image.

"Thank you for the offer," Reggie said, reaching his hand out. "I'll give it some thought, but I don't think that's enough for me to part with them today."

Howard handed the stamps over somewhat regretfully.

Reggie gave them his most wide-eyed, innocent look. "Is there a café somewhere nearby? I'd like to get something to eat. If I feel like it after that, I might come back."

Stephen narrowed his eyes at Reggie. He seemed to recognize that this very young man in front of him had more on the ball than he had originally guessed. "There is a café just down the street called Dupont's." He paused, still calculating, but not wanting to give too much away. "You mentioned earlier that your *uncle* had left you his entire collection. Do you have other stamps that are similar to these?"

"I do. And some that are much better."

Stephen's eyes positively glittered with greed. "Please come back after your meal. I am sure we can come to an equitable agreement that will make your trip from Oregon worthwhile." He pronounced the state incorrectly, like Ore-*gone.*

Reggie smiled, glad to see this faux pas. "I'll think about it. Thank you for your time." He dropped the page of stamps back into his pack and hurried outside. As he walked down the sidewalk, he glanced over his shoulder nervously, but didn't see anyone trailing after him.

His head was spinning. On the trip down, he had counted the sheets. There were twenty-six of them. If he could get a thousand dollars for each of them, that was more money than he had ever thought he might have. And that wasn't counting the most valuable stamp of all.

He saw a neon sign ahead that read *Dupont's Café*. He turned in, sat down and looked at the menu. He was afraid that even in a modest café, the prices would be terrible, but they weren't. He ordered a BLT and a Coke.

He was tempted to just take his booty and run, but one thing stopped him. Stephen was obviously a con man dressed in sheep's clothing, but that was exactly what Reggie needed. If he went to another store, he might run into someone who adhered to a strict moral compass. Questions might be asked. The police involved.

None of that would be good.

By the time he finished his BLT, he had made up his mind. He would take his chances with Stephen and Howard.

Since his acquisition costs had been essentially zero, he wasn't worried about wringing every last dime out of the transaction. It was more important to him to get a nice nest egg and escape without the threat of jail. That was the one area where he felt he could trust Stephen. He was sure the suave shop owner wouldn't want to risk getting himself in trouble with the law.

Reggie paid his bill and walked back to *Mint Condition*. The sign on the door said that it closed at five. He glanced at his watch and saw that it was already ten minutes after that, but the shop lights were still on and the door was open.

When he stepped into the store, Stephen seemed to light up.

"Mr. Harrelson. I'm glad to see you came back."

"Should I come back tomorrow? I see that it's after your closing time."

Stephen shook his head and made a tut-tut noise. "I will just turn off our sign and lock the door, then we can talk about things in peace. Come in, come in."

Reggie wasn't sure how he felt being locked inside with this relative stranger, but he felt that if push came to shove, he would be able to handle him.

Howard was waiting behind the counter. "May I see what other stamps you have?"

Reggie was a little unsure about putting all his cards on the table, but he had made the decision to proceed. He unzipped his pack and pulled out the stamps. All except the most valuable. He wanted to save that one.

He set the entire stack on the clean glass counter and kept his eyes on Howard. The short man's eyes went wide, and he sucked in his breath. He quickly leafed through the pile, his jaw falling a little more with each page. Finally, he looked up and said, "Did your uncle tell you what this collection is worth?"

"He gave me a pretty good idea," Reggie said.

Stephen stepped back around the counter after locking the door and said, "It will take us some time to put a proper offer together. Would you like to leave the stamps here with us overnight?"

"I would most definitely *not* want to leave the stamps here. I can come back tomorrow, if that works better. There's another shop I wanted to show them to as well. I can do that first thing in the morning, then come back here."

"My dear boy, that kind of leverage is not necessary. I think we both know why you came back and why I'm interested."

Howard looked at Stephen, surprised. Maybe Reggie and Stephen knew, but it was pretty apparent that Howard did not.

"Do you like espresso?" Stephen asked. "I have a fine espresso maker in the back. Why don't I make us one while Howard does what Howard does."

Reggie had vaguely heard of an espresso, but had no idea what it was, aside from the fact it was some form of coffee. "Sure, I love espresso."

Stephen disappeared into the back and Reggie could hear him humming and the sounds of something being steamed.

Howard, meanwhile, had gotten a notebook out and was jotting figures down, crossing them out, then rewriting them.

Reggie was very interested in what Howard was writing and doing his best to read upside down when Stephen reappeared holding two cups.

"I made us a lovely latte. I think you'll like it."

Reggie accepted the cup and saucer, took a sip, and opened his eyes wide. "That's something else."

"You like?"

"I love."

"Excellent. Now, you said you had some other stamps that were even more valuable than these."

"I do, but I prefer to sell these as one batch, then we can talk about the other."

"Do you have it with you? May I see it?"

Reggie didn't hesitate. "I'd really like to finish this first."

If Stephen was nonplussed, he didn't show it. His eyes did involuntarily wander down to the pack Reggie kept at his feet, however.

It took Howard several hours to come up with a value that Reggie knew was purposefully low. He wasn't hungry, though, and Stephen continued to make them delicious coffee drinks, so he didn't mind.

Finally, a little after eight, Howard and Stephen went into the back to confer.

When they came back, Stephen was holding a zippered bank bag. It appeared to be stuffed full.

"Our offer is based on us taking the whole collection. The risk that we will be able to recover our investment is completely on us."

"How much?"

"Twelve thousand dollars. It's all in cash right here." Stephen pushed the bag toward Reggie.

With that offer, Reggie knew that the collection was worth probably five to ten times that. He couldn't believe how lucky he had gotten. He touched his backpack with the toe of his sneaker, unconsciously checking in with the Inverted Jenny.

"We both know how low that is."

"We both know," Stephen answered, "how shaky the provenance is on these stamps."

There it was, out in the open for all to see. *We know you stole these, so take what you can get.*

"That's fair," Reggie said. He suddenly felt tired and wanted nothing more than to be back in The Armbruster, snuggled into bed, all that cash under his pillow and the best stamp of all still beside him.

"It's a deal."

"Excellent," Stephen said. He once again pushed the bag toward Reggie, who picked it up, unzipped it, and did a quick count. If it wasn't twelve thousand dollars, it was close enough.

"Now," Stephen said, "as to the other stamp?"

"Tomorrow," Reggie said, and couldn't keep the weariness out of his voice. "It's been a long day."

"Yesterday is but today's memory, and tomorrow is today's dream," Stephen said. "Kahlil Gibran."

"Sure," Reggie said. "Sure. I'll see you tomorrow."

"We open at nine," Stephen said, leading him to the door.

Reggie stepped out into the night, which was downright cold, but had no impact on him. He had more money in his backpack than he ever would have been able to dream of.

He was turned around at first, but then thought he had figured the right path to get back to his hotel.

He walked and dreamed.

There would be no bus ride home for him. He would buy a car and drive back. When he got home, he wouldn't bother with another apartment at Rivercrest. He would be able to rent whatever house he wanted. More importantly, he would have all the cash he needed to build an empire.

The dream was so real, he could almost touch it. So intoxicating that he wasn't really watching where he was going. He didn't notice the two men who slipped up behind him.

"Hey, kid," the smaller of the two men said. "What's your hurry?"

"Shit..." Reggie said. He turned to see that the smaller man had a knife and the bigger man a gun.

Reggie instinctively raised his hands.

The smaller man darted forward, his deadly blade catching the gleam of a streetlight as it moved toward Reggie's chest.

Chapter Thirty-Three

Reggie Blackwell opened his eyes.

"Gah!" He flinched and tried to turn away from the blade that was heading directly toward his heart.

Then, "Gah!" again, as he realized he was in total darkness and feared that he had been blinded.

His adrenaline spiked; his heart pounded. He twisted this way and that as if trying to escape from invisible arms that were holding him. He banged his right arm against something solid and a huge noise reverberated around him.

Then he saw a sliver of light and realized he wasn't blind, and that there wasn't anyone there trying to kill him. He took a deep breath and attempted to calm himself.

When he tried to stand, he found that his feet had gone to sleep, and he stumbled forward, banging into a wall of sheet metal. That caused another explosion of sound. He stomped his feet, trying to bring some feeling back into them.

"Where the hell am I?" Reggie groped around with his hands and found an indentation in the metal box he was in. He tried to pull it, but when that didn't work, he slid it open and fresh, cold air poured into the shed.

He gratefully stepped outside into that crisp night air. It was cold enough to sting his cheeks. He looked up and saw a few stars in the otherwise cloudy night sky.

He turned and looked beside him to see what his prison had been. It was nothing more than a cheap garden shed. With light coming in from the outside, he could see the lawn mower, the gas-powered weed eater, and the bags of lawn chemicals he had been sitting on.

He closed his eyes and tried to remember. He had a vague memory of falling asleep in a garden shed, but had a hard time recalling the when or why of it.

"Why the hell am I here?"

In this instance, Reggie meant standing outside a garden shed in the cold. If he applied that question to bigger issues, he would have made more progress than he had in his first three lives.

He looked around the neighborhood to get a better idea of where he was. He had been in Middle Falls just a couple of days earlier in his subjective memory, but he still felt a little lost.

A block down the street, Reggie saw headlights. Out of habit, he faded into the background.

A moment later, a Middle Falls police car with Deputy Naismith rolled by.

That seemed to be enough of a clue to help Reggie place himself. He walked a block and half and recognized Amanda's house. Just a few houses away, he saw a large house with white columns in front.

He smiled. Inside that house were the stamps he had just lost. Or at least, Reggie thought that was likely.

They were there in 1976, he thought. *So there's a pretty good chance they're there right now, too.*

Reggie had to fight himself to stop from going inside the house to see for himself. He realized that would be dumb, and he needed to be smart about things. Looking back at what had just happened in San Francisco, he realized he had not been smart at all.

Stephen had obviously called someone and told them to mug him and retrieve the money and whatever other stamps he had on him.

"Stupid," Reggie berated himself.

A sudden thought arrived, and he remembered *when* he was, in addition to where he was.

This is the night dad killed mom.

That thought put wings on his feet. He pounded the pavement, hurrying toward home. He arrived in record time and burst through the door to find an unfortunately familiar scene.

The house was dark and quiet. Elaine was lying quiet on the floor. His father was gone.

This wasn't exactly news to Reggie as it had been the first time he had stumbled onto this scene. But it was frustrating. He bit his lip and wondered why he couldn't have woken up in this life just an hour earlier, when he might have done something about this.

Then he remembered what had happened in his second life, when his father had killed him instead of his mother.

I've got to start planning these things out in advance.

He knelt beside his mother, who he knew was alive, but beyond help. Still, there was nothing else for it. He needed to play his part in what felt like a familiar drama.

Reggie went into the kitchen and pulled the Middle Falls phone book out. He found the number for Middle Falls General and dialed it.

"Middle Falls General, this is Cathy."

It was the same woman Reggie had spoken to in his first life, though that memory had faded away into mist.

He had essentially the same phone call with her that he'd had in his first life, though he wasn't nearly as panicked or forlorn. The distance of a few lifetimes can numb someone to almost anything.

Cathy ended the call by telling him an ambulance was on the way and that he should leave the porchlight on.

Just as he had in his first life, Reggie turned the porchlight on and saw that it was burned out. This time, he remembered where the bulbs were and switched them before the ambulance arrived.

He used the last few minutes before the EMTs got there to sit beside his mother and say goodbye. He didn't intend to go and visit her in the hospital this time. He didn't see any point in it.

"I'm sorry, Mom. I hate to see you like this. Next time, I'll try to get here before he does this to you."

The ambulance arrived, Elaine was taken away to die in the hospital, and Reggie tried to put together a new plan.

He knew he was in a tough situation at the moment. He was barely fifteen, at least physically, and he didn't have enough money to even buy a candy bar at Smith's.

He did have the advantage of knowing a few things, though. He knew his old man would probably show up the next day with the woman from the bar. If things played out like they had in his first life, he would get arrested and leave the cash he had sitting in the suitcase in the front yard.

That would be a start.

In his previous life, Reggie had tried to get revenge on Amanda Jarvis. That was still on his agenda, but he wasn't going to do it in such a way that he got sent to Plain Hill for three years. An image of Carson flitted through his mind, but he quickly dismissed it. Carson had shown that Reggie wasn't really all that important to him after all.

Most importantly, he knew where there was something that he could steal that was easy to carry and would really set him up in this life. He just had to think of a better way to convert that asset into cash. Obviously, what he had done in his previous life hadn't worked very well.

Given a fresh start like this, Reggie might have considered just going back to school, studying hard, and maybe trying to make something of himself.

The thought never even crossed his mind.

He went into his bedroom, got undressed and fell asleep almost immediately. As seemed customary in the first sleep of a new life, he slept like the dead and didn't wake up until almost noon the next day.

At that moment, the only thing he really wanted was to be able to go to Artie's for lunch, but even turning the house upside down, he couldn't find any money.

He ate the can of SpaghettiOs again. Reggie wasn't very philosophical, but staring into the orange pasta in the can, he wondered if this was actually the exact same food he had already eaten.

He shrugged. It tasted just fine to him in any case.

He couldn't think of anything to do with his day. He didn't really have anything he needed to do until his father would—all things being equal—come by the house and end up getting arrested.

That was a few hours away, though, and Reggie found himself at loose ends until then. He didn't want to just sit around and watch daytime television, so he grabbed his jacket and headed outside.

He passed the unmarred *Crampton Village* sign at the beginning of the neighborhood and decided to sneak out later that night and paint it again. Things didn't feel right to him without his little bit of graffiti. It was the one way he had made a mark on the town.

Reggie knew there was some small risk in walking around town on a school day. Someone might try to collar him and report him to the school for skipping, but Middle Falls didn't have a truancy officer. Unless he did something stupid—which had kind of been a hallmark of all his lives to date—he didn't think anyone would bother him.

He walked aimlessly through the back streets and soon found himself back in the very nice neighborhood where Amanda lived.

And, not coincidentally, where the stamp collection lived. He walked right past Amanda's house. He remembered that she had a sort of quasi-date set up with him later that week, but wasn't worried about that. She would have to find herself another sucker to groom.

Just a few houses past the Jarvis residence, he saw the two-story white house with the four columns in the front. He melted into the background across the street and settled in to do a little reconnoitering.

There was a single car in the driveway, an older two-door that Reggie didn't recognize. It didn't look like it belonged to anyone who would have lived in that house, though.

Reggie sat there long enough that eventually the school bus came down the road. A boy got off the bus and walked into the house, head down. He walked in such a herky-jerky motion that Reggie recognized him, though he couldn't quite remember his name after all the years that had passed.

The arrival of the school bus told Reggie that it was time to head for home. He didn't want to miss being home when Willis arrived. He had this fear that the woman who was with him might grab the suitcase and take off and then Reggie knew he really would be stuck.

He made it home, turned on the TV, and settled into the couch just before the door opened and Willis Blackwell came through.

The first time this scene had played out, father and son had an intense conversation, but Reggie didn't feel the need to do that this time. In fact, he really wanted to avoid it.

At the same time, he knew that if the timing was going to work out the same, he needed to delay Willis from leaving immediately. So, as if by rote, Reggie followed his father into the bedroom and asked him why he had treated his mother so badly.

Reggie hadn't cleaned up the bloodstain from the floor this time, and had watched how carefully Willis stepped over it, so he knew he had seen it.

Willis gave him the same lame reasons he had before, and Reggie had a hard time even pretending to be interested in any of it.

"Who's the woman?"

Willis looked a little surprised at Reggie even knowing there was a woman outside, since he hadn't seen him look out the window at all.

"Oh, right," Willis said. "It's Mrs. Mind Your Own Damned Business."

The first time they'd had this conversation, Willis had peeled off a few pity dollars from his roll and given them to Reggie, but this time, that didn't happen. He stuffed the whole bankroll into the inner pocket of the suitcase.

Reggie was okay with that. He figured he'd have it all soon enough and he didn't want to have to even appear to be grateful to his father.

Willis seemed to be getting into a worse and worse mood. He slapped the suitcase shut, said, "Well, Reg, don't take any wooden nickels," and headed for the front door.

Reggie followed close behind, a little panicked that he hadn't done enough to detain Willis before he left. If he just got in the car and sped away, Reggie wasn't sure what he would do. He tried to think of a question or some way to stop his father, but he drew a blank.

Willis stepped jauntily down the concrete steps off the porch and set the suitcase down outside the front door of the car. He opened the driver's door and slid in, then leaned over and kissed the woman waiting for him.

Reggie couldn't keep the revulsion off his face. He still thought she was the ugliest woman he had ever seen. She kept her eyes open when Willis kissed her and must have said something, because his father turned his head to look at Reggie, standing on the porch. He gave a dismissive wave toward his son, then started to get out of the car to retrieve his suitcase.

Reggie panicked. He craned his neck and looked down the street, but there was no patrol car. No Chief Deakins.

He looked down and saw a stray brick leaning up against the steps. He had no idea why it was there, but he had a use for it. He jumped down, picked up the brick and threw it at the car.

Reggie wasn't much of an athlete, but this was his moment. The brick flew straight and true and hit the windshield dead center. It bounced off, leaving a web of cracks behind.

"You stupid little shit," Willis said. He flushed and Reggie recognized the expression on his face. It was the same one he had seen when Willis had killed him in his second life.

Balling up his fists, Willis stepped toward Reggie, who jumped back inside and slammed the door closed.

Willis turned the handle before Reggie had a chance to lock it.

Reggie put his shoulder into the door, but knew he wouldn't be able to keep his father out for long. He was too small.

Willis really put his shoulder into the door and knocked Reggie over backwards. He landed on the dried pool of blood his mother had left there the night before.

Reggie closed his eyes, ready to accept his fate.

That was when he heard the siren. He opened his eyes and saw Deakins had arrived. Better late than never.

Before Willis got to Reggie, who was now scooting on his butt away from his father, Deakins stepped through the door.

"What have we got here?" Deakins boomed.

Willis Blackwell seemed to shrink three sizes at that moment. He unclenched his fist and turned to face Chief Deakins.

"Turn around, Willis, and put your hands behind your back."

Willis didn't bother to ask, "What for?" He did as he was told.

Deakins ignored Reggie, but hauled Willis outside.

The bar floozy had slid over behind the wheel. "Is there any reason I can't go, Chief?"

"None at all," Deakins answered. "Being stupid and hanging around with losers like Blackwell here isn't a crime. If it was, I'd have to build a bigger jail." Laughing a little at his own wit, he took Willis by the shoulder and led him toward his prowler. He opened the door, pushed Willis inside, then turned back to the woman. "You'll need to get that windshield fixed, though. Can't have you driving around town like that for long."

The woman shot a hateful glare at Reggie, then slammed her door and maneuvered the car so she could get away.

Reggie ran down to the yard and picked up the suitcase. Looking into the backseat of the police car, he caught his father's eye.

Slowly, with a large smile, Reggie raised the middle finger of his right hand.

Chapter Thirty-Four

Reggie slept well the second night in his fourth life. He was essentially accustomed to the rhythm of dying and reawakening now and had come to accept it the way he did the sun coming up each morning.

He was eager to get started on his plan, but one aspect was out of his control. He couldn't really do anything until he had stolen the stamps again.

That had been a huge stroke of luck that would have set him up nicely in his previous life if he had handled it correctly. As soon as he had shared the Inverted Jenny with the librarian, though, he knew it was going to make his life miserable in Middle Falls. It was much too small a town to be able to have someone know you have a valuable stolen item in your possession and not have it come back to haunt you.

This time, he would *know* what he had and would make sure that no one else did.

Reggie was frustrated in his attempt to get the stamps, though. He realized that he had essentially gotten lucky that first night. He had thought no one was home or he wouldn't have broken in. Once inside, he was doubly fortunate to not have been discovered by *CH*.

He hadn't bothered to go to the Middle Falls Public Utility District and the electricity was turned off. He knew he could have lived there in darkness for the few days he thought he would still be in the house, but having the power turned off felt too close to the disastrous flophouse he had found in his previous life.

That afternoon, he paid the late bill and the fee to get reconnected. It was almost a waste of money, but it made him feel better.

For the next few days, Reggie cased the Hollister house. He saw a maid come in early in the morning and leave after dinner. She seemed to stay in the house all day, so hoping to catch it empty during daylight hours was out.

There was also a woman who lived in the house, though she hadn't been anywhere in sight when Reggie had stolen the stamps. He had to remind himself that had been in 1976, and this was only 1973. Lots of things could happen in three years, like a wife leaving her husband.

Finally, once the son—Reggie remembered now that his name was Michael—came home from school, he typically stayed there.

Around 5:30 or so, *CH*—which Reggie had looked in the phone book to see was Clayton Hollister—came home from work.

All of that activity meant that there was never really a time when the house was empty.

Reggie could have just waited patiently until that happened, but patience was never one of his virtues.

After he had watched the house for ten days, he decided to risk another nighttime excursion. It wasn't ideal, but if he got caught, he would rely on the fact that he was just fifteen years old and that he had no record in this life. A simple breaking and entering probably wouldn't result in too much trouble for him.

Reggie skipped school all that time and on the day he had decided to break into the Hollisters, a strange woman came to the door of the Blackwell home. She had knocked persistently for several long minutes while Reggie hid quietly inside.

Once she left, Reggie checked and saw that she had left a card behind, tucked into the door. The card said she was Eunice Overton, with Oregon Child Protective Services. She had jotted a quick note on the back of the card: *Reggie Blackwell, please reach out to me. I can help you.*

That let Reggie know that his time of freedom was coming to an end. He was about to be placed on that conveyor belt he'd been running from for three lifetimes. He was more sure than ever that it was time to break into the Hollister home and make things happen.

He hated the idea of breaking into a house that he knew was occupied, but he felt like the benefits outweighed the risks. He had a new idea as to how to sell the stamps safely, and with them in hand, he would be ready to start the life he wanted.

He started his adventure by going to the bus station. He bought a ticket heading south that left at noon the next day. This time he knew he was going to San Francisco and didn't expect to have anyone hot on his heels, so he didn't feel the need to pay for a ticket to Los Angeles.

Then he went to Artie's to splurge on a burger basket and a strawberry shake.

He hung around Artie's for a while, watching the people come, get their orders and leave. It felt to him that they were all living lives that he couldn't understand. They all seemed to have families, a safe place to live, and jobs that didn't involve breaking into houses in the middle of the night.

Reggie wondered what that kind of life would be like, but decided that it was too far beyond his reach. He not only didn't know how to even start a life like that, but he wasn't sure it was what he wanted. None of his second chance lives had turned out great, but he enjoyed the freedom of not having anyone tell him what to do.

It was pitch dark when he left Artie's. Still, he walked carefully through the neighborhood where the Hollisters lived. He wanted everything to go perfectly this time.

There were still lights on in the Hollister home when he arrived at his hiding spot across the street. That was fine. He was planning to wait several hours until he figured everyone in the house was sound asleep.

His plan was to jimmy the lock on the back door, then go through the kitchen and straight to the office where he hoped the stamps would be. There was no need to look for candlesticks or go up the stairs and hope to get lucky with the watch or money clip again. They were all small potatoes compared to getting away safely with the stamps.

Reggie settled in for a long wait, sitting with his back against a tree in the yard across the street. He actually fell asleep himself for an undetermined time. That wasn't really a problem, but he didn't have a watch, so he didn't know how long he'd been asleep or how late it was.

He rubbed his eyes and stared at the Hollister house. It was quiet as a tomb there. Looking around the neighborhood, he saw that all the houses were quiet. He thought he must have been out for at least an hour or two.

It was a cold October night and that had seeped into his bones a little, so he stood up and stretched, twisted, and tried to get a little circulation moving. His stomach gurgled with the Artie's burger. Breaking into a house he knew was occupied was a new experience for him.

Finally, he decided he was just putting it off, and padded quietly across the street and down the long driveway. The lock on the back door was just as he remembered it from his previous life and it didn't give him any trouble this time either.

Reggie stepped inside and stood stock-still, listening. The whole house was quiet.

He took two steps into the kitchen and his tennis shoe squeaked against the linoleum. He froze, listening. When he didn't hear anything, he knelt down and slipped his shoes off. He would go sock-footed into the office.

In his previous life, it had been 1976 when he had broken in, but to Reggie, it had only been a few days earlier. He was struck by how similar everything looked. The kitchen, dining room and living room furniture all looked exactly as he remembered. He decided that maybe that was the way it was when you were rich. You bought really good stuff and then just kept it.

The one thing that was different was the television set. Instead of the console that Reggie recognized, there was a long cabinet with a hinged top that had a record player on one end and the television on the other.

He slipped past that and turned the knob on the door that led into the office. There was an audible click, but nothing to loud. Still, Reggie froze and listened for three heartbeats, then stepped inside.

Everything looked essentially like it had the last time he had been in that room. There were lots of pictures framed on the wall, all of which were of the man he had seen sleeping in the master bedroom in his previous life. There were pictures of him standing and smiling with people who must have been very important, though Reggie had no idea who they were.

His heart skipped a beat when he looked at the wall directly behind the desk. There was just a single framed item there. It was the Inverted Jenny stamp. Reggie looked to his right in a panic and saw that the same leather-bound book was there. He hurried to it, picked it up and looked inside. Even in the low light, he could see page after page of stamps, but the upside-down airplane stamp was not there.

He reminded himself that he was standing in the office three years earlier than that. For some unknown reason, in the intervening years, Clayton Hollister had taken the stamp off the wall and protected it in the book.

He knew that the stamps in the book were rare and would be worth a lot of money on their own, but his greed told him he needed the most valuable stamp to accomplish what he wanted. He set the portfolio of stamps on the desk and reached for the framed Inverted Jenny.

It didn't lift easily off the wall. In fact, it didn't lift at all. It was as if it was glued in place. He shimmied it, put his weight into it, and finally felt it give a little. He used that leverage to move it back and forth, back and forth, until it finally came loose from the wall.

Reggie didn't think he'd made any noise getting the frame down off the wall, but with his prize in his hands, he only had one thought in mind: escape.

He grabbed the book of stamps and put it on top of the frame, then hurried out of the office.

He had just turned left toward the kitchen and freedom when he froze.

There was someone in the kitchen. The refrigerator door was open and the light from inside it illuminated that end of the kitchen.

Michael Hollister, the boy he had gone to school with, was standing there with a glass bottle of milk to his lips.

It was impossible to say who was more surprised. For a moment, both Reggie and Michael froze.

Michael seemed to put the pieces together first. With unnerving quiet, he replaced the milk bottle in the fridge and closed the door.

"Uh, hey," Reggie said. "I know this looks bad, but I can explain."

Michael smiled at Reggie and made a gesture that said, *Sure, go ahead. Explain what you're doing in my house at this hour, holding my father's valuable stamps.*

Of course, Reggie couldn't explain. Instead, he just set the frame and the portfolio on the kitchen linoleum and said, "I'm just going to go now."

"I know who you are," Michael said. "Reggie Blackwell. The kid whose father killed his mother. Everybody knows about it."

"Yep, you got me," Reggie said, a sinking feeling in his stomach. He thought he might be about to purge the entire Artie's burger basket and strawberry shake onto the clean kitchen floor. His first thought was that he was about to once again find out what would happen to him as a first-time offender.

He never got the chance to find out.

"You're right, I do have you," Michael said. "Bad luck for you."

Michael's smile was frightening to behold. Casually, he reached across the counter and pulled one of the bone-handled knives out of the block. The blade gleamed in the moonlight that came in through the kitchen window.

That gave Reggie a terrible feeling of déjà vu. He tried to run around Michael and make it to freedom, at least temporarily.

He failed. Michael caught him, spun him around, and sank the blade deep into his chest.

Chapter Thirty-Five

Reggie Blackwell opened his eyes.

Once again, his first word in his new life was "Gah!" He clutched his chest, trying to deflect a blade that was no longer there.

He was once again wrapped in complete darkness, but he had been here recently, so he didn't panic this time.

Even so, his shoulders sagged, his chin dropped to his chest, and he sighed. He was starting all over again. He had dealt with some harsh things in that short life. Finding his mother on the floor, but too late to save her. Confronting his father to the point of having to pitch a brick at *Mrs. None of Your Business's* car.

Then, the topper, getting stabbed again. That made two lives in a row. Repeating it did not improve the experience.

Reggie was not an introspective man. But after running his face headlong into a brick wall several times in a row, he contemplated a change. Maybe he should try a different angle this time. Forget about the stamps and taking the bus to San Francisco. Forget about setting up his small criminal empire for good.

Those somewhat noble thoughts were quickly followed by this: *But then what?*

He realized that if he didn't follow his plan, failure though it had been up to this point, what else was there for him?

To go back to school and be the object of derision until Eunice Overton grabbed him and stuck him in with some foster family, where he would probably be the subject of worse intentions?

No thank you.

Reggie had spent many years as the guest of the State of Oregon Penal System in his first life. He wasn't surprised to find that many of the men he met there came from the foster family system. These were hard men with hard shells, but once he really got to know them, they let their walls down long enough to share what that experience had been like.

Reggie was sure that there were many good-hearted people in the foster-care system. But there were also a large number of people who got in it for the wrong reasons. He wasn't interested in rolling the dice on that one.

Besides, he thought, *what's the downside of what I'm doing? I mess up, I die, and I wake right back up in this stupid shed.*

He drew a deep breath, stood up, and tried to shake some feeling back into his feet. He opened the door and stepped out into the cold night once again.

There was no real reason to hurry. He had tried that last time, and had still gotten there too late to help his mother.

Instead, he went through the motions of the next twenty-four hours like an actor in a play. He went home, apologized to his mother again, made the phone call to Middle Falls General and spoke to Cathy. He waited for the EMTs to come and take his mom away, then collapsed into the sleep of the dead one more time.

This life, he didn't bother to leave the house at all the next day, but just spent it watching television and waiting for Willis Blackwell to show up. This time, he threw himself into his playacting to keep his father there long enough for Deakins to arrive.

He did a good job of playing on his father's sympathies, because this time Willis tossed him some bills before trying to make good his escape.

Right on schedule, Deakins showed up, cuffed his father and hauled him away, leaving the suitcase sitting on the lawn.

Reggie didn't bother to flip off his father this time. He was feeling too tired to summon up that much anger.

The next day, he paid the light bill. Again.

Late that night, he took a different path. He hadn't been back to Sal's Pawn Shop since early in his second life.

This life, he went back in the middle of the night. He was pleased to see that the same crappy lock was on the door and he again wondered why Sal wasn't broken into more often. He could only think that there were a lot of honest people in Middle Falls.

This time around, he knew that Sal was upstairs and that any noise would bring him down the stairs.

Reggie crept silently around the store. He didn't want to steal anything too valuable. He was hoping that Sal wouldn't even notice what was missing for some time.

He ignored the case with the jewelry and instead moved to the long glass cases where the handguns were stored. These were not fine pieces of American engineering. In fact, they fell more under the category of *Saturday Night Specials*. That is, they were small caliber, low-quality handguns that could be bought for very little money. There were enough of them in the case that Reggie hoped Sal wouldn't notice that one was gone. Like the crappy lock on the front door, the lock on the case didn't present any challenge to Reggie either.

He picked up a .22 revolver. It was lightweight and would be easy to conceal. It also wouldn't have a lot of stopping power. If you hit someone dead center, it might stop them, or it might just make them mad.

He gently placed the .22 back in the tray and picked up a .380 ACP. Heavier, not quite as easy to hide in your clothes, but if you hit someone with it, they would know they'd been shot.

Reggie pulled out the bottom drawer and rooted around until he found a box of ammo for the .380. He grabbed the box and slid it into his coat pocket. Just having the gun on him made him feel a little safer. He was tired of bringing his fists to a knife fight.

Less than a minute later, he was standing on the street, the door locked—though not convincingly so—behind him.

He was getting paranoid after having so many things go wrong, so he hurried from one shadowy spot to another until he was back at home.

After waiting and waiting for a prime opportunity in his previous life, he decided to just break into the Hollister place the next night. Waiting hadn't gotten him anywhere.

By the time he got to sleep, it was past three in the morning, which allowed him to sleep past noon.

He tucked the gun and bullets under the sink and took off to Artie's for lunch. He had his regular—though the waitress had never seen him in this life and didn't recognize him at all. After he polished that off, he went to the bus station and bought yet another ticket heading south at noon the next day.

It was still early in the afternoon, well too early to start his stakeout at the Hollisters, so he went home, hoping to catch the afternoon movie. He thought that if he kept living through these same days over and over, eventually he would have the television listings memorized.

When he got home, he retrieved the gun and loaded it. He put the rest of the bullets in the bread drawer. He knew that even if Michael tried to kill him again, it wouldn't take that many bullets for the issue to be decided.

Holding the .380 in his hand, he felt a bit like a bad man, even though he still looked like a scrawny high school freshman. He even entertained a brief fantasy of Michael accosting him in the kitchen again and him blasting away, filling him full of lead. That was a bad idea, and he knew it. A dead teenager would bring even more heat than stealing one of the world's most valuable stamps. It would mean leaving Middle Falls and probably never returning, at least in this life.

He set the gun on the kitchen counter, turned on the TV, and found the movie on Channel Eleven. Today's showing was *Hang 'em High*, starring Clint Eastwood.

"Perfect," Reggie mumbled as he plopped down on the couch.

He had barely gotten into the movie—which wasn't long on plot, really—when there was a knock at the door. It wasn't the stern rapping that Chief Deakins used, or the petite tap-tap of the woman from Child Protective Services, either.

Reggie moved to the window and slid the curtains back ever so slightly.

It was Harold.

Reggie was so surprised that he opened the door without thinking about it. He had gotten used to things kind of repeating in this early part of his life, and Harold had never come to visit before.

"Hey, man," Reggie said.

"Hiya, man," Harold answered. He looked somber.

"You all right?"

"Am *I* all right?" Harold answered. "Yeah, I'm fine. I just came to check on you."

Right, right, Reggie thought. *To you, it looks like my mom just died and my dad is on the hook for it.*

"I'm good," Reggie said, then realized that probably wasn't the best answer. "I mean, I'm doing okay."

"Is it okay if I come in? I won't stay long."

"Sure, come on in. I'm the man of the house, now. I say who comes and goes, and I say to you, 'Come on in, good sir.'"

"Thanks," Harold said.

Having him there made Reggie a little self-conscious about how the place looked. It wasn't any worse than it had been when his mom was alive, aside from the bloodstain on the floor that Harold pretended not to notice. Still, there was a reason why he had usually gone to Harold's house instead of vice versa. He knew that Harold wouldn't care, he wasn't that kind of friend. But *Reggie* cared. Harold's house wasn't anything like the Hollisters' or the Jarvises', but it was a nice three-bedroom rambler in a much better neighborhood than Crampton Village.

Harold didn't make a point of looking around, but Reggie noticed that his eyes did flit to the gun that was sitting out on the kitchen counter.

Reggie almost made a joke out of it—*You can never be too careful in this neighborhood*—but decided it was best to just ignore it. That was how he solved a lot of his problems.

"You gonna be in school tomorrow?" Harold asked.

Reggie squished up his face and answered honestly. "Prolly not."

"You dropping out?"

"Probably, yeah."

"Well, that's why I wanted to come by. When my mom and dad heard about what happened, they asked me to come talk to you."

Reggie had to think about that. Where was he in this cycle? Was his mom dead already? Did everyone know? Or did they still think she was fighting for her life? He decided that she was probably dead already, but he wasn't sure.

"Mom and dad think you should come live with us."

"What?" Reggie was well and truly surprised.

"We've got an extra bedroom. You could stay with us and still go to school. I think that would be good, don't you?"

"What, and give up all this?" Reggie said with a small laugh.

Harold didn't laugh, though he did give him a pity smile. "I'm serious. You can grab some things and come with me right now if you want. Mom's making meatloaf tonight, which isn't that great, but she's usually a pretty good cook."

Reggie was stunned and trying to recover. It was not just a completely unexpected offer, but it was a lot to take in so suddenly.

"The only thing is," Harold said, "you'd have to stay in school."

"Of course, yeah," Reggie said. He felt tears welling up and his throat was suddenly thick. He had been on his own for so long, he couldn't imagine what it would be like to have someone else to count on. If he ever could rely on someone, though, it would be Harold. They had met in kindergarten and had been best friends ever since.

"Please tell your mom and dad thank you for me," Reggie started, but Harold held up his hand.

"If you're about to say no thanks, then don't answer right now. Just think about it, okay? The offer's open."

Reggie shut his mouth. He couldn't have even said why, but he was about to do exactly that—say thanks, but no thanks. Instead, he said, "You got it. Let me sleep on it, and I'll let you know tomorrow."

"Good enough," Harold said, slapping his hands against his legs and standing up. That made Reggie smiled. Harold had kind of seemed like a middle-aged man ever since he had known him.

Harold couldn't stop his eyes from wandering to the gun on the counter, but he just said, "Okay, talk to you tomorrow, then."

When he was alone again, Reggie tried to process this new possibility. He wondered what would have happened if Harold had made that offer when Reggie really was a fifteen-year-old boy. He thought he probably would have jumped at the chance. Instead, he had gone to Amanda's house and everything since had seemed to spin off of that.

Reggie knew that he wasn't really that same teenage boy, though. He was a much older and more experienced man living inside this young body. He couldn't imagine what it would be like to live under someone else's roof. Even with people as kind as Harold's parents.

Reggie filed the idea away where he filed almost everything—somewhere deep in himself where it would never be retrieved.

He grabbed the gun off the counter and sat down to watch the movie. It would be dark soon, and he could go to the Hollisters'.

Chapter Thirty-Six

Reggie took a deep breath and pushed open the back door to the Hollister home. It was his third time doing so and both of the first two times had given him problems. He was planning on a quick in and out this time.

He stepped inside and removed his shoes. No squeaks across the clean linoleum this time. He went straight through the kitchen, turned right at the dining room and moved through the living room without stopping to look at anything.

He opened the door to the study as quietly as possible and stepped inside. The room was mostly dark and filled with shadows. Reggie tried to be just another one of those shifting shadows.

He went straight to the bookcase and pulled the leather case off the shelf. He didn't bother to look inside. He knew what was in there.

He remembered the difficulty he'd had getting the Inverted Jenny off the wall, but also what had finally done the trick. He repeated that and had the frame down in under a minute. He gathered up the book and set it on top of the frame and was ready to go.

Total time in the house to that point: ninety seconds.

He carried his booty balanced on his left arm and pulled the gun out of his jacket pocket. If he ran into Michael this time, he would shoot first, then run before anyone else arrived on the scene.

He had given a lot of thought to the exceedingly strange way Michael had reacted to him in his previous life. He'd always thought

Michael was a weird kid, but the way he had smiled, almost as though he was looking forward to killing Reggie, had been beyond any level of weird previously assigned to him. It was almost as though Michael had been waiting for a chance to kill, which made no sense to Reggie.

In any case, he was ready this time. He stepped into the kitchen, holding his breath and saw that it was empty. He smiled and relaxed slightly. Freedom was just a few steps away.

He hurried to the back door, locked it, and stepped outside, pulling the door quietly shut behind him.

His first step onto the cold concrete step told him that he had forgotten his shoes inside. He looked through the glass and could see them sitting there.

"Shit," Reggie muttered. "Always something."

He set the frame and stamp collection down on the stairs, took his ASB card out of his wallet, and jimmied the door open again. He grabbed his shoes, sat down on the steps, and put them on. One more time, he locked the door and headed for home.

Reggie felt nervous the whole trip back to Crampton Village. He knew that somewhere out there, Naismith was probably patrolling the neighborhood and would enjoy hassling him if they crossed paths. The frame and stamps would be hard to explain. The gun would almost certainly mean he would get pulled in to sort things out in the morning.

He made it home without seeing a single pair of headlights though. When he closed the door behind him, he was finally able to breathe normally.

For once, everything had gone to plan. Now he had his starter bankroll from his dad, his ticket to San Francisco and the stamps. The only issue was that the best stamp was locked away behind the heavy glass of the frame. He went onto the back porch and got some tools, then went to work trying to liberate it.

The frame frustrated all his efforts. It was almost like it was built to be burglar-proof. Finally, fed up with the whole thing, he picked up a small ball-peen hammer and tapped at a corner, far away from the stamp itself. Nothing happened.

He tapped harder. Same result. He muttered a curse word and slammed the hammer down. The glass didn't exactly shatter, but it did break into large shards. Reggie leaned over breathlessly to examine if the stamp had been damaged. It was unmarred.

With the glass broken, he was able to disassemble the rest of the frame, which was kind of a work of art on its own. After some careful work, he was able to remove the stamp and the small piece of fiberboard it was attached to. It would fit into his pack and that was good enough for him.

He looked at the clock and saw that it was 3:30 a.m. His adrenaline had been running on high since he entered the Hollister house and now, with that gone, he was exhausted. He was afraid he might sleep past his bus leaving the next day, so he set his alarm clock for 10:30 and went to bed.

Reggie was probably right about missing his bus. When the obnoxious buzzing of the alarm went off, he was so deep asleep that it went on for almost a minute before he woke up.

The rest of that day went as it had on his last trip to San Francisco, with the exception that he didn't have to worry about the cops being on the lookout for him. There was no way anyone knew he had the stamps this time.

He was still nervous and uncertain, though. He knew he had to have a different plan for moving the stamps and what he had done in his first life had not worked. Where everyone else on the bus had something to keep them occupied, Reggie just had his worries.

He got off the bus and walked straight to The Armbruster again. Reggie didn't mind an adventure, but he did take comfort in a certain sameness as well.

He was put in a different room this time. When he opened the curtains, he saw he was staring out at the top of a parking garage next door, where the last time he'd had a view of a nearby brick wall. Neither one mattered. He wasn't there for the view.

This time, he didn't bother looking for a coin collecting store. The more he had thought about it, the more he had realized that he would either find someone who would toss him out on his ear upon hearing his story, or someone liable to shank him in the back, like Stephen had.

That didn't mean he wasn't going to deal with Stephen in this life, though. It just meant that he was going to do it more intelligently.

Reggie once again opened the San Francisco phone book and turned to *Attorneys* in the yellow pages. There were a lot of lawyers practicing in a city that size. Reggie found twelve pages of listings. That felt a little overwhelming, but he knew the only way out was through. He tore the pages carefully out and took the elevator downstairs.

He stepped outside, wondering if he might see the same cabbie miraculously waiting for him. There was nothing but an empty parking space where the cabbie had been during his previous lifetime.

Reggie realized that he had no idea how to summon a cab. He went back into the front desk and asked the clerk if they could call a cab for him. In a more upper end hotel, there would have been a concierge who could handle such requests. At The Armbruster, everything fell on the front desk clerk.

The man who had checked Reggie in had already looked at him askance when he had checked in, wondering why someone so young was getting a room. Reggie had made up a lie on the spot, saying that his parents would be along soon and that they wanted him to have a room ready. He registered the room in his father's name and that seemed to satisfy the clerk.

Now, the same man looked down his nose at him and said, "May I ask where you are going?"

Reggie considered whipping out the Yellow Pages he had stolen from the phone book upstairs, but knew that wouldn't help the situation. "My dad asked me to pick something up for him, and it's too far to walk." He reached into the pocket of his jeans and showed a few of the bills he had there. "He left me the money to take care of it."

In a way, that was actually true. Willis had left him the money, though not intentionally.

It seemed that the desk clerk was looking for a reason to not call the cab, but couldn't come up with anything. Finally, he picked up the phone, dialed a number and spoke to someone on the other end. When he hung up, he looked at Reggie and said, "A cab will be here shortly. You can meet them out front."

"Thank you," Reggie said, though he didn't mean it. He didn't like the clerk's attitude.

When the cab pulled up, the cab driver looked a little surprised to pick up such a young passenger at a hotel, but just said, "Where to?"

Reggie pulled the pages out of his backpack and looked them over. He didn't want anyone with a big fancy ad. Maybe just a line listing. He found one of those and gave the cabbie the address.

Without a nod from the driver, they were careening up and down the hills of San Francisco. They pulled up in front of a nice building in the middle of the business district. Too nice for Reggie's taste.

"No, this isn't the place I want." He flipped through the pages until his eye fell on a kind of sleazy-looking guy with slicked-back hair. The ad read "Been in an accident? Let Big Frank fight for you."

Reggie held the ad out to the driver. "Is this address in a good location?"

The driver tipped his head back to read the ad, then shook his head. "No. You'll probably want a real lawyer, not someone like this."

"Perfect. That's what I want. Let's go there."

The cabbie shrugged, as though he would never figure out people, but reentered traffic. Ten minutes and several miles later, they pulled up in front of a disreputable looking strip mall. There was a convenience store, a cigar store, and, sure enough, a window with a hand-painted sign that read, *Big Frank, esq.*

"Yep, this is who I want," Reggie said. The meter read $3.25, so he peeled off four singles and gave them to the driver. "Keep the change." He grabbed his pack and walked straight to Big Frank's. He had no idea what he might find inside, but was a little surprised that the waiting room was fairly full. The people that were waiting looked like they might have been in a hospital waiting room instead of an attorney's office. There were people with crutches, their arms in slings, and several people wore neck braces. Reggie felt completely out of place.

He walked up to the receptionist, who was flipping through a *Glamour* magazine and chewing gum. When she looked up, her eyes were hard, as though she spent much of her life doing battle. When she saw such a young boy standing there, her expression softened.

"Whaddya need, hon?"

"I need to see Big Frank."

The receptionist nodded at the waiting room. "He's busy today. Are you selling something for one of the schools?"

Reggie shook his head. "Nope. I want to retain him to handle a sale of some valuable merchandise for me. I'll pay him a percentage of each sale."

The woman's head tilted back, and she laughed, though it was mostly silent. Finally, she looked at Reggie and said, "Every day when I come in here, I think I've seen it all, then someone like you walks in." She leaned forward, a little confidentially. "Listen, if you want to wait a while, I can squeeze you in, but it will probably be a couple of hours."

"I've got all the time in the world," Reggie said, which, including all his bonus lives, seemed to be completely on point.

"You can go next door to the store and get a Coke and a comic book if you want. It'll be a while."

"Thanks," Reggie said, giving a broad smile. "I'm going to do just that."

And he did, though he had no interest in comic books. He went next door, bought a Coke, a bag of chips, and a Daredevil comic.

He returned to the waiting room and had his snack while ostensibly reading the comic. In reality, he was just watching the people around him. He thought he had most of them pegged. Some of them might have actually been injured, but he thought most were using an accident as a lottery ticket of sorts, looking for a payoff.

Slowly, the number of people in the room dwindled. Reggie went outside, found a trash can and dropped his trash in, including the comic. He hadn't actually read a word of it.

He still had to wait a while, even when the room had emptied out.

Finally, a little after 5:00, the receptionist began to gather her things, readying to go home. When she had everything arranged to leave, she said, "Mr. Fontana will see you now."

That threw Reggie. Was he seeing someone else, or was this Mr. Fontana the same guy as Big Frank? Reggie tried that name on for size in his brain. Frank Fontana. That sounded like someone out of a comic book or Hollywood movie.

The receptionist led Reggie down the short hall where he had seen people limp all afternoon. She opened a door, leaned in, and said, "Night, Frank."

A large man with a five o'clock shadow and a swarthy complexion said, "See you tomorrow, Francine. Lock up behind you."

Reggie stepped in the office, which looked like a cheap attempt at chic to him. There were paintings on the wall, but that wall was made of the kind of wood paneling that a lot of the houses in Crampton Village had. Reggie knew cheap when he saw it.

"You've got five minutes, my friend," Frank said in a voice that wasn't completely unfriendly. "Then I've got a date with a double martini."

"First, I've got a question. Can you represent me, even though I'm not eighteen yet?"

"Yes."

"So I can rely on your discretion?"

That was such an unexpected question that Frank barked a laugh. "If you retain me, you will be protected by attorney-client privilege and you can count on my complete discretion."

Reggie reached in his pocket, pulled out a twenty-dollar bill and placed it on the desk. "Is this enough to act as a retainer?"

Frank's eyes twinkled. He stared at the bill for a few moments, then said, "Why don't you tell me what you need from me, but keep it vague."

"Sure," Reggie said. "I've got something I'd like to sell, but I don't want to do it directly. I want to hire someone to act as an intermediary between me and any potential buyer."

Frank narrowed his eyes at Reggie. This wasn't what he expected a fifteen-year-old-boy to sound like. "If I was to accept an arrangement like that, it would take a lot more than twenty dollars."

Reggie reached into his bag and pulled out one of the pages of stamps. He laid it on the desk. "Let's say I have stamps that are worth tens of thousands of dollars. Maybe a lot more than that. I'd be willing to pay ten percent to whoever acted as the middle man."

"Sounds like there would be some risk."

"That's why I'm asking an attorney who will know the law and can protect themselves and me."

Frank twisted his neck left and right, which made an impressively loud cracking sound. "Fifteen percent."

"Ten percent will probably come to a lot more than that room full of fakers I saw out there today."

Frank didn't seem to be offended at that characterization of his clientele. He contemplated that for a long minute, then reached a meaty hand across to Reggie.

"Deal."

Chapter Thirty-Seven

Reggie Blackwell had made so many mistakes over his lives, it would have been difficult to track them all.

Hiring Big Frank to help him distribute his stolen stamps was not one of them.

Frank Fontana was what the criminal elements might have admiringly called *an honest crook*. That is, he might have pirouetted around and over certain laws and turned a completely blind eye to others, but if you were on his side, you were good.

Truth be told, he kind of admired the chutzpah of what appeared to be a fifteen-year-old boy hiring him.

After Frank and Reggie struck a deal, Reggie trusted his instincts and left all the stamps—including the Inverted Jenny—with Frank.

Reggie asked for a phone book, looked up *Mint Condition Coins and Collectibles*, and told Frank to ask for Stephen. He may have had Reggie murdered in an earlier life, but Reggie didn't hold a grudge against him for that, and at least he knew he would be interested.

Frank was, unsurprisingly, a better negotiator that Reggie had ever been. Where Reggie had managed to turn all the other stamps into twelve thousand dollars, Frank more than doubled that amount to twenty-seven thousand dollars. Even paying Frank his ten percent commission, Reggie came out way ahead.

Frank wasn't able to handle everything immediately, so Reggie ended up staying at The Armbruster for several days while he waited. He was kind of at loose ends in a strange town, but he was confident he wouldn't have to make Willis's money last forever, so he lived pretty well.

There was no Artie's in San Francisco, but there were a lot of other fast-food places and inexpensive coffee shops that fit his appetite.

He spent several afternoons and evenings going from one movie theater to another. He saw *The Exorcist,* which he had never seen before and which scared the wits out of him. After that, he went to see Paul Newman and Robert Redford in *The Sting.* That one went down a lot easier.

He took one day and caught a ferry out to Alcatraz. He kind of enjoyed being in the most famous prison in America, knowing that he could walk away any time he wanted to.

A full week after Reggie had first walked into his office, Frank left a message at The Armbruster that he could come to see him.

This time, when Reggie showed up, Francine the receptionist didn't leave him cooling his heels for hours. Instead, she showed him right in.

Frank handed him the contracts he had drawn up for the sale of the non-Inverted Jenny stamps, then copies of the checks he had collected. He went over the math with Reggie so he knew he was getting a fair shake.

Finally, he produced a check for twenty-four thousand, three hundred dollars, drawn on his office account.

Reggie gave the check the fish eye.

Frank noticed and smiled. That smile might have been frightening, but to Reggie it was reassuring.

"Come on, kid, we'll go out the back door and I'll take you to my bank. That's probably the only way someone your age will actually get the money."

"How about the Inverted Jenny?" Reggie asked.

"That one's a pretty big freakin' deal," Frank said. He narrowed his eyes at Reggie. "But you knew that, didn't you?"

"Yessir."

"It's going to take a little time to move that one, but I think that one alone will get you two or three times what all the others did put together."

Reggie had known it was valuable, but that honestly made his head spin. If it really did net him out three times what he had, he would have a hundred thousand dollars. That amount seemed so big, he couldn't even quite grasp it.

Frank loomed over Reggie while they slipped out the back and walked toward the bank. Frank's legs were so long, Reggie had to half-run to try and keep up.

Frank looked down, his homely face serious. "You trust me, don't you, kid?"

Reggie nodded and simply said, "I do."

Frank nodded as though that was the answer he expected. "Good, because you can. You've got to choose who you trust wisely, though. I don't know what you're gonna do with all this money, but when people find out you've got it, you're gonna have a lot of new friends. *Capiche*?"

"Got it," Reggie said, and maybe he did.

"Do you have a permanent address?"

Reggie thought about that, then shook his head.

"You'll need to call me with an address, then, when I get the funds in, I'll send you a cashier's check and a letter from me confirming it. You'll be able to take that to whatever Podunk bank there is where you're from. But, don't trust them just because they're a bank, either. They'll probably cheat you if they get the chance."

"Thanks, Frank."

"Just watch yourself, kid."

Twenty minutes later, they were in and out of the bank and headed back to Frank's office. Frank had convinced him to get almost all the money in traveler's checks, so if he got mugged, he had a shot at getting the money back.

Reggie wanted to hug Frank before he left, but Frank didn't really look like the hugging type. Instead, he said, "Go on now, I've gotta go back to the hard work of taking insurance companies to the cleaners."

Reggie left the law offices of Big Frank, Esq. feeling lighter and more hopeful than he had in a long time.

The reality was, even having started this life with a crime, he had enough money that he could have set himself up in an honest life. He had the head start that he had wanted for so long.

That thought never really crossed his mind. Reggie just thought that he finally had enough money to do what he wanted to do.

That started with buying himself a few things. He went into a nicer department store than he'd ever been in in his life. He started in the men's department but was soon scooted over to the boys' section.

No matter, his money went further there. He bought himself three new pairs of jeans, new underwear, new socks, and a new suitcase to carry it all in. On the way back to The Armbruster, he threw his old pack and his old clothes away.

When he had been in San Francisco in his previous life, he had dreamed of buying a sports car and driving home. He had enough money to do just that now, but at age fifteen, he had no driver's license, and he was barely tall enough to see over the dashboard.

He hated the thought of the long bus ride ahead and considered buying a plane ticket instead. That would have gotten him from San Francisco to Portland in less than ninety minutes, but then he had no idea how he would get back to Middle Falls from there.

Finally, he gave up on the idea and resigned himself to another long bus ride.

In the end, it wasn't so bad. He had a lot of plans to make.

Chapter Thirty-Eight

Reggie had plenty of money. Twenty-four thousand dollars was a lot in 1973, and he had the expectation of more money—a *lot* more money—still to come.

The challenge was how to live without being scooped up and put into a foster care system he didn't want to be in. He had a plan, though he wasn't sure it would work.

When he arrived back in Middle Falls, he actually decided it might help to go back to school. If Eunice Overton found her way to his door again and he was living a footloose and fancy-free life, that would almost certainly count as a strike against him.

The last thing he wanted to do was go back to school, but he decided it was the best thing to do anyway.

He got off the bus from San Francisco just after noon on a Thursday in late October. He went straight home, unpacked his new clothes, and hid his money in various locations around the house. He put the traveler's checks on the counter in the kitchen.

He looked around the house. It was the same sad, forlorn place it had always been, though he hadn't been aware of how rundown it was in his first life. He knew he had enough money to both pay the mortgage and fix it up if he wanted to stay here. He just had to decide if that was what he wanted.

He went to bed early that night. He had slept a little on the bus trip back to Middle Falls, but it had been fitful. He wanted to be fresh for everything he needed to do the next day.

Having been gone from school for several weeks in this life, Reggie was once again the center of attention when he walked back onto the Middle Falls High campus. He ignored it all and went straight to the office, where he asked to speak to Mr. Macintosh, the principal.

Students didn't usually get ushered right in to the principal's office by request, but Mrs. Sears, who was the power behind the throne at MFH, did just that.

Mr. Macintosh, an earnest, slightly harried-looking man, looked up from the paperwork in front of him, obviously surprised.

"Well, hello, Mr. Blackwell. Come in, have a seat. We thought we'd lost you."

"I know, and I'm sorry. It's been a tough couple of weeks."

"Of course it has," Mr. Macintosh agreed. "Of course it has. So you're here to see me about your unexcused absences? What's it been, two weeks or a little more?"

A lot more, Reggie thought. *Lifetimes.*

"Yes, sir. But I'd like to be able to come back to class, if that's all right."

"That number of unexcused absences is usually a reason for a parent conference at a minimum." Macintosh froze as if he suddenly became aware of what a terrible thing to say that was. He flushed a little, but tried to hurry on to cover up his faux pas. "But I can make an exception here, of course." He grabbed a note pad from the corner of his desk and scribbled a note. "Show this to your teachers and let them know they can give you some makeup homework for the modules you missed. I'll take care of the paperwork in the office."

Reggie realized that this was about as good of an outcome as he could have hoped for and he decided to skedaddle while the skedaddling was good. He did remember to put a somber expression on his face, appropriate for a teenager in his predicament.

"Thank you, Mr. Macintosh. I just need a second chance."

The fact that Reggie had actually been given a second, third, fourth, and fifth chance eluded him at that moment.

He stepped back into the hallway and almost instantly regretted his decision to return. From his subjective viewpoint, it had been decades since he had walked these halls. He sure didn't remember anything he needed to get along.

He decided to use his status as the poster boy for tragedy by going back to Mrs. Sears.

"Mr. Macintosh said I can go back to class, but I think I've forgotten everything while I was away. You know…" He left the words dangling in the air.

Mrs. Sears did know. Everyone knew. She jumped up to try to help. "Certainly, Reggie. What do you need?"

"I can't even remember my locker, or my combination, or what my classes are. Do you have all that?"

"Of course I do," she said soothingly. "Stay right there." She disappeared into the file room for two minutes, then returned with a piece of paper with all the information Reggie thought he needed.

"It's still first period, isn't it?" Reggie knew he sounded confused. Way *too* confused for a student that had only been away for two weeks, but he knew he would need to press his luck a few times.

"Yes, of course," Mrs. Sears said. She pointed to the schedule she had written out for Reggie. "You've got American History with Mr. Ward in Room 117." She pointed down the hall, but Reggie kind of had the layout of the school still in his head.

"Thank you, Mrs. Sears. I really appreciate how kind you and Mr. Macintosh are being."

Mrs. Sears cocked her head and gave him her sincere *bless your heart* smile.

The rest of the day wasn't easy, but he managed to get by.

At each class, he showed the note Mr. Macintosh had written and asked for whatever additional homework he had missed. He had no intention of actually doing it, but he did ask for it.

Lunch was a little awkward. He decided to go ahead and sit with Nelson and Harold, but where their conversations had always been easy, now they seemed labored. Part of it was the passage of so much time for Reggie, another part was that he was now a grown man that couldn't come close to remembering what they had talked about when they were the same age, and a final part was that he had rejected Harold's very kind offer to stay with him.

Nonetheless, Reggie made it through and thought that his second day at school would be better.

As soon as the final bell rang, he hurried toward downtown, grateful to be away from the constantly prying eyes and buzz of conversation that followed him wherever he went.

His first stop was at The First Bank of Middle Falls. He took Big Frank's warning to be careful about them to heart and so just brought one of the smaller traveler's checks with him.

He waited in line, then asked if he could open a child's saving's account. The teller shuffled him over to a man in an office who asked him a few basic questions, then said, "And how much would you like to start your account with?"

He was undoubtedly thinking it would be ten dollars or under, but Reggie laid the smallest of his traveler's checks on the desk. It was for fifty dollars.

"That's quite a lot of money," the man observed. "Do you have any identification?"

Reggie twitched his cheek. "Just my ASB card."

The man reached his hand out, wriggling his fingers impatiently. "That will do."

"How did you come into this much money?"

It's none of your damned business, is it? Reggie thought.

"It's a gift from my uncle."

In a small town, everybody tended to know everybody else, that didn't extend to this man. "Lucky boy," the man said, and Reggie knew that at least one person in Middle Falls didn't know he was the tragic boy of the moment.

He left with a blue passport savings book in his pocket. He wished he had gotten all the traveler's checks in smaller amounts, so he could trickle them into the account. He hoped that after they got used to him making regular deposits with them over time, he would be able to deposit the larger ones.

With that errand out of the way, Reggie crossed the street and went through a door in a small, unassuming building.

He didn't have hundreds of choices of lawyers in Middle Falls like he had in San Francisco. There were only three options. Two were decent-sized firms that each employed five to six lawyers at various stages of their careers.

The third was Marvin Shipman, a one-man operation. That's what led Reggie to his office.

When he stepped inside, he just found an entryway. To the left, there were stairs, to the right, there were generic offices. A sign on the wall to his left read "Marvin Shipman, Atty at Law" with an arrow pointing up the stairs.

He climbed the wooden steps, which led to a single door at the top.

Not sure what he would find, he opened the door tentatively. What he found was some form of controlled chaos. There were three desks and all of them were covered in files. There was one man who sat at the farthest desk. He didn't seem to hear Reggie come in and continued to bend over a pile of papers, turning them one by one.

Reggie stood silently for a long minute, then cleared his throat.

The man looked up, surprised. He had obviously been in a world of his own.

"Sorry," the man said, fumbling at his glasses, then focusing on Reggie. When he saw how young he was, he returned his attention to the file in front of him. "Sorry, my school donation fund is tapped out. No more money until next year."

"I'm not asking for money. I want to give you some."

The man looked up, obviously skeptical.

"Look, kid..." the man started, but Reggie interrupted him.

"I want you to help emancipate me. I can pay."

An hour later, he left Marvin Shipman's office. The attorney wasn't sure they would be able to pull off having Reggie emancipated, but after he questioned him, he thought they at least had a chance.

The big hold up was whether or not Reggie would be able to support himself.

Between the money he already had and the money coming from the eventual sale of the Inverted Jenny, Reggie knew he had that covered. The issue was, he couldn't claim the stolen money as his. He also knew he would need a better story than a fictional uncle who had left him the money.

He told Shipman that his mother had died with a small life insurance policy that would leave him ten thousand dollars. Not a fortune, but Shipman thought it might be enough if Reggie showed some other form of income, like a part-time job. Shipman told him that he would need to be able to prove that he had the insurance money when they went to court, but he thought that would probably be four or five months away at least. Reggie assured him he would have the money before then.

The good news was that Shipman could use the filing of the emancipation paperwork to keep the rest of the world at bay. He had given Reggie a few of his cards and told him to hand them to whoever came to his door.

Reggie walked out of the office into the gathering gloom of another Middle Falls early evening. It got dark early in late October.

He looked at the neon sign of Artie's, but went instead to Smith and Sons. He had decided to make a few changes in this life. Going back to school was the tough one, followed by hiring a lawyer to help emancipate himself. He also decided to learn how to cook at least the basics. Artie's was great, but it couldn't make up the majority of his diet.

Instead of just buying frozen TV dinners and canned food, he went to the small butcher counter at the back of the store and bought three one-pound packages of hamburger. He bought some buns as well, which brought a memory of his mother to mind. When he had asked to go to Artie's, she would always say, "We've got Artie's at home." Then she would fry up some hamburger meat and put it between two pieces of Wonder Bread.

After a while, Reggie had learned to stop asking.

He picked up a small bottle of ketchup and a jar of Nalley's pickles. Feeling brave, he walked down the aisle and picked up a box of Hamburger Helper beef stroganoff. He looked at the directions on the back of the box and figured he could do what it said.

It had been a full day and Reggie was worn out by the time he lugged his bag of groceries back to Crampton Village.

He opened the door and immediately saw the dried bloodstain he had chosen not to clean. He set the groceries on the counter, then picked up a rag and drew a bowl of water.

It took a lot of scrubbing, but eventually the stain was mostly gone. He reminded himself that in the next life, he should clean it up right away.

Ignoring the problem didn't make it better.

The irony of that realization did not occur to him.

Chapter Thirty-Nine

The next day, the alarm went off early again, but Reggie didn't really mind.

His life had lacked any real kind of structure since he had died the first time. In all his years of prison, he had become accustomed to being somewhere at a specific time, doing what he was supposed to be doing.

Then, he was making license plates and doing thousands of loads of laundry.

Going to Middle Falls High was easy by comparison.

There were still some slings and arrows flung his way, but he was able to handle them.

People stopped pointing at him and gossiping behind his back after just a few days. He didn't do anything to add fuel to the fire and it soon burned out naturally.

The exception to that was Amanda Jarvis. She had taken it as a personal affront that Reggie had stood them up on that Friday a few weeks earlier. She did everything she could to heap scorn on him and line her toadies up to do the same. There was no better scorn-heaper than Amanda.

Reggie had a different perspective than he had in his first life, though. He had been through the wars and he was still there. When Amanda sneered at him or made a biting comment as he passed her in the hall, he just smiled and nodded. That seemed to infuriate her even more.

He was also much more wary around Michael Hollister. Every time he saw him in the halls, he moved to the other side. He couldn't shake the satisfied, almost happy smile that Michael had when he saw him standing in the kitchen.

Reggie started behind on everything because of his two weeks of absence. Unfortunately, he hadn't been a good student to begin with and having decades of time pass since he had studied anything didn't help the situation.

He had some advantages in this life, though. For one thing, he didn't care whether he learned anything or not. School was basically just a front while he fought his emancipation battle in court. Once that was settled, if it was in his favor, he planned to drop out immediately. Legally, he would be an adult, able to do whatever he wanted to do.

His second advantage was that he was richer than any other student at MFH. People like Amanda and Michael may have come from well-off families and received generous allowances, but none of them had the money that Reggie did.

He used that to his advantage. In each class, he identified a student who was smart and looked like they might be willing to do his homework for a few dollars.

If Reggie was developing a superpower, it was the ability to identify people who would skirt the law or the rules if it profited them.

He was lucky enough to have one of those students, Cameron Burton, in three of his classes. That simplified things as he only needed to negotiate with him to take care of half his schedule.

Reggie found that it was surprisingly inexpensive to hire teenagers to do the work he didn't want to do. It only cost him sixty dollars to get his homework handled for the entire semester. He did have to emphasize to the brainiacs that he just wanted C-level work. He knew that excellent work would be suspicious. The fact that he had to explain this to the smart kids proved to him that there are brains, then there is common sense.

His plan at the bank worked well. Once he had the account opened, he was able to slowly add in the rest of his traveler's checks over time without really raising any eyebrows. Reggie knew that it was possible at some point that some enterprising bank official might wonder why there was twenty thousand dollars in a student savings account, but he hadn't run into that problem yet.

He was essentially laundering the money from the sale of the stamps because when he did make a withdrawal, it was completely clean money.

His case to be declared emancipated dragged on and on.

In Oregon in the early 1970s, case law for minor emancipation wasn't as settled as it later became. In fact, at least in this life, Reggie became part of establishing precedent.

He had hoped to get the legality of it settled by spring, but the case dragged on and on. At a minimum, it had kept anyone from trying to force him into the foster care system, and he was happy with that.

During the months while he waited for the case to be adjudicated, Reggie kept his nose clean. He didn't want to do something stupid and be declared ineligible.

He essentially lived like a normal Middle Falls teenager through the end of 1973.

Christmas might have been a little lonely, but Harold invited him over to have Christmas dinner with his family.

Reggie felt he should probably do something for them, since they had offered to put him up. When he showed up at their door on Christmas Day, he had two packages under his arm. He had bought Harold a scientific calculator that he'd had to special order from the five and dime. He bought Mr. and Mrs. Calkins a very nice set of steak knives.

When Harold opened his present, he just said, "Woah," then looked embarrassed.

Reggie opened what Harold had gotten him. It was a small pocketknife.

The disparity seemed to bother Harold, but Reggie was quite happy with it. He hadn't expected anything.

When the Calkins opened their steak knives, they exchanged a look that said Reggie had probably miscalculated. He should have gotten them something smaller.

Miscalculation or not, it was a nice evening and the meal was one of the best Reggie had ever had. Ham, mashed potatoes, yams, fruit salad, and pumpkin pie for dessert.

"If I ate that way every day, I would weigh two hundred pounds," Reggie said.

Everyone laughed a little at that, since he probably weighed 130 pounds soaking wet.

When the calendar turned to 1974, Reggie stuck with his normal routine. He still kept his nose clean. He did like to take long walks through the best neighborhoods in Middle Falls in the middle of the night, but never crossed the threshold of a single house.

Finally, in May, his emancipation case came before a juvenile court judge.

Reggie would have helped himself by having a job, but with so much money—his share of the Inverted Jenny was almost a hundred thousand dollars—it was impossible to get motivated to work at Coppin Hardware or sweeping up at Smith and Sons for two dollars an hour.

He didn't dare put that much money in his account, but he did deposit twenty-five thousand of it, so his balance was almost fifty thousand dollars.

Since the poverty level in American in 1974 was an income of five thousand dollars per year, Marvin Shipman was able to argue effectively that Reggie would not become a burden on society before he turned eighteen.

Reggie was also able to produce statements that showed he had paid the mortgage and utility bills on time for the previous six months. Shipman also produced the previous year's statements for the same bills that showed how much more responsible Reggie was than his parents.

There had been some concern that the court would ask to see some paperwork for the non-existent life insurance, but once the judge looked at his bank balance, he stopped asking questions.

He gave Reggie a small lecture on responsibility and what his ruling would mean for him. That from that point on, if he got into trouble, it would come with all the weight of being an adult.

That was an aspect that Reggie hadn't considered, but he didn't dwell on it. He just decided he wouldn't get caught.

Reggie decided not to drop out immediately after the ruling came down. He had found he enjoyed going to school. And, as long as he could pay someone to do his homework, there wasn't much downside to it.

Middle Falls High let out the first week of June, so he decided to finish out the school year and then just not go back after the summer vacation.

Meanwhile, with all his ducks in a row, he made a few changes to his family house. He hired a handyman to do some basic cleanup. He found a listing in the Middle Falls Yellow Pages for a company called *Rent a Husband* that promised there was no job too large, no job too small.

Reggie didn't need a husband, but the picture that went with the small ad made him laugh, so he dialed the number and made an appointment.

The next day, a beat-up old pickup pulled in front of the house. A squat man with a red complexion stepped out of the truck, looked at the sad state of repair of the fence, the yard, and the house and let out a low whistle.

Reggie stepped out onto the small porch and nodded. "You said no job too big, right?"

"Yes, I did, but you've got to remember, I'm an old guy. I've only got so many more years to live."

Reggie liked him immediately.

The handyman approached Reggie and stuck his hand out. "Stan Fornowski."

"Reggie Blackwell."

"Reggie, good to meet you. Your dad home? He must have been the one to call me."

"Nope. That was me. This is my place, such as it is."

"Okay," Stan said, recovering quickly. "What is it you're wanting done?"

"I want this place to not be such a hellhole."

"I appreciate the sentiment, but we'll have to be a little more specific." He went back to his truck and got a clipboard with some blank paper on it. He and Reggie walked around the house deciding on what needed to be done. That included tearing the old fence out and replacing it with a new one, doing the same for the gutters, replacing two cracked windows, and doing some foundation work. And that was just the outside.

"I don't do yard work," Stan said, "but I've got someone I can get to do it. Do you want me to include that in my bid?"

"Yes, please."

Stan looked levelly at Reggie. "This is a pretty big job, son. It's not going to come cheap."

Reggie met his eyes. "That's no problem. Do you think you can get it done by the end of the summer?"

"If we get started on it right quick, yes. If I need to, I'll hire someone to help me out."

"Good. Then we can start on the inside when the weather turns."

Stan laughed a little, but just nodded and headed back to his truck. "I'll have a bid for you on this by tomorrow. We can get started on Monday if it looks okay to you."

Stan delivered the bid and though it was fair, it was still over fifteen hundred dollars.

Stan and Reggie shook hands, and Reggie told him he would have the entire payment up front when Stan showed up on Monday. He could already tell that Stan was one of those guys he'd be able to trust.

Reggie felt a little awkward hiding inside while Stan and his hired hand worked, but he didn't feel confident enough in his own handiness to offer to help. Instead, he just took cold drinks out to them and made sure they knew they could come in and use the bathroom.

As the work continued, they found more and more that needed to be done. Stan crawled under the house and came out shaking his head.

"Your rim joists have rot in them. That's gonna be a job. And there's no vapor barrier underneath, not to mention there are some varmints that have made themselves at home there."

Reggie flashed back on the hole in the floor and the family of racoons that had made themselves at home in a previous life.

"Let's just get 'er done. I'm going to live here for a long time. I want it to keep standing straight."

Having the nicest house in Crampton Village was a bit like having the best-looking zit on a teenager's acne-scarred face, but that's how it turned out.

The Blackwell place slowly evolved into the jewel of the neighborhood.

The neighbors took turns standing out in their yards and watching the transformation. They put their heads together and gossiped, but that's all it was. Reggie wasn't doing anything wrong that might attract attention.

In July, Reggie realized that he was older than fifteen and a half in this life and so went down to the Department of Licensing and got his learner's permit. He even asked Stan if he could drive his pickup around town a little.

Stan wouldn't go for turning him loose on the streets of Middle Falls, but he did take him to the high school parking lot—it was the biggest paved open space in town—and taught him how to drive a stick shift.

This life was coming together for Reggie Blackwell.

Still, he remained stubbornly, resolutely, unrepentant.

No matter how many good people were thrown in his path, no matter how many opportunities he received, he kept his head down, walking the same path.

Chapter Forty

Reggie didn't return to school when it started again in September. It had been fine as a transition point in this life, but he had plans to put into action.

Oddly, those plans included hanging out at the Bulldog Den, which an outside observer might have interpreted as goofing off.

When he first started going, the place was still being run by a white-haired older man who had obviously seen his fill of teenagers and kids. He'd had enough and wasn't going to take any of their nonsense anymore.

Reggie couldn't remember when Steve Anderson had told him his family had bought the place, but he knew he was there in 1976, and he hadn't seemed to be brand new at the time, so he knew he would be along eventually.

Reggie had lived through multiple lives by this point and thought he had a handle on how things worked. If he interacted directly with someone, he changed what happened to them. That's why his father had killed him instead of his mother in his second life.

But if he didn't have anything to do with a particular situation, it seemed to happen the same way life after life.

Any changes he did make had ripples, but ripples are subtle, and Reggie was not keen on subtlety.

When he started hanging out at the Bulldog Den again, Reggie didn't spend any time playing pinball. Instead, he focused on learning how to play pool.

Like any establishment that had pool tables, there were the sharks and the minnows.

The sharks were excellent players, though they often tried to pretend they were not. The minnows were terrible players who often tried to pretend *they* were not.

Reggie had shot the occasional game of pool when he was living in Corvallis with Carson, but he was still one of the minnows. He had a couple of things that the other kids who hung out at the Bulldog Den didn't have, though. He had all the time in the world and a nearly endless pile of quarters to put into the coin slot.

He was still living off his initial big hit with the stamps, so he didn't bother to have any kind of a real job. If he wanted to spend five or six hours a day practicing his pool, he could. Also, he once again put his money to work for him.

When there were sharks playing, Reggie tended to grab a Coke from the snack bar and sit on a stool watching them. Eventually, he identified someone he thought he could get along well with. He waited patiently until that guy was shooting by himself one day.

Reggie approached him and said, "I've been watching you play."

"Yep," the boy said. "I've been watching you watching me play. You a weirdo or something?"

Reggie shrugged. "No more than anyone else. I'd like to be a better pool player. I was wondering if I could pay you for some lessons."

That was such an out of left field idea that the guy scrunched up his face and looked more carefully at Reggie. Finally, he said, "How much?"

"How about I give you ten bucks and I pay for the games? When you feel like you've given me ten dollars' worth of lessons, you tell me, and we can take it from there. I'm Reggie. Reggie Blackwell."

"Jim," the boy said. "Jim Cates." He paused, then said, "That'd be okay, I guess, but only when there's no one else here. I don't want anyone to get the idea that I'm open for business."

"That's fair," Reggie said. "Totally fair. When do you want to start?"

Jim looked around at the deserted place and said, "Now's as good a time as any."

During those first few games, Jim winced a lot when Reggie took his shots. He shook his head. From time to time, he said, "Oh my God, you're terrible." But he didn't abandon his new student and over time, Reggie got better.

Also over time, Jim and Reggie became friends. There was never any mention of another ten dollars.

Reggie never did get good enough in this life to beat Jim, but he did become a more than competent pool player. That made it easier to pass the time.

In October 1974, just before Reggie's 16th birthday, the old guy who ran the place disappeared and several new faces appeared behind the snack bar. One of those new faces was Leslie Anderson, who went by the nickname Wimpy. That wasn't a great nickname, Reggie thought, but it was probably better than being a dude named Leslie. Wimpy was Steve Anderson's father, and he took the place of the old man behind the snack bar.

Steve Anderson was there, too. He was too young to take over running the place from his father, but Reggie figured that if things followed the same course as they had, that would happen in the next year or two.

Steve hung around the Den a lot. He was already a good pinball player, but the first time Reggie saw him pick up a pool cue, he knew that both he and Jim had more than met their match.

There were good players, great players, and naturals. Steve was a natural.

Since his family owned the place, he wasn't allowed to hustle any of the other kids for their lunch money, but Reggie never saw him lose more than one game in a month, let alone two games in a row.

With everything going right in this life, Reggie didn't feel in a terrible hurry to move things along, but instead took things as they came. After the imprisonment in his first and second lives and the chaos he had lived with since then, it was kind of nice to just relax and enjoy life.

The day after he turned sixteen, Reggie asked to borrow Stan's old pickup to take his driver's test.

Stan had become more or less a constant fixture in Reggie's home. He had finished the outside work by September and was now doing the inside work. He had started by removing the old wooden paneling on the walls and installing sheet rock one room at a time. He taped, textured, then painted it.

Each time Stan finished a job, Reggie had three more ready for him. After he had seen the newer dual-pane windows that Stan had replaced the broken windows with, he wanted to do that to the rest of the house. He wanted to install new flooring and thought that hardwood floors should replace the old, musty carpeting. It seemed like a never-ending cycle, and both Reggie and Stan were fine with that. Stan enjoyed the work and not having to hustle up other jobs, and Reggie liked having Stan around.

Stan told him that he wouldn't loan him his pickup to take the test because it would be tough to parallel park, but he did show up in his wife's four-door Ford sedan and loaned him that instead.

Reggie passed his test and celebrated by buying a 1973 Chevrolet Impala. It wasn't the sexiest car, and Reggie did drool a little over the new Camaro on the lot, but the Impala made a lot more sense. He was yearning for the freedom a car would bring, but didn't want to attract too much attention. Even after paying for the remodel on the house, he was still flush with cash, but he didn't want to advertise that fact.

By Christmas, Stan had completed Reggie's list.

On the outside, the Blackwell house looked like a well-kept but modest house. On the inside, it was a bit of a showplace. Reggie allowed himself to run a little wilder there. He had Coleman Furniture deliver a complete living room set, with a matching sofa and loveseat, side tables, a coffee table, and lamps. He had the bathroom remodeled in a peach color, and the kitchen got all new avocado appliances. All of it would be thought of as embarrassingly seventies in another ten years, but in 1976, Reggie felt like he was living his best life.

He bought a Curtis Mathes twenty-eight-inch color television and a Bang and Olufson stereo system, both special ordered through Coleman's.

When his pool instructor Jim Cates told him that he was having trouble at home and might be out on the street soon, Reggie invited him to move in. Reggie had long since moved into what had once been his parents' room, so he moved Jim into the bedroom he had once shared with his brother.

Jim happily accepted and when he saw how nice the house was, he asked where Reggie had gotten all his money.

Reggie used the same story he used everywhere, that it came from a life insurance policy from his mother. No one ever dug any deeper on a sensitive topic like his mother's murder, so that went down just fine.

In the spring of 1975, Stan came back to Reggie's to fix a few things that the winter had undone. That didn't take long. Stan did excellent work and what he fixed tended to stay fixed for quite some time.

When the work was done, Reggie, Stan, and Jim all stood out on the new and improved lawn that had been put in the year before.

Stan looked around the neighborhood and though he didn't say anything, it was obvious what he was thinking. Where Reggie's house was now pristine, all the other houses in the neighborhood were in disrepair.

"I know," Reggie said, responding to Stan's unspoken thought. "It's a little rough in Crampton Village." He nodded across the street at the house where the blue tarp on the roof flapped lazily in the breeze. "Could you fix that?"

"Sure," Stan said. "I wouldn't be willing to put a new tarp down. That's not a good fix. But I could patch up the hole and replace the new shingles." He squinted at the roof. "Looks like that's just got one layer on there. I could put a second layer over the top for not too much money. It would just depend on how much they want to spend."

Reggie shook his head. "It wouldn't be them spending it. It would be me."

Stan looked at him like was crazy. "What? Why would you pay for someone else's roof to be patched?"

"I've got my reasons," Reggie said.

"I know you've come into some money, but if you keep spending like that, it won't last long. You've got to have a plan."

Reggie smiled. "I've got a plan, it's okay. Let's go knock on their door and see if they're home. When could you start on it?"

"Depends on what we're going to do. Maybe tomorrow, maybe next week, if I need to order some supplies."

"Good. Let's go talk to them."

Jim had no idea what Reggie's plan was, but he was a smart enough cookie to just keep quiet and wait until he knew more.

Reggie went across the street and knocked on Mr. Leach's door. It took him a long time to answer because he used a walker to get around. He wasn't all that old—only in his late fifties—but had lost a lot of his mobility when he was wounded as a paratrooper in World War II.

When Reggie explained what he wanted to do, Mr. Leach gave him the same look that Stan had. He turned his head this way and that, trying to figure out what the angle was.

"Really," Reggie said. "I just want to help."

"I don't like charity," Mr. Leach said. He looked up at the loose tarp. "I know it's an eyesore, but my benefits don't seem to go as far as they used to."

Reggie didn't want to put too fine a point on it, but he did glance down at the walker. "It's not charity. You did a lot for the country and this is just a small thank you."

Mr. Leach couldn't find anything to argue with about that, so he gave his permission.

"I'll leave you two to figure out the details, then. Stan, just let me know how much it will be."

That began the year of the renaissance of Crampton Village.

Reggie and Stan didn't make every house in the neighborhood look as good as Reggie's, but they did at least a few things to every house. Straightened up or built a fence. Fixed a broken sidewalk. Supported a front porch that was listing badly. Hacked down years of overgrown weeds and planted grass.

Reggie was surprised at how little it all cost him. He knew he wouldn't be able to keep up this level of spending forever, but he believed soon enough that he would have money coming in again. In the interim, he felt like doing the work in the neighborhood was a good investment.

Everything was working according to plan.

Chapter Forty-One

Reggie had never considered the time he spent at the Bulldog Den as wasted time or goofing off. He thought it was an investment in helping him to build his future crew.

He would have preferred to do that in a more adult environment like the Do-Si-Do, but he was still only sixteen years old. Since he had been turned away from that fine establishment when he was eighteen, he knew there was no way he would be able to get in for quite some time.

That being the case, Reggie decided to build up his team with what was available to him.

He thought there would be advantages to that. For one thing, there seemed to be a few Middle Falls teenagers who were like himself. That is, they had bad situations at home, like Jim, or they found themselves suddenly without parents or guardians.

Reggie wasn't the only one who wanted to stay out of the foster care system, so if he could extend a hand and offer them a way out, he did so.

The challenge was that the Blackwell house, though much nicer now, was still small. It was a little less than nine hundred square feet and had only two bedrooms.

The kids who needed a place to stay weren't choosy, though. Reggie bought two new bunkbeds and put them in his old room. That allowed him to recruit three others beside Jim. He thought that was enough, at least for a start.

If he hadn't been vigilant, the house could have become a mess. It was a bit like Never Never Land and the kids he adopted could have run wild as a form of Lost Boys.

Reggie didn't let that happen, though. He liked order and made sure it was maintained. He was their age physically, but was the equivalent of a house mother. He laid out the rules, which included *no dishes left in the sink, no food left on the counter*, and *pick up your clothes*, then he enforced them.

The four boys who got to live with Reggie knew they were lucky to have found shelter in the storm, so they toed the line.

All the boys were still in high school, and that was the final rule. They had to attend.

When they pointed out that Reggie didn't go to school, he told them that if they wanted to go to the trouble and expense of becoming emancipated, they could drop out as well. Otherwise, he knew they were making themselves vulnerable to getting picked up and dropped into the foster care system.

To all appearances, Reggie had turned his life around. He was a neighborhood hero for helping those in need. He was an angel for taking in at-risk boys and not asking anything in return.

Appearances can be deceiving.

Reggie hadn't had a sudden change of heart and become a do-gooder.

He had made the changes in Crampton Village because he was sure it would insulate him from prying eyes.

Crampton Village was just a neighborhood, not a town. But if it *had* been a town and had elected a mayor, it would have been Reggie. He didn't just fix things for people that couldn't afford to do so, he listened to their problems and helped out where he could. He organized huge barbecues and street parties, buying all the food himself. He almost single-handedly turned the little gathering of houses into a true neighborhood.

He endeared himself to the people of the former *Crapped-On Village* in much the same way that Al Capone had done in Chicago decades earlier. The people in that neighborhood had protected him not because they were afraid of him, but because he provided soup kitchens and helped out those in need when the police and government were nowhere to be found.

Reggie's offering shelter to the boys was not any more altruistic.

He chose each of the boys, including Jim Cates, because he thought he saw a willingness to either bend the rules of society or color outside the lines altogether.

He was building a team.

It was a very young team, it's true, but he was in no hurry. He still had enough money to get by for years, thanks to the Hollister stamp collection. If he could take care of the boys and essentially groom them for future roles in his gang, he was fine with that.

The only downside for Reggie was that he got a little bored while the four boys—Jim, Hank, Bart, and Ike—were at school.

He tried just staying home and watching television, but daytime TV in the mid-seventies was a desert of soap operas and game shows, neither of which were attractive to Reggie.

Most days, he took the Impala down to the Bulldog Den, where he practiced his pool and hung out with Steve Anderson. It wasn't unusual for the place to be completely empty except for the two of them. There was something in Steve's manner—a quiet confidence and competence—that was a real draw to Reggie.

One sunny September afternoon in 1976, in the very heart of Middle Falls' Indian Summer, Reggie was mowing the lawn. Crampton Village was quiet except for the dull roar of the lawnmower engine. Reggie had taken over the maintenance of the yard, not because he didn't want to pay someone to do it, but because he found that he enjoyed it. There was something satisfying about making patterns this way and that with the wheels of the mower.

He finished the mowing, switched the engine off, and was going to retrieve a rake when he noticed something strange coming down Crampton Village Road.

It was a dog, which wasn't all that unusual. Even the poor people had pets, though they tended to be of the mongrel variety. This dog didn't appear to be any particular breed, either. It was smallish, with a tangle of long black and white fur.

What *was* unusual was the expression on the dog's face. Where most dogs jogged along in a zig-zag pattern, pulled this way and that by a smell here, a slight noise there, this dog kept its head up. It never took its eyes off of Reggie's face. It was a little eerie how focused on him it was.

The little dog was undoubtedly homely, and yet there was something undeniably attractive about it.

Reggie walked to the fence and stared down as the dog approached.

It walked straight up to the gate and sat on its haunches, as though Reggie might have ordered a mutt and here was the delivery.

"Well, aren't you just a little bundle of Mushu." Reggie shook his head. "Wait, what? What in the world made me say that?" He laughed a little at the ridiculousness of that statement.

The dog's pink tongue lolled out the side of its mouth. It didn't seem to object to being called a strange name like Mushu.

Reggie opened the gate and the dog padded through as though it was home. It sat on its haunches and looked up at him expectantly.

"If I feed you, you're never going to want to leave, are you?"

The little dog snuffled and that seemed like an agreement.

"I don't have room for a pet around here. I've got four boys I'm already wrangling."

Still, Reggie went inside the house and the little dog followed. Reggie shut the door behind him and noticed that he had a shadow. "Oh, no. You belong outside. No piddles on the floor for me." He picked the dog up and examined its undercarriage. "You're a little bitch, huh? Well, bitch or not, no dogs inside casa Blackwell." He opened the door and set her down on the porch. She didn't try to rush back inside, though she did look a little reproachfully at Reggie at being pushed out.

He went into the kitchen and got down a small saucer and a plate. He poured some milk into the saucer, then retrieved some leftover hamburger from their dinner the night before and put it on the plate.

"I should have my head examined," he said as he carried the small feast out to the little beggar on the front steps. He set both the milk and the meat down in front of the little dog.

She just looked at it. Then at Reggie. Then back at the food.

"Well go ahead, silly dog. Go ahead and eat."

As if she had been waiting for permission, the dog did just that. She was a skinny little thing, but she didn't eat like she was starving. She lapped delicately at the milk, then took tiny bites of the hamburger. She ate slowly, but finished every bit.

When she finished with her meal, she curled up at Reggie's feet, seemingly quite content.

"Oh, no you don't, you little beggar. That's it for you. I'll spring for a meal for you, but I'm not going to put a roof over your head."

He picked the dog up and carried her out to the fence. He opened the gate and set her down.

She didn't try to run back in, but cocked her head at Reggie as though asking, *Are you sure?*

Her response was so human that it made Reggie smile, but did nothing to change his mind. "Go on now, you'll have to find your next meal somewhere else."

The little dog stared at him for a long minute, giving him a chance to change his mind

He didn't. Instead, he went back to where the mower was and pushed it into the garden shed in the backyard.

He didn't give the little dog another thought.

Chapter Forty-Two

Time passed.

By 1977, all of the boys had matriculated from Middle Falls high school. Three of them—Jim, Hank, and Bart—had turned eighteen over the previous eight months and were legally adults. Ike was the baby of the Lost Boys. He had skipped second grade and so wouldn't have that birthday until September.

Nonetheless, Reggie thought it was time to put the next phase of his plan into motion. He made a big pan of spaghetti, which was a staple in the house, served at least once a week. Along with some garlic bread, it filled up the stomachs of even teenage boys.

When everyone sat down around the dining room table, which was a little crowded with six people, since Steve Anderson had also been invited, Reggie said what passed for grace. "It's hot, dig in, everybody."

The next few minutes were marked by the passing of the bowl of spaghetti and plates of hot bread, or the filling of milk glasses. Meals did not take long in this house. Everyone ate industriously until they saw the bottom of their plates and there were no more refills available.

When the food was gone, Reggie knew they were about to get up and disperse to the living room, where they would take turns playing the new Atari 2600 that he had bought as a graduation gift for the house.

"Hold on, everybody. I've got something to talk to you about."

The scraping of chairs was reversed, and everyone sat back down. Reggie was the same age as they were, but there was a definite hierarchy in the house. The same age or not, Reggie struck the other boys as older, somehow, which of course he was.

Aside from setting the rules and making sure they were adhered to, he didn't lord that over them, though. It wasn't a democracy in the house, but Reggie was at least a benevolent dictator.

All five boys did their best to look at Reggie, though, truth be told, both Bart and Ike let their eyes wander toward the living room, where a game of Space Invaders was waiting for them.

"I won't take long," Reggie said, grinning at them, "then you can get back to your game." He took a deep breath then plunged ahead. "Do any of you have any idea what you want to do next, now that you're out of school?"

Steve shrugged. "I guess I'm locked in at the Den. Otherwise, nope."

"Stay here and live off of you?" Jim said with a smile, then shook his head. "Don't have a clue."

The rest of the boys nodded their agreement.

"Listen, I'm not going to kick any of you out, but I won't be able to carry all of us forever."

That put a worried look on most everyone's face. They had known on some level that this couldn't go on forever, but they hadn't thought the end would come right after dinner that night.

"But, if you want, there's something we can do about it. I've got a few plans we can put into action."

"Great," Hank said. "You're the boss, man. Whatever you've got lined up, I'm in. I always figured I'd end up putting my forty hours in at the box factory. If you've got something better than that, I'm in."

Reggie nodded. "Good. But listen. These plans are a little risky. They're not exactly legal." He paused to gauge the reaction of everyone around the table. He liked what he saw. "But they will be pretty profitable, I think." He shrugged nonchalantly. "There's risk too, of course. There's always risk. But if you don't mind that, I think we can make things work."

Asking an eighteen-year-old boy to consider risk is like asking a blind man what color the grass is. It's a foreign concept to them.

Jim scrunched up his face and was the first to speak. "No one ever did me any favors in this life." He looked meaningfully at Reggie. "Until I met you. You've been way more family to me than the one I grew up with. I trust you. Whatever you've got lined up for us, I'm in."

Jim might as well have spoken for everyone else. Around the table, there were nods of agreement.

Reggie had expected that from the four who lived with him. He looked at Steve, though. "What do you say, man? You in or out? You've still got a family and a place to go."

Steve sat quietly for a minute, contemplating. "I know I'm lucky that I do still have a good relationship with my family and a place to go. I don't want to piss that away." He nodded and smiled. "But you guys are like my family, too. I'll keep my gig at the Den, but I'm in too."

"So what do we do first?" Jim asked.

"First? First, you guys go play your game and enjoy the night. I'll start getting everything else put together."

Reggie had been preparing for this for a long time. Months earlier, he subscribed to a magazine intended for locksmiths. The articles proved somewhat interesting, but what he really wanted was the pages of classified ads offering different lock-opening kits. He had ordered one of each, found the system he liked best, and had half a dozen of them shipped to the house.

He spent a month teaching himself the ins and out of his chosen equipment, then another month teaching his young charges. By the end of that time, they could open anything except the most advanced lock system almost as fast as if they had a key.

He drove all of them to Eugene—the Impala was crowded with six of them, but they were all thin—and bought everyone new clothes for the new enterprise. The gang all thought the clothes were cool, but only Reggie really got the joke. Everything he bought them, from pants to shirts to beanies, were black. It was his little nod to the girls who had once started him on a life of crime.

Reggie's plan from there was simple. They wouldn't work in Middle Falls. It was just too small a pond for them to fish in. Instead, they always drove to a new town a few hours away, and spent a week scouting neighborhoods and casing houses. They hit all their targets in one night so there wasn't time for word of a crime wave to spread through the community. As soon as the houses were picked clean, they left town and drove at least an hour away before the sun was even up and people noticed their finery was missing.

They didn't try to pawn or fence the merchandise immediately. Even moving several hours away, Reggie was sure that would have been traced back to them. Instead, they stored their loot in a heavy-duty shed that Reggie had Stan Fornowski build for them in the backyard. It took up the majority of the backyard and was against several Middle Falls building codes, but no one in Crampton Village was going to turn him in. Reggie had an excellent lock and security system installed on that shed. He was cautious in other ways, too. They kept the loot from each heist in the same bin or shelf in the shed, but when they did drive somewhere far away to hock it, they never took too much from the same job.

That system worked for a few years, and they made enough that everyone got a share, but overall Reggie wasn't as happy as he could have been. The big roadblock was always converting the stolen merchandise into cash.

If they got lucky and found something that was obviously valuable, like a coin collection, Reggie used the same system as before. He would send it to Big Frank in San Francisco, who would represent him in the sale for only ten percent.

For other things, though, smaller items like silverware, museum-quality vases, or fine crystal, they had to run things through a pawn shop at a significant loss of potential earning.

That was when Reggie got one of his crazier ideas. He had only been to Sal's pawnshop once in this life, and that was to steal a gun. He had no beef with Sal in this life. Even so, he didn't want to reach out to Sal directly. He still looked young and knew he wouldn't be taken seriously.

He reached out to Big Frank again and asked him to negotiate a purchase and sale agreement for the pawn shop.

Big Frank did and after some back and forth, Sal agreed to sell the shop to Big Frank "and/or assigns."

The *and/or assigns* was Reggie, of course.

By then, he didn't have enough cash on hand to buy the shop outright, but did negotiate to put twenty-five percent down with a balloon note due in five years.

Reggie was confident that the pawn shop would be profitable enough to pay for itself by then. After all, all the inventory they brought in to launder would be free.

Reggie had no interest in running the pawn shop himself. Instead, he talked Steve into walking away from the Bulldog Den and taking it over. That didn't cause too much heartburn for Steve. By then, his little brother was ready to take over the Den.

With Sal's Pawn Shop in play—Reggie decided to leave the name the same—their little crime empire took off.

Reggie spread the business out to other illicit businesses. Mail order scams, insurance fraud, anything where a young man with a dream and very little conscience could put a plan into play.

Things went well over the next decade.

Mrs. Stephenson, the mean old woman next door, who hadn't been nearly so mean to Reggie in this life, when he was like the Robin Hood of Crampton Village, died.

Reggie bought her house, which gave him room to move most of his roommates next door and have at least a little more privacy.

In many ways, this life was everything Reggie had dreamed it would be. Virtually nothing went completely wrong. There was the occasional close call, but nothing that couldn't be handled.

Reggie never left the house he had grown up in.

Was he happy in this life?

Happiness is elusive and impossible to maintain for entire lifetimes.

He *was* content in this life, though.

More than anything, he wanted to do things exactly the way he wanted to do them. He accomplished that.

It was, in some ways, a successful life. It was, in almost every way, an unexamined life. In fact, it was that very lack of forced introspection that pleased Reggie the most.

To an outside observer, Reggie Blackwell's fifth life might have seemed a little staid, a little boring, and yes, a little criminal.

Criminal was a word that he didn't think or worry too much about. He didn't have what another person might have thought of as a moral compass. His compass constantly pointed ahead, nowhere else.

That same outside observer might have also pointed out that Reggie had, in some ways, recreated the environment he had spent most of his time in during his first life.

He wasn't imprisoned, but he did live a semi-cloistered life with the boys, and eventually men, he chose to trust.

In any case, Reggie wasn't interested in what any outside observer might think about the life he chose to live.

In fact, he approved of this entire stretch of events so much that when he eventually died of cancer in his late fifties and woke up in the tiny gardening shed in 1973, he set out to recreate it.

He did just that, again and again.

Time and again, he lived essentially the same life, then died, always in his late fifties. Reggie was not destined to be long-lived. Each time he felt the encroaching darkness of inevitable death, he smiled, ready to start over and do everything again.

And that's what he did. Once, twice, ten times, then twenty-five times, and eventually so often that he lost complete track of what life he was on.

Each time he woke up in that shed in 1973, he was aware that he couldn't save his mother, but that didn't bother him so much anymore. From his perspective, she had been dead for centuries.

Each new life, he was equally aware that he had a huge to-do list that he needed to start checking things off of.

That started with getting an ambulance for his mother, then stealing the stamps from Clayton Hollister, taking the trip to San Francisco and engaging Big Frank to represent him, and so on and so forth.

Things didn't always go perfectly. There was still randomization in the world. In several lives, he got a different judge during his trial to be emancipated. A judge who was not as sympathetic or wanted paperwork that neither Reggie nor Marvin Shipman—who he hired each life like clockwork—could produce. Those were harder lives, and each of them reinforced the idea why he wanted to avoid the foster system. He was glad to leave each one behind for a clean start.

Reggie may have lost count of his lives, but The Machine never did.

For many cycles, Reggie lived the same life with only minimal changes. On his seventy-fifth life, something different finally happened.

In the end, what seemed like a minor change to his lives changed everything.

Chapter Forty-Three

That seventy-fifth life started just like the long string of lives before it.

Reggie always felt reinvigorated at the start of each life. It was a charge to go from being older and deathly ill to being so young and healthy again. There were always so many things that needed to be done in order to set the life up that he wanted.

This particular life ran normally through all the familiar early points. Reggie stole the stamps, sold them, got emancipated, paid Stan to remodel the house—again—and moved the Lost Boys in with him. He bought Sal's Pawn Shop and was settling in to enjoy the fruits of the labor he had put in.

It was November 1983. Reggie had just bought a VCR and was hooking it up to the same Curtis Mathes television he bought each life. He liked them because they seemed to run forever without giving him any trouble.

Adding the VCR was something a little new this life. As much as Reggie wanted to keep his lives the same, he had to admit that watching the same movies and shows over and over again had gotten a little old. He hooked the VCR up to the TV and settled onto the couch to learn how to program it to record different shows. He was looking forward to being able to record *The A-Team* and *Magnum, P.I.*

Cable television had finally come to Middle Falls and Reggie had plans to record an entire library of his favorite shows now that there were so many channels to choose from. As always happened when he tried to read something more complicated than a Dick and Jane book, he had trouble focusing on the directions. He tossed the VCR's instruction manual onto the couch in frustration and decided to wait until Jim got home. He was the best in the house at figuring stuff like that out.

There was a quiet knock at the door and Reggie answered it without looking through the peephole. He had very little to fear in this familiar life.

A young boy who looked to be thirteen or fourteen stood on the porch. It was raining outside and though he stood under the overhang of the porch, he was already soaking wet. Reggie was a little surprised. This was something new. No young urchin had come knocking at his door in any of his previous lives.

"Yes?"

"I'm Sonny. You're Reggie Blackwell, aren't you?"

"Yep. What can I do for you?" Reggie wasn't completely unfriendly, but he was pretty sure he didn't need anything that this young boy was selling.

Sonny shifted back and forth on his feet, trying to figure out what to say.

Reggie took him in, from his worn-out tennis shoes to the jeans that didn't seem to fit right and the old coat that was completely wrong for this cold weather. He realized that he could almost be looking at an image of himself at the same age.

Reggie stepped back from the door and said, "While you're trying to figure out what you want to say, you better come on in. It's cold out there."

Sonny looked at the nice hardwood floor Reggie had and said, "Maybe I should just stand here. I don't want to drip on your floor."

Reggie raised a hand, telling Sonny to wait, and went down the hall to the bathroom. He grabbed a towel off the rack and tossed it to the soaking wet boy. "Here, dry yourself off, then you can tell me what you need."

Sonny ran the towel vigorously over his hair, then wiped his face dry. "Thanks." He looked seriously at Reggie and said, "What I need is a place to live."

That was unusual. Yes, Reggie ran a sort of home for wayward boys, but they always came from his own circle of friends. In all his lives, no one had ever approached him directly, asking to be let in. He had no interest in accepting applications.

"What made you come to me?" Reggie was honestly curious.

Sonny shrugged. "I was talking to Ike at the Bulldog Den. He told me about what you did for him. I thought you might do the same thing for me."

Reggie didn't answer immediately, but he was lining up all the reasons why he couldn't help the boy. Jim and Steve and the others were essentially the same age as Reggie. This boy was quite a lot younger. After so many lives living with the same comfortable people, Reggie wasn't at all sure he wanted to add a new element in this one.

"What are you, anyway? An eighth grader?"

Sonny shook his head. "I'm sixteen. I'm just small for my age." He seemed to be gathering his courage to say something.

Reggie noticed and stayed still.

Quietly, almost in a whisper, Sonny said, "I can't go back there."

"Back where?"

"To the Johnsons. The foster family I was assigned to. I just can't." He looked at Reggie with clear eyes. "You don't have to take me in. I know you don't owe me anything. I just thought I'd ask."

"You say you can't go back. Do you want to tell me why?"

Sonny had been holding eye contact, but now he averted his eyes. "No."

"Where will you go from here?"

That sounded a lot like Reggie had already decided to say no, and Sonny understood. He took a deep breath with a shudder in it. "I'm just going to leave town."

It was obvious that he wasn't trying to play up the drama, but Reggie knew what that meant. He didn't have anything with him unless he'd dropped a pack off somewhere before he'd arrived. He was probably leaving Middle Falls with the clothes he had on and nothing else.

⟪ ⟫

REGGIE KNEW THE LIKELY fate of a young boy who was small for his age in those circumstances, but he really didn't want to take the kid under his wing. He had just gotten things the way he liked them in this life.

At the same time, he couldn't turn him away.

"Listen. You can stay here for a little while, but we've got rules here. Number one is, you'll have to keep going to school."

Sonny's face lit up at the first part of that sentence, then fell. "I don't think I can go back to school."

"Why not?"

"Because the courts assigned me to the Johnsons. They get paid for every month I'm with them and they want that money. If they know where I am, where to find me, they'll make me go back. I understand why you have that rule, but I just can't."

Reggie glanced at the new VCR sitting on top of the television set. Just a few minutes earlier, trying to figure that out had been the biggest problem in his life. Now, this. He looked up at the ceiling, as if for guidance. He shook his head and said, "I must be crazy, but I'll help you. If I do, you'll have to stick to the rules completely. Got it?"

"Got it, but what can we do about me going to school?"

"I've got a lawyer we can see."

It had been ten years since Reggie had used Marvin Shipman for his own emancipation process, but he took Sonny and went back to the same law offices. Somehow Marvin never seemed to grow any bigger or go completely under.

When they climbed up to his second-story office and sat down across from Marvin, Reggie said, "He's part of the foster system. Will that make it easier or harder for him to be emancipated?"

"Theoretically, it should make things easier for us. If the judge sees that he's already costing the state money and might get off the payroll if emancipated, that should work in our favor. He'll need to be gainfully employed, of course, unless he's also come into a life insurance policy?"

Reggie hadn't been sure that Marvin was capable of making a joke, but there it was.

"He's working at a store I own." That wasn't true at the moment, but Reggie could put him to work at the pawn shop at any time. "And I'm happy to sign a two-year lease that allows him to stay in the house for a dollar a month."

Marvin tapped his pencil against his legal pad, then said, "I'll draw up the paperwork. Let's have you back to sign everything tomorrow afternoon."

On the way back down the stairs, Sonny shook his head. "I didn't think you'd even let me stay with you, now you're doing all this. I owe you a lot."

"It's no big deal." A smile came over him that made him look ten years younger. "Hey, you want to hit up Artie's?"

Just as it had with Reggie himself, filing the emancipation paperwork allowed Sonny to go back to school and not worry about being shipped back to the Johnsons or any other foster family.

Sonny was almost ten years younger than everyone else who lived at Reggie's house, but that didn't pose a problem. Everyone seemed to take him under their wing. He was easy to get along with, carefully followed the rules, and was soon adopted as a little brother by all the guys.

As promised, Sonny went to work at the pawn shop where he immediately proved to be invaluable. He had an instant knack for figuring out electronics that stumped everyone else. Back at the house, long after everyone had given up on programming the VCR, for instance, Sonny had done it in less than fifteen minutes. He tended to look at Reggie and the others like they were old and out of touch, even though they were only in their mid-twenties.

Like it had with Reggie, the emancipation process dragged on for months. Sonny had his seventeenth birthday before the hearing arrived. He joked that by the time they actually saw a judge, he might not need to be emancipated any more because he might be of legal age.

In the end, the process went smoothly for Sonny, just as it had for Reggie. He was granted his emancipation request and knew that he wouldn't have to go back to the Johnson family under any circumstances.

The rest of that life was unchanged. Adding Sonny into the family just enhanced everything, and in retrospect, Reggie knew that those seventy-five lives he had lived before were a little emptier without the youngest addition to the Lost Boys.

Beyond that single change, though, things went on unimpeded, for the most part. When the next life rolled around, Reggie thought about possibly trying to reach Sonny before he was ever put into the system, but there were so many landmines involved with doing that, he gave it up.

All of the Lost Boys had terrible things in their past. That's how they found their way to Reggie. When Sonny showed up for the second time, Reggie tried to get him to talk about it, but Sonny refused. In the end, Reggie decided that he didn't have much choice but to allow Sonny to find his way to him when the time was right.

In that second life, Reggie was unsure if Sonny would even show up again. He had lived so many lives without him that he thought it was possible it had been a one life occurrence.

Time and again, though, Sonny showed up at Reggie's door. Once the path was established, it seemed to reoccur each life.

Chapter Forty-Four

Sonny had a gentle personality that made it easy to be his friend and everyone felt protective of him, especially for the first few months after he showed up at the house each lifetime.

Life after life, Sonny went to work for Reggie at the pawn shop, but he also participated in the other aspects of the life they led.

His natural ability with electronics made him the go-to guy in the gang when they faced a house that had a complex alarm system. He could get everyone in and out of the house without anyone being the wiser.

He never grew much, though, so if it was a job where there was heavy lifting to be done, Sonny would stay in the vehicle and act as lookout and driver.

Life after life passed with no more than the occasional blip of a change in circumstances. A number of the Lost Boys got pinched now and again and spent a little time in jail. Reggie always hired the best criminal attorney available for each one, which normally kept them from having to do any serious time.

If one of them did end up doing a few months in the county lockup, Reggie made sure that he did everything he could to make their stay in the Graybar Motel go by as quickly as possible.

Sonny even got arrested a few times, but it was always after he had been emancipated, so there weren't any terrible repercussions from it. He just did his time like anyone else and came out not wanting to go back there.

These patterns went on for life after life. Reggie might have gotten bored and wanted to break the pattern—maybe spend a lifetime traveling, or at least moving out of Crampton Village, but he never did.

He wouldn't have been able to say why, but more than anything, he didn't want to be put in situations where he had to look inside himself and contemplate making real changes. In pursuit of that, Reggie was very stubborn.

If something hadn't changed, it's possible the whole cycle could have gone on for an eternity.

There's always something, though. A fly that lands in the ointment and changes everything.

For Reggie and those in his chosen family, that change happened fifty-four lives after Sonny had first appeared. Reggie lived a little over forty years on average, so he spent over two thousand years living those same circumstances over and over.

He didn't mind a bit. In fact, he hoped it *would* go on forever.

It all changed when Reggie offered to pay for Sonny's emancipation again. He had done that so often by then that it was just another rote part of his life, like stealing the Inverted Jenny or hiring Big Frank to offload them.

Every life, he hired Marvin Shipman to represent Reggie and every life Sonny was granted his emancipation.

Something different happened on the day of the fifty-fourth version of the same hearing.

When they walked into the courtroom that day and Reggie saw who was sitting on the bench, his eyes went wide and he said, "Oh, shit. What's *she* doing here?"

"Who?" Marvin asked, looking around the courtroom. "You mean Judge Grand? There was a last-minute switch because Judge Harrison is sick. It shouldn't make any difference."

Reggie knew differently. His own emancipation suit had been turned down twice over his many lifetimes, and both times, it was when something had happened and Judge Grand had been on the bench. Sitting there in the courtroom, though, it was too late for Reggie to do anything but cross his fingers and hope.

The hope was in vain, and the die was cast for the rest of this drama.

The judge ruled on the spot and denied the emancipation request.

Sonny seemed crushed.

Reggie was pissed. "Can we appeal?"

"Not a decision like this, no," Marvin said. "I'm sorry."

"Will she try to drop Sonny right back in the system?"

Sonny looked anxiously at Marvin, hanging on the answer.

"No. That's essentially out of her purview. But it does put you at risk of being scooped up and dropped back into the system at some point, unfortunately."

"Let's get out of here before they change their minds about that," Reggie said.

They walked home without even thinking about stopping for a celebration at Artie's. There was nothing to celebrate.

Reggie rolled things over in his mind the whole way home. When they walked inside, he laid out what would happen.

"You're seventeen now. That means there's less than a year that they can put you back into the system. I don't think at your age, they're going to bother looking too hard for you."

Fear flashed in Sonny's eyes. "You don't know the Johnsons."

Reggie noticed the fear and for the hundredth time, wondered what had happened to him there to cause such extreme reactions. "Don't worry. We're not going to count on that, though. Here's what we're going to do."

Reggie laid out his plan, which combined aspects of several other things he had been considering.

They put the plan into action the next day, when Ike and Sonny drove to Portland. Reggie had been contemplating doing something new in this life—he was considering setting up a second outpost somewhere away from Middle Falls, and since they needed to find a place to stash Sonny, it seemed like as good a time as any. Portland wasn't too far away and being in such a metropolitan area put them within easy driving distance of a lot of plush neighborhoods.

Ike didn't really want to leave Middle Falls, but like the good soldier he was, he rented a small house for him and Reggie and signed a lease that would at least get them past Sonny's eighteenth birthday. That would keep him out of the system permanently.

There was still a small possibility that someone might go looking for Sonny, but Reggie couldn't imagine that any search would extend clear up to Portland.

It was an ideal, if not elegant solution.

Until it wasn't.

Two months after the move, the phone rang early one morning, and Reggie answered.

"Hello?"

"Reg, it's Ike."

Reggie heard the strain in his voice and immediately knew there was a major issue. "Trouble?"

"Yeah, the two of us were out on a little maneuver last night and things went sideways."

"You on your one call?"

"Yeah."

"I'll get our lawyer on it. We'll get you bailed out pronto."

"Thanks, boss. That's not the real problem though."

That brought Reggie up cold. "What's the real problem?"

"When they found out how old Sonny was, they shipped him off to Juvie. He's back in the system now."

Chapter Forty-Five

Reggie went to work immediately. The first challenge was finding out where Sonny was. Since Reggie had no idea where to start a project like that, he called someone who did.

Fifteen minutes after Reggie heard from Ike, Marvin Shipman was on the job.

Thirty minutes after that, he called Reggie back. "They've got him in a juvenile holding facility in Portland. Since he is a first-time offender, underage, and he was only driving the vehicle and not actually doing the breaking and entering, he's probably going to get off pretty light. I talked to a few friends who know the system and they say there's a chance they'll let him go with a promise to appear at a later date."

"I'm not sure they will," Reggie asked. "Will they really let him go, or will they assign him back to a new foster care family? If they do that, it will be okay, but I think he'll just run if they try to put him back with the same family he was with before."

"I'm a little out of my element here, Reggie. Until recently, you were the only juvenile case I ever handled. I'll keep making calls, and I'll keep you informed."

Reggie had a sick feeling in his stomach that day. He felt helpless, which was unusual for him after he had lived essentially the same life so many times. He wasn't used to this feeling of uncertainty.

He paced back and forth in the living room of the house.

Steve closed the pawn shop down at midday and came home. All the other guys who were out on different jobs did the same. Marvin managed to arrange bail for Ike and even he made it back to the house by the time darkness settled in.

It felt a little like a vigil as everyone sat around looking at each other, waiting to hear something that they could act on.

Reggie made a pot of coffee and everyone drank that while they batted ideas around. They all felt helpless and wanted to do something. *Anything.*

When Reggie looked at the men gathered in his living room, he felt proud. They were a group of ruffians and thieves. They had essentially adopted Sonny though, and it was killing them that they were so helpless.

It wasn't so much that Sonny was in the system—that had happened several times before. This time, it was that he was in the system, was under eighteen and so ran the risk of being sent back to the Johnsons.

Finally, it got so late that everyone knew that nothing was going to happen that night. They dispersed to their own houses or bedrooms, and Reggie was left alone in the living room.

By the next morning, there was still no word.

Reggie was climbing the walls. Just to do something, he called several Portland attorneys and asked for the names of lawyers who *did* specialize in juvenile matters.

Getting the chance to talk to those attorneys was not as easy as finding their names, though. Attorneys—especially those who specialize in family matters—have to insulate themselves from random calls requesting information and help.

It was mid-afternoon before Reggie managed to talk his way through several levels of secretaries and actually speak to one of those attorneys.

"Benson," the voice on the other end of the phone said. "You've got one minute."

Reggie was ready for that. He gave a concise, honest rundown of what had happened and what the possible stakes were.

Arch Benson sighed on the other end of the line. "I understand the urgency, Mr. Blackwell, but I'm buried in paperwork already and I have to prepare for a court appearance in front of a judge that hates my guts at 9:00 a.m. tomorrow."

"I'm not asking you to handle the case. I just need some information, like where in the system he is and whether he's been put into custody or with a new foster home. I'll gladly pay you five hundred dollars for thirty minutes of your time if you'll make the calls. You're the only person I've reached who might actually find out for me."

"My rate is a hundred dollars an hour."

"And I'm willing to pay you ten times that rate for you to make a few phone calls."

There might have been attorneys somewhere who would have said, "No, that's fine. I'll just charge you my normal rate."

Arch Benson was not one of those attorneys. After a short pause, he said, "I'll make the calls. Give me your number and I'll put my secretary back on. She can give you the process to wire the money to me. No money, no information. Capiche?"

Reggie hung up, glad that he had finally accomplished something, but afraid that he had gotten in touch with someone too late to do anything that day. He looked at the clock and realized that he needed to hurry down to the bank before it closed so he could wire the money.

He did that and hurried home. When another hour passed and the phone hadn't rung, he was sure he would have another sleepless night.

At five minutes to six, the phone finally rang. Reggie answered on the first ring. "Hello?"

"Mr. Blackwell, this is Arch Benson. It took more than a few phone calls to untangle this, but I've got the information you requested. It's a bit unusual, but apparently there was a flag in the system to be on the lookout for this young man. He's been released from custody with a promise to appear at a future date. He was picked up by his foster family."

"A new foster family he was assigned to?"

"No. The same family that apparently had been looking for him for quite some time." There was a pause as Benson looked at his notes. "The Johnson family in Middle Falls."

Reggie dropped the receiver into the cradle, then immediately picked it up again. He listened for the dial tone, then made the first of several calls.

In less than an hour, all of what could have been called *The Blackwell Gang* were once again gathered in the living room.

When the last of them arrived, Reggie said, "I've tried to do everything the right way with this. We went to the courts first. Then we tried to hide him. None of that worked. We're going to have to do things a little differently."

Jim Cates, the first person Reggie ever brought into the house, was the first to speak. "Whatever you need, we're here. What are you thinking? Going in and getting him, no matter what?"

That had been Reggie's first thought, but in the time that had passed since he found out where Sonny was, he had calmed down a little.

"Not if we can help it. We can't just take it easy, though. I'm worried about the kid. He told me a long time ago that if he was forced to go back there, he'd do something stupid. I believe him. He's never lied to us."

Steve was always level-headed. "Maybe if we show up and just try to talk with them, we can figure something out. Sonny always said that the money was important to them. Maybe we could negotiate."

Reggie hadn't even thought about that possibility, but it was something he was more than willing to do if it was possible.

"How much," Steve wondered, "do we think they get for keeping the kid?"

No one knew, but Reggie took a guess. "Maybe two or three hundred dollars a month?"

"Okay," Steve said. "It's ten months until Sonny turns eighteen. Let's say it's three hundred bucks a month. That's three grand. I'll put up a third of that."

Immediately, everyone around the room chimed in, offering their own money.

Reggie raised his hand to quiet them down. "You guys aren't giving anything, though I appreciate it." He looked around the room. "But this is something I want to do. I'll grab that and a little more from my rainy-day fund and take it with me."

"We'll all go," Jim said. "A show of strength."

Reggie shook his head. "I'm not sure a show of strength is what's needed here. I don't think these people are going to be much trouble. Steve, let's just you and I go. The rest of you guys stay here. We'll come back with Sonny."

"Do we even know where these people live?" Steve asked.

Reggie looked a little embarrassed. "No."

"Hang on, I'll look them up." He pulled the Middle Falls phone book out and turned to "J" in the White Pages. "Okay, there are six Johnsons listed. Any ideas what their names are?"

"Sonny always just called them *those bastards*," Reggie said. "Tear that page out and we'll figure it out. It's Middle Falls. Nothing is more than five minutes away, right?"

In this life, Reggie had allowed himself the luxury of buying a car he wanted—a deep blue 1980 Lincoln Continental. He and Steve got in and headed for the first address on the list. It was a modest house in an area near the edge of town.

"Looks kind of small for a family that's taking in foster kids," Steve said.

"I agree, but let's check it and make sure." Reggie got out of the car and hurried up to the front door. There were lights on inside and he felt a knot in his stomach. He wasn't sure what he would do if they were the right people and tried to blow him off.

It turned out, he didn't need to worry about it. A woman who appeared to be in her seventies lived in the house by herself.

Reggie apologized for the mistake, but before he left, the old woman gave him a clue. "Did you say you were looking for someone named Sonny? I think that's the name of the boy my son is fostering. I thought he had disappeared, though. That's what so many of those kids do. They're so ungrateful for what Quinn does for them."

Reggie couldn't stop his lip from curling back in disgust, but did manage not to say anything to her that might cause her to call and warn her son.

When Reggie got back in the Lincoln, he said, "Is there a Quinn Johnson on the list?"

Steve clicked on the overhead light and ran his finger down the list. He nodded. "Yep. Last one."

"That's our target," Reggie said. He knew the neighborhood. It wasn't far from where he stole the stamps from Clayton Hollister at the beginning of each life, though it was in an area that wasn't nearly as nice.

They knew they'd found Sonny, but both of them remained silent on the drive. Nothing about this situation felt good to either of them.

"Take a right up ahead," Steve said.

Reggie turned on his blinker and took the right, but then took his foot off the gas and coasted to a stop.

They wouldn't need to try and figure out which house it was.

Two police cars and an ambulance were parked in front of a two-story house on the right. The lights of all three vehicles lit up the neighborhood.

Reggie and Steve looked at each other.

They both knew that whatever had caused those flashing lights, it wasn't going to be good.

Chapter Forty-Six

Reggie rolled up behind one of the police cars, and killed his lights.

He was, in all probability, the biggest criminal in Middle Falls, but he had no fear of talking to the police. In this life, he'd never even been interrogated, let alone arrested or imprisoned.

Reggie and Steve sat in the car for a few minutes. The windshield wipers slowly wiped away the falling mist. As they watched, two EMTs pushed a gurney down the front steps. There was a body shrouded by a sheet on it, but the face was covered.

"I hope he killed the son of a bitch," Steve said.

"Me too. If he did, he'll have a damned good lawyer."

Reggie squinted through the darkness, trying to judge the size of the form on the gurney. Did it look like a full-grown man, or an undersized seventeen-year-old boy?

A deputy that Reggie did not know—he was happy to *not* know any of the Middle Falls police department anymore since the retirement of Chief Deakins—approached the driver's side window.

Reggie rolled the window halfway down and felt the cold rain blow in on him.

"Excuse me, sir," the officer said, "can I ask what your business is here?"

There was no easy answer to that question. *I'd like to know if that's my friend dead on the gurney* didn't seem like an appropriate response. *Just saw the flashing lights and wanted to see what was going on*, wouldn't get any traction either.

"Sorry, we'll move along."

"Good," the cop answered, then walked toward the house, though he stopped to make sure that Reggie really did move the car.

Reggie took a deep breath, then put the Lincoln in gear and pulled around the ambulance. He drove down the block, then turned around in a driveway a block down. He pulled off to the side and parked on the street. There was no law against parking there and they were out of the immediate line of sight of the cop who chased them away.

They watched the scene continue to unfold in front of them for the next ten minutes. Their frustration rose, but neither one could think of anything else to do.

Finally, the two EMTs loaded the gurney into the ambulance. One of them went back inside to retrieve some equipment. The other climbed into the cab and lit a cigarette.

"There's my chance," Reggie said. He hopped out of the car and jogged toward the ambulance. He stood outside the driver's side window, but the man behind the wheel didn't seem to be interested in rolling the window down.

Reggie fished into his front pocket and brought out a fifty-dollar bill. He held it out toward the man.

The window instantly came down.

"Yeah?"

"Can you tell me what happened here?"

The driver looked meaningfully at the bill. Reggie handed it over.

"Some dumbshit kid attacked a guy with a knife. He's dead."

Reggie's heart sank. "The guy? Or the kid?"

"Oh, the kid. He was just a little shit. The old guy managed to knock him down and took the knife away from him. Put it through him a few times."

Reggie closed his eyes. The image of Quinn Johnson stabbing Sonny multiple times was not one he wanted in his head, but it was there forever now. He couldn't stop the tears that leaked from both eyes. He hadn't cried in many lifetimes, but he was afraid that if he started now, he might not ever stop.

He exerted the same iron will he'd had since he'd been fifteen years old in his first life and got a hold of himself.

"Sorry, buddy. Is the old guy a friend of yours? He's all right. Just got a little nicked up."

Reggie nodded dumbly, then turned and walked back to the Lincoln.

From behind him, the EMT said, "Thanks, man. This'll come in handy."

Reggie didn't hear him. At that moment, there was a rushing in his ears and he couldn't hear anything else.

When Steve saw Reggie's face, he didn't have to ask the question. He knew. He cursed quietly under his breath and looked out the window.

There was nothing to say.

Both of them felt like they'd gotten hit by a truck.

Reggie had lived for thousands of years and had managed to insulate himself from this kind of pain for all of them.

He loved people, like the Blackwell gang, in his own way. But he hadn't exposed himself to the possibility of devastation since the day he had first found his mother on the floor of their home.

Now, that façade, built up over millennia, was crumbling, brought to the ground by a vulnerable teenage boy he had managed to protect over and over, but not in this life. A boy who had never sought anything except the freedom to not go back to a place he couldn't tolerate.

The two men drove back to the house in Crampton Village. Again, when they went inside, there was no real need for questions.

Steve just shook his head and glanced at Reggie out of the corner of his eye, as if to say, *Don't ask. It will be too much for him.*

It was hard on all of them. They all loved and cared about Sonny. But the rest of the Lost Boys had only known him in this lifetime, and it had been for less than a year. Reggie had known him so much longer.

Even with his perspective and knowledge of what happened after death, at least for some people, it didn't change the devastation he felt.

Reggie didn't speak at all, but went down the hall to his bedroom. It was late and pitch dark outside. That matched the darkness in Reggie's heart. Over and over, a scene played out in his head. Sonny attacking Quinn Johnson, then losing the knife and being stabbed over and over until he couldn't fight any more, then slumping to the ground.

Like he had once done on the night when his mother had been killed, Reggie stretched out on his bed without getting undressed.

He felt a fury of emotion in his chest, but he didn't give into it. Like he had so often over his many lives, he kept it in check, though this time the effort seemed to cost him more than it ever had before.

He heard—but didn't pay any attention to—the sound of the other Blackwell Gang members either leave the house, or go to bed in the other room.

He didn't sleep, but just rode the wave of thoughts in a tight circle, round and round.

When light came through the bedroom window, he got up and made a pot of coffee. He sat at the kitchen table, drinking cup after cup in an unconscious mimicry of his mother on his first-ever fifteenth birthday.

When he had as much caffeine in him as he thought he could tolerate without getting shaky, he went back to his bedroom and pulled a shoebox down from the top shelf of his closet. He sat on his bed, opened the lid, and pulled out the .380 ACP.

He had stolen it as part of the start up of every one of his lives. In all those lives, all those times he had it with him, he had never fired it once. He had never even pointed it at another human being.

He checked the load and, satisfied, slipped the gun into his coat pocket. He stepped out the front door. The Lincoln was parked where it always was, but he walked right past it. This was a mission to be undertaken on foot.

It felt good to be out of the house and moving.

It took him fifteen minutes to arrive back at the neighborhood where Quinn Johnson lived. The house was quiet. Aside from a few muddy tracks along the front of the yard, it looked like nothing exciting had ever happened there.

Reggie walked past the house once, scoping things out. There was a wooded lot across the street and that was what he was looking for. He walked to the end of the block, then turned around and came back, casually walking into the woods.

He found a spot where he could observe the Johnson house.

He had to wait in the same spot for quite some time, but that was okay with him. He was willing to wait for days if he needed to.

When the front door opened, he perked up, but it was just a middle-aged woman. She hurried to her car—a late model Toyota—and got in. She started it and disappeared toward downtown.

Reggie settled in to wait again.

In the middle of the afternoon, a mail truck came down the road, distributing mail at each house. Reggie faded back another few steps.

Fifteen minutes later, the front door opened again.

An older man with a few days' growth of beard and a ponderous gut stepped outside. He was wearing boxer shorts and what looked like a too-small woman's robe that he didn't bother to try to tie at the front.

Reggie didn't hesitate.

He stepped out of the woods and walked across the street at a steady pace. He raised his hand and said, "Hey, Quinn." Not friendly, but not angry, either. He didn't want to have to chase him down.

Something tripped the man's radar, though. He squinted at Reggie coming out of the woods, turned, and headed back to the house.

Reggie didn't want to have to break into the house to get at him. For all he knew, Johnson had guns inside. Reggie certainly wasn't afraid of death, but he had a mission to carry out.

Johnson made it back to his porch and was reaching for the door knob when Reggie got within easy firing distance. He didn't have time to aim carefully, but his first shot found its intended target.

The bullet ripped into the upper right leg of Quinn Johnson, who tumbled forward, smashing his face against the front door and knocking it open. He tried to take advantage of that by crawling inside.

Reggie was on him too fast. He reached him at the threshold and kicked him forward into the living room.

Johnson turned and held his hands up defensively. "What? Why?"

"You know why," Reggie said. "The same reason Sonny came after you."

Johnson blanched, but said, "Wait, wait, wait."

Reggie didn't wait. He pointed the gun at the man's midsection and pulled the trigger. Once, twice, three times. Any one of those shots might have been eventually fatal, but they weren't immediately, even in combination.

Johnson's face twisted in shock and agony, but he stopped talking. Instead, he tried to simultaneously hold his intestines in and to crawl away.

Reggie put his shoe against Johnson's shoulder and leaned over until his face was close. "This is from Sonny."

He put the gun against Johnson's forehead and pulled the trigger.

Chapter Forty-Seven

Reggie had not been concerned about being caught. Starting a cold-blooded murder in broad daylight on a residential street in a town the size of Middle Falls guaranteed that he would be apprehended.

Still, he didn't want to be captured there at the scene.

He exited the house, went back into the woods and walked across them until he came out on another street a quarter mile away. From there, he turned toward home. He dropped the gun down a storm drain. Not a perfect solution, but he didn't want to take it home with him.

He didn't run into anyone before he made it back to Crampton Village, which was a good thing.

Once he was safely inside, he went to the bathroom. Looking in the mirror, he saw that he had blood spatter all over his face. He took a washcloth out of the cupboard, soaped it up, and washed his face clean.

He walked back into the living room just as Jim came in through the front door. Jim took one look at Reggie and said, "You did it, didn't you?"

There was no reason for Reggie to hide anything. He just nodded.

"He's on greased skids heading straight to hell then," Jim said. "Good. You should get out of here. Grab enough money to last you, get in the Lincoln and go. Wait. Soon enough, they'll have an APB out on that vehicle. Take my Chevy."

"Thanks, Jim, but I'm not going anywhere."

"Unless you were really sneaky," Jim started, but Reggie interrupted him.

"I wasn't sneaky. I don't know how long it will take them, but they'll be here eventually."

"Then let's get you the hell out of Dodge."

"No," Reggie said shaking his head. "This is murder. It's not something that's going to blow over. I don't want to be on the run my whole life. It's just not worth it. I'll be right here waiting when they come looking for me."

"I should have taken the bastard out then."

Even under the great stress of the moment, that made Reggie smile. "I know you would have, but you're not cut out for that kind of work. Sit down."

Jim sat.

"I'm going to need you and Steve to step up and take care of things for however long I'm away. Maybe forever."

"I don't want to think about that."

"I don't either, but it's the way it is. You guys know our systems. I haven't really done anything other than take a cut of everything for a long time now. We're a well-oiled machine."

"You know that's not true," Jim said. "We know what you do for us. What you've been doing for us for a long time."

"It's been a good run, hasn't it?"

Jim nodded, thinking of the previous eighteen years.

Reggie, meanwhile, was thinking of the many lives they had spent as friends.

"I'll use what I need to get the best defense team I can, then give myself a healthy account balance at the prison. I want you guys to share everything else. I'll deed the houses and the pawn shop over to you and Steve. All I ask is that you take care of the other guys."

Jim, as tough as they came, looked away, trying to disguise the tears in his eyes. He shook his head, but Reggie knew he would do what was asked of him.

"I think that's everything for now. I'm tired. I haven't slept a wink since this all went down. I'm going to go grab some shuteye."

Reggie did retire to his bedroom again, but sleep was still elusive.

Exhaustion eventually overtook him, and he slept through the rest of the afternoon and through the night.

He was woken up the next morning by a loud rapping on his front door. In his sleep-sodden state, it reminded him of Chief Deakins knocking the same way so many lifetimes before.

He put his feet on the floor and rubbed his hand through his hair. He had no intention of running from whoever was there, but he didn't mind making them wait a minute.

The rapping continued, almost metronome steady. Eventually, a man's voice said, "Reggie Blackwell? We need to talk with you."

Reggie went to the bathroom, flushed, then looked in the mirror. He looked older than he actually was, unsurprisingly.

When he finally answered the door, he found two Middle Falls police officers. They stood back a few feet, hands resting on their guns.

Reggie looked at them calmly. "Yes?"

"Reggie Blackwell?"

"Yes."

"Turn around, please. Put your hands behind your back."

Oddly, that brought the ghost of a smile to his lips. He flashed back once again to the many times he had heard Deakins say those same words to his father.

He did as he was told.

The younger of the two officers snapped the cuffs on his wrists.

The moment before he did that was the last free moment of this lifetime for Reggie Blackwell.

Reggie did as he said he would—he hired the best defense attorney available, reaching all the way to Portland to find him. They did everything they could, but the evidence against him was overwhelming.

Two neighbors had seen Reggie hail Quinn Johnson and shoot him on his porch. They both testified to that, and Reggie couldn't even be mad about it. They were just doing their civic duty.

One of the officers who arrested Reggie was the same young man who had shooed him away from the Johnson residence the day before. He also testified.

They never did find the gun that was used to commit the murder, but the prosecution was easily able to overcome that.

Reggie was found guilty of first-degree murder. If he had stormed the house that first night and shot Johnson then, he might have been able to plead out to manslaughter. It was the fact that he went home, slept on it, retrieved his gun, and then lay in wait for Johnson to come outside that showed premeditation and sealed his fate.

Almost anyone would be devastated by being found guilty of murder and being given a life sentence.

Reggie was more sanguine. He knew that was exactly what it was—a *life* sentence. Unlike almost anyone else, he knew that when this life was over, he would find himself young and free once more.

It had been thousands of years since Reggie had been a prisoner, but he was able to adjust well. The members of the Blackwell gang never forgot him or left him to rot on his own. One or two of them showed up every visitor's day and made regular deposits into his commissary account.

The years passed slowly for Reggie, but that was okay. He had a lot to think about.

With nothing but time on his hands, Reggie finally reflected on his original life.

For the first time, he truly grieved the loss of his mother, dredging up feelings that had been stored away for so long they might have been lost.

Grief is only delayed, never lost.

There were many nights in this life where Reggie lay on his bunk, tears running down his face as he finally allowed himself to feel everything he had avoided so long.

That process took years. Reggie thought he would never get through it all in this lifetime.

He was wrong again.

There were two ends of the spectrum of grief.

One end was where he had lived for so many lifetimes—avoiding dealing with it at all, shutting it out.

The other end was what he did in prison—living in it, feeling it, absorbing it, and making it part of himself.

Eventually, the tears ran out. The grief—for his mother, for Sonny, for the loss of his whole family, everything that had happened to him—became manageable. It didn't go away, and he suspected it would likely never go completely away. But it became smaller. Something that he could look at in his mind, touch on, but not be consumed by.

Having his physical body imprisoned forced him to slow down, reflect, and truly change.

By the time he had worked his way through all of that, he was in his mid-fifties. He knew that if things worked the same way they always had, he would grow sick and die soon. That thought filled him with happiness.

He was eager to escape the physical limitations of this life, but more than that, there were things he wanted to accomplish when he woke up.

Chapter Forty-Eight

Reggie Blackwell opened his eyes.

He sighed with contentment. His previous life had seemed longer than any ten of those that had gone before it. It wasn't just being imprisoned; it was that he had recognized that he had been imprisoned within his own unbending unwillingness to look inside himself.

When he finally did so, he found, as humans often do, that although what was there was terrible, it was not nearly as bad as the fear of looking at it.

And now, here he was, fifteen years old and sitting in the same garden shed he had woken up in so many times before.

He stamped his feet a bit to get the circulation going, then stood up, stretched, and slid open the door.

It was, as always, a cold night in Middle Falls. To Reggie it felt bracing. He stepped back into the shadows and waited, as he always did, for the Middle Falls police prowler to roll by him.

Once it did, he walked toward home, anxious to get started on the life he had planned.

Part of what had confounded him as he had made his plans was that each life, he started things at such a disadvantage. He had always justified his lives of crime as being necessitated by that poor start. If he didn't follow that same path, how would he survive?

When he had taken the time to examine his lives, he realized that while it might be a valid excuse for starting his lives out that way, that didn't come close to justifying the more than forty years of crime that followed.

He was planning on doing things differently this life. He still wanted some of the same things. He knew he wanted to rekindle his friendship with Jim Cates, Steve Anderson, and the rest of the gang.

Then there was Sonny. He wanted to help him in this life. Most importantly, he wanted to do it *before* he fell into the orbit of Quinn Johnson. That was one of several parts of the plan where he didn't know exactly how he could accomplish it. There were parts of this life that he was going to have to figure out on the fly.

After so many lifetimes of repeating the same process over and over, that felt as fresh and welcome as the cold night air.

Reggie made his way home and once again found his mother on the floor. He had always left her there, but tonight, that felt wrong. It was a struggle, but he lifted her up and laid her gently on the couch with a pillow under her damaged head. He knew he couldn't save her; that had been proven over and over. Still, he wanted to give her as much dignity as he could. He kissed her cheek, then went into the kitchen, got a rag, and cleaned up the bloody spot on the floor. After that, he got the new lightbulb and changed it out with the burned-out bulb on the front porch.

He called the hospital, made arrangements for the ambulance, then waited patiently for their arrival.

When his mother was carried away, he went to bed and slept late into the next morning, just like he always did.

He waited for his father the next day, delayed him enough that he was arrested by Chief Deakins again. He scooped up the suitcase and was ready for phase two.

Given his preferences, he would have toughed it out with just the assets he had. He knew that wasn't realistic, so he had to choose between stepping off the path momentarily or giving up on so many of his goals.

He kept his goals in sight.

He had robbed the stamps from Clayton Hollister so often that it had become rote. He did it again, though he vowed this would be the only time he took something that wasn't his.

The next day, he went to Artie's for his traditional meal, though something had changed. As he sat in the dining room looking up at the menu, his normal strawberry shake no longer sounded right to him. When he approached the waitress, he switched to chocolate for the first time.

It was delicious and tasted like a new life.

He went through the same San Francisco routine as he had so many times, hiring Big Frank, getting the first tranche of money, then coming back to Middle Falls to wait for the big payday from the Inverted Jenny.

That was where he stepped foot onto the road less traveled.

In his previous lives, he had often gone back to school just to have something to do, then had dropped out when the new school year began.

This time, he did things differently.

First, while he was in prison in his last life, he finally realized he had dyslexia. That's why he always had so much difficulty with his reading. On one of Steve's visits, he had asked him if he could help with the problem.

Steve could.

For the next few years, he brought a speech-language pathologist along with him when he visited. Steve thought it was admirable that Reggie, who was locked up for the rest of his life, was still trying to improve himself.

Reggie knew the truth. He was trying to improve himself for his next life and all potential future lives.

There is no known cure for dyslexia, but the pathologist gave Reggie strategies to learn how to deal with the issue. She brought books and worked with him an hour at a time once a month for more than two years.

Steve gladly footed the bill for her services. Business had remained good for the Blackwell gang, even with Reggie permanently locked away.

Now, Reggie was reaping the benefits.

He was never destined to be a fast reader with perfect comprehension, but when he used the tactics he had been taught, he was at least able to get by.

What surprised Reggie was that he found he actually enjoyed reading.

In this life, he was committed to not just going to school, but to doing the work himself rather than paying other students to do it for him.

When he applied all his focus and willpower on something, he tended to succeed. So it was with school. He was already a little behind the eight ball when he reinvented himself, with an exceedingly poor GPA, but by the time he graduated, he had brought his overall grade point average to above a 3.0.

Another change that Reggie made in this life was that he didn't just hire Stan Fornowski to do all the upgrades on the house and property. He had been alongside him so many times that he was capable of doing most of the work himself. He still hired Stan for some of the trickier things, like installing the new double-pane windows and jacking up the house to replace the floor joists. Other things, like ripping out the flooring and replacing it or hanging drywall, he could do himself.

That gave Reggie almost as nice a house as he'd had in previous lives while spending much less on the projects.

That was important, because the financial head start he had given himself was all he was going to get in this life. He decided that in this life, he would pay more attention to the stock market, so maybe he would have a clue what to invest in during his next life.

He hired Marvin Shipman and once again was given his emancipation.

He knew that he had been about ten years older than Sonny, but because he had never talked about it, he had never known how old Sonny was when he went into the foster care program.

He solved that by hiring a private investigator and asking him to check up on Sonny once a month. He thought that way, he could get a heads-up when things went wrong in his young friend's life and he could find a way to come to the rescue.

In the meantime, he formed the same friendships with Jim, Steve, Hank, Bart, and Ike just as he had so many times in previous lives.

The big difference in this life was that when it came time to convert his friends into a gang, he didn't do it.

He still made a big meal for everyone this time, but when it was finished, instead of hustling them down the chute to a life of crime, he made a different pitch.

There were six of them sitting around the table when he said, "I've got an idea I'd like to pitch you."

"I'm in," Jim said.

"Let's wait until you hear the idea, first, okay?"

"Okay, but I mean it. I'm in." He paused, then grinned and said, "What is it?"

"I'd like to start a company with all of you."

Around the table, everyone nodded and said, "I'm in," even though Reggie hadn't begun to explain his idea.

"You guys are too much. Listen, it's going to be a lot of hard work for a long time. Really, it will probably be kind of hard work for the rest of our lives."

"I knew it," Bart said. "You're gonna make us all work at the box factory."

Ike laughed and high-fived Bart.

"No," Reggie said, "but there will probably be times when you'll wish you were working at a regular nine-to-five job. But, the upside is, we'll all be equal partners in this business."

Around the table, everyone smiled and nodded. They were liking it better and better.

Reggie took a deep breath and said, "I want us all to start a home security business."

Steve cocked his head and said, "I'm not sure any of us know much about home security."

"Don't worry," Reggie answered. "I've got a lot of experience you don't know about. I'll train you guys."

"So we'll be like what, then?" Hank asked. "Security guards? Do I get a gun?"

"That will be part of it. We'll talk about guns later. Eventually, you'll all get your own trucks to do your rounds. That's not all of it, though. I've been looking into electronic home security systems. We can sell them, install them, then charge a monthly fee to monitor them. One upfront cost, then we can make money off each system for years."

By the expressions around the table, it was obvious that this was all a foreign concept to them. Reggie had expected that.

"Don't worry, I've been thinking a lot about this. I'll walk us through it."

That was very true, though he had done most of his thinking about it while he was imprisoned the lifetime before. He couldn't think of anyone better to install security systems and guard properties than someone who had broken into thousands of houses over more than a hundred lifetimes.

Soon enough, everyone agreed and retired to the living room to play the new Atari 2600 that Reggie had just bought them.

The company started small, but Reggie had saved enough of his initial windfall to fund the first year while they got established.

Year one was touch and go, but that was kind of exciting for Reggie, too. After living the same life over and over, it was enjoyable to not know every outcome.

Ironically, one of the first calls to Blackwell Security came from Clayton Hollister, who wanted their most advanced, deluxe system installed. Reggie insisted on handling that one himself. He was curious to talk to the man he had seen only once, so many years earlier.

Reggie installed their top-of-the-line system while Clayton Hollister followed him around, telling him the story of how he had lost many thousands of dollars in valuable stamps a few years earlier.

Reggie shook his head sympathetically. "Too bad we weren't in business yet. We could have saved you a lot of money."

Clayton smiled. That expression, sitting uncomfortably on his face, immediately made Reggie a little nauseous. "Eh, it's all right. I had them overinsured."

Year two was much smoother, and by year three, it was obvious that the company was going to make it.

By year five, the company was paying all six partners a generous salary and they were able to hire out some of the grunt work.

In January of 1982, the investigator that Reggie had hired reported in that something major had happened in Sonny's life. On a trip to see a show in Portland, his parents had been in a car accident and were killed.

"Sonny is in a juvenile care facility," the investigator said, "but he'll be transferred out of there to a foster family in the next month."

That meant Reggie didn't have long to put things in motion. He'd already made some preliminary arrangements, but knew he needed to jump into action.

He called one of his teachers from high school and asked if he could come in and talk to the class that Sonny was in about working in the security field.

"Can't it wait until Career Day?"

"It could, but I'm going to have some job openings that teenagers can do and I'd like to see if I can identify them."

That worked, and both Reggie and Steve went to talk to the class a few days later. Reggie really did have a few lower-level grunt work jobs that he could hire students to do, but he was really only interested in one.

It was a bit of a shock to see Sonny after so long. From Reggie's subjective viewpoint, he hadn't seen him in more than forty years. When Sonny had first shown up at his door in the previous life, he had looked beaten down and ready to flee. Today, he seemed somber, which was natural with the death of his parents less than a month before. He looked healthy, though.

Reggie and Steve gave a talk about the new field of home security and could see that none of the students were really interested in it. At least, none of them were interested until Reggie pulled one of the security systems out of a case. Then Sonny's eyes lit up.

Reggie smiled. Sonny always liked electronic gadgets.

Steve handed out job applications to everyone and encouraged them to apply if they wanted a summer job.

The bell rang, and while everyone was leaving, Reggie called Sonny over. "I saw your eyes light up when I brought our systems out. Something you're interested in?"

Sonny shrugged. "Maybe, someday. Right now, I've got a lot going on and I don't know where I'm going to be."

The teacher, Mr. Roberts, interjected, "Sonny's going to be staying with a foster family."

"Amazing," Steve said. "My mom and dad are a foster family." As though it was a new idea, he snapped his fingers and said, "You know what, if you want to fill out an application, we can probably get you a job *and* a place to live."

Sonny looked suspicious. He scrunched up his face and said, "I'm not sure it's going to work like that."

"Totally up to you," Steve said. "But if you want to try, I'm game."

Sonny was right, of course. The system didn't work like that. Though Steve and Reggie had talked Steve's parents into being approved to be a foster family, that didn't mean there was any way they could get Sonny assigned to them.

At least through the regular way of doing business.

Reggie still had his instincts, though, and over the next few days, he found people who worked within the system who were either having some financial problems, or were just interested in some easy money.

It cost a bit, but money was something that Reggie never worried about.

Within two weeks, Sonny had been assigned to Steve's family.

He was safe.

There had been a lot of moving parts to get this life to where Reggie wanted it, but he had made it. He had gotten his life on the straight and narrow, he had brought the gang back together, and he had kept Sonny from being sent to the Johnsons.

What really bothered Reggie, though, was that it was inevitable that other kids *would* be sent to live in that house.

He didn't think he could live with himself if he didn't do something about it.

When he had killed Quinn Johnson in the previous life, he had done it in the heat of the moment.

He killed him again in this life, but was much more calculated about it.

Quinn Johnson was a birdwatcher. That was about the safest, most-low key hobby anyone could think of, with the possible exception of being a rockhound and agate hunter.

It was safe unless someone was stalking you.

Reggie stalked Quinn for more than a month, waiting for his opportunity. He got to know the man's schedule and where he liked to go. Several times, he followed him on his birdwatching trips.

Finally, he took his opportunity. In the previous life, he wanted to scare and hurt Quinn Johnson as much as possible. This life was different. This was simply removing a threat before harm came to another innocent victim.

Reggie waited until Quinn walked down a path off the Forest Service Road just outside of Middle Falls. He killed him with two quick shots to the head.

No one saw him.

Chapter Forty-Nine

The rest of this life went as smoothly as any life ever did for anyone.

There were bad things that happened, as happened in every life.

Ike, one of the original six partners, was hit by a drunk driver on the way home from a job and killed. He was only forty-two when that happened. He had a wife and a child. Reggie made sure that his wife got everything coming to her, plus more.

Sonny turned out to once again be the electronics genius that he always was. He ended up designing one new system after another that kept their company at the forefront of the industry.

Huge national corporations identified him and tried to lure him away to Los Angeles or New York, but Sonny was happy in Middle Falls. He often spoke about the day that Steve and Reggie came to talk to his high school class as the luckiest day of his life.

He had no idea.

One thing that happened in every life was that Dr. Jarvis the orthodontist was caught in a billing scandal in the early eighties. He lost his license, his practice, his house, and his wife.

Amanda, who had never really prepared to be anything other than wealthy and pampered, did not adjust well to this new set of circumstances. She developed both a drinking and drug problem, and by the time she was thirty-five, she was no longer beautiful. She looked at least twenty years older.

Reggie passed her from time to time and always said, "Hello, Amanda."

She never seemed to recognize who he was.

Reggie was more open and interested in what went on around him in this life.

He was asked to run for mayor of Middle Falls in 1988. That idea struck him as hilarious, but no one else knew all his background.

He did run, and he won. He was reelected to a second term in 1992, then stepped away to give someone else a chance.

Reggie never moved out of the small Crampton Village home he was born in.

He never again spray-painted the sign.

As he had so often, he began to feel poorly when he was in his late fifties. He didn't mind. This had been an exceedingly good life, and as he grew weaker, he went over it again and again in his mind, setting a blueprint to repeat it.

If his dull and criminal life had repeated a hundred and twenty-seven times, he was more than prepared to give this life at least that many chances.

Afterword
Universal Life Center

Reggie Blackwell opened his eyes.

He made a quick gasping sound. He was not in the darkness of the garden shed. He was immediately certain that he was not in Middle Falls. He had absolutely no idea where he might be.

He sat in an almost featureless room—completely white with a number of rows of benches.

A woman with long blonde hair sat beside him. She reached a hand out and touched his arm. She smiled a sweet smile and said, "It's all right. It's jarring to wake up here, I know. Everything is fine, though."

Reggie asked what almost everyone asked who woke up in this room. "Where am I?"

"This is the Universal Life Center. I am Karrina. I've been your Watcher for many lifetimes."

"My *Watcher*?"

"You were my very first person I ever watched over. I was so inexperienced. I tried the best I could to help you. I sent Carson, then Harold, even Mushu, but you just weren't ready. Watchers have to learn lessons, too. With you, I had to learn that there is no hurrying what will not be hurried."

Reggie squinted, as though trying to follow all that. He vaguely remembered a Carson in his first and second life, and he did remember his friend Harold, but he had no recollection at all of someone named Mushu.

"I wish I could have done more, but some things cannot be changed. Speaking of that, there's someone who's been waiting for you."

"For me? I can't imagine who."

Karrina looked over her shoulder and in an instant, his mother appeared in front of him. He almost didn't recognize her. She was younger than he'd ever seen her, and so lovely it brought tears to his eyes.

"Mom?"

"Hello, Sweetheart." She enveloped him in a hug.

"Please don't tell me you've been waiting for me all these lifetimes."

"Yes and no," she answered. "Time is very different here."

Reggie thought on all the lives he had lived before the last one. "Could you see me there?"

His mother shrugged. "Sometimes. Most of it wasn't any of my business. I am not a Watcher. I've just been resting." She sat beside him and reached a hand out. "I did see every time you found me on the floor. I heard every word you ever said to me. I knew how you loved me."

"I'm sorry. I wanted to save you."

She smiled. "There was nothing you could do about that. I chose that path and you couldn't change it."

Reggie wanted to ask why she would choose such an awful path for herself, but decided there was time enough for that later.

He looked at Karrina. "So, what's next?"

"That's the lovely part. Next is whatever you want it to be."

Coming Soon

The Indomitable Lives of Tuesday West[1]

Book #22 in the Middle Falls Time Travel Series

---

1. https://www.amazon.com/dp/B0DR9Y2YLS

THE INDOMITABLE LIVES OF TUESDAY WEST

A Middle Falls Time Travel Story

SHAWN INMON

2. https://www.amazon.com/dp/B0DR9Y2YLS

Author's Note

As I've mentioned in previous Author's Notes, some books come to me easily, others are more difficult. *The Unrepentant Lives of Reggie Blackwell* falls into the latter category.

Because I start with just a blank page and not much of an idea what the story would entail, I never know going in how challenging a book is going to be.

For Reggie's story, I really only had a single idea: what if someone didn't really *want* to try and find redemption. Reggie was perfectly content to live his larcenous but safe life over and over, at least until Sonny appeared on the scene.

I suppose some readers might read a sexual element into the relationship between Reggie and Sonny, but as the creator of the story, I can say there is none. Reggie is, in fact, essentially asexual. Whether that is a matter of nature or nurture, I'll leave to others to decide.

The first thing I ask myself when I've hit upon a theme for a book is *why?* *Why* was Reggie the way he was?

Sometimes, I wait until later in a book to reveal why someone is the way they are. Why was Evan Sanderson so remote and offbeat? We didn't find out until we met his mother. Why had Richard Bell lived such a regretful life? Again, we didn't find out until very near the end of his story.

With Reggie, I wanted to drop us right into his life at the pivotal point that influenced all the rest of his lives. I spent more than thirty thousand words—almost a third of the book—covering just a few days of Reggie's life in 1973.

By the time we had finished with what happened with his mother, father, brother, and what Amanda had done to him, I think we have a pretty good idea of what had shaped him.

Amanda Jarvis, by the way, is one of a large group of recurring characters in this story. She first appeared in *The Unusual Second Life of Thomas Weaver*, as the pretty girl at the kegger that talked Thomas into spending time with her cousin from out of town. I hadn't initially planned on including Amanda again, but when I closed my eyes and waited for the story to drop into my head, there she was.

What other recurring characters did we have from previous books? Chief Deakins, of course, Ann and Zack Weaver, Stan Fornowski from Joe Hart's book, Sal Parker, who appeared in both Hart Tanner and Richard Bell's books, and Michael and Clayton Hollister. I guess an honorable mention should be given to the *Inverted Jenny* stamp, which also played a critical role in *The Redemption of Michael Hollister*.

Of course, I can't forget Mushu, who I always think of as our canine Mary Poppins. She shows up when she's needed and leaves when the job is done. The fact that Reggie turned away the ministrations of Mushu showed, to me, how lost he still was.

One of the interesting things about this book was that Reggie made it to the Universal Life Center without living a spotless life. I did that on purpose.

Many people think of the ULC as a stand-in for heaven, but I see it differently. To me, it is more like a way station in our lives' journeys.

For Reggie, the critical thing was to learn how to adapt and change, which he did in his final life. Even though that life started with another theft and even though he murdered a person who needed it, he still did enough to make it from point A to point B. Only The Machine really understands what that takes.

I present the foster care system in a poor light in this story, from Reggie's fear of it to the unknown bad thing that happened to Sonny. I want to say that this is more of a story instrument than any personal indictment of the system. I'm sure that like any organization, there are both good and bad actors, with the good undoubtedly outweighing the bad.

Linda Boulanger designed the cover for this book, as she's done for twenty others in the series. There's a reason I keep going back to her—she's talented, responsive, and has created the faces of Middle Falls.

My friend Terry Schott helped me a lot at several key spots in this book. When I finished the last few chapters, I wasn't happy. Terry was insightful enough to help me find what was wrong *and* helped me find a great fix for it. He is invaluable to my writing process.

As is Melissa Prideaux, who has been my editor for my last twenty books. She knows my strengths and weaknesses and helps me with both. I would hate to ever tackle a book without her.

My final line of defense against my tendency to make mistakes (I often get dates and names wrong, along with other malfeasances) is my invaluable team of proofreaders. They've been with me a long time now, and I am endlessly appreciative of Dan Hilton, Kim K. O'Hara, Marta Rubin, Steve Smith, and Kurt VanderSluis. They make the end product you are holding in your hands so much better than what I give them!

All remaining errors are my responsibility and mine alone.

Thank you for following along as we peep on the lives of the residents of my favorite small Oregon town of Middle Falls. You are the reason I sit down to write every day.

Shawn Inmon

Tumwater WA